The Ugly Side of Me

The Ugly Side of Me

Nikita Lynnette Nichols

Urban Books, LLC
97 N18th Street
Wyandanch, NY 11798

The Ugly Side of Me

ISBN 13: 978-1-62286-821-6
ISBN 10: 1-62286-821-8

First Trade Paperback Printing December 2015
Printed in the United States of America

10 9 8 7 6 5 4 3 2 1

Distributed by Kensington Publishing Corp.
Submit Orders to:
Customer Service
400 Hahn Road
Westminster, MD 21157-4627
Phone: 1-800-733-3000
Fax: 1-800-659-2436

The Ugly Side of Me

by

Nikita Lynnette Nichols

Dedication

I always have so much on my plate. I work a full-time job, have so many deadlines to meet, and write full-time, and still I'm always on the grind for my favorite people. So, to all my readers, Facebook fans, book club members and supporters, this book is for you. Y'all keep me busy, and for that I'm forever grateful.

Acknowledgments

I have to give credit where it is due. I must send a shout-out to Deborah Pearson for the lovely photo she shot of my book-cover model, Yolunda Rena Cooper.

Other titles by
Nikita Lynnette Nichols

Prologue

My best girlfriend, Anastasia Baker, aka Stacy, left about twenty minutes ago. It was good seein' her, but then again, it's always good to see Anastasia, because she makes me laugh even when I don't really feel like it. And lately, I haven't felt like laughin' about a darn thang. But leave it to Anastasia to tell those lame jokes of hers to bring a smile to my lips.

It felt good to laugh since I haven't done it since the last time she was here, which was about a week and a half ago. Anastasia had told me on many occasions that my behavior sometimes made her want to deny that she knew me. And she'd been telling me that for the past six years, but it wasn't until I got to this place that I fully understood what she meant. And now that I'm here, I'm almost ashamed to tell you my name. But it's all good. We all do dumb things in life that cause us a little embarrassment from time to time.

In my case it was ignorant things, stupid things, horrible things that put me here. But to be honest with you, I really don't understand just how I got to this place. The past few weeks of my life are a blur. I mean, how does a thirty-four-year-old graduate from Spelman, with her master's degree in business displayed on her mantelpiece, inside a frame made of fourteen-karat gold, behave the way that I did? I don't even remember half the things the prosecutor said that I had done.

Anastasia claims I'm a few ribs short of a full slab, and I'm starting to believe that. Maybe I *am* crazy. I must be. In order to do the silly crap that I did, I must have lost my ever-loving mind. With any luck, I'll be found innocent by reason of insanity.

I see women on television, in soap operas and reality shows, who put themselves out there with no self-respect whatsoever, and I always yell at them, "You dumb broad. What are you? Stupid or something?" And today I feel like one of those dumb, stupid broads from TV. I know you're asking yourselves, *How can she talk about herself like that?* But, hey, call a spade a spade. I'm a big girl. I can take it. Once they put you in here and slam those bars shut, you grow the heck up real quick, fast, and in a hurry.

Yeah, that's right. I got locked up for doin' some silly stuff I ain't had no business doin'. I think the lyrics to the theme song from *Baretta* say it best: "Don't do the crime if you can't do the time." I'm guilty as sin, though. Yeah, I did the crime. I showed my natural black behind, and because of that, I'm lookin' at eighteen to twenty easily.

Y'all wanna know what I did? I know you do, and I'm gonna tell you too. I really don't wanna put my business out there, but women need to know, especially black women. If you're sprung out over a dangalang like I was, I advise you to get unsprung before you end up in the cell next to mine. I had to learn the hard way that no man's dangalang is dipped in platinum.

My name is Rhapsody Blue, and this is my sorry story.

Chapter 1

Mid-morning on a Saturday in June, I lay on the sofa in Dr. Janet Buckles's office. I was there for my routine biweekly chat with her. I inserted a Charms Blow Pop lollipop in my mouth and withdrew it. It was lime green, the same color as my blouse. Lime green was the color that represented mental illness.

"I see you got your green on," Dr. Buckles said to me.

I glanced down at my blouse, then looked at her. I sucked on my lollipop again, swallowed the sweet and sour taste before I spoke. "I wear lime green only when I come here. I don't wear this color in my everyday life."

She cocked her head to the side. "Why? It's such a pretty color on you. It kinda makes your dark skin glow." Dr. Buckles moved her shoulder-length hair away from her right ear and turned it toward me. I saw that she wore green studs in her lobes. "The emerald is my birthstone."

I sucked on my lollipop. "You wore those for me?"

She nodded her head and smiled. "I noticed that you always wear green when you come for your sessions."

"Only here, though," I reiterated. "Nowhere else."

"Why?" Dr. Buckles asked me again.

I had been diagnosed with Tourette's syndrome when I was six years old. I'd never forget getting my butt whupped each time I yelled an offensive slur. Finally, my parents had marched me into Bishop T. A. Clark, Jr.'s office at the church and had laid me over his desk.

My mother had been fit to be tied. "You better lay hands on her, Bishop, 'cause if she yells out and calls me a dirty fart bag one more time, I'ma kill her."

"Can't you perform an exorcism on her?" my father had asked the bishop.

I distinctly remembered Bishop Clark picking me up from his desk and holding me tight in his arms. That man prayed for my soul and my deliverance from whatever was attacking me and making me shout out nasty things. Well, after that didn't work, my folks took me to see a psychiatrist, and that was when Dr. Buckles broke the news that I was crazy and would be that way forever.

"I don't want to be pitied," I said, snapping out of my thoughts of the past.

"For wearing the color green? You don't have to be ashamed of your illness, Rhapsody. Tourette's syndrome is not uncommon. Have you had any episodes in the past two weeks?"

I sucked on my lollipop. "Nope."

Dr. Buckles smiled slightly. "That's good, right? No tics or anything at all?"

I shook my head from side to side. "Nobody made me mad in the past two weeks. The ugly side of me comes out only when I get pissed off."

Dr. Buckles nodded her head and wrote something on the notepad she had in her hand. "I still don't think you need to take any medication, Rhapsody. You seem to be managing your TS just fine."

Tourette's syndrome is a neurological disorder characterized by repetitive, stereotyped, involuntary movements and vocalizations, called tics. Tics that involve involuntary movements include rapid eye blinking, facial grimacing, shoulder shrugging, and head or shoulder jerking. The most dramatic tics are those with the element of self-harm, such as punching oneself in the face, and vocal tics, such as uttering socially inappropriate words. Because tic symptoms often do not cause impairment, most people with Tourette's syndrome require no medication for tic suppression.

Tourette's syndrome occurs in people from all ethnic groups; males are affected about three to four times more often than females. It is estimated that two hundred thousand African Americans have the most severe form of Tourette's syndrome, and as many as one hundred thousand exhibit milder and less complex symptoms, such as chronic motor or vocal tics.

Dr. Buckles stopped writing on her notepad and looked at me. "You're doing so well, Rhapsody, that I think we can start to schedule your visits for only once a month, rather than keeping them at twice monthly. What do you think?"

"I think so too, Dr. Buckles."

"Okay, well, I think we're done for now. Is there anything else you wanna talk about or share with me?"

I sucked on my lollipop some more. "Nope. I'm good."

Dr. Buckles stood, and so did I. "Then I'll see you in a month."

Chapter 2

On Monday evening I was driving home from work in my copper-colored, late-model Mercedes-Benz, heading toward my duplex in Oakbrook Terrace, a rich community west of Chicago. Yeah, I said "Mercedes-Benz" and "Oakbrook Terrace." That's right. I was living large, if I do say so myself. I was thirty-four years old, manless, and childless. I didn't have any dependents. It was only me in my household. When I ate, my whole family ate, so I had plenty of money. I wasn't loaded, but I made a nice living working as a traffic director for the Chicago Transit Authority. So was there any reason why I *shouldn't* have been living where I lived or driving what I drove?

My best friend, Stacy, said I was boojee, but she talked outta the side of her neck sometimes. I had the right to be sitting on top of the world. I wasn't born with a silver spoon in my mouth. I was raised on Drake Street, right off of Fifteenth Street, in the heart of the West Side of Chicago. It was common for crackheads to stand on every corner all day, every day. I didn't need my mother or an alarm clock to wake me up for school in the morning because I had the police siren, which was right on time each and every day. And the siren always meant that someone had been shot or stabbed or had gotten raped during the night. I remembered how my girlfriends and I would play in the park around the corner from my house when we were growing up. We sometimes used the chalk outline from a dead body to play hopscotch.

Forget teenage pregnancy. Back in the day it was adolescent pregnancy. One of my hopscotch friends was pregnant at the age of eleven. Her name was Phoebe, and she hadn't even gotten her period yet. Me neither. Phoebe was a pretty girl with soft, long black hair, and she wore it like Pocahontas. It was parted down the middle and woven into two long braids that came way past her shoulders. Phoebe's parents weren't of the same race. Her mother was black, and her father was a Puerto Rican man. Phoebe was so pretty that not only did the boys stare at her, but the girls would stare at her too and wish they could look just like her. I was one of those girls who envied Phoebe. But she was the one girl in the neighborhood whom all the other young girls our age were warned to stay away from, because she was hot to trot.

I knew Phoebe was messing around with fifteen-year-old Derrick Holmes, aka Skeet, because every time the kids on the block played "Catch a girl, kiss a girl," Skeet always made sure he caught Phoebe. Eventually, time told that they were doing more than just kissin'. Skeet was her baby daddy.

One thing I can say about my mama, Lerlean Blue, was that when it came to me, she didn't play that. I was Lerlean's only girl and the youngest in a family with two boys, and my mama was on my behind like stink on poop when it came to my period. I'd never forget the day I first got my period. I was in gym class, jumping double Dutch, wearing the required red school shirt and white shorts. The night before, Lerlean had washed and pressed my hair the old-school way. I'm talkin' about sittin' at the kitchen table, next to the stove, as the hot comb lay in the fire while my mama talked on the telephone. She held the receiver in the crook of her neck, with her left shoulder hunched up to press the telephone to her ear. She never did this without a cigarette dangling from her lips.

Lerlean was the only woman I knew who could smoke a cigarette all the way up to the butt and talk on the telephone without any of the ashes falling off. I remembered the crackling sound the hot comb made when it came into contact with the green Ultra Sheen hair grease Lerlean had piled on my scalp. Every time I heard that crackling sound, I would slump down in the chair to keep that hot comb from touching my forehead, my ears, or the nape of my neck.

"Girl, sit your tail up in this chair. I'm tryin' to get to this kitchen," my mama would fuss, and then she'd go right back to laughin' and talkin' to whomever she was on the telephone with. Of course, we all knew "kitchen" referred to "naps," and I had plenty of them.

After she pressed my hair, my mother would part it down the middle, then part it across from ear to ear to make four shiny braids. Then she would put a pair of my clean panties, which we called bloomers, on my head and send me into her and my father's bedroom to kiss Daddy good night before tucking me into my bed. I loved my daddy. He was the only father I knew who let his little girl decorate his hair and beard with pink and yellow barrettes.

Anyway, back to gym class and jumping double Dutch. I thought I was cute, especially since Sherman Douglas, the cutest boy in my class, was watching. When I knew I had his undivided attention, I really showed off as my teammates sang, "D-i-s-h. D-i-s-h. *D* is for double Dutch. *I* is for Irish. *S* is for single. *H* is for hop. D-i-s-h. D-i-s-h. *D* is for double Dutch. *I* is for Irish. *S* is for single. *H* is for hop."

After I impressed Sherman Douglas, since no other girl could beat my score in double Dutch, we moved on to Chinese jump rope. We used to connect the ends of rubber bands by intertwining them with one another to make a long rope. Two girls would stand facing each other about five feet apart, with the Chinese jump rope down around their ankles.

"Jump in. Jump out. Jump side to side. Jump on. Jump in. Jump out," everyone would chorus.

The girls standing with the rope around their ankles would move it up to their knees, then up to their thighs. Just like with double Dutch, I was the master at Chinese jump rope.

On that particular day, I was getting down, showing off for Sherman, when I heard, "Ooh, Rhapsody, you bleedin'." It came from one of the girls holding the Chinese rope.

Wouldn't you know it? Just when I had Sherman right where I wanted him, my period came for the first time, right through my white gym shorts. That I felt embarrassed was an understatement. I literally wanted to lie down right there on the gymnasium floor and die.

Now back to what I said about my mama not taking any crap when it came to my period. Lerlean kept a calendar hanging on the wall in her bedroom, and she marked the days of my period every month. Every twenty-eight days, like clockwork, she was on top of me.

"Did you get your period, Rhapsody?"

"Yes, ma'am," I'd answer.

See, in Lerlean's household—notice that I didn't say, "In my *father's* household," and that I said, "In *Lerlean's* household"—my daddy didn't run nothin'. And my brothers and I couldn't answer a question and leave it at that. We had to put a "ma'am" after it.

"Let me see," she would say to me.

It didn't matter if we were in the living room or outside in the backyard. I had to pull down my panties and show the color red on a maxi pad to prove to my mama that I was on my period. I used to think Lerlean was crazy and strict as heck for doing that to me, but guess what? That kept me in line, and to this day, I thank God that my mama was on me the way she was, because although I was a fast-tailed li'l girl, in my neighborhood I was one of the few, and I mean *very* few, girls to graduate from high school without getting pregnant or having an abortion.

During my freshman year I gave my number to a boy named Tyreek Avery, who was a junior at my school. When he called my house for the first time, Lerlean answered the telephone. I didn't know what she said to Tyreek, but I wasn't allowed to talk to him on the telephone that night and he never called again and he avoided me in school from then on. After she hung up on him, my mama stormed into my bedroom and told me a thing or two.

"Why you got these li'l nappy-headed fools callin' my house?"

"Tyreek just wanted to talk, Mama."

"Talk my behind!" she scolded me. "That ain't all he wanna do. He wants to get in your panties, Rhapsody." Then she cocked her head to the side and glared at me. "Are you messin'?"

I was shocked as heck that my mama would ask me such a question, but then again, Lerlean was never one to bite her tongue for anyone.

"No, Mama."

She cocked her head to the other side and glared at me some more. "Don't lie to me, Rhapsody. All I gotta do is take you down to the clinic and find out. Are you messin'?"

"No, Mama, I'm not."

"Let me tell you somethin'. You can go out there and get a baby if you want to, but you need to know that I'm not raising any more kids. These li'l boys will say anything to get you to have sex. Well, I ain't having it. So I'ma tell you this one time and one time only. Keep your legs closed. You're only fourteen years old, and I'm not gonna let you throw your future away because some li'l snot-nosed, musty boy told you that you were pretty. You *are* pretty, and I want you to stay that way, because there's nothin' pretty about a fourteen-year-old pregnant girl. And if you *do* mess around and get caught up, I'ma beat the black off you, then send you to live with him and *his* mama."

It took Lerlean only one time to preach to me. I was proud to say that my mama never had to put me out of her house.

I promised my parents that I would make something of myself someday. I went to college, graduated at the top of my class, and got a job immediately. I went to work for the Chicago Transit Authority, even though it wasn't in my field. But I didn't mind at all. Money was money. And I didn't care if I was called a sellout for living better or driving better. I felt that if someone wasn't paying my house or car note, then Stacy and everyone else who had a problem with my lifestyle could do what I used to hear my mama tell my daddy all the time. Kiss my entire black rump. And I had a big rump too, just like Lerlean.

Sometimes it could be hotter than hell itself in June. My air conditioner was blowing as I headed west on Interstate 290. I was cruising at forty miles an hour. According to a report on WGN Channel 9 news the night before, Chicago was ranked number one when it came to cities with the worst traffic. I was certainly a living witness to that. I was literally playing a game of stop and go. My commute to Oakbrook Terrace from the Loop was jacked up every single day.

I thought about the day I'd had. Mondays were always bad. It didn't matter where you worked or how much money you made. If you had four more days ahead of you to do the crap you hated to do, then Mondays were always bad. A few minutes before quitting time today, a woman had decided to end her life by jumping onto the tracks, into the path of an oncoming train. I had been standing by the time clock, ready to punch my time card, when the message came over the walkie-talkie from the control center. I'd been afraid to turn around and look into my boss's face for fear of what I might see.

"I know you heard that, Rhapsody," Mr. Duncan had said to me.

Darn. I had to do mandatory overtime. "Yeah, I heard it." I exhaled loudly and placed my unpunched time card back in its slot.

Then Mr. Duncan and I hopped into his company SUV and headed to the tunnel at State and Randolph Streets, so that he could investigate the incident while I did what I was hired to do, which was to reroute passengers. I'd been with the CTA for almost nine years, and it was my job to direct train and bus passengers to an alternate source of transportation each time there was an accident or derailment.

I hated working with the public, because people could be some of the most ignorant buttholes you could ever meet. For me, seeing a maimed body was the same as watching *The Young and the Restless* during my lunch hour. It had always been a part of my day. But trying to reroute passengers who had never seen anything so hideous was difficult.

Mr. Duncan and I arrived at the tunnel and pressed our way through the crowd of people staring at the body on the tracks. It was a mystery why we always arrived at the crime scenes before the police did. When I got to the edge of the platform, I saw a woman, who appeared to be in her early thirties, lying across the tracks, with pieces of her body strewn all around her.

"She was standing there. Then, all of a sudden, she just jumped right when the train was coming," an elderly Caucasian woman said. I immediately pulled her to the side and asked her to wait for the police to arrive, because they'd definitely want to talk with her if they ever got their sorry tails there.

Each time I managed to pull one passenger away from the edge of the platform, another would step in his or her place to get a look at the dead woman on the tracks. I softly tugged on a black man's arm to get him away from the edge of the platform. "Sir, step this way, please."

"I'm just trying to see," he said to me.

That was what I was referring to when I said that people could be some of the most ignorant buttholes you could ever meet. Who in their right mind would want to see bloody body parts sprawled across the tracks? I felt like pushing him off the platform so that he would land right on top of the dead woman. That way he'd get an up close and personal look at her and probably catch a case of hepatitis C.

It took about an hour to clear the tunnel of passengers; the police had arrived by then, along with the city coroner. That was when I noticed the young blond train operator sitting on a bench, with her head hanging down. I went and sat next to her.

"Are you okay?" I asked.

When she looked at me, I saw the bluest eyes. She didn't say anything, but I noticed tears streaming down her cheeks. Of course she'd be upset. What train operator wouldn't be in this situation?

"Would you like a bottle of water?"

She sniffled and blew her nose in the tissue she was holding. "I couldn't stop. There was nothing I could do. It all happened so fast."

She began sobbing loudly, and I pulled her into my arms and rocked her. I truly felt sorry for her. Witnessing someone jump in front of the train you were driving could traumatize a person for life. While I was consoling her, the CTA's urine laboratory technician stepped up to us and told her that she had tested positive for alcohol. She didn't have the five years of service needed to qualify for the employees' assistance program, where you could keep your job but get treatment for six months without pay.

Personally, I didn't feel that was right. Someone had jumped in front of her train, and she had had to take a piss test, like it was her fault. She placed her face in her hands and cried some more. Just like that, she was out of a job. Now, *that* was real trauma.

Too much excitement for a Monday had made me hungry. I saw that I was coming up on Seventeenth Avenue, and I couldn't help but see the huge Burger World sign from the expressway. After the day I'd had, I sure as heck wasn't about to try to cook anything. I put my right turn signal on and made my way up the exit ramp. I turned into the Burger World parking lot and drove into the drive-through lane, then placed my order.

"Your total comes to six dollars and seventeen cents. Please drive up to the window," the cashier told me over the intercom.

I proceeded to the window and held out a ten-dollar bill for the cashier to take when I saw him leaning out the window. He was fair skinned, high yellow, some might say.

He repeated the order I'd placed. "That was a cheeseburger deluxe, a small French fry, a medium root beer, and a slice of apple pie?"

He waited for me to confirm that the order was correct, but I was in a daze. I stared into the greenest eyes I'd ever seen in all my thirty-four years of life. He saw the ten-dollar bill stretched out to him but, I guess, decided not to take the money from me until I had answered him. He looked at me as I gazed through him. "Ma'am?"

I blinked three times. "I'm sorry. What did you say?"

He repeated my order.

"Yes, that's correct," I confirmed.

"Six seventeen."

I extended the money his way. He grabbed the bill, but I held on to it. When I didn't release it, he looked at me.

"Would you like something else?" he asked.

Yes. You on a silver platter. I let go of the money. "No, that'll be all."

A minute later he returned to the window with my change and my drink. "I'm sorry, but it's gonna be a three-minute wait for your fries," he said. "If you pull into one of the waiting parking spots, someone will bring your order out to you."

"I want *you* to bring it out to me." I had inherited my mother's raw tongue. Just like Lerlean, I was extremely outspoken.

"Excuse me?"

"I placed my order with *you*, and it was *you* who took my money, so I want *you* to bring it to me, and no one else. Because if my order is not right, I'll know who to blame."

I didn't wait for a response. I drove into a waiting spot, placed the car in park, and did a quick make-up check in my rearview mirror. I could tell from his smooth skin that I had at least ten good years on him, but I didn't care, 'cause if he was grown enough to work a job, then he was grown enough to work me.

From my purse, I withdrew a small bottle of Vera Wang perfume and sprayed the insides of my wrists and rubbed them together. I quickly ran my fingers through my

The Ugly Side of Me

shoulder-length locks; then I adjusted the air conditioner to blow full blast.

I was sitting in my Mercedes-Benz, enjoying the comfort of the air conditioner, when there was a knock at my window. I looked up and saw him standing there, holding a white paper bag. I pressed the button to lower my window, and he gently placed the bag in my hand.

"I'm sorry about the wait," he said, apologizing.

"It was no problem. Hot fries are always worth the wait."

You are worth waiting on too.

"Well, have a nice day, ma'am."

He had turned to walk away when I called after him. "Can you wait a second? I want to make sure my order is correct."

"I checked it myself, ma'am. You got exactly what you ordered."

I looked him up and down. *Humph. Not everything.*

I unwrapped the cheeseburger and saw it had been prepared the way I wanted. My French fries were hot and fresh. "You forgot something," I complained.

He looked at me. "And what might that be?"

"Ketchup."

"I didn't forget it. Condiments are given only upon request."

I looked deep into his jades. "Okay, well, I request three packets of ketchup."

He cracked a smile, which made me believe that he knew I was flirting with him. "Are you serious?"

"What do you mean, 'Are I serious?' Of course I'm serious. Who eats French fries without ketchup?"

"I just figured you to be a barbecue sauce kind of woman."

"Is that right? I like barbecue sauce, so you can bring me some of that too."

"I'm gonna have to charge you for the barbecue sauce."

"You can charge me for barbecue sauce, soy sauce, tartar sauce, and hot sauce as long as I get to see you again."

He smiled. "Hold that thought." He disappeared inside Burger World and returned with three packets each of barbecue sauce and ketchup. "Here you go. The barbecue sauce is on the house."

"Thank you, but you still forgot something."

"Ask me how I knew you were gonna say that. What did I forget this time?"

"I want you to figure it out."

"Ma'am, I'm on the clock. I don't have that kind of time."

"First of all, my name is not ma'am." Dang. Did I look that old to be called ma'am? That was what I called women my mother's age. "It's Rhapsody, okay? Rhapsody Blue. Secondly, isn't it your responsibility to make sure that each customer is completely satisfied?"

"Something like that."

"Well, let me ask you a question. What's your name?"

He pointed to the tag on his shirt. "Malcolm."

"Malcolm, what should I do if I get too much ketchup or barbecue sauce on my fingers?"

He chuckled. "Lick them clean."

"Yeah, I guess I could do that, but what if I wanted to wipe them clean instead?"

Malcolm laughed out loud. "I forgot your napkins, didn't I?"

"Yes, you did. But I don't mind waiting while you get them."

Two minutes later Malcolm presented me with napkins. "At the risk of losing my job for spending too much time out here, I'll ask the question, anyway. Can I get you anything else?"

"Yes. Your age and telephone number." There was no shame in my game, but I needed to make sure he was legal.

"I'm twenty-one," Malcolm said.

I smiled, because he was old enough to handle what I wanted to do to him. I didn't have to worry about getting arrested. The moment I knew Malcolm was an adult, I went all the way in. "If I invited you to my bedroom tonight, would you come?"

He blushed first, then laughed out loud. Malcolm's yellow complexion turned crimson red right in front of me. He covered his mouth with a semi-closed fist and asked, "Are you serious?"

"As a heart attack," I answered. I wasn't smiling.

There was a long pregnant pause before Malcolm spoke. He stopped smiling and looked directly into my eyes. "How old are you, Rhapsody?"

"Does it matter?"

Malcolm shrugged his shoulders. "I don't know. It might."

"I'm thirty-four," I said and held my breath. He was so fine, and I wanted him badly.

When he nodded his head up and down, I became hopeful and released a sigh of relief.

"Yeah, we can do this."

Good. "What time are you off?"

"Nine."

After assuring me that he'd meet me in my bedroom after his shift was over, Malcolm and I exchanged cellular telephone numbers. I drove away from Burger World, feeling like a new woman. I was dry, and I looked forward to some young blood quenching my thirst.

Chapter 3

I couldn't get out of the parking lot fast enough before I called Anastasia, Stacy's government name.

"Stacy, I just found my husband."

I heard her sigh into the phone line. I knew what she was thinking. *Aw, heck! Here we go again.* "Before we go any further, Rhapsody, I gotta remind you that the Bible says that a man finds his wife, not the other way around."

"Well, I found this man at Burger World, and I'm keeping him."

"Burger World?"

"Yes, Burger World. He works there."

"Rhapsody, you work for the CTA, making boo coo money. What can a man working in a fast-food restaurant do for you?"

"That's what I'm gonna find out, and guess what else, Stacy."

"I'm afraid to. Just tell me."

"He's twenty-one years old."

Anastasia shrieked. "*Twenty-one*? Rhapsody, are you crazy?"

It was just like her to jump off the deep end over something so minor. I longed for the day when I'd hear my best girlfriend say something like, "All right with your bad self. I ain't mad at ya."

"Stacy, calm down. Dang. Why can't you ever be happy for me? I tell you I met a young tenderoni, and you act like all hell has broken loose."

"I'm glad you mentioned that, Rhapsody, because all hell *will* break loose when you bust it wide open."

I rolled my eyes into the air. I didn't feel like listening to another one of Anastasia's self-righteous sermons. "He's legal, Stacy."

"And that makes it all right?"

"*Whatever*. Besides, it's about time for this kitty kat to come out of hiding."

"Rhapsody, you're going straight to jail for messing with these li'l boys."

"Well, be that as it may, just be down at the jailhouse with my bond money when I call. And trust me when I tell you this, girlfriend. Malcolm doesn't look like a boy. I got a good look at his biceps and pecs through his uniform shirt, and they were screaming out my name."

"Oh, I get it. You just want a boy toy to play with," Anastasia said.

"No, not necessarily, but if the opportunity presents itself, I can't make any promises to walk away from it. You'll never understand, Stacy. You lie next to a man *every* night."

"I'm married. I can do that. Just take a cold shower and you'll be all right."

"You think it's that easy? Just take cold showers about four times a day? That's your advice to me? I ain't never been celibate, and I ain't tryin' to be."

"Cold showers could help."

"Well, let me just tell you that that is a myth. I can remember a time when I sat in a tub of cold water and it started bubbling like I had dropped two Alka-Seltzer tablets in it. You know my vajayjay stays hot."

Although Stacy didn't want to, she couldn't help but laugh at me. "Ooh, I can't believe you said that. But for real, though, Rhapsody, you need to get saved. And God will keep those that want to be kept."

Here she goes again with this holy, holy, saved and sanctified crap. "Like who? You? Girl, please. When was the last time *you* said a prayer? You go to church only on Easter and Mother's Day. So, when you get the calling and preach your first sermon, I'll be sitting on the front pew, but until then, you need to shut up and stop judging what *I* do."

"Why you gotta cuss me out like that, Rhapsody? I'm tryin' to help *you* out. You're making this personal."

"You never cussed me out, Stacy?"

"No."

"You're lying. Didn't you cuss me out last Thursday, when I bought myself a Fendi bag without buying you one to match it?"

"And that was a good reason for cussing you out. You don't do no mess like that."

"Look, can we change the subject? I'm getting a headache."

"Uh-uh. We're gonna finish this. Why not get involved in an extracurricular activity to take your mind off of sex?"

"Like what?" I asked.

"I don't know. Heck, anything. How about bike riding?"

I thought about it. "Uh-uh. The seat pressing against my inner thighs will make me horny."

Anastasia exhaled. "Oh, Lord. Well, how about doing aerobics at the gym?"

I thought about that also. "Nope, because all that sweat on my body will become hot and sticky, and I'll end up in the sauna, doing nasty things to myself."

"Oh, my God. You know what, Rhapsody? I'm starting to believe that there's no hope for you. What about knitting or crocheting? You can't get into trouble with that, can you?"

"I sure can. Having access to that much yarn or rope will make me tie a man up and take it from him."

She was fed up with me. "Okay. Do whatever you wanna do. I tried. Where are you headed?"

"Home. I hate Mondays. Today was the day from hell. If I never see another train or bus, it would be too soon."

"I caught the tail end of the news, but I couldn't quite make out what happened."

"Right at the start of rush hour this evening, some woman decided to jump in front of an oncoming train at the State and Randolph station. We had to shut the power off on the entire red line. So my boss made me work overtime, rerouting passengers. Needless to say, I didn't have a good evening."

"It's a shame when folks commit suicide like that."

"I don't have a problem with people committing suicide. I get upset when they do it on my dime and time. If you wanna knock yourself off, don't inconvenience half the darn city. Do it the normal way. Just close all the windows in your house, turn the gas on in the kitchen, then sit at the table and wait for your neighbor to find you."

Anastasia laughed. "Girl, you're stupid. There's nothing normal about committing suicide."

"That ain't true, Stacy. It depends on what you're going through. Like in my situation, if I don't get any nooky in the next twenty-four hours, ain't no telling what I might do."

"Rhapsody, please, you ain't *that* crazy. Being celibate does not make you wanna kill yourself."

"Yeah, okay. Today is Monday, and if I don't get any nooky by this time tomorrow, don't be surprised when you find me on my kitchen floor, lying next to the stove."

Anastasia was done with me. "Bye, heifer," she said and disconnected the call.

Immediately my telephone rang. I saw my folks' home telephone number displayed on the caller ID.

"Hey, Mama." I knew it was her. My father never called my cell.

"Hi. I saw the news. Rough evening?"

I exhaled a loud sigh. "Yes, ma'am. Not only did a person commit suicide, but I witnessed a young train operator lose her job too. She had alcohol in her system and not enough years on the job to stay employed."

"My Lord," Lerlean said. "That's terrible. Did you pray for her and the person who committed suicide?"

I frowned. "Huh?"

"Did you pray for them? A tragedy happened, Rhapsody."

"Mama, no amount of praying was gonna put the maimed woman's body back together, and no amount of praying would have saved the train operator's job. It is what it is."

I appreciated the fact that my mother was a praying woman, but there were times when she worked my nerves. In Lerlean's world everything—every event and every occasion—was a reason to pray. If it rained too hard, she'd pray for the Lord to take the rain away. If it didn't rain at all, Lerlean could be found on her knees, praying for God to bring the wet stuff. If she wasn't trying to drag me to church, then she was trying to make me pray about something.

Like my folks, I was a member of World Deliverance Christian Center and had been all my life. I was baptized by Bishop Thomas Arthur Clark, Jr. When he retired from the pulpit, his son with the same name took over the church. We called the young bishop by the nickname Art. Art was the same age as me, and he could surely bring forth a good word, but whenever he preached, it seemed that he was speaking directly to me. And he always made eye contact with me, like he knew my dirty secrets. Somehow Art always knew when I had lain with a man, 'cause the Sunday after I had committed the sin, he'd preach about fornication and forgiveness. It never failed.

I considered myself a born-again Christian. I believed in God. I believed that He died on a cross for my sins, and I believed that on the third day, Jesus rose from the grave and ascended to heaven. I was baptized when I was five years old. Couldn't nobody tell me that I wasn't saved. But I hated when folks tried to force religion on me. I prayed when I wanted to pray.

What could I say? I loved sex. I loved how it made me feel. Sex was the one sin that easily beset me. I knew I needed to sit under Bishop Art and his wife, First Lady Felicia, because I knew my deliverance would come, but I didn't wanna be delivered from sex. I did, however, mail my tithes and offerings to the church faithfully. Now, that was the one thing I didn't play with. I always gave God His money, because I realized that it was because of Him that I was alive and healthy. I should've been dead a long time ago. But God kept me, and for that, I was thankful.

"I know a tragedy happened, Mama. But what could I have done?"

"Prayer changes thangs, is all I'm sayin'."

"No one knows that better than me," I sighed. I was ready to end the conversation.

"You should come to Bible study with me tonight. Bishop Art is teaching a series on knowing your strength in God."

"Not tonight, Mama. I'm tired. It's been a long day, and I just wanna go home, shower, and get into bed." There was no way I was gonna be honest with Lerlean and tell her that I was expecting company in my bed in a few hours.

"Rhapsody, you always have an excuse why you can't come to church. Whether it's to Bible study or Sunday morning service, you can never make it."

She was right.

"I know, Mama. I'm always so busy."

"Too busy to worship the Lord? What if God was too busy to tend to *your* needs?"

"That's why I send my tithes, Mama. I pay God to take good care of me."

I could tell I had pissed her off when she yelled out, "God don't need your money! He *is* money. He's air, He's light, and He's the sun, moon, and stars. He ain't God because you're paying Him to be. He's God because He's God. God's got His hand on you because He wants it on you."

Again, she was right. I lived a great life. God had blessed me with a wonderful job. My health and strength were good. I really had no real excuse for why I couldn't attend church. "Okay, Mama. I promise to go to church, but not tonight." There was no way I was gonna give up the opportunity to have my legs suspended in the air. "I'll meet you at church on Sunday morning."

"I've heard that lie before."

After what Malcolm and I were getting ready to do, I was for sure gonna go to church and get myself forgiven. "I'll be there, I promise."

Just after nine thirty that evening, I was lying across my bed, watching the news, when a commercial announced that the most delicious hamburgers in the Windy City could be found at Burger World. Immediately, I thought of Malcolm and wondered what he was doing at that moment. I wanted to call him but thought it would make me seem desperate. In all actuality I *was* desperate, but Malcolm didn't need to know that.

I turned onto my side and clutched my pillow. I was picturing his dark green eyes when the telephone on my nightstand rang. I wasted no time answering it on the first ring. I hoped that it was Malcolm calling to say that he was on his way to my house.

"Hello?"

It was Anastasia. "Hey, it's me."

I gave a sigh of frustration into the telephone. "Oh, what's up?"

She knew me well, and she also knew it wasn't her voice I wanted to hear. "Well, heck, I love you too."

"I'm sorry, Stacy. It's been a long day. I was almost asleep," I lied.

"Is that all it is, or were you expecting a certain young man with the smell of Similac with iron on his breath to call?"

"Who are you talkin' about?"

"Don't play with me, Rhapsody. You know who I'm talkin' about."

"I ain't thinkin' about that boy."

"I'm glad to hear that, because that's exactly what he is, a boy. It won't work, girlfriend."

"What won't work, Stacy?"

"Whatever it is you're daydreaming about doing with him. He's way out of your league, and you two are not on the same level. Don't start anything with him that you can't finish."

"Look, Stacy, I haven't given Malcolm another thought since I saw him. I doubt if he'll even call."

"But what if he does?" she asked.

"Then I'll tell him I was only flirting and didn't mean anything by it." I lied to Anastasia just to get her off the line. Yes, I had flirted with Malcolm, and I had meant every word that I said to him.

"Yeah, okay," Stacy said. I knew she didn't believe me.

"I'll talk to you in the morning," I said and disconnected the call.

Fifteen minutes later, I answered my front door, wearing a short red lace teddy with thin spaghetti straps supporting my heavy double D breasts. Malcolm stood in the doorway in awe of me. He was lookin' good. With that bulge in his pants, he couldn't hide the fact that he was excited to see me too.

"Can I help you?" I asked seductively.

He smiled. "You called *me*."

Yeah, I had. I was weak. I had called Malcolm to confirm that he was still going to pay me a visit that night. I couldn't hide the fact, not even to myself, that I was desperate. "Come on in, and I hope you brought your appetite with you. I have strawberries and whipped cream in the refrigerator."

"I'm not a strawberry type of guy." He scanned my body, slightly pausing when his gaze reached the area beneath my belly. "I do like cherries, though," Malcolm said seductively.

I looked at him and smiled. "Well, in that case, let's skip the appetizer and get right to the main course."

Malcolm stepped into the foyer and pulled my torso to his. He could feel my cleavage pressing into his chest. "What's on the menu?"

I ran my tongue along his entire mustache from left to right before answering him. "My cherry."

A dose of young blood was exactly what I needed. Malcolm gave me what I wanted, how I wanted it, and where I wanted it. He whispered words in my ear I had never heard before. Young Malcolm rocked my thirty-four-year-old world as he turned me every which way but loose. He kissed, he licked, he massaged, and he caressed my entire body before turning me out, all the way out. We did everything but swing from the ceiling fan. I appreciated the fact that every ten minutes, Malcolm asked how I felt or if I liked what he was doing to me. My answer was a continuous yes. He even asked what my pleasure was, and before I could finish describing my fantasy, Malcolm was already mastering it.

I did my best to last with him, but eventually, I begged Malcolm to stop. My thighs were so sore that I could only pray that I'd be able to walk in the morning. Malcolm and I lay spent in the middle of my king-size bed with only sweat between us. I hoped and prayed that God would forgive me for what I had just done.

"That was good, Malcolm," I moaned.

He chuckled. "I aim to please."

"I hope we can do this again."

"We can definitely do it again."

I was lying on Malcolm's chest, drifting off to sleep, when he gently eased out from under me and sat up on the bed.

"You're not leaving, are you?"

"I have to open up the restaurant in the morning," he answered as he reached toward the floor for his pants.

I purred like a kitten. "Do you have to go right now?"

Malcolm leaned over to me and kissed my lips lightly. "Yeah, I gotta get home and get some sleep."

He walked into my master bathroom and started the water in the shower. Malcolm had told me he lived with his mother, and so I wondered why he felt the need to shower if he was going home and straight to bed.

Chapter 4

On Tuesday morning, while I was driving to work, my cellular telephone rang. I saw that it was Anastasia calling.

"*Good morning*," I sang.

"My, my, my. Aren't we bright-eyed and bushy tailed this morning? I take it that you had a good night's sleep."

"Well, I had a good night, *that's* for sure. Actually, the word *good* is putting it mildly. There wasn't much sleeping going on, though."

"Tell me you didn't, Rhapsody."

I giggled. "I don't know what you're talkin' about."

"Don't play with me. You called that boy, didn't you?"

"First of all, Stacy, his name is Malcolm, and he's a grown man."

"Barely," Anastasia stated sarcastically.

"So what?" I shot back at her. "Grown is grown, and the answer to your question is yes. I was on fire, and Malcolm came to extinguish me. And I'll tell you something else. His body should have a note from the surgeon general attached to it that reads, 'Warning. One stroke of this *will* be hazardous to your health.'"

Anastasia didn't find that humorous at all. "Humph. So what happens now?"

"What do you mean?"

"Where do things stand with you and this boy?"

I exhaled loudly. She was pissing me off big-time with this "boy" crap. "Stacy, do you think it's possible for you to refer to him as Malcolm?"

"I'll do my best. Are you and *Malcolm* an item now? Are you gonna see him again?"

"Dang, Stacy. What's up with the third degree?"

"I just have one more question for you, Rhapsody."

I rolled my eyes at no one in particular. "What?"

"What's Malcolm's last name?"

"Look, Stacy, I don't know. Finding out Malcolm's last name, birthday, and Social Security number wasn't a priority for me last night. I just wanted to get done. Okay?"

"That's a shame."

"Whatever. I gotta go, 'cause I'm on my way to work to earn some money. Not every woman has the luxury of being a devoted housewife like you."

I disconnected the line and tossed my cellular telephone on the passenger seat. To heck with what Anastasia was preaching about. Every single night she lay on a huge, hairy chest, so of course, it was easy for her to tell me what I should and shouldn't be doing. Now, a single woman with the same issue as me might have something to say that was worth listening to, but Anastasia, on the other hand, needed to mind her own freakin' business and keep her darn mouth shut.

Traffic was moving nicely, and I saw that I had ten minutes to spare, so I decided to pay Malcolm a morning-after visit at Burger World. I got to the drive-through menu board, all set to hear his voice, but I heard a female's voice over the intercom instead. I placed an order for a ham and cheese biscuit and a small coffee with cream and sugar, then drove around to the pickup window. I handed over the money and looked at the cashier.

"Is Malcolm here?" I asked.

"No. He's off today."

What? "Oh, really? Did he call in sick?"

"No. It's his regular day off."

I went over in my mind what Malcolm had said to me at two in the morning. *I have to open the restaurant in the morning. I gotta get home and get some sleep.*

Without waiting for my meal, I sped away from the window and drove to a parking spot. I quickly placed the car in park and called Malcolm's cellular telephone number, the only number he had given me. My call was immediately sent to his voice mail.

"Yo, what's up? This is Malcolm. Leave a message, and I'll holla back. Peace."

The beep couldn't come fast enough before I turned up. "Malcolm, this is Rhapsody. Remember me? I'm the one you screwed for three hours last night. Guess where I am right now. I'm at Burger World, and I just found out that you're scheduled to be off today. Let me tell you something. You ain't gotta lie to me, okay? As far as I'm concerned, last night was just a one-time thang. You don't owe me squat, and I don't owe you squat. So, you can just lose my number, you trifling jerk."

I was mad as hell. Malcolm had lied to me. The night before we had kinda made plans to see each other again. We had been all hugged up and twisted in each other's arms like a pretzel. I didn't feel like what we had done was a one-night stand. Malcolm had kissed my forehead and the rest of my face softly. It had felt like we were making love and not just having meaningless sex. I thought I had meant something to Malcolm, so I didn't understand why he had lied.

I got back on the Eisenhower Expressway and headed toward the Loop. My heart was beating out of my chest, and I felt a spell coming on. I couldn't control the tics. I tried not to, but I threw the back of my head into my headrest three times. My eyes connected with those of the woman driving on my right side, going at the same speed as me. She saw me and looked at me like I was insane. I sped up to get away from her gaze, but she caught up with me. I suppressed the bad words that were forthcoming. I shook my head vigorously from side to side. I wanted to shake the bad words away.

Please, God, not now, I silently prayed. I needed the Lord to stop what was getting ready to escape from my throat. *Please keep it inside, Jesus.* I looked at the woman as we drove side by side on the expressway. She kept watching me. Tears had begun to fill my lower eyelids, because I couldn't control my reaction. "Slut, whore, butthole lips!"

My passenger-side window was down, and so was the woman's driver-side window, so she heard my words. She frowned at me, shook her head, then sped up to get away from me. I wanted to catch up to her and apologize, like I had done to hundreds of people during my lifetime when I had exploded in anger, but I didn't bother chasing the woman. I just cried all the way to work.

Chapter 5

Lucille Ella-Jean Washington was a sixty-four-year-old paraplegic, a result of being in the wrong place at the wrong time. Two years and four months ago, she was standing in the parking lot of the Jewel food store on Ninety-Fifth Street and South Ashland Avenue in Chicago, unloading groceries from a shopping cart and placing them into the trunk of her car, when gunshots pierced the air. Before Lucille had a chance to run for cover, a bullet struck her lower back, paralyzing her from the waist down and confining her to a wheelchair for the rest of her life. She was the second person to become a victim of a gang cross fire in the same month and in the same parking lot.

"Now, that's what I like to see."

Lucille turned and rolled away from the stove. She sat a plate of fried honey-flavored country bacon on the kitchen table. She looked at her son, who was standing in the doorway. "What are you talkin' about, Malcolm?"

"I'm talkin' about waking up to see a woman do what she's supposed to be doing."

"Is that right?" she asked.

"Please believe me."

"Come on over here, boy, and give your mama some sugar."

Malcolm strolled over to Lucille and knelt to kiss her right cheek, but before his lips could touch her face, Lucille smacked them with the back of her hand.

He frowned. "Ow, Mama. What was that for?"

"That was for talkin' crap," Lucille fussed. "And it's lucky for you that I can't move my legs, 'cause if I could, I'd put my foot deep in your behind."

"You would, huh?"

Lucille mocked her son's famous last words. "Please believe me."

Malcolm got a plate from the dish rack, then sat at the table and filled it with bacon, scrambled eggs, and waffles. "So, I guess you got a thing about women serving men."

"I ain't got nothin' against a woman serving her man, but you ain't my man. I *am* your woman, though."

"How do you figure that?" Malcolm asked.

"Get me the butter out of the refrigerator."

Malcolm did as he was told, then sat down at the table.

"Get me the maple syrup out of the cabinet and pour me a glass of milk."

Without hesitation, Malcolm obeyed. He sat down at the table again. "Is there anything else you want?"

"Uh-uh. But you see how you just served me and asked if I wanted anything else?"

"Yeah. So?"

"So that's how I figure that I'm your woman."

Malcolm scowled at his mother. "You think you're all that, don't you?"

"Let me tell you something, boy, and don't you ever forget it. Lucille Ella-Jean Washington is all that and then some."

"You sure about that?" Malcolm asked.

"Please believe me," she replied, mocking him again.

They were laughing, talking, and enjoying breakfast when they heard Malcolm's cellular phone beeping in his bedroom, indicating there was a message on his voice mail.

"Malcolm, that phone has been beeping for the past hour," Lucille complained. "Why don't you check the message?"

"Because I know who it is and I don't feel like being bothered by that chick right now."

"What chick?"

"This girl I met yesterday. She's calling so we can hook up, but I ain't feelin' her." Earlier Malcolm had seen Rhapsody's number flash across his cellular phone screen but had let the call go to his voice mail. He wouldn't dare confess to Lucille that he had already hooked up with Rhapsody.

"Well, if you're not feelin' her, why did you give her your number?" Lucille had forbidden Malcolm from giving the home telephone number out to women. They showed no respect when they called in the wee hours of the morning and woke her up. She had told Malcolm that he could do whatever he wanted to do with his cellular number, but that had also rung at the midnight hour.

"It's a guy thing, Ma. I like to keep my options open."

"Every month it's a different girl and always the same bull crap. You better not come around here with no babies, Malcolm."

"You ain't gotta worry about that, Lucy. I'm a pro at what I do."

Malcolm knew that a sure way to get under his mother's skin was to call her Lucy.

"You know what, Malcolm? One of these days God is gonna put just the right amount of strength in my legs long enough for me stomp a hole in your back big enough for me to walk through. I miss kickin' your behind. You know that? But one of these days I'm gonna be like a storm up in here."

Malcolm finished his glass of orange juice, then leaned back in his chair and belched loudly. "Like Hurricane Lucy?" He laughed.

The front door opened, then closed. Malcolm looked over his shoulder to see his sister, Cherise, coming toward them. Every morning before work, Cherise stopped by to help their mother with her bath.

When Cherise got to the archway of the kitchen, Malcolm began making wind noises with his lips. "Watch out, Cherise. Take cover. Hurricane Lucy is in here."

Lucille looked at him and rolled her eyes.

"What are you doing, Malcolm?" Cherise asked. She smacked the side of his face softly with the back of her hand.

Lucille quickly responded, "What he does best. Acting like a fool."

Cherise walked over to her mother and kissed her cheek. "Good morning."

"Good morning. How's my favorite son-in-law?"

"Sean is your *only* son-in-law. He's fine, and he sends his love."

"Are you pregnant yet?" Lucille asked Cherise.

"Mama, must you ask me that every day?"

"Yep. I'm hoping you'd get tired of me asking and go ahead and make me a grandma."

"You don't need me for that. Malcolm can handle that."

"I sho can. What do you want? A boy or a girl?" Malcolm asked with a mouth full of food.

"I want an angel. All I would get from you are demons. And I taught you to swallow your food before you speak," Lucille fussed at her son.

Malcolm swallowed, then looked at his sister. "You see how she treats me?"

"Better you than me." Cherise adjusted the brakes on Lucille's wheelchair. "Are you ready for your bath?"

"It's almost nine o'clock. Aren't you gonna be late for work?" Lucille asked Cherise.

"I have a late meeting this morning. What time is your therapy session?"

"Not until ten thirty."

As Cherise rolled her mother toward the bathroom, she paused. "Do you hear that?"

"Hear what?" Lucille asked.

"That beeping sound."

Lucille yelled over her shoulder. "Malcolm, please do something about that darn phone. And if you don't want the heifers to call, then don't give them the number."

Malcolm stood from the table, placed his empty plate in the sink, then went into his bedroom and closed his door. He picked up his telephone and lay on the bed, then listened to his voice mail.

"Malcolm, this is Rhapsody. Remember me? I'm the one you screwed for three hours last night."

Malcolm's eyes bucked out of his head.

"Guess where I am right now. I'm at Burger World, and I just found out that you're scheduled to be off today."

Malcolm sat up on the bed. "What are you doing there?" he asked out loud.

"Let me tell you something. You ain't gotta lie to me, okay? As far as I'm concerned, last night was just a one-time thang. You don't owe me squat, and I don't owe you squat. So, you can just lose my number, you trifling jerk."

Later that morning, at Bethany Hospital, Malcolm sat in the waiting room on the fifth floor while Lucille attended her therapy session. He couldn't get Rhapsody's phone call out of his mind. It didn't take a rocket scientist to figure out she was pissed beyond words, but for the life of Malcolm, he couldn't understand why. He'd met her only yesterday, and maybe it was too soon for them to have slept together, but why the attitude? All because he said he had to work and really didn't?

Truth be told, Malcolm never stayed the whole night with a girl. It wasn't because he didn't want to, but because Lucille had made it a rule that before she woke up in the morning, Malcolm had best have his behind in the house. She depended on him to help her out of bed and into the bathroom every morning. If there ever came a time when Malcolm wasn't there to assist her to the bathroom, he would have hell to pay.

Due to the fact that Lucille could no longer drive, she had given her Toyota Camry to Malcolm. She had asked only that he agree to take her to therapy twice a week and become her chauffeur whenever she needed to go anywhere.

Eight months ago, on a Saturday morning, Lucille had woken up at 7:00 a.m. with a full bladder, only to find that Malcolm had yet to return home from one of his wild nights out. She wore adult diapers daily, and it wasn't unusual for Lucille to relieve herself while still in bed. Her frustration that morning had stemmed from the fact that she had to lie in a soiled diaper for an hour and a half. Lucille had got angry that Malcolm had forfeited their agreement. She had reached for the telephone on her nightstand, then had called the police to report her car stolen. With the help of the tracking device, her car was found within twenty minutes. It was three miles away, in the parking lot of the apartment complex of Deidra Jackson, a twenty-three-year-old bombshell. Deidra was one of Malcolm's latest conquests, one whom Lucille didn't particularly like.

Lucille had told Malcolm that Deidra was so dumb that if he asked her to make him a bowl of Frosted Flakes, she would look through a cookbook for the recipe first. The first time Malcolm brought Deidra home to his mother had been the last. From the moment he walked through the front door with his trophy on his arm, Lucille had sensed something was different about Deidra. She hadn't quite been able to put her finger on what it was, but she had known that time would tell. And when time *did* tell, it told it all.

When Lucille had pointed to the sofa and had said to Deidra, "Have a seat," Deidra had looked at the sofa and replied, "No, thank you. I already have one of these at home."

The look on Lucille's face as she turned to her son was priceless. Malcolm read her question in her eyes. "What the devil's hell did you bring in my house?"

Malcolm quickly grabbed Deidra's hand and guided her to the sofa. Lucille sat in her wheelchair across the living room and tried to figure Deidra out. She had beautiful long black hair; Pocahontas had nothing on the girl. Deidra's face was round and full. With her eye make-up done to perfection and shiny bronze lip gloss, her mocha-colored skin was flawless. Just like all the other trophies Malcolm had brought home to his mother, Deidra was curved in all the right places. Lucille thought it was such a waste of life to have all that beauty and a bag of rocks for a brain. She could only hope that somewhere behind those long eyelashes and sultry lips was an ounce of sense.

"Ma, Deidra can't stay long. She's on her way to choir rehearsal."

A church girl. There's hope, after all, Lucille thought. "Really? What church do you attend, Deidra?"

"I belong to the Church over the Tavern."

Lucille knew there was no way she could have heard her right. Her eyebrows shot up in the air. "Excuse me?"

Deidra leaned back on the sofa and crossed her legs. "I'm a member of the Church over the Tavern, located at sixteen-sixteen West Sixteenth Street, where Reverend Jack Daniels is my pastor."

Lucille made a mental note in her head to curse Malcolm from *A* to *Z* as soon as that whatchamacallit left her house. She wondered who Deidra's parents were. "Uh-huh, that's nice. Uh, what's your last name?" Lucille asked.

"It's Jackson, but you can call me Deidra Jackass."

"Excuse me?" Lucille said in a high-pitched tone and frowned. She couldn't believe her ears.

"My father gave me the nickname Jackass, and that's what everybody calls me."

Lucille's frown got deeper. The lines across her forehead were evident. "That's horrible, Deidra. Why would a father nickname his daughter Jackass? Doesn't that bother you?"

"Uh-uh. I'm used to it," Deidra said nonchalantly. "Hee hawl, hee hawl, hee hawlways calls me Jackass."

Lucille's mouth fell wide open when she heard a chuckle come from Malcolm's throat. Refusing to waste another fraction of a second of her life on this hopeless cause, Lucille didn't say another word as she rolled her wheelchair into her bedroom and slammed the door shut.

"I don't think your mother likes me," Deidra said to Malcolm.

Of course she didn't. Malcolm had picked up on it the moment he and Deidra had walked in the front door. He also knew Lucille was in her bedroom, sharpening up her personal vocabulary for him later.

"Why do you think that?" he asked.

"I can tell. I've been reading people's minds since I was a little girl. I'm a psycho."

Malcolm knew Deidra meant to say that she's a psychic, not a psycho, but he didn't correct her. He decided that if he simply asked Deidra to keep her mouth shut when they were out in public, no one would know that she was dumb all day long.

Deidra asked Malcolm's permission to use the bathroom before she left for choir rehearsal. Ten minutes later she exited the bathroom and asked for a toilet plunger. After Deidra left, Lucille opened her bedroom door and rolled her wheelchair to the bathroom door and saw Malcolm working the plunger. One look at her face and Malcolm knew he was in trouble.

"Go ahead and cuss me out. I know it's coming." He chuckled.

"I ain't gonna cuss, and I don't think anything is funny. It's really sad, to be honest with you. You can't do any better than that, Malcolm?"

"Can I be honest?"

"Of course," Lucille answered.

"It ain't about Deidra's brain."

Lucille knew where her son was headed. Malcolm had been chasing girls since he could walk. "Humph. Then it must be the booty."

Malcolm smiled, then nodded his head and continued plunging.

"I believe sex is gonna be your death, Malcolm. You best be careful."

He stopped plunging and looked at his mother. "Well, if I'm gonna die, can't I die with a smile on my face?"

Lucille shook her head from side to side and rolled toward the kitchen. "I see it's useless tryin' to talk some sense into you. When you finish, pour bleach in that toilet and let it sit for a half hour. And the next time that heifer gotta poop, take her down the street to the gas station."

At 1:15 p.m. a nurse rolled Lucille into the waiting area.

"How did your therapy go?" Malcolm asked his mother.

"The same as it always go. It was strenuous and a total waste of my time."

"Ma, you say that every week, but every week you look forward to coming."

"That's because I'm trying to build enough strength in my legs to stomp a hole in your back."

The nurse standing behind Lucille's wheelchair laughed out loud. She looked at Malcolm. "That's exactly what she said she was gonna do to the fitness instructor when he told her he wanted to try acupuncture during her next therapy session."

Standing six feet, two inches tall, Ivan McGee weighed 265 pounds easily. Solid muscle protruded through his sweaty tank top as he bench-pressed 185 pounds of steel early Tuesday afternoon at the Cardio Palace Gym. A spotter stood at the head of Ivan's workbench, looking down at him as Ivan strained to push the heavy plates away from his chest. Ivan was close to the end of his fifth set of eight repetitions each. The spotter witnessed various veins bulging from Ivan's forehead and neck.

"That's it, man. Just three more. Come on, dude. You can make it," the spotter said, encouraging him.

With every fiber of his being, Ivan let out a loud roar and forced the heavy weights away from his chest, then locked his elbows in place. "Grab it. Grab it," he strained to say.

The spotter grabbed ahold of the bar and helped place it on the stand above Ivan's head. Out of breath, Ivan looked up at his helper, whose name he didn't know.

"Thanks, man. I appreciate it."

The spotter bumped his fist against Ivan's. "It's all good."

When he walked away, Ivan lay, spent, on the bench, breathing heavily. Suddenly, his cellular telephone, which was lying next to his keys beneath the bench, began to ring.

"What up? This is Ivan," he said, giving his standard greeting.

"Where you at, fool?" Malcolm asked.

"At the gym, gettin' my sweat on. Something *you* need to be doing. Why?"

"You know that chick I told you about yesterday?"

Ivan chuckled. "Malcolm, you told me about three chicks yesterday."

"I'm talkin' about the older broad. The one driving the Benz."

"Oh, yeah. What about her?"

"She summoned me to her house last night, man."

Ivan sat up on the bench and wiped sweat from his forehead. "Yeah. And?"

"And I went, fool."

"So let me guess. You tapped that, didn't you?"

"Ivan, I waxed it. Twice."

Ivan pumped his fist into the air, as if he was congratulating Malcolm. "Oh, snap. For real, dude? So you feelin' her or what?"

"I don't know. She's trippin'."

"Trippin'? How?"

"Let's meet at Betty's Soul Shack, and I'll let you hear what she left on my cell."

Chapter 6

At lunchtime I stood at the salad bar at Pete's Grocery Store on Wabash Avenue and placed huge chunks of fresh fruit, including watermelon, cantaloupe, pineapple, honeydew melon, and strawberries, in a plastic container. Then I took it to the checkout lane, along with a sixteen-ounce bottle of Evian water. My total came to $12.16.

"Cash, debit, or credit?" the elderly Caucasian lady asked me.

I gave her my brand-new plastic friend with the MasterCard logo. It had arrived in the mail two weeks ago, and I had yet to use it. "Credit."

The cashier swiped the card, waited a moment, and gave me my card back to me. "Your purchase was declined." She had an attitude and couldn't have said it any louder.

Another Caucasian lady, who was much younger than the cashier, stood in line behind me. She heard what the cashier said and giggled. I became furious at the thought of these siddity women having a field day at my expense.

I looked at the cashier. "Not that it's any of your business, but this is a new card, and I activated it yesterday."

"Oh, sure," the cashier responded sarcastically.

I gave her back the card. "Try it again."

The cashier swiped the card and again the word *declined* was displayed on the readout panel.

"It's denied again," she said, much louder this time. She knew she had an audience.

I heard another giggle come from behind me, which pushed me over the edge. I glared at the cashier. "Oh, so I guess you and this prejudiced trick standing behind me think I can't afford twelve dollars and sixteen cents, huh?" I snatched my card from her hand. "I just told you that this is a brand-new check card."

At my outburst, the cashier's eyes bucked out of her head. She knew I was pissed, and she tried to keep me from causing a scene, but it was too late. She started to panic. "Uh-uh. I was just saying that when the cards are denied, it's usually because there is no money in the—"

"I heard what you said," I snapped at her. "You were implying that because I'm black, I don't have any money. There could be a number of reasons why this card isn't working. Heck, maybe your machine is jacked up. You ever thought of that?"

"Everything has been working all morning and afternoon . . . until now," she said sarcastically.

I had to calm myself down before I caught a case. I placed the card in my purse, then searched my wallet for cash and purposely avoided my five-dollar, twenty-dollar, and fifty-dollar bills. I gave her a crisp hundred-dollar bill.

The cashier looked at the bill, then at me, then at the bill again. I knew she was wondering why I just hadn't given her the cash to begin with. My wallet was filled with money, and I could've given her cash, but I wanted to use my new credit card.

She slowly and gently took the bill from me, and it was a good thing she did. Had she snatched the money out of my hand, I was gonna mop the floor with her prejudiced behind.

"Um, I don't have any change for this," she said. "Do you have anything smaller?"

Ain't this a trip? Who ain't got no money now? I returned her nasty attitude. "No. One hundreds are all I carry."

She was heated. She stormed off with my money.

That's right. Go on over to the customer service counter and get change. I turned around and faced the broad behind me with a huge smirk on my face. I was holding up the line, but I didn't care. She quickly averted her eyes to read the tabloid she was holding. I just stood there, looking at her, while I waited for my change. She kept her face down and stared at the page. I knew that she knew that I was looking at her. In my mind I dared her to look at me just so I could say, "What the heck you lookin' at?" But she never raised her eyes. I hated when I had to demand respect, but sometimes it was necessary.

When the cashier returned, she carefully placed my change in my hand. I checked my watch and saw that I still had a half hour before my lunch break was over. So I decided to get the oil in my car changed at one of those ten-minute lube places.

I drove to the Oil Express two blocks away from the grocery store and told the mechanic that I wanted a basic oil change. "And before you ask if I want anything else," I said, looking sternly into his eyes, "the answer is no. I don't want a new oil filter or new wiper blades. I don't need my tires rotated or anything other than what I just told you. Just change my oil."

"Yes, ma'am," was all he said.

I took my fruit salad and bottle of water and went and sat in the waiting area. To kill time, I called Anastasia to see what she was up to.

"Oh, heeyeck to tha naw," she answered. Not "Hello" or "Good afternoon." I imagined Anastasia's neck dancing as she spoke to me. "I know good and well you ain't crazy enough to call my house and talk to me like you ain't act like a total fool on the phone with me this morning."

She was right. I had been out of line earlier. Anastasia could be a bit overbearing sometimes, but her heart was always in the right place.

"I'm sorry, Stacy. You forgive me?"

"Should I?" she asked me.

"I'll buy you that Fendi bag just like mine."

"In that case, you're forgiven. So, what's going on?"

"I'm sitting in Oil Express, waiting on my oil to be changed, but I called to tell you what happened in Pete's Grocery today."

Before I could get into the story, the mechanic was at my side. "Excuse me, ma'am."

Didn't I tell this fool that I didn't want anything else done to my car? "Hold on a minute, Stacy." I looked up into his eyes. "What?" I asked irritably.

"Uh, I just want to let you know that our records show that you were here less than two months ago."

I shrugged my shoulders. "Yeah. And?"

"Your mileage is well over four thousand miles since you were last here."

Who cares? I couldn't understand why he was bothering me. I shrugged my shoulders. "And your point is?"

"Well, I just wanna say that you're putting a lot of miles on your car."

I snapped, "Don't you think I know that? I do a lot of driving. That's why I'm here gettin' the oil changed, so change it." I dismissed him and brought my cell phone back to my ear. I exhaled loudly to show him that he was working on my last nerve *and* the one before it. "Anyway, Stacy, my new debit card wouldn't work at Pete's Grocery and—"

"Excuse me, ma'am," the fool interrupted again.

Without telling Anastasia to hold, I looked up at him again with my eyes blazing. "What is it?"

"Huh?" Anastasia asked.

"Hold on, Stacy. I ain't talkin' to you," I said to her.

The mechanic became nervous at the look in my eyes. "Uh, it's just that four thousand miles is a lot for two months. If you don't mind me asking, where are you driving every day?"

No, he didn't just ask me that.

I felt like Linda Blair when she was possessed by the devil in the movie *The Exorcist*. My head turned three hundred-sixty degrees on my shoulders. "*If I don't mind you asking?* You're darn right, I mind you asking. And I mind you wasting my time with unnecessary bull. What the heck does where I'm driving got to do with you changing my oil? Is this your first day on the job or what? I didn't come in here for a lesson on mileage. Maybe I should speak with your manager, because it ain't none of your business where I drive. Just do what I'm paying you to do, which is to change my oil."

The mechanic lowered his head and walked away. Again, I brought the telephone to my ear.

"Can you believe this, Stacy?"

"Rhapsody, I'm gonna pray for your mouth *and* your attitude."

"Humph," I said. "You better pray that this mechanic don't get his behind kicked." My shoulders jerked back and forth five times. I hated when folks pissed me off, because it always triggered an attack.

Chapter 7

Malcolm and Ivan sat in a booth inside Betty's Soul Shack. As soon as the waitress walked away from the table with their orders, Malcolm dialed his voice mail, then stretched his hand with the cellular telephone across the table. Ivan grabbed the telephone and brought it to his ear. His mouth dropped wide open at Rhapsody's message.

"Oh, snap. What did you do to her, man?"

Malcolm chuckled. "I told you that I waxed that butt."

Ivan handed the telephone back to Malcolm. "Well, she doesn't sound like she had a good time. She's pissed."

The waitress returned to their table and sat two glasses of raspberry lemonade before each of them. "Your orders will be right up," she said to them.

Malcolm drank from his glass. "Rhapsody is mad only 'cause I didn't spend the whole night with her. I told her I had to open the restaurant this morning and I needed to get home and get some sleep. It turns out that she stopped by the restaurant this morning and found out that today is my regular day off. So she thinks I blew her off."

Ivan shrugged his shoulders. "Well, you *did* blow her off. Why did you lie to her?"

"Man, please," Malcolm said. "You think I want chicks to know that my mama would kill me if she woke up in the morning and I wasn't home?"

"How old did you say Rhapsody was?"

"I don't know. I think she's thirtysomething."

Ivan's eyebrows rose. *"Thirtysomething."*

"Early thirties, Ivan."

"So what? Heck, thirty is thirty. You got a cougar on your hands? What were you thinking, Malcolm?"

"Man, look, to be honest with you, I didn't think Rhapsody was gonna call me, but when she did, I remembered how fine she was and what she was driving, so I went to see her. And she doesn't look her age. Rhapsody's body is bangin'."

Ivan shook his head from side to side. He smelled trouble. "When a woman leaves a voice-mail message like that on a dude's cell phone after only one night of screwing, it means she ain't wrapped too tight. So, what are you gonna do?"

"I'll call her when I think she's calmed down a little bit."

"Malcolm, you better slow your roll," Ivan advised his best friend. "This Rhapsody chick doesn't sound like she's playin' in the minor leagues. You got me scared of her, and I haven't even met her. She's givin' off some bad vibes, man."

Malcolm couldn't disagree. He nodded his head. "Yeah, I know."

The waitress was back with their meals. "Here you go." She placed their plates on the table before them. "Enjoy."

Both Malcolm and Ivan thanked the waitress, and then she walked away.

After inserting a forkful of homemade macaroni and cheese into his mouth, Ivan looked across the table at Malcolm. "Do you remember what happened two years ago, when you had Gisele Matthews on you? She tried to set fire to the shirt and pants she bought you while you were wearing them. And last year Ressia Thompson did her best to run you down with her Jeep."

Malcolm swallowed meat loaf and mashed potatoes as he nodded his head. "Yeah, I remember. Those broads were lunatics."

"It's only been a month since Jasmine Sprawls came into Burger World and announced to every one present that you're a no-good piece of crap. And you know *crap* wasn't the word she used. And now you got a thirtysomething cougar pissed because she caught you in a lie. Sounds to me like you need to put your junk on strike, man."

Malcolm laughed, then wiped the corners of his mouth with a napkin. "Nah, Ivan. I can't do that. But I *will* say this, though. If I died tomorrow, sex won't owe me nothing."

Chapter 8

After another tedious day at work, I decided to stop by Anastasia's house in Bellwood on my way home. She opened the door, looking beautiful. From the size of her belly, no one would have guessed that she had given birth to my goddaughter, Chantal, only four months ago.

"Stacy, girl, you're looking great, as always," I said. "And I love your haircut."

"Thanks, sis," she said, running her hand along the back of her new feather cut. "Come on into the kitchen." Anastasia led the way toward the rear of the house, and I followed.

"Ooh, something smells good up in here. What are you cooking?"

Anastasia brought her index finger to her lips to silence me. "Shh. I just laid Chantal down."

I poked my head into the nursery and got a glimpse of my god baby sleeping in her crib, then went into the kitchen, where Anastasia was.

"I'm making smothered pork chops with white rice and gravy," Anastasia said to me. "You want to stay for dinner?"

"Is there enough?" I asked, hoping there was enough, because I was starving.

"I just gotta defrost two more chops. It's no big deal."

I sat down at the kitchen table and watched Anastasia take a freezer bag full of pork chops from the freezer and sit it in a bowl of warm water.

"How's Chantal doing?"

"She's good. The catnaps ain't no joke, though."

"Well, you look well rested to me," I said, admiring Anastasia's pretty face and hair. "Got your hair done and your make-up on."

Anastasia went to the stove and removed the lid from the skillet and poked the frying pork chops, testing them for tenderness. "Well, you know I still gotta look good for my man."

"Speaking of Trevor, where is that fine husband of yours?"

Just the mention of his name brought a huge smile to Anastasia's lips. "He called ten minutes ago and said that he's on his way home from work. He'll be glad to see you, Rhapsody. Trevor asks about you all the time."

"Stacy, you are so lucky to have a man like Trevor. He's the ideal husband."

I loved the way Trevor took care of his family. He went to work every day, brought home his paycheck every two weeks, and allowed Anastasia to run the house with it. Trevor was tall, dark, and handsome. He treated his wife with the utmost respect; I had never witnessed him raise his voice at her. He was mild, and so was his attitude toward life. And the way Trevor attended to their baby, Chantal, melted my heart. It seemed as though he bathed her, changed her spoiled diapers, and fed her more than Anastasia did.

After flipping the pork chops over in the skillet, Anastasia turned to look at me. "I'm not lucky. I'm blessed. Luck comes by chance. God intentionally *gives* blessings."

Aw, heck. Here we go. She's gonna preach. I was hungry as all get out, so I had to sit through it.

"I had to go through a lot of pain and suffering to get Trevor. He wasn't cheap. You remember me tellin' you about my ex-husband, who almost killed me mentally *and* emotionally?"

I nodded my head.

"For years that fool had me convinced that I would never amount to anything. He wanted me to change my appearance to look like a skinny tramp he was messin' around with. He wanted me to *look* just like her, *be* just like her, and *act* just like her. But it wasn't happening, so eventually I had to get away from him."

"Well, look who you have now. Trevor is every woman's dream," I said.

Anastasia took two pork chops from the freezer bag, rinsed them with water, and laid them on a plate of seasoned flour. "Yeah, he is," she said. She battered my two pork chops and placed them in the hot skillet, from which she had already removed four chops.

I just sat at the table, thinking about her fabulous life with her husband and brand-new baby girl. "I wish I could find myself a good man."

Anastasia placed the top on the skillet, then turned to look at me as I pouted at her kitchen table. She wiped her hands on a dish towel, then went and leaned back against the sink. She looked at me. "See? That's your problem right there, Rhapsody."

I didn't have a clue what she meant. "I ain't got a problem."

"Yeah, you do," she insisted. "Everywhere you go, you take out your binoculars and scope for men. You gotta stop doing that. You make yourself look real desperate when you approach men all the time." Anastasia pointed her index finger at me like she was scolding a two-year-old. "I can guarantee you this one thing. The moment you stop lookin' for a man . . ." She paused, looking directly in my eyes, making sure she had my undivided attention. "Is when the right one will come find you."

I didn't say anything behind that. I sat in silence and absorbed every single word Anastasia had just said to me.

When she didn't get a response from me, Anastasia went over to the stove and turned the fire down beneath the skillet. She then pulled a chair out from the table and sat down across from me. She leaned her elbows on the table and looked at me. "A penny for your thoughts. You're a million miles away. Are you all right?"

I wanted to confide in Anastasia and tell her about the message I had left on Malcolm's voice mail, but her point about me being desperate would be proven, and I didn't know if I could handle that right then.

"Rhapsody?"

Tears came to my eyes. That was when Anastasia got up from the table and removed the skillet from the fire and sat it on top of another burner. She then came and sat back down at the table, in the chair right next to me. She pulled a napkin from the holder in the center of the table and gave it to me.

"What happened, sis?"

Sniff, sniff. I held the napkin up and turned away to wipe my tears and blow my nose, which had started to run. "I did something so stupid today, Stacy."

"Like what?"

"I decided to pay Malcolm a visit at Burger World on my way to work. I got there and found out that today was his scheduled day off. When he got up to leave me last night, he told me that he had to go home and get some sleep because he needed to open the restaurant this morning. So when I found out that he had lied to me, I called his phone and went off on him on his voice mail."

Anastasia's shoulders drooped. It was evident that she was disappointed in my behavior. "Rhapsody, tell me you didn't," she pleaded.

"I did more than that, Stacy. I totally snapped on him. And that was at seven o'clock this morning, and now it's almost six in the evening. I haven't heard from Malcolm. He hasn't called to apologize."

"What has *he* got to apologize for? You cussed *him* out. If anyone is owed an apology, it's Malcolm."

I really didn't understand her logic. "Stacy, *he* lied to *me*. How do you figure I owe him an apology?"

"Before I answer that, let me ask you a question," she said. "You said you did something stupid today. Was that what you were talkin' about?"

"Allowing Malcolm to get under my skin is what was stupid."

"No, Rhapsody. Getting angry is showing emotions, and that's not stupid. Leaving that type of message on his telephone is what was stupid. You and Malcolm have no ties to each other. Heck, you just met him yesterday, and you screwed him yesterday, which was also stupid. But you can't get mad just because he didn't want to spend the night with you, girl."

"I'm not mad because Malcolm didn't want to spend the night. I'm mad because he lied to me about why he had to leave."

Anastasia shrugged her shoulders. "Rhapsody, what difference does it make? If he didn't want to stay the whole night, it was his prerogative to leave. You need to get a grip."

She was starting to piss me off. "I need to get a grip? *Really,* Stacy? Well, tell me something. How do you manage to keep your husband on such a short leash?"

"I manage because my relationship with Trevor is great. I make sure that his needs are met. I keep his belly full, and when he's horny, I fulfill my wifely duties. Trevor knows that he doesn't have to go out into the street to be told that he's a handsome man, because I remind him of that *every* morning, before he leaves this house. And another thing, Rhapsody. A man doesn't like to feel that his woman has her hand wrapped around his testicles. It wasn't good for you to call Malcolm and leave that message, especially if he's really not out there creepin'. And technically, he's not your man. Leave him alone and let him breathe, because what you're gonna end up doing is making him think that if you're sweating him and accusing him all the time, then he may as well go ahead and cheat, because according to you, he's already guilty."

"Now, there is one thing that I love about Trevor. He makes me feel secure. When he leaves for work in the morning, he calls from his cell to complain about how bad the traffic is. Then he calls to let me know that he has made it to work safely. He calls home in between meetings and vents about what his boss is doing. He calls at lunchtime to thank me for puttin' an extra Hostess Twinkie in his bag or for the little love note he found wrapped in his sandwich. Every day, at quitting time, Trevor calls to let me know that he's on his way home and asks if he should stop at the convenient store or dry cleaners. And when he walks through the front door, he doesn't leave out of it again until the next day."

"Not that I care to know, but I know what Trevor is doing twenty-four hours a day, seven days a week. I've never had to ask him where he's going or who he's been with. Trevor knows all about my past relationship, so he takes it upon himself to keep my mind at ease. That's what a good man does for his woman. I know that that doesn't guarantee that Trevor isn't cheating, but I *will* say this. When he's not *beside* me, he's on the telephone, talkin' *to* me. If he can screw a chick *and* hold a lengthy conversation with me at the same time, then he's a bad boy. And another thing. If Trevor *is* messing around, then *she* must be paying for their escapades and buying her own furs and jewelry, because Trevor puts his paycheck, un-cashed, in my hand every other Friday. If there comes a time when that changes, *then* we'll have a problem."

"Now, I've said all of that to say this, Rhapsody. *My* re-lationship is tight. Trevor is a married man with a four-month-old daughter. He has responsibilities. He lived his life in the fast lane years ago. Malcolm, on the other hand, is twenty-one years old. He's just starting to see what life is all about. He probably hasn't even had his heart broken yet. He's young, energetic, and full of spunk. It will be impossible for you to tame him and put him on lockdown. And trying to take ten years off your life to become one of his peers is even more ridiculous. So, I'll say this in a way that you, Rhapsody, can understand. Malcolm's dan-galang is not made of platinum."

I had taken to heart everything Anastasia had said to me and I was beginning to let it sink down in my soul until she made that last statement. It was obvious that Trevor had never put it on her the way Malcolm had put it on me last night. "See, that's where you're wrong, Stacy. Malcolm's dangalang *has* been dipped in platinum, and there are diamond solitaires surrounding the base of it."

I guess what I had just said shocked the heck out of her, 'cause she just glared at me, then stood and went back to the stove.

"You ain't got nothing to say?" I asked her.

"Nope, not a thang," Anastasia answered. Then, with-out turning around, she said, "Do yo' thang."

Chapter 9

After eating dinner, I hopped back in my car and arrived home at a quarter to nine. I had had a good time with Anastasia and Trevor. From the moment he'd walked in the front door, she had been all over him, like he'd been gone for months.

I'd loved the look on Anastasia's face when Trevor presented her with a dozen white roses. I'd asked him what the occasion was, and he'd told me that there was no occasion, and that just because it was Tuesday, Anastasia got flowers. That had messed me up. Was it possible for me to be happy for Anastasia and jealous of her at the same time?

I was having strong mixed emotions. I ain't never had a man buy me flowers just because it was Tuesday or Wednesday or any other day of the week. I remembered a time when I was at the Taste of Chicago with a guy I was dating. His name was Braxton. We were walking and eating when I saw a woman selling long-stemmed lilies. I asked Braxton to buy one for me. He looked at me and said, "For what? It ain't your birthday." Braxton was a trifling, cheap bastard if I ever saw one. I guessed it had slipped his mind that I had paid for those darn tickets we were redeeming to eat with. And everybody knew that if you wanted to eat good at the Taste of Chicago, you were gonna spend plenty of money.

I wasn't hating on Anastasia; she was my girl. But I wondered when a Trevor would come into *my* life. After we had eaten, the three of us had sat in the living room and had chatted. By that time Chantal had woken up and was ready to eat. I sat my jealous self in the La-Z-Boy recliner and watched Anastasia cradle her baby girl and breast-feed her. Trevor sat next to his wife on the love seat, with his arm around her shoulders, and caressed Chantal's head with his other hand. Both mother and father were making cooing noises as Chantal nursed.

My presence had been long forgotten. Since that was obviously a family moment, I decided to leave them to their private time. I thanked my best friend for dinner and kissed her cheek; then I knelt down to kiss Chantal's forehead. Trevor walked me to the door and opened it for me. He told me how good it was to see me and that he was glad that I had stopped by. He then reached for the vase on the cocktail table, where Anastasia had sat her beautiful bouquet, and pulled a single white rose from it and gave it to me. I looked at Anastasia, who was smiling at me, and then I looked at Trevor and asked what the rose was for.

He said, "You make my wife smile, so you get a rose."

Trevor walked me outside, all the way to my car, and opened the door for me. Once I had secured my seat belt, he kissed my cheek lightly and told me to be careful. "Make sure you call us when you get home so we'll know you made it safely."

Trevor shut my door and stood on the curb as I drove away. In my rearview mirror, I saw him still standing on the curb, watching until my car was out of sight. I wanted a real man so bad.

Even after Anastasia tried to talk some sense into my brain, I was still pissed because Malcolm hadn't rung my telephone. I knew he must've gotten my message by then. Maybe Anastasia was right. I should've just left Malcolm alone and gone back to living my boring life.

I had sworn off men five years ago, when I found out that Jerome, the man I was engaged to, was the father of my cousin Cherelle's baby. Cherelle was my father's brother's daughter. My first cousin. Ain't that a trip? I should've figured something was going on when Cherelle, Jerome, and I stopped hanging out together as much as we used to. When Cherelle's belly started to show, she would often tell me that two was company and three was a crowd. So she opted to stay at home when Jerome and I went out.

And funny little things started happening when we were all in the same room, like Jerome and Cherelle not saying anything to one another or purposely not looking at each other. Folks did that when they didn't wanna be found out. But, hey, I knew I had to be trippin', cause Cherelle and I had grown up together. We were the same age and were as close as sisters. Jerome and I had been together for about eight months, and we'd never really had any problems, so I thought our relationship was solid. Humph. I was in for a rude awakening, because when Cherelle's baby boy was born, she named him Michael Jerome Blue.

When Cherelle first told me that she had given her son my man's name, I was uncomfortable with it. But she explained how special Jerome and I were to her and how we were really the only friends she had. And since her baby's daddy was unknown, even to me, Cherelle said she felt the closest to Jerome. She assured me that if her baby had been a girl, she would've named her Rhapsody.

Well, a month went by, and baby Michael got sick and needed blood. It was 3:00 a.m., and my entire family was in the emergency room at Advocate Christ Medical Center in Oak Lawn. It was funny how out of all my uncles, aunts, first cousins, and grandparents, no one matched baby Michael's blood type. So, we were all sitting in the waiting room, praying for a miracle and trying to figure out which long-distance cousin we could call at three in the morning to come and get tested for blood, when I looked up and saw Jerome walking through the sliding glass doors.

I jumped up to hug him and thank him for coming, because I knew he'd want to be there for Cherelle and baby Michael, but then I thought about something. I hadn't called Jerome, so who had? All the attention was on baby Michael. Who would take time out and call *my* man? And the way he hugged me was way off. Jerome had always pulled me close to him and kissed my forehead, but that time the hug wasn't tight, and there was no kiss. I looked into his eyes and was on the verge of asking him what he was doing at the medical center when his eyes answered my question before I even got the first word out.

He was as nervous as heck, and I knew why. Jerome had been screwing around with Cherelle all that time right under my nose. Michael Jerome Blue was my man's son. Well, after I went off on Jerome and caused a scene, and after I threatened to whup Cherelle's behind the minute she stepped foot out of the nursery, I was thrown out of the medical center. It turned out that Jerome's blood was an exact match for baby Michael's.

It had been five years since I'd seen or heard from Cherelle or Jerome. My mother had told me that he married Cherelle, but she divorced him after only eight months because she found out that at the same time she was in the hospital, delivering baby Michael, Jerome had another son being born at Rush University Medical Center. He was named Jerome too. So, while Cherelle and Jerome were playing me, *he* was playing both of *us*.

Mama Lerlean used to always tell my brothers and me that what went around came back around. I guessed Cherelle got what was coming to her. I didn't really care about Jerome, because he was only a man and they were a dime a dozen, but Cherelle was my blood, and she should have known better.

I hadn't had a committed relationship since. But I missed the sex I had had with Jerome. That was when I entered my promiscuous years. I allowed myself to accept booty calls at the midnight hour. Truth be told, I was addicted to sex and had been for a long while. I thought about it morning, noon, and night. I really believed that because Lerlean had had such a tight grip on me when I was living at home, I got buck wild when I got on my own. I was like a sheltered kid going off to college. I lost my doggone mind when I got out into the real world. Sex, sex, and more sex had become my life. Hundreds of men had passed through my bedroom. If my walls could talk, they'd probably nominate me to be listed in *The Guinness Book of World Records* for the girl who had had the most sexual partners.

I attended Spelman College, an all-female school, and it was directly across the street from Morehouse, an all-male school. My mother chose the college I attended. Neither I nor my father had a say-so in the matter. I completed grades one through eight at a public grammar school. And my mother didn't have a problem with that. I guess she thought she'd lose her tight grip on my vajayjay if I went to a co-ed college. And even though I went to a women's college, that was exactly what happened. When I learned that pectorals and six-packs were just a stone's throw away, and I could see them come and go from my dorm room window, I lost my mind.

I was like a kid in a candy store when I went to my first frat party. The testosterone was thick in the air, and it smelled heavenly. Red plastic cups filled with alcohol were unlimited. I lost my virginity to the first boy who asked what my name was. There was no curfew in college. No one was watching me. For the first time in my life, I was free from Lerlean's prying eyes and her lectures. I became addicted to sex in my freshman year of college and had been addicted ever since. I just loved to screw. At times it didn't even matter who the man was. As long as he had a condom in his pocket, we were good to go.

In my bedroom I pressed the PLAY button on the answering machine, which sat on my nightstand, while I got undressed. Anastasia's fried pork chops were heavy in my stomach, and I was ready to get into bed.

"Hey, sis. It's Danny. You know Mom and Dad's fortieth wedding anniversary is coming up. Walter and I thought it would be good if we gave them a surprise party. What do you think? Give me a call when you get in." *Beep.*

"Hey, sis. It's your big bro. What's up? It's almost nine o'clock. Where are you? I know you ain't got a man keeping you busy, so what are you doing out of the house?"

I looked at the answering machine. "Shut up, Walter."

"Listen, Danny and I want to do something special for Mom and Dad. Can you believe they lasted forty years? Call me." *Beep.*

I hung my work uniform in the closet and went into the bathroom and inserted the plug in the tub and ran my bathwater. I didn't return either of my brothers' calls. Walter and Daniel were the cheapest men on the earth. Each and every time *they* decide to do something for *our* parents, they put the burden on *me*. Walter was a thirty-eight-year-old gynecologist, but he never seemed to have any money. Had he stopped inserting his dangalang in every vajayjay he examined and making babies, he would've been a rich man.

Daniel was thirty-six and was the CEO of Blue Construction Company. He was pulling in major bank, but he'd squeeze juice from a penny because he was extremely cheap. Every dime Daniel made went to the bank, and there was nothing wrong with that. But he could afford to take Antoinette, his girl of one year, to a nice fancy restaurant sometimes. Daniel's idea of a date was pushing the ON DEMAND button on his remote control and purchasing a movie for $3.99 and ordering in a pizza. But, hey, if Antoinette didn't have a problem with his cheap behind, then more power to her. There was no way I'd be spreading my legs for a CEO of any darn thang and not eat at Lawry's steakhouse at least twice a month.

See, what Daniel and Walter wanted to do was have *me* make all the arrangements and book the hall for our parents' vow renewal. Then they would put me in charge of the catering and make me send out the invitations, select the cake, and do everything else by myself. They figured that since I was a female, I would do a better job at planning a party. If I tried to get their opinion on something, they'd tell me to just go ahead and do what I wanted and we would split the cost three ways.

Well, that tactic didn't work when I planned our parents' thirty-fifth anniversary party. Daniel had a problem with the menu I selected, and Walter wasn't pleased that I had invited our lesbian cousin, who brought along her wife. But had Walter taken the time to go over the guest list, like I had asked him to do, he would've known they were on the list. Who was he to judge, anyway? And if Daniel had gone with me to the food tasting, he would've known that I had selected roast beef instead of roasted chicken, which was what he wanted.

Then they had a problem with the cake I chose. I was the one making all the decisions, so I chose carrot cake. They wanted a vanilla cake. So since the two of them had their butts on their shoulders throughout the entire party, they decided that they weren't going to give me what they owed me, which came to thirty-five hundred dollars. When they said they weren't gonna to pay me their share, I cussed them out and didn't speak to them for two months.

The distance between my brothers and me took a toll on my mother. Each day we didn't speak to one another, Lerlean cried herself to sleep at night, and that upset my father. He called my brothers on a three-way and said, "I'm sick of listenin' to your mother cry at night. If she develops an ulcer over this beef you have with your sister, I'm gonna put a cap in both of y'all's behinds, so you better fix it."

"But, Daddy, Rhapsody—"

"But nothing. Fix it, Walter, and fix it now."

"Daddy, you don't understand what—"

"Daniel, I don't wanna hear nothin' you gotta say. Just fix this with your sister."

Three days later I received two separate money orders in the mail for $1,750.00 each. My brothers had reimbursed all my money. I loved my parents and would do anything for them, but I wasn't going through that drama again.

I sat on my bed and lowered my head. I exhaled loudly. "Lord, I really need You to help me. I need You to make me a better person. I don't wanna talk to my brothers, I'm jealous of my best friend's life, and I fornicated last night. I know that eventually I'll call Danny and Walter back, and I'm sure that I'll learn to be happy for Anastasia, instead being envious of her. But with Malcolm, Lord, I'm gonna need for You to really help me with this situation. I know what I did was wrong, and I'm sorry for giving in to the lust of my flesh. I promise, Jesus, not to mess with him no more. I need You to keep me."

Before I got in the tub, I called Anastasia's. Trevor answered on the first ring.

"She and the baby are asleep, Rhapsody, but I'm glad you made it home safely."

"Okay, Trevor. I'll call her in the morning."

After speaking with Trevor, I soaked in the tub for forty-five minutes. When the water got too chilly for me to stay in any longer, and my fingers and toes were white and wrinkled enough, I drained the tub and got out. I rubbed Johnson's baby oil on every inch of my body; then I stood at the sink and brushed my teeth. I heard the telephone ring and thought it was my brothers calling again. I went into my bedroom to answer the telephone on my nightstand. I saw ANONYMOUS on the caller ID. I decided not to answer, because anonymous calls were usually bill collectors, and I had plenty of overdue bills. Then I changed my mind and grabbed the receiver just before the voice mail picked up the call.

"Hello," I said.

"Rhapsody?"

My heart skipped two beats at the sound of his voice.

"Who's calling?" I knew who it was.

"Oh, so now you don't know my voice?"

Since Malcolm had pissed me off that morning, I was more than happy to return the favor. "Anthony?"

"No, this is not Anthony."

"Robert?"

He exhaled. "Try Malcolm."

"Malcolm? I'm sorry. I don't know anyone named Malcolm. . . . Oh, Malcolm, from last night. Now I remember."

"*Now* you remember?"

"Uh-huh. What's up?" I tried to be calm, cool, and collected, but I was so excited to hear his voice.

"Well, I was hoping you could tell *me* what's up with the bogus message you left on my cell this morning."

Dang, he sounded sexy as heck, but I had to be strong. I had just asked God to forgive me for messin' with Malcolm. I needed to kick him to the curb.

"What's your primary language, Malcolm?"

"What?"

"What language do you generally speak?"

"English."

"The message I left on your phone was in English, and it's self-explanatory. But tell me what part you didn't comprehend and I'll try to break it down in more basic terms."

"I don't understand why you're giving me this attitude. We just met yesterday."

"And we knocked boots yesterday. Maybe you're used to hopping from chick to chick, but I don't flow like that, Malcolm."

"You don't know what you're talkin' about. I don't hop from chick to chick."

I knew Malcolm was lying to me. He was too fine to play it straight. "Humph. I can't tell by the way you hopped out of my bed early this morning, talkin' bout how you had to go home and get some sleep to be at work early. You lied to me, which meant you left my bed and got into someone else's."

"Yeah. My own."

I rolled my eyes. "Whatever, Malcolm. You're busted, okay? Ain't no need for you to keep lying, 'cause I really don't care. Remember the voice mail I left you? You don't owe me nothin'. I'm done with it."

"Look, Rhapsody, I'ma tell you the truth." He paused, then sighed. "My mom is a paraplegic, and she can't do a lot of things by herself. One of those things is getting up and into the bathroom in the morning. And she gets up pretty early, so I need to be home."

I was all set to hear some lame crap come out of Malcolm's mouth, but not that. There was no way he could be lying. No man would lie on his mama. "And you felt you couldn't tell me that?"

"I don't like to talk about my mother's condition, because folks want to know what happened to her and how it happened, and I really don't wanna relive that day."

"Well, I think taking care of your mother is honorable, and I'm sorry for leaving that message on your phone."

"So, we're cool?"

I wasn't mad anymore. "Yeah, we're cool."

There was a pregnant pause before Malcolm spoke. "What do you have on?"

I glanced at myself in the mirror above my dresser. Talking on the telephone with Malcolm, I'd completely forgotten I was naked. "Baby oil."

"You want some comp—"

"Yes," I said immediately. All that I had begged God to forgive me for and keep me from not even half an hour ago had gone out the window quick, fast, and in a hurry.

The area between my thighs was already pulsating when Malcolm drove his car into my driveway. "I'm not gonna have sex with him, Jesus. We're just gonna talk," I said out loud.

My mother had once told me that God knew that we were going to sin even before we knew it ourselves. Of course, I knew that I was gonna have sex with Malcolm that night. I knew it when I first heard his voice on the telephone. So why was I standing in my living room, dressed in lingerie, looking out the window at Malcolm as he exited his car, already sinning in my mind about what I was gonna do to him, while trying to convince God otherwise? I was kinda hoping that God would cause Malcolm to have car trouble, or maybe he'd suddenly get called in to work. I needed Jesus to intervene and keep me from doing what I desperately wanted to do. But then again, I didn't. I craved that young man that night.

I opened the front door before Malcolm had a chance to ring my doorbell. "Come on in."

Malcolm stepped into the foyer and closed the door behind him. "I see you're ready for me," he said, admiring my attire. He was so young and fine.

"The question is, are *you* ready for *me*?"

Malcolm stood in front of me and unzipped his pants and let them fall to the floor. His mouth didn't need to answer my question. Just looking at him told me he was ready. Malcolm had a great body, which an unexperienced woman might be afraid to even go near. But I refused to be intimidated. I knew Malcolm had to be home in a few hours. That gave me just enough time to show him what a cougar could do.

Chapter 10

Wednesday morning Lucille was on her way into the kitchen to prepare breakfast. She rolled her wheelchair past Malcolm's bedroom and saw him struggling to put his uniform shirt on. She noticed that Malcolm was wincing in pain with every move he made. He was looking in the mirror, facing away from her, when she yelled out to him, "What the heck is that on your back, Malcolm?"

Malcolm closed his eyes, hung his head, and exhaled. He didn't offer his mother an answer, but he knew she was referring to the passion marks that had been branded on his back.

"It looks like somebody slashed your back with a rake," Lucille fussed. "Were you in a fight?"

Malcolm knew that there was no way he could tell his mother what had really happened to his back. He conveniently forgot about the pain and quickly put his shirt on and buttoned it. "I don't know what you're talking about."

"I'm talking about those long marks across your back. Take that shirt off," Lucille demanded.

She rolled her wheelchair into his room but stopped two feet from the door. Malcolm unbuttoned his shirt and walked over to his mother.

"Turn around."

He hesitated, then turned his back to Lucille. As she reached up to pull his shirt down, Malcolm held his breath. He squeezed his eyes shut when his mother shrieked.

The scratches started at the bottom of Malcolm's neck and traveled downward to the middle of his back, taking the shape of an almost complete letter *A*. It had happened at the height of orgasm.

"What the heck is this?" Lucille shrieked. "Who did this to your back?" Her eyes were blazing.

Malcolm was pissed with himself. In the past he'd been at the top of his game when his mother charged him with questions like "Where have you been?" or "What were you doing?" He had always been prepared with a good answer, but he hadn't expected her to see him get dressed this morning. He couldn't fabricate anything that could explain the marks on his back. When Malcolm was sixteen, Lucille slapped his face because he'd allowed a girl to put a hickey on his neck. She'd told Malcolm never to allow a female to put marks on his body, under any circumstances.

There were eight long, deep scratches, and Lucille saw dried blood along each one. She grabbed Malcolm's left arm and forcefully turned him to face her. "How did this happen, Malcolm?"

It happened last night," he said.

"Don't play with me, boy. I didn't ask when it happened. I asked *how* it happened."

Malcolm refused to tell his mother the truth; he didn't part his lips to speak.

Lucille looked into his eyes. "You're not gonna say anything?"

For a long thirty seconds Malcolm stood in his bedroom, looking down at his mother, who was sitting before him. Lucille knew how the marks had got on his back, but she wanted a confession, which wasn't forthcoming. The fact that he wasn't intimidated anymore by her stares pissed her off. He was a grown man, and although Lucille had never wanted Malcolm to reach manhood, it was inevitable and she had to accept it. She turned her wheelchair away from him and left his bedroom.

"Take that darn shirt off and come into the bathroom," she called from the hallway.

Malcolm hung his head and followed his mother.

Lucille wheeled her chair into the bathroom, positioned herself next to the sink, then grabbed a cotton ball and isopropyl alcohol from a cabinet. "Turn around and kneel down," she demanded after soaking the cotton ball with the alcohol.

Malcolm did as he was told and moaned loudly each time Lucille pressed the burning antiseptic against his open wounds.

"Is this how you sounded last night, Malcolm? Does this feel good to you?"

Malcolm groaned loudly when Lucille purposely allowed a drop of alcohol to run along the length of the last scratch. "Ma, can you please hurry up?"

Lucille bandaged his back with gauze and told Malcolm to get out of her sight. He was happy to oblige. In less than ten minutes, Malcolm was dressed and out of the house. Through the living room bay window, Lucille saw Malcolm drive away from the curb.

"Lord, I wanna kill him."

On his way to his physics class at Richard J. Daley College, Ivan's cellular telephone rang, and he recognized Malcolm's number.

"What's up, fool?"

"*Man*, a whole lot of crap," Malcolm complained. "Where you at?"

"On my way to class right now. I got about ten minutes, though. What's up?"

"Rhapsody, dude," Malcolm sighed. "She got me in trouble with my mother this morning."

"What did she do?"

"She messed up my back. I got scratches all over. My mom caught me gettin' dressed this morning and went off. I thought she was gonna kill me."

Malcolm couldn't see Ivan shaking his head from side to side. "Dude, why you let that broad do that to you? I told you she wasn't wrapped too tight."

"I didn't *let* her do it, Ivan. She just did it."

"How did you end up at her house? You told me you were just gonna *call* her."

"Ivan, I called the girl and explained why I couldn't spend the night with her. She understood about my mom, then apologized for leaving that message on my phone. So I asked what she had on, and she said she was wearing baby oil."

Ivan knew where Malcolm was going with the conversation. "And you just had to go over there, right?"

Malcolm chuckled. "Yeah, but I was in for a big surprise when I got there. Rhapsody answered the door darn near naked and smelling good. But check this out, man. She took me to her bedroom and tied me up to the bedpost."

Ivan shrieked, "What?"

"Dude, Rhapsody ain't no amateur."

"Malcolm, are you nuts? Never let a woman tie you up. I can't believe you allowed that."

"I think I was hypnotized, Ivan."

"If you were tied up, how did you get the scratches on your back?"

Malcolm thought about the question Ivan had just asked him. "Man, to be honest, I don't even know."

Ivan shook his head from side to side again as he pulled into a parking spot. He couldn't believe how careless Malcolm was. "I gotta get to class. This is too much for me.

But let me give you some advice before I go." Ivan put the car in park. "Something ain't right with this Rhapsody chick. From all that you told me about her, I think she's bipolar or even schizophrenic. And I can't say for sure, but it sounds to me like she may have scratched your back on purpose."

"Why would she do that?"

Ivan exhaled loudly. Sometimes Malcolm acted as though he was fifteen instead of twenty-one. "Dude, are you *that* naive? Rhapsody did it to mark her territory. Aren't you supposed to be scoring with Alicia this weekend? How are you gonna explain the marks on your back?"

Malcolm hung his head. "Aw, man. I ain't even think about that."

"Trust me," Ivan said. "Scratching up your back was Rhapsody's way of blocking you from gettin' your freak on with anybody else. Because if another chick sees those marks, she ain't gonna mess with you."

Chapter 11

When I punched my time card at work, I found out that I was gonna have a great day. Mr. Duncan was scheduled to be in meetings all day. He'd be out of the office, and I'd have the whole day to do nothing. Mr. Duncan had left a note clipped to my time card, telling me to update some files. I ripped the note into shreds and put the scraps in my purse to throw away when I got home.

No, I didn't see a note, Mr. Duncan. Are you sure you left it on my time card? I already had my lie together.

I was glad he would be out of my hair that day because I needed to balance my checkbook and catch up on my reading. Anastasia had recommended *I Ain't Me No More*, a novel written by best-selling author E. N. Joy. Anastasia was a huge fan of E. N. Joy, and I was looking forward to relaxing with my coffee and my Kindle Fire. I'd get to sit at my desk and peruse the novel while I waited for a train or a bus to either derail or run into something.

I went to the employees' lounge to prepare myself a cup of coffee. As I poured a packet of sugar into my white Styrofoam cup, I heard, "You don't need sugar in that coffee, girl. You're sweet enough."

I recognized the raspy voice before I turned to see Willie Boston. A motorman with thirty-two years under his belt, Willie was literally a thorn in my side. Almost every morning he brought his behind upstairs, to my office, which was nowhere near the train platform, his work location, just to get on my nerves.

"Good morning, Willie. How are you?" I didn't know why I didn't say, "Good morning," and leave it at that. Asking Willie how he was doing made it seem like I was interested, when the truth was, I really didn't care.

After making my coffee light and sweet, the way I liked it, I threw the stirrer in the trash can and headed for my desk, with Willie on my heels. He was so close to me that had I stopped, he'd have bumped into my butt, which I was sure he would have enjoyed.

"Girl, you look like you were born in those pants."

I sat at my desk and exhaled loudly to let him know that he was two seconds away from getting cussed out. "What do you want, Willie?"

"A date."

I was on the verge of telling him that he couldn't afford me, but he actually could. With the amount of overtime he did each year, Willie was banking in the ninety Gs easily. But he had a wife and grandchildren; plus, he had at least fifteen years on my father.

"Willie, I don't date married men or men who can be my daddy's daddy. I tell you this all the time."

"What are you talkin' about? I don't look my age."

He was right about that. He didn't look his age. Sixty-six years had treated Willie very well. I could've counted the number of gray hairs on his head. His goatee was always trimmed to perfection. He had natural charcoal-gray eyes that would melt any woman. And I had to admit, Willie always smelled good. If it wasn't Hugo Boss, it was Issey Miyake or Prada.

But Willie had a flaw. He had so much gold in his mouth, if he stood ten feet away from a third rail, he'd get electrocuted. And with every other tooth longer than its neighbor, he looked like a vampire. If I allowed Willie to pleasure me, he'd probably give me a hysterectomy.

"And you know I can buy you anything you want," he continued.

Willie was starting to make me think about how I could benefit from his request. It would be really nice to have my mortgage and car note paid, 'cause Malcolm's minimum-wage-earning behind sure as heck couldn't pay them.

I considered spending time with Willie, but not on a date. I raised the stakes high. "Willie, there's nothing that you can buy me that I can't buy for myself, but what can you do for me in the bedroom? I'm a freak, and I need a man who can hang with me." He was so old, I imagined myself having to blow dust off of him before I touched him.

"Girl, you ain't said nothin' but a word. Willie Boston can throw down at least twice a week," he bragged, pulling his pants up on his waist.

Did he say, "Twice a week"? Out of respect, and because I didn't want to embarrass Willie, I didn't laugh in his face. Twice a week didn't cut it for me. I got hot just about every day. I sat and thought about my options. A sixty-six-year-old who could perform only on Mondays and Thursdays, with a bonus of living mortgage and car note free, or a twenty-one-year-old who could literally have me howling at the moon every night, with me paying my own bills.

I chose the latter. "Sorry, Willie. No can do."

"Oh, well. I tried," he said, glancing at his watch. It was almost 8:00 a.m., time for him to get a train into service. "You don't know what you're missin', girl."

Willie left my office, but he would be back before the week was over with the same crap. As far as what he said about me missing out on something, I wasn't missing out on a darn thang. I pulled my cell phone from my purse and dialed Malcolm's number. I wanted to know if he could meet me in my bedroom that night.

"Hi there," I greeted in a high-pitched voice when he answered. I was excited to hear his voice.

I noticed hesitation before Malcolm responded to me. "Hi." His voice was dry.

"Are you all right?"

"Yeah, I'm cool."

He didn't sound cool to me. "Are you sure?"

Malcolm sighed. "Thanks to you, my mother is pissed with me."

I didn't understand. "Why? You left my house in plenty of time to get home."

"She saw what you did to my back, Rhapsody. She's mad as hell."

"Oh." I didn't know what else to say.

Not only was his mother pissed, but apparently, Malcolm was pissed too. "I gotta go," he said.

"Um, what are you doing tonight?" I asked, hoping for a rerun of the night before, minus the fingernails.

"Nothing. Why?"

I was hopeful. "I thought we could hook up again."

"I'll have to get back to you. I might have plans."

A second ago he didn't anything to do. "Malcolm, how do you go from not having nothing to do to all of a sudden having plans?"

"I just remembered that I usually hang out with Ivan on Wednesday nights."

"Doing what?"

"Excuse me?" he said in a high-pitched voice, like I had no right to ask the question.

"Who's Ivan, and what are y'all doing tonight?" I didn't stutter, and I felt justified asking.

"Well, if you must know, Ivan is my best friend, and we'll probably shoot some hoops or go to a club."

"A club?"

"Yeah."

"What club, Malcolm?"

"Probably Mr. G's. What's up with the third degree?"

"Look, I ain't trying to get in your business, okay? But how about comin' to see me before you get with your boy?"

"I was with you last night and the night before that. Ain't you had enough?"

"No, I haven't." I chuckled. "You can do whatever you wanna do tonight. Just come by and hook me up first."

By lunchtime, I was done reading. I'd managed to complete the novel *I Ain't Me No More* in only four hours. *Kudos to author E. N. Joy,* I thought. She definitely got two thumbs-ups from me. She was a Christian fiction author, and I wasn't too sure about reading that genre, but Anastasia had assured me that E. N. Joy's books weren't preachy.

I wasn't looking forward to telling Anastasia that she was right, because she couldn't handle compliments coming from me. "See, Rhapsody? You should listen to me more often," I could hear her say. I leaned back in my chair and stretched my arms and legs. I had nothing to do, but I wasn't complaining. I loved when the CTA had perfect days.

I suddenly realized that I hadn't spoken with Anastasia that day. I picked up the desk telephone and called her home.

"Hey, girl. What's up?" She sounded chipper, as usual.

"It's lunchtime, and I'm tryin' to figure out what I want to eat."

"Chantal and I are on our way to meet Trevor for lunch."

"That's nice. Where are you meeting?"

"I made sandwiches, and I got chips and dip, cheese, grapes, and sparkling punch. We're gonna surprise him with a picnic in the park."

See, that was the kind of relationship I wanted with a man. I dared not try to have lunch with Malcolm. He would probably make me sit in Burger World and would serve me onion rings and a milk shake. "I love your life, Stacy," I sighed.

"Don't let the happy times fool you. Trevor and I have our moments."

"Yeah, but you two never give up on one another. Whatever you're faced with, you work it out together, and I admire that."

"It takes a lot of prayer, Rhapsody. Nothing worth having and holding on to comes easy. Speaking of prayer, Sunday is Chantal's dedication at church. You, being her godmother, need to be there."

"Oh, I'll be there. I promised my mother I'd come to church, and I gotta get on the altar and repent for some thangs."

"The baby dedication ceremony takes place after morning worship, but Sunday school starts at nine o'clock."

"Well, I'll be there for morning worship. I can't do Sunday school, though."

"Why not?"

"Because that's too much church, Stacy. I'll end up falling asleep. Besides, I ain't tryin' to learn about Fatback, Tupac, and the Big Negro in the diary burner."

Anastasia hollered so loud, she almost burst my eardrums. "Rhapsody, you are ignorant! It's Shadrach, Meshach, and Abednego in the fiery furnace, you fool."

"Well, heck, I didn't know."

She couldn't stop laughing at me. "Fatback, Tupac, and the Big Negro. Girl, no you didn't. And what is a diary burner, Rhapsody?"

I shrugged my shoulders. "I don't know, but I've been sayin' it all my life."

"I just can't do this with you today. That just goes to show that Sunday school is *exactly* where you need to be. God is gonna get you for that one, Rhapsody. I ain't lying. I'll talk to you later, girl."

I could still hear Anastasia laughing at me before our call was disconnected.

Chapter 12

On the way home from work, I decided to do something special for Malcolm. Instead of hopping into the bed right away, I thought I would feed him first. It was the least I could do.

I stopped at the local grocery store in my neighborhood for the ingredients to make lasagna. I was glad to find everything I needed and was home before six o'clock. The first thing I did was sit a pot on the stove and boil water for the pasta. I went into my bedroom to undress and saw the light flashing on my answering machine. I pressed the LISTEN button while I changed the sheets on my bed.

"Rhapsody, where the heck you at, girl? You think I ain't got nothin' better to do other than track you down? Me and Walter need to talk to you. And why aren't you answering your cell?" *Beep.*

"Probably 'cause I don't wanna talk to y'all, Danny." I placed the dirty sheets in the clothes hamper and got my brand-new burgundy silk sheet set from the linen closet and dressed my bed.

"This call is for Rhapsody Blue. This is Dr. Scimeca's office. Our records indicate that it's time for your annual Pap test. Please call the office to make an appointment at your earliest convenience." *Beep.*

"Hi, baby girl. This is Mama. I haven't talked to you this week. You know I get worried if I don't hear from you. And don't forget that you promised to be at church on Sunday." *Beep.*

"You can just call my cell like you always do, Mama," I said to myself. I erased all three messages and went into the kitchen to add the pasta to the boiling hot water. I picked up the kitchen cordless telephone and called Lerlean.

"Hello," my daddy answered.

"Hey, Daddy."

"Hey, daughter."

"How ya doing?"

"I'm all right for an old man."

"You're not old, Daddy. You're seasoned."

He laughed at me. "That ain't what your mama said today."

"What do you mean?"

"Today she got mad at me and said that I was old."

"You probably misunderstood her, Daddy. What did she say?"

"I couldn't open a can of Spam, and she said, 'James, your old behind ain't good for nothin'. All you gotta do is turn the darn key backward. Take your senile behind somewhere and sit down.' Then she said, 'If you can find the couch.'"

I laughed, because that sounded just like Lerlean. "I'm sure she didn't mean it, Daddy." The truth was I knew my mother meant every word she said to him. "Her arthritis was probably acting up."

"That's her excuse for everything," he said. "Every time she cusses me out, she blames it on her arthritis."

"Is she asleep?" I asked.

"Nah. She went to the riverboat with your aunt Gladys."

"How is Mama able to gamble and pull the handle on the slot machines if the arthritis in her arms is acting up?"

"Humph. That's what I wanna know."

"Well, she left me a message. Make sure you tell her that I called her back. Okay, Daddy?"

"Okay. Listen, your brothers are trying to get in touch with you. Why won't you answer them?"

"So they can bug the mess out of me? I don't have time for Walter and Danny right now."

"They said it was important."

I exhaled loudly. "All right. I'll call them when I hang up from you."

"Okay. I'll tell your mama that you called."

"Bye, Daddy. I love you."

"I love you more."

I sat a skillet on the stove, turned on the burner, and got my seasonings ready for the ground beef and the Italian sausage; then I dialed Daniel's number. Antoinette answered on the first ring.

"Hey, Ant. It's Rhapsody."

"Hey, girl. What's going on?"

"Did you get that rock yet?" I already knew that my cheap bother hadn't bought her a ring.

"Rhapsody, you know Danny and I are not in a hurry to get married."

"You're a good woman, Antoinette," I said. "Danny got the right woman, 'cause it sho can't be me. Is that cheap bastard home?"

"Ooh, Rhapsody." Antoinette chuckled. "Why do you talk about your brother like that? Danny is a good man."

"He's a cheap bastard," I reiterated. "And the sooner you realize that, Antoinette, the better off you'll be. You're wasting your time on him." I didn't care that Daniel was my brother. I called 'em like I saw 'em. I seriously doubted that Antoinette would take my advice, but I did my due diligence. If she was happy, then I was gonna be happy for her . . . God bless her.

Without saying anything further, Antoinette summoned Daniel to the telephone.

"What's up, sis?"

"You and Walter are hunting me down like blood-hounds. Y'all tell *me* what's up."

"Hold on a second while I get him on the line."

Daniel clicked over to dial Walter, and I heated my oven to 350 degrees and then blended together American cheese, Colby, and ricotta cheese in a bowl.

"Hey," I heard Walter say.

I jumped right in and addressed both of them. "Listen, before the two of you try to stick me like y'all did the last time we gave Mama and Daddy an anniversary party, I'ma tell y'all right now, I ain't doin' it."

"Well, hello to you too," Walter said with an attitude.

I coated the hot skillet with nonstick cooking spray and browned the meat. "Look, I got a date. Y'all better say what you gotta say real quick."

Daniel called himself mocking me. "A date? When did *you* get a man?"

"Screw you, Danny, and before you say anything, Walter, screw you too."

"What the heck are you cussin' me out for? I ain't said nothin'."

"Walter, I ain't forgot that crack you made on my answering machine last night. And why is it so hard for y'all to believe that I can have a man?"

"Because nobody wants to put up with your evil behind, that's why," Daniel answered. "When was the last time you been to church?"

I drained the noodles. "It ain't none of your business when I was in church last. When was the last time you shopped at a reputable grocery store? You still watching the sale papers and cutting out coupons? Y'all got sixty seconds to tell me what you want. I got thangs to do."

"You tell her, Walter," Daniel said.

"Why can't you tell her?"

"Because you're the oldest."

"She'll probably listen to you," Walter said.

Click. I hung up.

By 8:30 p.m. the lasagna was sitting on the cooling rack. I had cleaned the kitchen and taken my bath. I lay across my bed, dressed in a short pink lace and chiffon teddy. I didn't know what was taking Malcolm so long to get to my house. I called his cellular telephone and was immediately greeted by his voice mail.

"Yo, this is Malcolm. Hit me up after the beep." *Beep.*

"Malcolm, it's Rhapsody. It's gettin' late. Where are you? I expected you to be here an hour ago. Call me." I disconnected the call and glanced at the digital clock on my nightstand. *Eighty forty-two p.m.* I lay down on my bed and dozed off.

When I woke up, it was 11:45 p.m. It took me a minute to focus and look around my bedroom and realize that Malcolm hadn't come by. I got pissed when I thought of all the trouble I had gone through for him. I mean, I didn't even cook for my own self, let alone somebody else.

I went into the kitchen and looked at the lasagna I had made for him. It cost a lot of money to make lasagna. You got to buy the pasta and the spaghetti sauce and the ground beef and the Italian sausage and the ricotta cheese and the Colby cheese and the cheddar cheese and all the darn seasonings to make it taste good.

Just who in the heck did Malcolm think he was? I got pissed even more. I was so mad, I began to sweat. I dumped the entire pan of lasagna into the garbage can. I called his cellular phone again and got his voice mail. I felt my blood begin to boil. I stormed into my bedroom and looked at my brand-new silk sheets, which I'd paid an arm and a leg for. On an impulse, I went into the bathroom and opened the medicine cabinet and found my shears. I stormed back into my bedroom and sliced the sheets, pillowcases included. I sat down on the floor, breathing heavily.

"Rhino face . . . bbbbbarf bag!" I stuttered and shouted uncontrollably. My neck jerked back and forth, as though I had a bad case of constant hiccups.

Obviously, Malcolm had chosen to hang with his boy rather than be with me. I thought about that and got more pissed than I already was. I rocked back and forth. While I was sitting on the floor, boiling, I remembered something.

What club, Malcolm?

Probably Mr. G's. What's up with the third degree?

At midnight I was on Interstate 290, heading east. At Eighty-Seventh Street, I exited from the Dan Ryan Expressway and turned right, driving toward Ashland Avenue. I turned left into Mr. G's parking lot and couldn't find a parking spot. The lot was filled to capacity. Even with my windows up and my air conditioner blowing at a high speed, I could hear the bass coming from within the club.

One fool walked past me, wearing a bright yellow cape made out of rayon over a white satin button-down shirt. He had on bright yellow pants that matched the cape. On his head was a canary-yellow top hat with a white satin feather stuck in the white satin band. I almost ran into a parked car when I saw the yellow cane with a brass handle in his hand. The fool's pants were so long that I couldn't see the heel of his shoes, but I could imagine that he wore platforms to complete the ensemble. You couldn't call what he wore a suit or an outfit. It was an ensemble. If you took the cane away and put a wand in his hand, he would be mistaken for a magician.

Even though I was pissed at Malcolm, I couldn't help but laugh at this fool, who obviously thought he was superfly. He looked like a broken-down Huggy Bear from *Starsky & Hutch*. Whoever was still sewing crap like that for folks to wear needed to be put behind bars for life. It was just stupid.

I searched the parking lot for Malcolm's Toyota Camry and found it parked in between a metallic gold Ford Mustang GT and a candy apple–red GMC Envoy SUV. Both automobiles were late models. As a matter of fact, when I looked around the lot, I saw that Malcolm's car was about the cheapest one in the entire lot. I parked my Mercedes-Benz directly in front of the Camry and got out.

There was a long line of pimps and hoes standing outside the club, waiting to get in. I saw teal-green suits, powder-blue suits, and burgundy suits holding hands with women wearing fishnet bodysuits and sheer blouses and skirts. One chick wore her jeans so tight, they looked like they were taking her blood pressure.

I stormed right up to the bouncer. He was a big black bear–looking man, but I didn't care. I was at the club on a mission, and it was gonna get accomplished, even if I had to whup the bouncer's butt. When I cut through to the front of the line, I heard, "Oh, no she didn't."

I ignored the prostitute-looking broad who was standing behind me. I guess she thought she was cute. Obviously, she didn't own a full-length mirror, 'cause if she did, she'd have never stepped foot outside. Her double D boobs showed through the dress, which looked like Saran Wrap. I mean, why wear a clear plastic dress? She should've just come to the club naked, since all her body parts were exposed, anyway.

"You gotta get to the back of the line," the bouncer said to me.

"My sixteen-year-old son is in there," I lied effortlessly. "And if you don't want the PoPo here, I suggest you move out of my way."

The bouncer proved what had been said long ago. Black folks were afraid of the police, and that was because we were always doing some crap we ain't got no business doing. He stepped aside and allowed me entrance. Inside the club the cigarette smoke was so thick, I could hardly see in front of me. What happened to the no-smoking policy? Or maybe that didn't apply to clubs. I couldn't say for sure. I hadn't been clubbing in quite a while. I was more laid back, a lounge kind of chick.

To my immediate right was the DJ, and to my left was the bar. Every bar stool housed the booty of a tramp who was wearing too much make-up, too much weave, and way too much silicone. And why did broads always try to squeeze their big booties into way too small clothes? If you wore a size twenty-four wide, you didn't buy a size twelve petite. And women had the nerve to get an attitude when someone frowned at them or made a comment. Women should buy their right size. They would look better, feel better, and breathe better.

The way I was eyeing the heifers sitting at the bar was the way they were eyeing me. Unlike their hoochie mama attire, which was obviously the norm in that club, I had on a navy blue jogging suit and K-Swiss gym shoes. I was there to kick some butt, not to show mine.

I searched the dimly lit club, trying to be careful not to let Malcolm see me first. I didn't wanna give him time to react when I rolled up on him. I found him sitting near the back of the club, at a round table, with another man and two women. For about thirty seconds I observed the chemistry at the table. That was enough time for me to conclude that Malcolm was very friendly with the broad sitting next to him. She seemed to be hanging on every word he was saying in her ear. She was sitting so close to him, she might as well have been sitting on his lap.

I guessed that was the famous Ivan sitting across from Malcolm, with his arm around the other broad's shoulders. As she smiled and talked to Ivan, his eyes were focused on her chest. Apparently, he thought she communicated with her overexposed cleavage. The halter top she was wearing wasn't supportive at all. The eighteen-hour bra she wore was on its nineteenth hour. So, again, I asked myself the question, *Why not just come to the club naked?*

Between the four of them, I saw nine drinks on the table. Malcolm kissed the cheek of the chick next to him, then whispered something in her ear. She giggled and moved her hand from the table and placed it on his thigh. I watched her hand make its way up toward Malcolm's groin. At that point, I had seen enough, and I walked right up to the table.

"What the heck is going on here?" I barked.

The expression on Malcolm's face was priceless and a Kodak moment. His eyes were so wide open, he looked like a deer caught in the headlights. No one at the table spoke, including Malcolm. I kept my eyes focused on his.

"Why did you blow me off?" My eyes were blazing.

Malcolm was speechless; he didn't know what to say. He tried to remember my name. "Hi. Um, um . . ."

I was way past pissed. "Rhapsody, fool," I snapped, reminding him.

"Oh, yeah, yeah. Uh, Rhapsody, this is Sharonda and Leticia and—"

"Screw Sharonda and Leticia!" I yelled.

Both of the chicks' mouths fell open. I dared either one of them to say a word to me, because I was ready to fight. I looked at the guy sitting across from Malcolm.

"Are you Ivan?" I barked.

He acted as though he was afraid to answer. He hesitated before he spoke. "Yeah."

"Well, screw you too," I said.

"Hold up, Rhapsody," Malcolm said as he stood.

"No, *you* hold up, Malcolm. Why did you blow me off?" By that time I had attracted a crowd of spectators.

"What are you talkin' about?"

"You were supposed to come to my house this evening, remember?"

"Rhapsody, I never agreed to come by. I said that I would get back to you."

"So, you couldn't call and tell me that you *weren't* coming? I cooked for you. Do you know how much it cost to make a freakin' pan of lasagna?"

Malcolm threw his hands in the air. "Look, I'm sorry you went through the trouble, but that ain't my issue."

Now, why did he say that to me? It was at that exact moment when I realized Malcolm didn't know whom he was messin' with. I was too old of a cat to be scratched by a kitten.

My eyebrows rose. "It ain't your issue? How 'bout I give you an issue?"

The bouncer was at my side. "Is there a problem here?"

I kept my eyes focused on Malcolm's as I answered, "Nah, ain't no problem."

I gave Malcolm a stare that positively put fear in his heart. I could tell by the way his Adam's apple moved when he swallowed. I just put something on his mind. With my mission accomplished, I left the club.

Outside in the parking lot, I got my tire iron from my trunk and threw it at Malcolm's rear window, and it shattered completely. Huggy Bear and a few more people saw what I had done, but I didn't care. I was pissed beyond words. I got behind my wheel and burned rubber out of the parking lot.

I was a nervous wreck while driving on the expressway. What did I just do? Some teenage high school crap was what it was. Never in my wildest dreams would I have imagined myself doing what I did. What was I thinking? I was a grown woman, which meant I was too old to behave that way. It was ridiculous.

As I sped away, I kept looking in my rearview mirror for the police. There were witnesses; I knew someone saw my license plate. Tears started to stream down my face. I had met Malcolm only two days prior, and I tried to figure out how I had lost all my self-control and self-respect in such a short period of time. What if Malcolm pressed charges against me? How would I explain that to my parents?

I was afraid to go home. What if the police were waiting for me there? I needed a hiding place for a few hours, so I headed for Anastasia's house. I braced myself, knowing that she would cuss me out for showing up on her doorstep at 1:00 a.m. without calling first. My tears made it difficult for me to see clearly. I accidentally drove my Mercedes up on the curb right in front of her house, but I didn't care. I left my car right where it was and put it in park. Ten seconds later, I was pressing Anastasia's doorbell nonstop.

Trevor yanked the door open, ready to light into whoever it was, until he recognized me and saw the distraught state I was in. "Rhapsody?"

I was so emotional, I couldn't say anything. I placed my face in my hands and sobbed loudly. The next thing I knew, I was in Trevor's arms. "Calm down and tell me what happened. Did someone hurt you?"

Anastasia appeared and put her hand on my lower back. The look on her face was one of horror. "What happened to her?" she asked Trevor.

"I don't know. She won't say anything."

"Bring her into the living room, Trevor."

He guided me inside the house, helped me over to the sofa in the living room, and sat me down, then knelt before me. "Rhapsody, I need you to talk to me. Did someone hurt you?"

I still couldn't bring myself to say anything, but I shook my head from side to side. Anastasia sat on the sofa next to me. "Sis, you're scaring me."

I managed to pull myself together. "I'm sorry, Stacy. I'm so sorry to come here like this."

She pulled me into her arms and held me tight. "It's all right. Calm down. It's gonna be all right." She wiped my face with a Kleenex tissue Trevor had given her.

"Is there anything I can do?" he asked Anastasia.

"Help me get her to the guest room."

Trevor literally picked me up, carried me into the guest bedroom, and laid me down on the bed.

"Thanks, baby," I heard Anastasia say.

"What else do you need?" he asked her.

"Get a nightgown from my top dresser drawer and bring it to me."

When Trevor brought the nightgown to Anastasia, I heard Chantal crying.

"Stay with Rhapsody. I got the baby," Trevor said.

Anastasia didn't ask me any more questions. With Trevor out of the bedroom, she undressed me and slipped the nightgown over my head. She went into the bathroom to wet a small towel with warm water and washed my face clean of smeared black mascara and eyeliner. My best friend tucked me beneath the covers, then lay next to me and rocked me to sleep.

Chapter 13

"Aw, shoot," Malcolm whined when he saw the damage to his window.

Ivan stood in the parking lot, next to him. "Dude, you know who did this, right?"

"That crazy broad. I don't believe this, man. My mama is gonna kill me."

Huggy Bear approached Malcolm. "Dude, I saw who did this to your window. It was a woman. She drove away in a black Mercedes."

Malcolm nodded his head. "Yeah, I know who she is. Thanks, man."

A police car with bright blue neon lights flashing arrived on the scene.

"Who called the police?" Ivan asked.

Huggy Bear spoke. "I did. I didn't know whose car this was."

A Latin policeman exited the squad car, removed his flashlight from the holster on his belt, and walked toward Malcolm, Ivan, and Huggy Bear. With his flashlight, the officer surveyed the damaged vehicle, then shined his flashlight in each of the three men's faces.

"Whose vehicle is this?" he asked.

"It's mine, Officer," Malcolm answered.

The officer moved his flashlight beam toward Malcolm. "Can I see your license and registration?"

Malcolm gave the officer his identification from his wallet. He then reached inside the glove compartment for his insurance card and gave it to the officer.

"What happened here?" the officer asked Malcolm as he examined the documents.

"I came out of the club and saw my rear window like this. Somebody threw a tire iron through it."

"Do you have any idea who might have done it?"

"No."

"What?" The question came from the mouths of Ivan and Huggy Bear.

At the tone of their voices, the officer shined his flashlight in Ivan's and Huggy Bear's faces and studied their expressions before shining the light on Malcolm again. "You want to file a complaint?"

"No, I don't," Malcolm answered.

"You *don't?*" Ivan asked with raised eyebrows.

"Nah, man. I ain't got time for that. I gotta get home," Malcolm confessed.

"It'll take only a few minutes," the officer said.

"Nah, that's all right," Malcolm answered. He was anxious to leave. "I gotta go."

"Hold on a second," the officer said and walked back to his squad car with Malcolm's identification.

Malcolm shook Huggy Bear's hand. "Thanks for your help, but I got it from here."

"No problem, man. Be cool." Huggy Bear turned and walked away.

With Huggy Bear out of hearing range, Ivan spoke to Malcolm. "What are you doing, fool? Why didn't you turn her in?"

"Because I don't wanna make this any bigger than it is. I'll get the window fixed in the morning. I'm done with Rhapsody, though. That's for sure."

"Dude, tomorrow is Thursday. Don't you take your mother to therapy every Tuesday and Thursday morning?"

Malcolm hung his head. "Now what am I gonna do?"

The officer was back at Malcolm's side. "Who is Lucille Washington?"

"She's my mother. Why?"

"When I ran the plates, it showed that this car is registered to her."

"Yeah, it's in her name, but it's my car."

"You're not listed as a co-owner, and I can't allow you to drive this car in the condition it's in. Since she's the sole owner, Lucille will have to be notified. And she has to call her insurance company to file a claim, but first, she has to get this car towed to an auto body shop."

Malcolm felt his whole world crashing down all around him. Allowing his mother to find out about this was not an option for him. "Officer, please, my mother can't know about this."

"She's being contacted right now."

As soon as Lucille disconnected the call from the police department, she dialed Malcolm's cellular telephone.

He knew it was her before he looked at the caller ID. He sighed before he answered. "Hey, Ma."

"What happened, Malcolm?"

"Somebody threw a tire iron through the back window."

"You mean 'some woman,' don't you?"

His heart skipped two beats. "What?"

"A man gave a statement that he saw a woman deliberately throw something through the window."

Malcolm looked around for Huggy Bear, but he was nowhere to be seen. "Ma, I don't know anything about that."

"Uh-huh. I figured you would say that. Who's with you?"

"Ivan."

"I called AAA motor club," Lucille stated. "You stay there until they tow my car. Then have Ivan drive you home."

Hours later Ivan and Malcolm sat in Ivan's car outside of Lucille's house. Malcolm looked at the front door of the home he shared with his mother.

"Man, I don't even wanna go in there. Ain't no tellin' what she's got waiting for me on the other side of that door. She probably has the cast-iron skillet in her hand."

Ivan chuckled. He knew Lucille was very strict. "Yeah, you're probably right. But seriously, Malcolm, you need to stay away from Rhapsody."

"I plan to. I just can't believe this night. This is some wild crap."

"Yep," Ivan agreed. "Like a fatal attraction. You better be careful. Rhapsody seems like the type of woman that lurks in bushes and trees, just waiting to jump out at you."

Lucille opened the front door and rolled her wheelchair onto the front porch. "Bring your narrow tail in this house, Malcolm!" she yelled.

Ivan looked at her and chuckled. "Well, at least she ain't got a skillet in her hand."

Chapter 14

I woke up early Thursday morning to the voices of Anastasia and Trevor. Through the closed guest bedroom door, I could hear them moving around the house.

"Did you get her to talk?" Trevor asked Anastasia.

"No. She was too upset," Anastasia answered. "It didn't take long for her to fall asleep. As soon as her head hit the pillow, she was out like a light."

"I looked out of the living room window this morning and saw her car up on the curb, so I took her keys and parked it right," I heard Trevor say.

"I'm sure Rhapsody will thank you for that," Anastasia said.

"You couldn't get anything out of her last night?"

"Nope. Nothing. You want breakfast this morning?"

"Nah. I'm running late as it is. I'm outta here."

Five minutes later, I heard the front door open and close. Soon after, Anastasia knocked lightly, then opened the door to the guest bedroom before poking her head inside. "Rhapsody?"

"Good morning, Stacy," I greeted softly.

She smiled. "Oh, you're awake. It's almost seven. Are you going to work today?"

I sat up on the bed and propped the pillows behind my back against the headboard. "Nah, I don't think so. Would you get my cell from my purse? I need to call my boss."

"Of course," she answered. "You left it on the sofa in the living room." Anastasia left the guest bedroom and returned moments later with my purse. She gave it to me, then sat on the end of bed.

I pulled my cell phone from my purse and dialed Mr. Duncan's voice mail. "Good morning, Mr. Duncan. This is Rhapsody. I'm calling to let you know that I woke up with a migraine headache this morning and I can't make it to work today." I disconnected the call and laid the phone on the bed beside me.

"You feel like talking about it?" Anastasia asked me.

I looked at her. "What makes you think there's something to talk about?"

"Because I have never seen you like this before. And you've never rung my doorbell at one o'clock in the morning. Does this have anything to do with Malcolm?"

"Humph," I said. I sighed before adding, "It's has everything to do with Malcolm."

"Did you two have a fight?"

"No, not in the way you're thinkin', Stacy. I didn't get a chance to tell you that Malcolm called Tuesday night to tell me the reason he couldn't spend the night with me. Apparently, his mother is a paraplegic, and he has to be home early in the morning to help her out of bed. Then I apologized for leaving that bogus message on his cell phone."

Anastasia nodded her head. "Okay. That's good. And?"

I smiled seductively. "And we made up."

Anastasia rolled her eyes. "Spare me all the intimate details and fast-forward to last night."

"Yesterday I called Malcolm and invited him over. He said that he usually hangs with his boy, Ivan, on Wednesday nights. I told him that it was cool with me as long as he came by to see me first."

Chantal woke up crying, and Anastasia left the guest room. "Hold that thought," she said over her shoulder.

She returned with Chantal in her arms and sat down in the chair and pulled out a big black boob and shoved it in Chantal's mouth. "Okay. Go ahead."

"Well, since it seems that the only thing Malcolm and I do is screw, I wanted to do something a little different than hop in the sack when he got to my house, so I decided to cook for him."

"*You*? Cook?" Anastasia joked.

I chuckled. "I know, right? I had really planned to sit down at the kitchen table and talk over dinner so that we could get to know one another."

"Sounds okay so far. What happened?"

"I finished cooking, took my bath, and lay across my bed to wait for him. I accidentally fell asleep and woke up at a quarter to twelve. I called his cell and didn't get an answer." I exhaled. "The bastard never showed up, Stacy. He left me hanging."

Stacy tucked the first boob in her bra and moved Chantal to her other arm, then pulled out the second boob and shoved it in her mouth. "Then what happened?"

"I got pissed at the trouble I went through cooking for Malcolm, and then I realized that he told me where he and his boy were gonna be last night. So I threw the lasagna in the garbage and sliced up my brand-new silk sheets. Then I put on a jogging suit and drove to Mr. G's Club on Eighty-Seventh Street."

Anastasia shook her head vigorously from side to side, like she was trying to shake some words out of her brain. She frowned at me. "Hold up, Rhapsody. What did you say?"

"I said I drove to Mr. G's on Eighty-Seventh Street."

"Uh-uh. Before that," she said.

"I put on a jogging suit."

"Nope. Before that."

"I sliced up my silk sheets and threw the lasagna in the garbage?" I asked her, wondering if that was what she wanted to hear.

Anastasia nodded her head, confirming that those were the words she had wanted me to repeat. "That's what I thought you said. Why would you slice up your sheets and throw away your food?"

"Because I was pissed, Stacy."

"So darn what? You don't throw away food that you cooked, and you definitely don't slice up your expensive sheets. Why did you let the crazy out?"

As my best friend for so many years, Anastasia knew I suffered from Tourette's syndrome. Oftentimes, for support, she'd gone with me to the appointments with Dr. Buckles. But Anastasia had told me more than once that she believed that I sometimes caused some of my own episodes.

I didn't answer Anastasia, because I knew she was right. I had purposely sought Malcolm out the night before and had put on a show.

Anastasia tucked the second boob away, then laid Chantal on her shoulder, and began patting her back lightly. She rocked back and forth. "What happened when you got to Mr. G's?"

"I saw Malcolm and his boy sittin' at a table near the back of the club. They were cheesing all up in some heifers' faces. I walked over to the table and asked Malcolm why he stood me up."

"Oh, my God!" Anastasia said. "Please tell me you didn't do that dumb crap, Rhapsody."

"I did. I cussed him out. And, as a matter of fact, I cussed everybody at the table out."

"For what?" Anastasia asked in a raised voice. I could tell that she was reprimanding me.

"I told you that I was pissed." That was my only defense.

"Well, after you made a fool of yourself, what happened next?"

"I was so loud that the bouncer came and asked me if there was a problem. I was causing a scene."

Anastasia shook her head from side to side. "Humph, humph, humph. You left without a problem, right?" She was hopeful.

"Not exactly, Stacy. I left the club, then went outside and got a tire iron from my trunk and threw it through Malcolm's rear window. Then I jumped in my car and sped out of the parking lot. I came here 'cause I was too scared to go home. I thought the police would be lookin' for me there."

The look on Anastasia's face was one of horror. "Rhapsody, are you thirty-four or sixteen?"

"Look, Stacy, I know I was wrong, okay? It's just that—"

"It's just that your grown behind is sprung. There is no other way to put it. You are sprung out over a twenty-one-year-old dangalang, and it's a shame. You need to get your stuff together before you self-destruct."

"You think I should apologize to Malcolm, Stacy?"

Her eyes grew wide. "Do I think—" She cut her own words off and composed herself. She lowered her voice. "Yes, you should apologize *and* pay to get Malcolm's window fixed. But don't do anything just yet. Give Malcolm a few days to calm down a bit."

"Maybe I should go to Burger World and talk to him today."

"You know what, Rhapsody? Your head is as hard as a brick. What did I just say? Stay away from Malcolm until he calms down. Seeing you this soon will set him off."

"Yeah, you're right, Stacy. I'll wait until he gets off work, and then I'll call his cell phone. No sense in upsetting his day at work."

Anastasia stood and came over to me. She tapped her knuckles against my forehead. "Hello, Mr. Brain. Are you in there? Can you shut this dumb broad up and let me talk to someone with some common sense?"

I pushed her hand away. "That ain't funny."

"You're right. It's not funny. This whole situation is sad. Really sad. I'm trying to tell you that you're about to screw up again, but you won't listen to reason, so go ahead and do what you feel you have to do. I know one thing, though," Anastasia said over her shoulder as she turned to leave the guest bedroom. "If you ever ring my doorbell in the middle of the night and disturb my family again, I'ma call the police on you myself."

Anastasia laid Chantal down in her crib and then cooked breakfast for both of us. I swallowed the eggs and bacon so fast and was out of Anastasia's house before eight o'clock. I couldn't take her going on and on about what I should and shouldn't do about Malcolm. Don't get me wrong. Anastasia was my best friend, and I valued our relationship and her opinions, but she really needed to shut up sometimes.

I knew I was wrong in what I did, okay? I got that. But coming down on me harder and harder wasn't gonna change the fact that a wrong needed to be made right. I figured that if I could just get Malcolm alone, somewhere where it was just the two of us, I could explain my actions to him.

On my way home from Anastasia's house, I called Malcolm's cellular telephone.

"What do you want?" Malcolm yelled into the telephone. I knew he was mad at me, but darn.

"I'm sorry." That was all I could say. I was set to give him a long, drawn-out speech, but his greeting threw me for a loop.

"You crazy broad! Yeah, you're sorry, all right."

"Listen, Malcolm, I know you're upset, but—"

"Upset? Try mad and pissed off! You're a crazy broad, you know that?"

"Okay, I can understand your frustration, but I ain't gonna be too many more broads."

"You're gonna be whatever I say you are. What is wrong with you, girl? You don't own me. You ain't got no papers on me."

I exhaled loudly in Malcolm's ear to let him know that he was getting on my last nerve and the one before it. "If you would shut your mouth for one minute, you'd realize that I'm trying to apologize."

"Apologize for what?" He was still yelling. "For destroying my mother's car?"

I frowned. I was confused. "Your mother's car?"

"Yeah, it was my mother's car," he confirmed. "And you know what, Rhapsody? She chewed me a new butthole last night."

"Oh, my God," I said. I *really* felt bad when he told me that. "Malcolm, I didn't know it was your mother's car."

"It doesn't matter whose car it was. You don't damage other folks' property."

"Wait a minute," I said. "You told me your mother was a paraplegic. How is it her car?"

"Not that it's any of your business, but she was driving before she got paralyzed."

"Malcolm, I am so sorry," I said with much sincerity. "I'm going to pay for the window."

"I don't want anything from you. The insurance is going to cover it."

"Malcolm, the window won't cost but a few hundred dollars at most. It's not worth the risk of having your car insurance go up just for a broken window."

"I said, I don't want anything from you. Because of you, my mother took the car from me, and now I gotta take the bus everywhere I need to go. Cherise had to miss work today to take her to therapy."

"Who's Cherise?"

"My sister."

"Well, I don't know what else to say to you, Malcolm. I was wrong and out of line. And I'm sorry it cost you the car."

"Whatever! Just leave me alone." Malcolm disconnected the call.

Chapter 15

I took a hot shower when I got home from Anastasia's house. I was lying across my bed and looking at *The Price Is Right* when I thought about my best friend. I didn't like the way we had left things that morning. After she had warned me never to come to her house unannounced in the wee hours of the morning, she had cooked us breakfast. We'd eaten in silence; then I'd left. I did appreciate Anastasia, and I truly valued our friendship. I felt the need to call her and let her know that deep down inside, I knew she had my back and would tell me only what I needed to hear. Anastasia would never pacify me with the things I wanted to hear. She'd proven to me over and over again that she had only my best interests at heart.

I was reaching for the telephone on my nightstand to call her when I noticed the light on my answering machine flashing. I pressed the PLAY button.

"Hey, baby girl. It's Mama. I called your job, and your boss said that you were out sick today. What's the matter? Call me, okay?" *Beep.*

"Rhapsody, will you please call Walter or me? We gotta get this anniversary party together for Mom and Dad. You ain't that busy that you can't help us with this." *Beep.*

"Hey, girl. What's up? This is Clyde. Let's hook up tonight. Call me." *Beep.*

I erased all three messages. I didn't wanna give Daniel or Walter the time of day. And as far as Clyde was concerned, we couldn't hook nothing up. He needed to hook his raggedy mouth up with a dental plan. Every other tooth in Clyde's mouth was missing; when he smiled, you'd swear you were looking at piano keys. I dialed the number that was so very familiar to me.

"Hello."

"Hey, Ma."

"Baby girl, what's wrong with you?"

"I just got a little headache, that's all," I lied. "I didn't feel like going to work today. How are you?"

She exhaled. "I guess I'm all right. My arthritis in my right arm is acting up."

"Daddy told me you went to the riverboat last night. How were you able to pull the slot machine handles with your bad arm?"

"I pulled with my left arm, and I won six hundred dollars."

"Good for you. What are you gonna do with your newfound wealth?"

"Get me some new drapes in the living and dining rooms. Walter and Daniel have been calling here like crazy, looking for you."

"I don't know why. The dumb fools know I don't live there."

"They said you won't talk to them."

"Ma, you gave birth to two stupid sons, okay? I was on the phone with them last night, and between the two of them, they had nothing to say. All I heard was, 'You tell her, Walter.' 'You tell her, Danny.' Ain't nobody got time for that."

Lerlean laughed at me. "You are truly your mother's daughter."

"Daddy told me that you cussed him out last night."

"I sho did, and I'ma cuss him out again when I get off this phone."

"Why, Ma?"

"Because he ain't got no business tellin' nobody what I do. What goes on in this house stays in this house unless *I* tell it. It was nobody's business that I went to the boat."

"But, Ma, you can't get mad just because he didn't know how to open a can of Spam."

"Well, what the heck did he think the small key attached to the can was for? The front door?"

I chuckled. Lerlean was right. We were definitely mother and daughter, 'cause that was exactly something I would have said.

"Take it easy on Daddy. He loves you."

"Yeah, okay," she said. "I'm about to show him what love is. And don't forget—"

"I know. I know," I said. "I'll be at church on Sunday." I disconnected the call.

After talking with my mother, I called Anastasia. "I just want to thank you for your hospitality."

"You called him, didn't you?" she asked.

"What?"

"Don't play with me, Rhapsody. You heard me."

"What if I did call Malcolm?"

I heard her exhale loudly. "You just won't learn, will you?"

"For your information, Stacy, Malcolm and I had a decent conversation." I seemed to lie so effortlessly.

"Oh, really?" she asked. The tone of her voice told me that she wasn't convinced.

"Yep. I still feel bad, though. It was his mother's car that I damaged, and she took it away from him."

"His mother's car? I thought you said she's a paraplegic."

"She had the car before her accident."

"What kind of accident did she have?"

"I don't know. Malcolm didn't get into all of that. I hate the fact that he's gotta take the bus everywhere."

"Well, you work for the CTA. Get him a bus pass. It's the least you can do."

"Maybe it is. Maybe it ain't," I said. The wheels in my head were turning.

"The way you say that, it sounds like you're thinkin' about buying Malcolm a car." Anastasia chuckled at the thought.

I laughed in her ear. "Girl, please. I'll admit that I'm sprung, but I ain't *that* sprung."

Fifteen minutes later, I was dressed and driving nowhere in particular. With my checkbook in my purse, I would stop at the first car dealership I came upon. I was gonna get Malcolm back by any means necessary.

By 3:00 p.m. Malcolm's brand-new, silver, late-model Lincoln Navigator sat in my driveway with a gigantic red satin bow sitting on top of the hood. It cost me $250.00 to have it delivered. Another three hundred dollars added to that equaled the car note I would pay each month for the next thirty-six months.

Automatic everything, including a moonroof; an ebony leather interior; deep, heated bucket seats; and a top-of-the-line stereo system; plus a twenty-disc changer were just a few of the amenities Malcolm had to look forward to. Even my Mercedes-Benz didn't have some of the features Malcolm's SUV had, such as the two high-definition televisions adjacent to the interior ceiling light for the backseat passengers to enjoy. And a personalized dashboard would greet Malcolm each time he sat in the driver's seat. I couldn't wait to see his face when he heard, "Hello, Malcolm. Welcome to paradise."

I sat in the parking lot at Burger World, facing the door to make sure I didn't miss him when he exited the restaurant. I had no clue when his shift ended, but I was gonna sit and wait all afternoon and evening if I had to. But at exactly 4:03 p.m. I saw his fine behind appear. I started my engine and slowly eased my car next to him as he walked toward the bus stop.

I honked my horn one time and let down my driver's window. "Hey, handsome. You want a ride?"

Malcolm looked at me, then looked at his wristwatch. "Shouldn't you be at work?"

"I'm trying to offer you a ride, Malcolm. It's about ninety degrees out here."

"If it weren't for you, I *would* have a ride. And you ain't gotta tell me how hot it is. I'm already sweatin'."

"I can fix that."

Malcolm stopped walking and looked at me. "What are you talkin' about?"

"Get in, and I'll tell you."

He shook his head from side to side. "You must be smoking dope if you think I'm foolin' with you."

"Malcolm, that was cruel."

He shrugged his shoulders and kept walking. "You may as well know that I took out a restraining order against you."

I knew he was lying. "Is that right? Why haven't I been served?"

"My lawyer didn't serve you today?" He tried to look shocked, but it wasn't working.

I had to laugh at him. "First of all, if you're gonna tell a lie, at least make it sound like you know what you're talkin' about. A lawyer doesn't serve restraining orders. Sheriffs do. And if you *do* have a lawyer who's dumb enough to darken my doorstep with a restraining order, he'll get shot in his butt."

"I really believe you'll do something like that."

"I was joking, Malcolm."

He kept walking toward the bus stop while I cruised down the street. "No you weren't."

This back-and-forth banter was getting on my nerves. "Malcolm, I was joking. Now, get in this car."

"Rhapsody, you need to go on. First, you cuss me out on my voice mail, and then you scratch my back up. After that, you showed up at Mr. G's and embarrassed me. Then you bust my car window. And now you think I'm gonna let you drive me somewhere and kill me?"

I was offended. "Oh, so now I'm a killer?"

"I wouldn't put it past you," he said.

"Okay, Malcolm, I admit that I behaved badly the past couple of days, and I'm sorry. I bought you a gift, a very expensive gift."

Malcolm got to the corner and sat down on the bench next to the bus stop sign. "I don't want it."

I pulled my car over to the curb. "It's something I know you'll like."

"Where is it?" he asked.

"At my house."

Malcolm shook his head from side to side. "Nope. It's a trap."

"It's not a trap, Malcolm. Trust me, you'll want this gift."

"Oh, snap," Malcolm said excitedly as I pulled my car into the driveway and stopped next to the Lincoln Navigator. "Is this for me?"

"Yep."

I had barely placed my car in park before Malcolm was at the driver's door of the SUV. I got out and walked over to him. I could see all thirty-two of his teeth.

"When did you get it?"

"This afternoon."

I gave Malcolm the keys. He pressed the button on the remote to operate the keyless entry and hopped in.

"Hello, Malcolm. Welcome to paradise."

Malcolm's eyes lit up, and he covered his wide-open mouth. "How much did you pay for this?"

"A lot, and I'll be paying on it for the next three years."

"How much is the note?"

"Why? Are you gonna help me pay it?" I asked with an attitude. He was getting on my nerves with the questions.

"Calm down. I was just asking," he said.

I stood outside the SUV, next to him, as he fumbled with the knobs and buttons on the dashboard.

"Malcolm."

"Huh?" he said, preoccupied.

"Malcolm, look at me."

He gave me his undivided attention. "What's up?"

"Contrary to what people may think, I don't have a lot of money. Just because I have a nice job and I'm single, with no kids, doesn't mean that I'm rolling in dough. I made a huge sacrifice and bought this truck for you because I really like you, and I wanted to show you how sorry I was for doin' the fool."

He leaned out of the truck and kissed my lips lightly. "It's cool, Rhapsody." He began pushing buttons on the dashboard.

"And one more thing," I said.

He kept fidgeting with the dashboard. "I'm listening."

"This truck isn't a free ride for you. Just like it's costing me, it's gonna cost you too."

Malcolm looked at me, then shrugged his shoulders. "What do you mean?"

"I mean I want you at my beck and call. I don't care what you're doing or where you are, when I call, you better come."

Malcolm giggled. "Oh, so it's like that, huh? You puttin' my junk on a leash?"

"That's the way it is." I needed Malcolm to know how serious I was.

"A'ight. I'm down with that," he said. He settled back into the deep leather bucket seat. "I can't wait to show Ivan." He started the engine. I reached for the keys and turned the engine off. Malcolm looked at me like I was crazy. "What's the deal, Rhapsody?"

"You need to thank me for your gift." I walked toward my front door. Malcolm exited the SUV and followed me.

It was almost 9:30 p.m. when I woke up. I turned my night-light on and sat up on the bed. Malcolm was gone, but his cologne, mixed with the scent of sex, still lingered in the air. I reached for the telephone to test my powers. Why? Because I wanted to.

"This is Malcolm," he answered.

"Where are you?" I asked.

"Ivan and I are about to go get somethin' to eat."

"Come back to my house right now."

"What?"

"You heard what I said, Malcolm."

I heard him exhale loudly. "Rhapsody, I just left you a couple of hours ago. Plus, I'm already on the South Side, and I got my boy with me."

"Is that supposed to mean something to me? What did I tell you earlier?"

"Come on, Rhapsody," he whined.

"Either you come back to my house or I'm coming to get my truck."

"*Your* truck?"

"Yes, my truck!" I shouted into the telephone. "*Your* name ain't on the papers. Now, what's it gonna be? You choose."

There was a long pause, and then I heard, "A'ight. Let me drop Ivan off, and then I'll be on my way."

I disconnected the call and redialed Malcolm's number.

"I said I was coming!" he snapped at me.

"Go ahead and hang with your boy. You don't have to come back tonight."

"Why are you doing this to me?" he asked.

"I needed to make sure that you and I were on the same page so there won't be any misunderstandings."

"Yeah, we're on the same page."

"Are you sure, Malcolm?"

"Yeah, Rhapsody. What the hell?"

I didn't care that he was mad. "Good night, Malcolm."

Chapter 16

Malcolm threw his cellular telephone on the backseat. "I don't know if I'm gonna be able to deal with this crap," he said to Ivan. "She acts like she owns me since she bought me this truck."

Ivan giggled. "She *does* own you. I told you to leave that crazy broad alone, Malcolm. By accepting this truck under her conditions, you just wrote a check that your junk will have to cash over and over again. You sold your soul to the devil, man. I really believe that you got yourself into something that you may not be able to get out of." Ivan ran his hand along the smooth leather of the dashboard. "This *is* a bad truck, though."

Chapter 17

Sunday morning I walked into World Deliverance Christian Center with my head held high. Even though I had a whole lot to repent for and ask God to forgive me for, I figured that no one else in the church was a better Christian than me. Just like me, everyone there had sinned and fallen short last week. In my purse was an envelope that held a check for my tithes and cash for my offering.

I knew I was a sinner, and I made God work extra hard to keep my soul saved. I'd always paid more than the required 10 percent of my income. Between Sundays, if I wasn't cussin' somebody out, I was doing something I had no business doing, and for that God had to work overtime to keep me from going to hell. I made sure that He received the money I owed Him. I was never late with my payment.

What I wasn't ready for was the bishop's whoopin' and hollerin'. He could be a little long-winded. The bishop ain't seen my face in the place in a while, so I knew when he did lay his eyes on me, his sermon would have my name on it.

The vestibule was filled with saints, especially Sunday morning saints like me. The kind of saints that were holy only on Sundays. I could admit it. I did act a fool all week long, but on Sundays I tried to behave, but it didn't always work out that way. Sundays were when I went to God and begged Him to change me, fill me with His Holy Spirit, and guide me in the right direction. But as soon as

Monday morning came, I was right back to cussin', lyin', cheatin', and fornicating. I couldn't help it.

"Rhapsody? Is that you?"

I turned around and saw one of the many faces I had planned on avoiding. "Lady Felicia Clark," I said and smiled. I knew she was already looking through me, as she always did. Lady Felicia was a bloodhound. She was gifted in sniffing out foul souls, and she didn't mind calling them out. "How are you?" I asked her. I was hoping she'd answered my question and not read me, but I knew it was inevitable. Lady Felicia hadn't seen me in about three weeks. She was gonna get me for sure.

She took me into her arms and hugged me tight. Although I knew her embrace was genuine, I knew she was revved up. Lady Felicia let me go and looked into my eyes. "Girl, I ain't seen you in a month of Sundays. What have you been doing?" She lowered her head and peered into my eyes. "Or should I have asked, 'Who have you been doing?'"

At that moment I felt my bladder betray me. A trickle of pee escaped. I literally had to use my Kegel muscles to stop the flow.

"I know you, Rhapsody," Lady Felicia said to me. "Whenever you miss a few Sundays in a row, you're out there justa sinnin' and doin' all kinds of stuff that God don't approve of."

My feet were glued to the floor. I couldn't move to save my life.

"Look at ya," she said. She scanned me from the top of my head all the way down to my feet. Lady Felicia looked at me with disgust. "Just as speechless as the day is long. That ain't nothin' but pure guilt. You're gonna sit next to me this morning on the front pew. I'll tell the bishop to lay hands on you. That spirit of lust gotta be lifted from you."

Lady Felicia and I were the same age and had grown up together at World Deliverance Christian Center. We had even sung in the choir together as fellow sopranos when we were teenagers. But when she married the bishop, the Lord put a special anointing on her. Nobody could get nothing past her. She was always on point. If you had sinned and came into her presence, she'd know it.

Nope. It ain't gonna happen. I'm not sittin' next to you. "I'm meeting my mother here, Lady Felicia. I know she's expecting me to sit with her."

Lady Felicia was a powerhouse, and I loved her to death, but that wasn't the first time she had called herself putting me on punishment by making me sit next to her in church. Everyone at World Deliverance Christian Center knew that if someone was made to sit next to the first lady on the front pew, it meant that she had pulled their coattail and all eyes would be on that person. "I wonder what she did. Uh-oh. So-and-so must've done something awful. Wow, Lady Felicia got another one," they'd whisper.

The last time she had pulled my coattail and had sat me down next to her, she was in my face with an amen every time the bishop said something she thought pertained to me. That was why I had stayed away from church. I didn't like being put on blast like that.

"Sister Lerlean is working the usher board today. Sister Mildred Cox fell ill this morning and won't be here. Your mother was kind enough to fill in and take Sister Cox's place."

My shoulders sank. *Darn.* I felt like walkin' back out the church doors.

"Hey, Rhapsody."

I turned around and saw Kimberley Johnson. She and I had also grown up at World Deliverance Christian Center, and we'd been baptized together when we were seven years old. Thank God she'd shown up when she did. I needed a distraction.

I quickly grabbed Kimberley and hugged her. I whispered in her ear, "I'm so glad you're here. Rescue me, please."

Kimberley released me and looked at Lady Felicia. "First Lady, the bishop has decided to dedicate the infants before morning service. We're gonna need a few towels."

Lady Felicia exhaled. "That man is always changin' the order of service around. Are all the babies and parents in place?" she asked Kimberley.

Kimberley nodded her head. "Yes, ma'am."

Lady Felicia exhaled and started to walk away; then she stopped in her tracks and turned around. "Go on ahead to the front pew, Rhapsody. I'll be there in a moment."

"You gotta be in the pulpit with Elder Clark today, First Lady," Kimberley said to her. "The parents and babies are on the front pew this morning."

I let out a loud sigh, and I knew Kimberley heard me.

Lady Felicia looked at me and sneered like a werewolf. All thirty-two of her teeth were exposed, and I knew she was disappointed. She really wanted to get me but couldn't that day, and I was so grateful for that.

"I'll get . . . I mean, I'll see you next week, Rhapsody," Lady Felicia said to me.

Not likely. "Yes, ma'am," I sneered back.

She turned and walked away.

Kimberley giggled. "She had you cornered, huh?"

"Girl, you know."

"Lady Felicia is gonna get you sooner or later."

"It's gonna have to be later, then," I said.

"Where have you been, Rhapsody?" Kimberley asked me. "We've missed you around here. Why haven't you been to church, and why haven't you returned my phone calls?"

In the past two weeks Kimberley had left me four voice mails, asking me why I had missed the previous Sunday and if I was coming to church the next Sunday. I shrugged my shoulders. "You know how it is, Kim. Life gets in the way. I get busy."

"Yeah, we all do, Rhapsody. What, you're too busy to spend two hours in the house of the Lord, worshipping Him?"

"Of course not, but the longer I stay away, the harder it is to return. But I'm here today."

Kimberley nodded her head. "You sure you ain't here this morning just because the bishop is dedicating the babies? You're baby Chantal's godmother, aren't you?"

For some reason, I felt insulted. "I was gonna be here today whether Chantal was being dedicated or not."

"Okay," Kimberley said, half believing me. "So, you'll be here next Sunday, then?"

"Probably so," I said. *Depends on how much mischief I get into this week.*

"Why don't you get on a committee or join the adult sanctuary choir?"

"You're trying to get me to enroll in something that'll require me to be in church every Sunday, Kim?"

She chuckled. "It couldn't hurt."

I shook my head from side to side. "Nah. I ain't ready for that kind of commitment."

Kimberley looked at me pleadingly. "You used to be, Rhapsody." She cocked her head to the side. "What's going on with you? You ain't been to church in a while, and you don't even return my phone calls."

I shrugged my shoulders. I didn't have an answer for her. "Are Stacy, Trevor, and baby Chantal here?"

Kimberley stared at me. She wanted her question answered. When she realized an answer wasn't coming forth, she said, "Yeah, all the babies and the parents are already seated up front. And I know you just changed the subject, but it's not gonna stop me from calling you."

She turned away from me and entered the sanctuary, and I followed, thinking to myself, Did this chick just check me?

"Hey, baby girl," Lerlean greeted when she saw me enter the sanctuary doors. She was seated on the rear pew, dressed in a black skirt suit and wearing white gloves, like the three other ushers who sat on the pew.

I went to my mother and knelt to hug her. "Hi, Mama."

"I can't believe you showed up."

"Why? I promised to be here, didn't I?"

"Yeah, but I've heard that promise many times before."

"Rhapsody? Chile, is that you?"

I looked at the usher seated next to my mother, the one who had spoken to me. I couldn't stand Sister Glendora Mayfield. She was the most gossipin', finger-pointin', neck-rollin', judgmental woman on this side of heaven.

There she sat, on the ushers' pew, with that same old tired gray wig that she'd been wearing since I was in grade school. She had brushed that thang so much, it was thinning out. I swear, I could've counted the few strands that were still standing. The black suit, combined with the wig and the small wire-frame glasses that sat on the tip of Sister Glendora Mayfield's nose, made her look like a mortician.

"What brings you here?" Sister Glendora Mayfield asked me with a smirk on her face.

What kind of question was that? What brought anyone to church? I came to church to worship, repent, and praise God like everyone else.

I ignored her question. "How are you, Sister Mayfield?" I really didn't care how her evil behind was doing. I was being cordial only 'cause my mother was present. What I really wanted to say to her was, "Don't you have some bodies to embalm?"

"I'm fair to middlin'," she responded.

I didn't have a clue what that meant. "That's good," I said.

"Are you gonna join the church this mornin'?"

I looked at Sister Glendora Mayfield like she had two heads. That old denture-wearin', Sulfur 8–smellin', snuff-chewin', thick-ankled broad knew doggone well that I was already a member of World Deliverance Christian Center and had been since I was a young girl. Heck, many years ago she herself had wrapped me in a towel as soon as Bishop T. A. Clark, Jr., had brought me out of the baptismal pool. So why would she ask such a dumb question?

Lerlean looked at the expression on my face and chuckled. My mother knew that I wanted to cuss at Sister Glendora Mayfield.

"Isn't baby Chantal gettin' christened this morning?" Lerlean asked me. She distracted me from letting my tongue loose in the sanctuary.

I nodded my head. "Yeah. I'm looking for them."

Just then Anastasia tapped my right shoulder. "Rhapsody, wow. You made it."

Why was everybody so freakin' shocked to see me at church? I'd missed only a few Sundays, maybe four, but darn, folks were acting like I'd been gone a year.

"Of course I'm here, Stacy. I told you that." There was hostility in my voice, and she picked up on it.

Anastasia raised her palms in the air, as though she was surrendering something. "Okay, okay. Don't get all crazy on me."

"I mean, seriously, what's the deal with folks this morning?" I couldn't stand church folks sometimes.

"Bishop Thomas Clark is dedicating the babies before morning service," Anastasia said.

"Yes, I know," I responded.

She grabbed my hand. "Well, come on up front. Trevor and I saved you a seat next to us."

I knelt and kissed my mother's cheek again. "Bye, Mama."

"It's good to see you, Rhapsody," Sister Glendora Mayfield said.

I didn't respond to her. I followed Anastasia to the front of the church.

Trevor was seated on the front left pew, with baby Chantal lying in his arms. She was asleep. I saw four other sets of parents and babies seated on the front pew, as well, including Jessica Hampton and her husband, Fabian, with whom I had had a five-month-long affair three years ago. Jessica had never found out about Fabian and me. I was glad to see that their marriage was good and that a newborn baby boy completed their family.

"Look who's here," Anastasia said to Trevor.

Trevor stood and gave me a warm hug and a kiss on the cheek. "We saved you a seat," he said to me.

That was why I liked Trevor. He wasn't messy at all. He didn't seem surprised to see me at church, and he didn't ask stupid questions about why I was there. Trevor greeted me with respect, like he always did.

"Thanks, Trevor," I said.

We sat down on the pew, and Trevor put my sleeping goddaughter on my lap. Chantal was beautiful in her white satin christening gown and bonnet, which I had purchased two weeks ago.

I leaned over to my right and said to Anastasia, "She's so beautiful."

Anastasia straightened out the satin bib around Chantal's neck. "She was so fussy this morning."

"She's probably hot and uncomfortable in all this satin material. Why do you think all the babies be hollerin' and screamin' on Easter Sunday?" I said.

"I'm glad the bishop is doing this before morning service," Anastasia admitted to me. "I brought her a change of clothes. Let's just pray Chantal will sleep through the whole christening."

I saw the program director, who had been sitting on the front pew, approach the podium directly in front of us. She had to be a new member to World Deliverance Christian Center. I didn't recognize her face.

"Praise the Lord, Saints," she greeted.

The congregation gave a hearty "Praise the Lord."

"It is so good to be back in the house of the Lord one more time."

"Amen," the people responded.

The program director looked at all the babies dressed in their cream and satin christening outfits. "Bishop Thomas Clark has changed the order of the service. He's gonna dedicate the babies before morning service." She looked toward the sanctuary doors. "Let us stand and receive our bishops."

The congregation stood, and the organist played soft music. I hoisted Chantal on my left shoulder and watched the elder bishop T. A. Clark, Jr., and his wife, the former first lady, Minister Patricia O. Clark walk down the center aisle. Close behind them was their son, the reigning bishop of World Deliverance Christian Center, Thomas Arthur Clark, whom everyone called Art, wearing a long white robe. He held hands with his wife, our current first lady, Felicia Clark. They were trailed by Ministers Marissa Clark and Charlene Clark, who were the elder bishop's daughters. Behind the Clark sisters was a host of associate ministers.

Elder bishop T. A. Clark, Jr., and former first lady Minister Patricia O. Clark, along with Marissa Clark and Charlene Clark, entered the pulpit and took their seats. Bishop Art and First Lady Felicia stood just beneath the altar, next to the baptismal basin. I saw eight associate ministers sit on a set of pews designated just for them, next to the musicians. Two other associates stood with Bishop Art and Lady Felicia.

The organist kept the soft music going as the program director spoke into the microphone at the podium. "You may be seated," she announced to the folks. After we sat, she looked at all the parents holding their babies on the front row. "Brother Trevor and Sister Anastasia, please bring baby Chantal to the bishop. Also, if there are any godparents here today for baby Chantal, please come at this time."

The three of us stood, and I carried Chantal, who still slept on my shoulder, to the baptismal basin. I attempted to give her to Anastasia, but she shook her head from side to side.

"You can continue to hold her," she told me.

I thought it was a little weird for me to be holding Chantal, but I kept her on my shoulder.

"Saints," Bishop Art said. "The angels in heaven are singing this morning. God is pleased, and the enemy is mad. Why, you may ask? Well, because today we're gonna give souls back to Christ."

"Amen, Bishop," many folks said.

Bishop Art looked at me standing in between Anastasia and Trevor. "It's good to see you standing here, Sister Rhapsody."

I smiled at him. "And it's good to be here, Bishop."

"Trevor and Stacy," Bishop Art said, addressing them. "God has blessed you both with a beauty."

"Amen," I said, along with other folks.

"I suspect, Brother Trevor," Bishop Art said, "that when Chantal is sixteen years old, you'll need to get the shotgun and sit it by the front door."

The people laughed.

"So that when young June bug comes knocking, he'll know what time of day it is."

The people laughed out loud again.

"I already got that covered, Bishop. I'm way ahead of you," Trevor confirmed.

Bishop Art nodded his head at Trevor, then addressed Anastasia. "Sister Stacy, are you standing here willingly to dedicate your daughter, Chantal, to the family of God?"

Anastasia nodded her head. "Yes, Bishop."

"Will you both as parents," he continued, "raise Chantal in the way in which she shall go so that when she is old, she will not depart from it?"

"We will," Trevor and Anastasia responded in unison.

Bishop Art looked at me. "Sister Rhapsody, as god-mother to Chantal, do you vow to step in and raise her and provide for her and care for her should there ever come a time when her parents won't be able to?"

I nodded my head. "Yes, Bishop, I do."

Bishop Art took Chantal from my arms and laid her in the crease of his right arm. He dipped his index finger of his left hand in the baptismal basin, which was filled with holy water. Bishop Art wet Chantal's head with his finger, making the shape of a cross. "Father God, it is today that we dedicate Chantal Justice Baker into your Kingdom. Lead her, guide her, and be the light upon her path of life. In Jesus's name, amen."

"Amen," the congregation responded.

I looked over at Anastasia and saw tears streaming down her face as Bishop Art put Chantal in her arms. The little girl had slept through the entire ceremony.

As the next family made their way to the altar to dedicate their baby, Trevor, Anastasia, Chantal, and I returned to the front pew.

I picked up my purse, then turned to Anastasia. "I gotta go."

The look on her face was one of confusion. "Where?"

I didn't answer her. I held up my index finger and made my way to the rear of the church.

My mother saw me and stood from the rear pew. She met me at the sanctuary doors. "You leaving already?"

"Yeah. I feel a headache coming on." I opened my purse and pulled out a white letter-size envelope. I gave it to her. "This is my tithes and offering. Will you make sure the finance committee gets them?"

"Sure, baby," my mother said to me and took the envelope from my hand. "You go home and get some rest."

I kissed my mother's cheek and exited the church. I dialed Malcolm's cell number as I walked to my car. As soon as he answered, I said, "Meet me at my house."

He exhaled loudly. "Right now, Rhapsody?"

"Yes, Malcolm. Right now," I demanded, then disconnected the call.

As I walked to my car, I knew that I was a pitiful soul. I couldn't even sit through morning service without thinking about sex. But I needed it, and I wanted it, so I was gonna get it.

Three and a half hours later, Malcolm and I lay spent on my bed.

Chapter 18

Monday morning Lucille glanced at the clock on the living room wall, then looked out the window. "Malcolm?" she yelled. "Call Cherise and find out what's taking her so long to get here. She's gonna make me late for my appointment."

Malcolm walked into the living room. "I told her not to come. I'm taking you to therapy this morning."

"Have you forgotten that you're not allowed to drive my car? I don't wanna be sitting in the passenger seat when another one of your tricks decides to throw a tire iron through the window."

"You ain't even gotta worry about that, Lucy. I'm not driving your car."

"Well, then, how are you gonna take me to therapy, Malcolm?"

"In my truck."

Lucille frowned. "What truck?"

"The silver one that's parked outside, in front of the house." Until then Malcolm had hidden his gift in the garage. But since he was taking his mother to therapy that morning, Malcolm figured it was time that she knew about his new truck.

Lucille moved the vertical blinds aside and looked outside. Her eyebrows shot up in the air. "That's *your* truck?" She had noticed the big truck when she glanced out the living room window while waiting for her daughter. Lucille had assumed the big silver truck belonged to one of the neighbors.

"Yes, ma'am."

"When did you get it?"

"A week ago."

"A *week* ago?" she shrieked. "Did Cherise co-sign for you?"

"Nope. A friend bought it for me."

Lucille cocked her head to the side and looked at Malcolm. "What friend?"

"Her name is Rhapsody."

She frowned. *"What?"*

Malcolm sighed. He didn't feel like being interrogated. "Ma, let's just go, okay?"

"Wait a darn minute, Malcolm. Who is this Rhapsody, why did she buy you a truck, and why haven't I met her?"

"She's a lady I met last week, and you'll meet her soon enough."

Lucille tried to put two and two together. "You said you got the truck last week. Are you tellin' me that you met a woman and she bought you that big truck all in the same week?"

"Yes. Now can we please go?"

"No. We ain't going nowhere until I figure this out. Where did you meet this woman?"

Malcolm plopped down on the sofa and exhaled loudly. "Ma, can we not do this now?"

"Where did you meet her, Malcolm?"

"I met her at the restaurant last Monday."

"Uh-huh. How old is she?" Lucille asked.

"Why do you need to know that?"

Lucille's eyebrows rose. "You better answer me, boy."

"Rhapsody is thirty-four, but what difference does that make? Age ain't nothin' but a number."

Lucille put her left hand on her heart. "Oh, my God. Malcolm, you're going with a thirty-four-year-old woman?"

Malcolm leaned forward and placed his elbows on his knees. "Ma, would you calm down? It ain't no big deal, and we're not going together."

"Then what are you doing, Malcolm? If y'all ain't going together, then what . . . ?" Lucille stopped her sentence, because she had figured it out. "Oh, God. Oh, my Lord Jesus. Please help me, Lord."

Malcolm saw the hysterical state his mother was in. "Ma, you're gonna give yourself a stroke. Rhapsody and I are just friends, okay? Now, let's go."

"Is she the girl that put the scratches on your back last week?"

Malcolm stood from the sofa. "I'm not talkin' to you about this. Rhapsody ain't no big deal, and the truck ain't no big deal." With that said, Malcolm helped his mother out the front door and down the ramp on the porch and rolled her to the truck.

With Lucille buckled safely in the passenger seat, Malcolm positioned himself behind the steering wheel.

"Hello, Malcolm. Welcome to paradise."

Lucille placed her hand on her heart again and looked over at her son. "Are you out in these streets, hoeing, Malcolm?"

Malcolm laughed out loud, started the engine, and pulled away from the curb.

Lucille placed the back of her hand across her forehead and said, "Lord, please be a blood pressure pill right now."

Chapter 19

I got to work early and decided to call my brother Walter at his medical office. I knew that I couldn't avoid him and Daniel forever. I told the receptionist that I was his sister and was returning his call.

She placed me on hold. I heard two short beeps and then, "It's about time you called me back." As usual, Walter had an attitude.

"You better be glad I called at all. What do you and Danny want?"

"Well, since you refused to talk to us, we thought it would be less of a hassle to just send Mama and Daddy on a cruise to the Caribbean instead of planning a party."

"I think that's a wonderful idea," I said.

"I talked with a travel agent and was able to secure a nice package to three islands. It's a seven-day cruise, and it costs twenty-seven hundred dollars, with Mom and Dad's airfare included. We'll split the cost three ways. You, Danny, and I have to pay nine hundred dollars each by next Friday."

I frowned. "Walter, that gives me less than two weeks. I won't have nine hundred dollars by then." Because of Malcolm's truck note, I had gone from having extra money to living paycheck to paycheck.

"Rhapsody, me and Danny have been trying to hook up with you for a month. You should have gotten with us when we were callin' you."

My neck almost did a 360-degree turn on my shoulders when Walter tried to pull rank on me. I didn't take that crap when we were kids, and I wasn't gonna stand for it now. "I'ma check you right quick, Walter. First of all, neither you nor Danny earn my money. Therefore, y'all sho ain't entitled to tell me how to spend it. If I say I won't have the money by next Friday, then I won't have it."

"Then what do you *suggest* we do, Rhapsody?"

Walter put special emphasis on the word *suggest*, trying to intimidate me, but I wasn't moved. I came right back at him. "If you and Danny want to send Mama and Daddy on a cruise, then I *suggest* y'all pay for it." I disconnected the call. I was done talkin'.

Ten minutes hadn't passed before Daniel was callin' my cell phone.

"I just got off the phone with Walter, and he's highly upset with you," Daniel said to me.

I really wished he could've seen me shrugging my shoulders. "Danny, I don't give a flyin' fig about you, Walter, the pope, Barack Obama, or anybody else being upset with me."

"I just don't think it's fair that we should have to pay the whole cost of this cruise. They're your parents too, you know."

"Look, Danny, you own a construction company, and Walter is a doctor. Both of you got more money than either of you know what to do with. Y'all can pay for the cruise without denting your pockets. I'm the one who's strugglin'. I live from paycheck to paycheck." The monthly payments on Malcolm's truck were gonna kill me.

"That's because you spend all your money on massages, manicures, pedicures, and other crap that ain't important. Learn how to keep your siddity behind out of the malls."

He pissed me off. "Do you balance my checkbook, butthole?"

"Nah, but maybe I need to," he yelled back at me.

I disconnected the call, 'cause I was done talking to Daniel. Who in the heck was he to tell me how to spend *my* money? If I wanted to pay somebody to rub on me, that was *my* business. To heck with Danny and his brother too. My body shook. "Douche bags, elephant poop sniffers!" I screamed. That was why I absolutely hated talking to my brothers. They always caused an episode to come upon me.

I was so hot and bothered by Daniel's call that I had to go to the bathroom and splash cold water on my face to get myself together. When I got back to my desk, Willie Boston was waiting for me.

"Good morning, Rhapsody. I bought you a dozen of those Krispy Kreme doughnuts everybody's crazy about and a cup of coffee. It's light and sweet, just like you like it."

"Thanks, Willie, but you still ain't gettin' in my panties, okay?"

"Now, why you gotta be like that? I bought you breakfast, and this is how you treat me?"

Willie was right. I shouldn't take out my frustrations from dealing with my brothers on everybody else. "I'm sorry, Willie." I sat at my desk and offered him a doughnut, but he declined. I dunked a glazed doughnut in my coffee, bit into it, and moaned at the good taste.

"Dang, girl. Are they that good?"

"Yep, especially when you dunk them in coffee," I said.

Willie reached in the box and pulled out a glazed doughnut. "I wanna dunk mine too, but not in coffee."

"You want some milk?"

"Uh-uh. I wanna dunk my doughnut in you."

I was swallowing when Willie said that, and it caused me to choke. It took me a minute to clear my airway before I could speak. "Willie, get out of my office before I call your supervisor and tell her that you're away from your work area."

"Come on, Rhapsody," he pleaded. "Just let me dip it one time, and I promise I'll leave you alone."

"Get your broke behind out of here, Willie. I ain't playin'."

"I may be a lot of things, but broke ain't one of them. Name your price."

That was the second time Willie had propositioned me. I wondered if he was serious. "You can't afford me, Willie," I said jokingly.

He took a step closer to me and spoke sternly. "I said, 'Name your price.'"

Since he stepped to me, I stepped to him and looked deep into his eyes. "Nine hundred dollars."

Willie didn't blink or flinch. He reached in his pocket and pulled out a wad of bills that was bigger than my entire fist. He peeled away nine one-hundred-dollar bills and laid them on my desk. "Where's your boss?"

I looked at the money and swallowed hard. "He's on vacation this week."

Willie picked up his glazed doughnut from the desk and glared at me like a hungry wolf.

Fifteen minutes later, Walter and Daniel were glad to know that I had my share to pay for our parents' anniversary cruise.

Mr. Duncan had taken a vacation that week, and I was glad. My boss and I shared a small office that we'd outgrown over the eleven years that we'd worked together. He was due back in a week, right after the July Fourth holiday, which was next Monday. Mr. Duncan was treating his wife and his two young children to a week in Negril, Jamaica. The only thing he had talked about for the past two weeks was how he couldn't wait to lie on the beach and get a tan.

Mr. Duncan was Caucasian and very pale. I'd told him that if he came back looking like me, I'd talk about him.

It was too bad that he'd be gone only for a week, because I could've gotten used to being by myself. Sometimes when there wasn't anything tragic going on with the trains or buses in the city of Chicago, Mr. Duncan and I would spend the entire eight hours of the day staring at one another and arguing over stupid stuff.

Driving home from work Monday evening, I felt like a crackhead on the second day of detox. I was feigning for Malcolm big-time. The hurtin' he had put on me after church the day before had worn off. I called him on my cell phone.

"Hi, Malcolm," I greeted excitedly.

"Hey, I was just about to call you," he said. He sounded just as excited as I was.

I blushed. "Oh, really?" I responded seductively.

"Yep. I got some good news." Malcolm was in a very good mood.

I smiled. "I'm listenin'."

"My sister, Cherise, and her husband are driving my mother down to Memphis for the holiday to visit my uncle. And you know what that means, right?"

I shook my head from side to side. But I was still smiling. "Tell me."

"I'll be able to spend the entire week and all the holiday weekend with you."

My smile got even wider. "Ooh, Malcolm, that *is* good news. When do they leave?"

"They're hitting Interstate Fifty-Seven at around eight tonight."

"And you'll come after that?"

"Yeah. I need to be here and help get my mother packed and settled into my brother-in-law's van. I should be at your place at around nine. And I want you to be ready for me, okay? I ain't showin' you no mercy tonight."

I loved the way he teased me. "I'm always ready."

I unlocked my front door and entered my living room on cloud nine, singing, "You want me just as much as I want you. Let's stop fooling around. Take me, baby. Kiss me all over." That song was the jam back in the day. I bet Prince caused a whole lot of babies to be conceived off of that melody.

In my bedroom I pressed the PLAY button on my answering machine.

"Hey, girl. Trevor, Chantal, and I are having a Fourth of July barbecue next Monday. We want you to come. Call me when you get in." *Beep.*

"This call is for Rhapsody Blue. This is Dr. Scimeca's office calling again. Please call to schedule your annual exam." *Beep.*

I erased both messages, and then I called Dr. Scimeca's office and made an appointment for eight o'clock next Tuesday morning, the day after the holiday. With that out of the way, I undressed and hung my uniform in my closet, put on a silk pajama set, then sat down on my bed and called Anastasia.

"Hey, did you get my message?" she asked.

"Yes, I did, and I'll accept the invitation, but only if I can bring a date."

"A date?"

"Yes, a date, as in an escort, a beau, someone to lick barbecue sauce off of."

"And who might that be?"

"Who do you think?"

"Malcolm?"

"Bingo. He and I made up," I said excitedly. I folded my legs in a pretzel position and leaned back against my headboard.

"How did you pull that off?"

"With my charm and a little 'I'm sorry' token."

"Rhapsody, what did you buy him, and how much did it cost?"

"You'll find out next week. What time should we be there?"

"One o'clock. I know you bought him an expensive watch, and I'ma tell you somethin' Rhapsody. Buying a twenty-one-year-old man jewelry won't make him commit to you."

It was time for me to end the conversation. "Good-bye, Stacy. Malcolm and I will see you on Monday. Should we bring anything?"

"No, and why are you rushing me off of the telephone?"

"Because I don't wanna hear you preach today, okay? I had enough of that at Chantal's dedication yesterday. Besides, Malcolm is on his way, and I need to get ready for him."

"You ain't even stick around to hear Bishop Art preach. So what you mean, you heard enough of that yesterday? And speaking of yesterday, why did you rush out of the church like that?"

"I didn't feel like being bothered with church folks. Lady Felicia cornered me and pulled my coattail. She wanted me to sit next to her so she could tap my leg every time the bishop said something she thought pertained to me. And Sister Glendora Mayfield almost made me cuss her behind out right there in the sanctuary. I just can't do church folks, Stacy. I can't."

"So what does that mean?" she asked.

Anastasia couldn't see me shrug my shoulders. "I don't know. Maybe it's time for me to find another church home. A place where nobody knows me."

"Humph. You mean a place where nobody knows you so you can keep doing the crap you're doing and no one can call you out on it."

I didn't respond. She was absolutely correct. I lived my life the way I wanted to live it, and what I did was between me and my God. I didn't like when folks judged me, looked at me sideways, or tried to get in my business. God and I had an understanding. Nobody knew me better than Him. He knew I was a horny chick. He'd made me that way. So Anastasia, Sister Glendora Mayfield, Lady Felicia, and anybody else who had a problem with what I did really needed to stay inside their own glass houses.

"So, what are you and Malcolm doing tonight?"

"We're gonna do what we always do."

Anastasia sighed. "Girl, bye." She hung up on me.

Chapter 20

Malcolm arrived with Chinese takeout in one hand and a huge overstuffed duffel bag in the other. In the kitchen I sat on his lap and fed him shrimp fried rice with chopsticks. Instead of using a napkin to wipe the corners of his mouth, I used my tongue.

"Aren't you going to eat?" he asked me.

"Uh-uh. It's all about you, boo," I said. I was in seventh heaven. I felt like June Cleaver. I wanted to do everything I could to keep my man happy.

When Malcolm's belly was full, I stood and guided him to the bathroom, where a hot bubble bath with rose petals was waiting in my Jacuzzi tub. Along the ledge of the tub, I had lit spice-scented candles.

"All of this is for you," I said to him. "I want you to take off your clothes, get in the tub, and relax."

I didn't have to tell him twice. Malcolm was naked and was leaning back in the tub in less than two minutes. He closed his eyes and exhaled loudly when the jets started beating his muscles. I knelt next to the tub, reached across him, grabbed the soap sponge, and lathered it with liquid soap. I caressed his body with the sponge, and Malcolm lay there, enjoying his bath. As I glided the sponge over his hairy chest, Malcolm looked at me.

"I ain't never had a chick bathe me before."

I smiled at him. "Do you like it?"

Malcolm took the sponge from my hand, then guided my arm to his pelvic area beneath the water. He moaned. "Can't you tell?"

I stood and dropped my red satin robe to the floor, then stepped between Malcolm's legs and sat with my back against his chest. It was my turn to moan and exhale as he caressed my body with the sponge.

"I'm loving the fact that we'll live together for a whole week, Malcolm."

Without saying a word, Malcolm reached in front of me and drained the tub. He stood and grabbed my hand to stand me up, and we both stepped out of the tub. Malcolm dried my body, then lowered the toilet lid and laid the towel over it and sat me down. He grabbed my bottle of baby oil from the sink and massaged a handful on every inch of me. After I watched him dry his own body, he led me to my bedroom. He switched on my boom box, and we heard Rick James and Teena Marie singing the heck out of "Fire and Desire."

Malcolm instructed me to lie on my stomach. Moments later he straddled me and massaged my back and shoulders while Rick and Teena serenaded me.

"You turned on, you turned on, you turned on my fire, baby."

I felt hypnotized. Almost like my equilibrium was off. Malcolm worked his magic on me that night. "Fire and Desire" was the appropriate song for the mood I was in. An hour of total bliss was very much needed and very much appreciated.

When I woke up on Tuesday morning, Malcolm was standing at my dresser, looking in the mirror and tying his tie. I sat up on the bed, with my hair strewn all over my head.

In the mirror, he looked at me and said, "Now, you know I gotta be at work in thirty minutes. Why you gotta wake up lookin' like that?"

"Like what?" I asked.

"All sexy and stuff."

I ran my hands through my tousled hair. "Malcolm, please. You know I look a hot mess."

He turned and walked toward me while untying his necktie and unbuttoning his shirt. "I got about five minutes to spare. Lay back down."

After the quickie, something dawned on me.

"I thought Tuesdays were your regularly scheduled days off." I remembered going to Burger World last Tuesday morning, after our first night together. The cashier had told me it was Malcolm's day off.

"No one gets the same schedule every week. My days off rotate."

"Oh," was all I said before sighing. "Well, I guess I better get on up and get ready for work myself."

Malcolm kissed my lips lightly. "I'll see you after work."

I couldn't wait to come back home and continue to play house.

Chapter 21

At noontime Malcolm was summoned to his superior's office. He knocked on the slightly opened door before poking his head inside. "You wanna see me, Mr. Wright?"

"Yes, Malcolm. Come on in and have a seat."

Seated across from Mr. Wright was a Caucasian male who looked to be the same age as Malcolm. Malcolm took the seat next to him.

"Malcolm, this is Jesse Aikens. This is his first day on the job. I want you to show him the ropes and make him feel comfortable. Jesse is a team player. I'm sure he'll fit right in."

Malcolm shook the young man's hand. "Welcome aboard. It's nice to meet you."

"You too," Jesse responded.

"Okay, first I'll introduce you to everyone, and then we'll get you started on French fries," Malcolm said.

Immediately, Jesse looked across the desk at Mr. Wright, who swallowed hard before speaking to Malcolm.

"Uh, Malcolm, I want you to take Jesse under your wing and show him your skills as restaurant manager."

Without knowing it, Malcolm frowned. *"What?"*

Jesse felt that this was his cue to leave. "Uh, I'm gonna visit the bathroom. Excuse me."

"What the heck is going on?" Malcolm asked when Jesse shut the door behind him.

Mr. Wright leaned back in his chair and exhaled. "Malcolm, his last name is Aikens. Can't you put two and two together?"

Malcolm thought about the question and realized Jesse was related to the chief executive officer of Burger World, whose name was Dominick Aikens. "Who is he? A son or a nephew?"

"A grandson."

"But this is *my* store, Mr. Wright."

"I know that Malcolm, but it's out of my hands. You've got to train him."

Malcolm sat back in his chair and crossed his legs. "Man, this is some bull." He looked at his boss. "I gotta train somebody to become my boss?"

"You're right, Malcolm," Mr. Wright said. "It *is* some bull."

Chapter 22

At 2:45 p.m. I got a call over my walkie-talkie radio from the control center. The operator stated that in the Loop area downtown, on State Street, a man had been hit as he stepped in front of an oncoming bus.

"Is he dead?" I asked the operator.

"No, but he's banged up pretty ugly."

That was an oxymoron if I had ever heard one. How could something be pretty and ugly at the same time?

I got pissed 'cause it was the beginning of rush hour and just about time for me to go home to my pretend husband. Now I had to go and redirect traffic because some hopeless bastard had thought he had bumpers on his butt. I hoped the bus driver had torn the man's leg completely off. It would serve him right for walking in front of a big rig that was going at least twenty miles an hour. I couldn't stand a dumb fool.

By 6:00 p.m. I was frustrated as heck. I was still downtown, rerouting passengers who were fit to be tied at having to take an alternate route home. To be honest with you, I understood their anger. Just like me, the passengers would get home two hours later than usual, all because of one blind fool. But one particular woman got on my nerves so bad. She complained and complained and complained. I was gonna slap her for real. Everybody was mad and inconvenienced, but she behaved as though she had been singled out to have a bad evening.

"This just doesn't make any sense. The CTA should be prepared for something of this nature," I heard her say.

I didn't say anything that time, because my boss, Mr. Duncan, had instructed me to always be cordial and considerate to the passengers, as they paid our salaries. But the fat broad kept going on and on like a Duracell battery. She, along with about twenty-five other passengers, was waiting for the next bus to take her over to Michigan Avenue and head south.

"What's taking this bus so long to get here?" She kept on. "I knew I should've driven today. This is what I get for foolin' with the CTA, anyway. Now my whole evening is screwed up."

That broke the camel's back. That was when I lost it. She had drilled the last nail into her coffin. I turned to her and laid my job and my salvation on the line. "Trick, what the heck is you complaining about? You think you're the only one standing on this bus stop? All of us out here is having a jacked-up evening." I knew I was out of line, and I knew God was gonna get me, but at that time I didn't care.

The passengers standing close to me all moved inches away. They probably thought that a fight was about to break out.

The complaining broad looked at me. Her neck danced as she spoke. "I'm running late for bingo. I'm supposed to call out the numbers."

She was trippin' because of bingo? *Really?* "Well, can't somebody else holler out *B* seven, *N* twenty-two, or *G* forty-five?" I asked her.

She didn't respond.

Humph. If anybody had a right to be mad, it was me. I was the one missing out on something. I had a young tenderoni with plenty of energy at home, waiting on me.

***

I arrived home and saw Malcolm's Navigator parked in my driveway, and I started singing a song by Chanté Moore, substituting my name for hers. "Rhapsody's got a man at home."

I found Malcolm sitting on the living room sofa, looking like the evening I had had. I could tell that he was miserable.

"Hey, boo. How was your day?" I asked.

He exhaled. "You don't wanna know."

I kicked off my work boots, sat next to him, and rubbed his bald head. "It can't be any worse than the afternoon I just endured."

Malcolm kissed my lips softly. "You wanna bet?"

"You wanna talk about it?"

He leaned back on the sofa and patted my hand. "Tell me about your day first. Why were you late getting home?"

For years I had been waiting for a man to ask me that. To ignore his own problems and focus on me. To ask how my day was. I thought it was a shame that not one of all the thirty- and forty-year-olds I'd dealt with had cared more than twenty-one-year-old Malcolm. I laid my head on his shoulder and explained my afternoon step-by-step to him.

"Rhapsody, why didn't you just redirect the passengers to the number six bus to take them over to Jackson? That way they could've caught the number twelve and headed south. It would've saved you and everyone else an hour."

Malcolm had just turned what was supposed to be a pleasant conversation into an unpleasant one. I'd been successfully rerouting passengers for three years without a complaint from anyone.

"Don't tell me how to do my job, Malcolm. Do I run over to Burger World and tell you when to flip the hamburgers?"

"I don't flip hamburgers. I'm a manager, I think."

I cocked my head to the side and look at him curiously. "What do you mean, 'you think'?"

"A young white dude was hired today. He's the grandson of the owner, and I've got to train him to be a manager. There's only one manager per restaurant on the day shift."

"Maybe you're training him to work at another location," I said.

"Nah. I didn't get that impression from Mr. Wright."

"You think your job is in jeopardy?"

Malcolm nodded his head slowly. "I'll probably be demoted to cashier."

I rubbed his arm. "I'm sorry, boo. I wish there was something I could do."

Malcolm looked at me. "Can you hook me up with the CTA?"

"What do you wanna do?" I asked.

He shrugged his shoulders. "I don't know. Heck, anything at this point."

"I'll give my girl Audelia a call. She works in personnel, and she owes me a favor."

I reached for my purse, which I had sat on the cocktail table. I pulled my cell phone out of it and searched for Audelia's name in my contact list. I hadn't spoken with Audelia in over three months. She and I had been hired together as car servicers and had cleaned the interiors of rail cars on the midnight shift during our first four years with the CTA. We'd been assigned to work on the brown line, in the garage located at Kimball Avenue and Lawrence Avenue. That was where I had met Miguel, a Mexican and also a car servicer. Miguel was a mad cutie, but he was a little too rough for me. He'd told me that while growing up, he had seen how his father dominated his mother, and that was how he treated his women.

Audelia had thought that Miguel was cute, so I had introduced them, and they'd been together ever since. They had produced two children, who were gorgeous. Hispanics made beautiful babies. I was Audelia's maid of honor at their wedding, and she'd told me that she would always be indebted to me for introducing her to Miguel. I hoped she hadn't forgotten what she'd said.

"Hey, Rhapsody," she answered.

"Hey, girl," I greeted. "Just calling to see how you're doin'. It's been a while since we talked."

"Yeah, it has. What's going on?"

I exhaled. "Girl, it's the same old, same old. Strugglin' to pay these bills."

"I know that's right."

"How's Miguel?" I asked.

"He's fine. He just left to go to work."

"Is he still on the brown line?"

"Girl, yeah. Miguel ain't going nowhere. I told him that I could hook him up with something better, but he claims he likes cleaning trains. As long as he continues to buy Pampers and pay this mortgage, I don't care where he works."

I laughed. "I heard that, girl. How are the kids? How old are they?"

"Adrina is three going on fifty-three, and I have to put my foot in her li'l behind almost every night. Miguel's mother has her too spoiled. When she's at her Nana's house, Adrina is allowed to do and say anything she wants. My mother-in-law lets the kids eat candy for breakfast, and when they get home, Adrina feels that just because she's the queen of Nana's house, she's queen of Mommy's house also. And every evening I have to remind her flipped-mouth behind that this isn't Nana's house. It's Mommy's house."

I laughed at Audelia. "Ooh, girl, sounds like you got your hands full."

"I'm tellin' you, Rhapsody, that li'l girl is something else. Last week Adrina asked for a Popsicle. I told her she couldn't have one, because lookin' at her ruby-red lips, I could tell that she'd had enough sugar. The li'l heifer screamed at me, 'I want a Popsicle!'"

My mouth dropped wide open. "Oh, my God. What did you do, Audelia?"

"I grabbed her hand and tried to twist it off of her wrist."

I chuckled. "Ooh, wee. These kids nowadays are gettin' out of hand."

"That's right, they are. Now, Juan is six years old, and he's only gotten out of pocket one time. He went through a phase about eight months ago when he all of a sudden started shuttin' his bedroom door whenever he's in there. Whenever I'd walk past his bedroom and see the door closed, I would open it. Then he got into the habit of locking it from the inside, talkin' about he needed his privacy."

"*Privacy?*" I shrieked. "At six years old?"

"Yes, girl, *privacy.* He's too young to be masturbating—at least I *think* he is—and there's no television or telephone in his bedroom, so what kind of privacy does he need at six years old? Miguel told me to leave him alone and allow him to express himself, but screw that crap. Ain't no six-year-old living in *my* house is gonna be closing and locking doors. For all we know, his li'l behind could be building a doggone bomb in there."

I chuckled. "You're sho right about that, Audelia. How did you get him to leave the door open?"

"I took the door off of its hinges, that's how. At six years old, I gotta see every move and hear every peep Juan makes. I refuse to be on the ten o'clock news, saying that I didn't know my son was capable of doing something crazy."

I laughed out loud. "That's that old-school upbringing, Audelia. More mothers should be like you."

"I just can't tolerate silly stuff, Rhapsody. The government already took prayer out of the schools, and now I hear they wanna remove 'In God We Trust' off of the dollar bills. People don't realize that without prayer and God, we may as well lie down and die, 'cause we're screwed, anyway. And personally, I think Jesus was a perfect boy who grew into a perfect man without sin because Mary beat his behind."

I laughed at Audelia and hollered, "Girl, you're crazy."

"Think about it, Rhapsody. The Bible describes Jesus's hair as being like sheep's wool, which means some blackness ran through His veins. Now, you know li'l nappy-headed boys must get their butts beat daily to keep them on the right track. The Bible also says, '*Train up a child in the way he should go, and when he is old, he will not depart from it.*' Jesus was absolutely perfect, without a flaw. You can't tell me that Mary didn't set that example. When I get to heaven, I'm gonna ask Jesus if his mom whupped his butt, and you know what His answer will be?"

"What?" I asked.

"I bet He'll say, 'Heck, yeah.'"

I laughed out loud again. "Audelia, that's too funny. You ain't changed a bit, girl. Listen, I need a favor," I said.

"Okay."

"My friend needs a job. Can you hook him up?"

"What's his name, and how old is he?"

"His name is Malcolm Washington, and he's twenty-one."

"Humph. A friend, huh? What are you doing with a twenty-one-year-old male friend, Rhapsody?"

"I'm screwing him," I answered boldly. Malcolm was still sitting on the sofa next to me. When he heard me say that, he looked at me with raised eyebrows.

Audelia hollered and then said, "Well, all righty then. He must be good."

"Better than good," I assured her.

"Okay, Demi Moore," she said to me. "Go on with your bad self. Is he working now?"

"Yeah. He runs the Burger World joint in Maywood, but it doesn't pay much. He needs something that pays at least eighteen bucks an hour."

"You think he'll be interested in driving the trains?"

"Will he make at least eighteen bucks an hour?"

"Oh yeah. Much more than that," Audelia said.

"Then he's interested."

"Okay. Headquarters will be closed on Monday for the Fourth of July holiday. Have Malcolm come see me first thing Tuesday morning."

"I sure will. Thanks, Audelia. I really appreciate this."

"You're welcome. You know there will be a background check done on Malcolm. He's gotta be clean, because he'll definitely have to drop some urine in a plastic cup. Drug tests are mandatory."

"Got it," I said to Audelia, and we said our good-byes. I disconnected the call, looked at Malcolm, then smiled. "You're in."

"For real? Just like that?"

"Just like that," I said. "Of course, you'll have to pass a drug test first."

"I gotta have a needle stuck in my arm?"

I shook my head from side to side. "No, but you'll have to pee in a cup, and that'll show if there's any drugs in your system." I lowered my head and glared at Malcolm. "You're clean, right?"

He nodded his head once. "I should be."

I frowned. "Should be? What does that mean, Malcolm?"

"I haven't smoked a joint in a while. I should be good."

"Okay," was all I said.

"When will that happen?"

"Next Tuesday morning at the CTA headquarters down-town, on Lake Street. Go to the tenth floor and ask for Audelia Alvarez-Costa. Make sure not to mention my name to no one. When you get to the receptionist, you don't need to say, 'Rhapsody Blue sent me.' Just say that you have an appointment with Audelia. Got it?"

He nodded his head again. "Yep. So, what job am I going for?"

I shrugged my shoulders. "I don't know. It depends on what the CTA is hiring for. Later you and I can look at their Web site and see what jobs are posted. If you see something you like, you can tell Audelia on Tuesday morning."

"Why did you tell her that we're screwing?"

I shrugged my shoulders again. "When she asked why I had a twenty-one-year-old friend, I didn't see a reason to lie to her."

Malcolm was literally under me when his cell phone rang after 10:30 p.m. I was in a deep sleep, with half my body on the bed and the other half on top of Malcolm. He felt how heavy I was when he had to push my torso aside to reach for his cell phone on the nightstand.

"This is Malcolm," he answered sleepily.

"Where you at, fool?" Ivan asked.

"I'm at Rhapsody's house."

"You sound like you were asleep."

"I was," Malcolm said.

"But the night is young. I'm at the Fifty-Yard Line. Why don't you come through?"

"Nah, man. I can't get up."

"Come on, fool. What do you mean, you can't get up? You ain't *that* tired."

Malcolm raised his head from the pillow and glanced down at my thigh draped across his waist. He tried to move it, but to no avail. "Ivan, believe me when I tell you that I really can't get up. I'm on lockdown."

Chapter 23

The following Saturday morning my mother called my house before the sun was up.

"Are you still in the bed?" she asked me.

I rolled off of Malcolm to lie on my back. "Ma, it's still dark outside," I moaned sleepily.

"It's Saturday, Rhapsody."

"I know that, Ma," I said sleepily.

"The new Filene's Basement store opens in Schaumburg today. They're having a grand opening sale from seven to noon."

"Thanks for telling me, Ma, but I don't need anything from Filene's Basement. If I need anything, I'll come to *your* basement."

Even though I was talking as low as I possibly could, Malcolm stirred and got up to go to the bathroom.

"Rhapsody, get up and get dressed. And then come and pick me up," Lerlean demanded.

"Come and pick you up for what, Ma?"

"To take me to the mall. Ain't you listening to what I'm sayin'?"

I heard the toilet flush, followed by water running in the bathroom sink. Malcolm came back to bed and snuggled up next to me. "Ma, I'm tired."

"From what?" she asked, like I didn't have a life.

From screwing all night long. "Just tired."

"Well, I was tired, too, thirty-four years ago, when I had to push your big head out, but I did what I had to do to bring you into this world. I had stitches all the way from my vajayjay to my butthole, but I guess you don't appreciate that."

I rolled my eyes.

"That's all right," she continued. "You know I don't wanna let your father take me to the mall. He'll bug the mess out of me, saying he's ready to go ten minutes after we get there. You know what? Don't even worry about it. I'll just call a taxicab."

I exhaled as loudly as I could into her ear. I hated that my mother had never learned to drive. She absolutely refused to get behind the wheel of a car. She once told me that at the age of sixteen she had witnessed a head-on collision. From that moment on, my mother had vowed never to operate a vehicle.

I sighed loudly. "I'm on my way, Ma."

I disconnected the call and threw the telephone down on the bed. Malcolm moved close to me and began nuzzling my neck and fondling my breasts. "What's wrong?"

I didn't answer him. I just moaned at the pleasure he was giving me, but I didn't have time to let him satisfy me, because I had to take Lerlean shopping. I pried Malcolm's fingers away and went to start the water in the shower. I swear, my mother could dry up a wet dream.

Don't get it twisted. I loved my mother with all that was within me. But she was the type of woman who loved to window-shop without a dime in her purse. I was the exact opposite: I didn't enter a mall unless I had some serious money. Window-shopping pissed me off because I saw so much stuff that I wanted but couldn't afford. Lerlean, on the other hand, would be at the mall when the security guard opened the doors, and then she'd close it down and walk out with only a pair of ten-dollar panty hose. That was what she called mother and daughter quality time. But I'd rather be at home, in my bed, lying on my back, with my thighs wrapped around Malcolm's waist.

It was hard for me to leave him that morning. I could sense within myself that I was becoming addicted to Malcolm. I couldn't say for sure if I was in love with him, but I did know for a fact that I was very much into him. If I were honest with myself, I'd realize that I was addicted the first time we did the nasty. I wondered what Malcolm's response would be if I asked him to marry me. I was so sprung that I was willing to let him quit his job and stay home as long as he was naked when I walked in the front door every evening. Malcolm wouldn't have to cook, clean, do laundry, or pay bills. The only chore he would have was to lay pipe. Humph, Malcolm didn't know how good he could have it.

"What do you think of this blouse, Rhapsody?" Lerlean asked. She held up a taupe-colored blouse that tied on the side for a sarong look.

"It's okay, but I prefer the lilac one," I said.

"I'm gonna try them both on." She took both blouses and went to search for the fitting room.

See, that was what I was talking about. The blouses were exactly alike, just two different colors. There was no need to try on both. Heck, if one was too big or too small, then so was the other.

I followed my mother and found a seat right outside the fitting room. I crossed my right leg over my left knee and got comfortable, 'cause I knew I'd be at Filene's Basement for a long while. Lerlean was trying on her first two items, and it was 7:15 a.m. And that meant I had at least another five hours of her modeling everything in the store to look forward to.

As I looked around Filene's Basement, I noticed that my mother and I were the only black women shopping there. A woman walked into the fitting room, carrying the same blouse Lerlean was trying on, but hers was in a different color than the two Lerlean had. In the woman's hand was a Carson Pirie Scott & Co. bag, a Lord & Taylor bag, a DSW bag, and a Neiman Marcus bag. I checked my watch. Unless those stores opened earlier than 7:00 a.m., the woman was a helluva shopper. If Daniel could see the woman and all her bags, he wouldn't sweat *me* so much about spending money.

Lerlean came out of the fitting room and stood in front of me, wearing the lilac blouse.

"Well, what do you think?" She turned all the way around to show me every angle.

"It's cute, Ma. I like that color on you."

"Really?"

"Uh-huh. That light shade of purple makes your skin glow."

"This blouse comes in turquoise too," she said.

"Yeah, I just saw a lady go into the fitting room with a turquoise-colored blouse. I bet those blouses would look cute with a pair of white Capri pants," I said.

"I bet they would too. It would be nice to have an outfit like this to take on the cruise you and your brothers are sending me and your father on."

And let the begging begin. Here we go. As usual, Lerlean tried on clothes and fell in love with them without a dime in her pocket. Normally, it would be up to me to keep her from pouting for the next five hours. But I had a surprise for my mother that day. Because of Malcolm's new ride, I didn't have an extra dime in my pocket. So I sat there and didn't say a word while she tried on nine more different outfits. And she modeled every one of them for me.

"Ooh, I can wear this to the captain's dinner," she said when she modeled a floor-length tropical sundress.

"Ooh, this would look pretty when we go into the village to shop," she said when she modeled a yellow halter top paired with blue jean Capri pants. "Ooh, I can lounge around the pool in this number," she said when she modeled a black-and-gold swimsuit. "Ooh, your father would rape me if he saw me in this negligee," I heard her yell out at me from the fitting room. "But, oh, well, I guess I can't take anything new on my cruise. It sure would be nice to have at least one pretty outfit," I also heard her say from the fitting room.

Next thing I knew, with my checkbook in my hand, I was standing in line with Lerlean and all nine outfits that she had tried on. She was my mama. What was I supposed to do? I planned to make a trip to my credit union the next morning to make a withdrawal from my savings account. I would deposit the money in my checking account to cover the check I was writing today. Or I could summon Willie Boston up to my office for another dip.

Saturday afternoon my father was sitting on the front porch when I parked my car next to the curb. I got out of the car and retrieved my mother's bags from the trunk. Lerlean got out of the passenger seat. Then she and I walked toward the house that my parents had owned since before I was born.

"Hey, Daddy," I greeted when my mother and I reached the porch steps.

"I see you and your mama been out spending my retirement money again."

"What money you got?" Lerlean asked him.

"I got all kinds of money," he stated firmly.

"Well, I ain't seen none of it. You must be givin' it to your hoes."

My mouth dropped open. "Ma, I can't believe you said that."

"You don't hear half the stuff she be sayin' to me," my father said. "Her mouth is so bad, she cusses in her sleep."

I had to laugh at that, because I knew he wasn't fabricating anything. My mother had a mouth on her, and she would let her tongue loose at any given moment. And I had to admit that I was definitely Lerlean's daughter. I had it honest. I was the heir to her bitter tongue.

I chuckled. "For real, Daddy? What do she say in her sleep?"

"She be sayin', 'Hell, damn, shit.'"

Lerlean got angry. She placed all her weight on her right leg; then she put her right hand on her right hip. My mother looked directly into my eyes and said, "Nah, that ain't what I say. *I'll* tell you what I be sayin' in my sleep, Rhapsody. I say, 'I wish this old bastard would get off his rusty butt and find a freakin' job. I'm sick of him hangin' around this damn house, buggin' the freak out of me. And I need a damn dishwasher, 'cause I'm tired of washin' the damn dishes. Every time I ask this bastard to do somethin', he claims his back hurts. If the bastard don't start helpin' me around this damn house, I'ma leave his butt here all by his damn self.'" Then she looked at my father and said, "*That's* what I be sayin' in my sleep. And if you're gonna quote me, quote me right."

My chin was on the ground. I was actually in awe of my mother's skills. She was a professional cusser, and I had inherited her tongue. I wanted to give her a round of applause, but I knew that would only offend my father.

"You see what I'm talkin' 'bout?" my father asked me. "And she got the nerve to sit in church every Sunday like she's saved, sanctified, and full of the Holy Ghost." He looked at my mother. "With a mouth like the one you got, God don't hear your prayers."

Lerlean's neck rotated when she spoke to him. "Well, He ain't gotta hear all of 'em, just the one when I ask Him to make yo' behind disappear." She took her bags from my hands. "Now see what you did, James? You done took me out of my anointin'. Now I gotta go in the house and get back right with the Lord. Come on in here," she said to him as she ascended the porch steps. "We gotta start packing for our honeymoon."

Lerlean went inside the house and left me and my father alone. Daddy could do nothing but shake his head from side to side.

I smiled at him. "You love it, don't you?"

"After all these years, she still does it for me."

I kissed my father's cheek and left.

I drove into my driveway and was upset because Malcolm's truck was gone. The mauve-colored carpet in the living room had just been vacuumed. I could tell by the zigzag lines. In my bedroom I saw that he'd made the bed nice and neat. My shower walls were wet, and I could still smell Dove soap. In the kitchen every dish from last night had been washed and was drying upside down in the dish rack. Malcolm was different from my father. That was for sure. I sat down at the kitchen table and called his cellular telephone.

"Where are you?" I asked when he answered.

"I'm at work."

"You didn't say you had to work today."

"I didn't say I *didn't* have to work, either."

"Are you gettin' smart with me?"

"What if I am? What are you gonna do about it?"

"I might just drive to Burger World and whup your tail," I said jokingly.

"Well, come on, if you're bad enough, but you know you can't handle this."

"I *can* handle you."

"Humph. Not according to last night. Remember how you were complaining? 'Hurry up, Malcolm. I'm tired. My leg is cramping up,'" he teased me.

I laughed out loud. Malcolm was thirteen years my junior, and he reminded me of that every time we slept together. His stamina and longevity gave me a run for my money. "You think you're all that, don't you?"

"That's what you tell me."

"We'll see who whines tonight."

"It won't be me, that's for sure," Malcolm said in a matter-of-fact tone.

"What time are you off?"

"Seven o'clock tonight."

"Okay. I'll see you then."

I disconnected the call with Malcolm and dialed Anastasia's home number. Trevor answered on the first ring.

"Hello?"

"Hey, Trevor. It's Rhapsody."

"Hi. How are you doing?"

I hadn't had a chance to thank Trevor for what he did for me when I came to their house in the middle of the night, after I showed my behind at Mr. G's Club. It would have been awkward to bring up the subject during Chantal's christening at church. "Much better. I wanna thank you for taking care of me last week, Trevor. I really appreciate it."

"Rhapsody, you don't have to thank me for that. You and Stacy are like sisters. It's my job to take care of both of you."

When Trevor mentioned me and Anastasia being like sisters, I remembered how she had undressed me and washed my face, then had rocked me to sleep that night. "Yeah, we are sisters. Is she home?"

"Yeah. Hang on a second."

I heard him call Anastasia's name, and I could also hear Chantal having a fit about something.

"Hey, girl. What's up?" Anastasia asked. She sounded like she was out of breath.

"You tell *me* what's up. Why is my goddaughter hollerin' at the top of her lungs?"

"Because I'm tryin' to wean her off my boobs. She's hungry, but she doesn't wanna take the bottle."

"She's only four months old, Stacy. Why are you weaning her this soon?"

"Because Chantal eats too much, and I can't produce milk fast enough to keep her li'l chubby butt satisfied."

"Well, what are you gonna do about her hollerin'?"

"I can't do *anything* about it. Her pediatrician says that when she gets hungry enough, she'll drink the formula from the bottle."

"What are you and Trevor doing today?"

"Trevor can't do anything, 'cause I'm on my way to get a mani and pedi."

"You're leaving your husband with a fussy baby?"

"Heck yeah. Chantal and I are joined at the hip Monday through Friday, while he's at work. Saturdays are for me. He's her daddy. He's supposed to listen to her fuss. What are you and Malcolm doing today?"

"Malcolm is working until seven o'clock tonight."

"Well, come on and get your hands and feet done with me."

I looked down at my cuticles. It had been over a month since I had visited a nail shop. "I guess I could use a fill-in, but my money is funny." Since I had purchased Malcolm's truck, I couldn't afford any pampering.

"Come on and go. I got you."

"You ain't got a job."

"But I got a husband," she retorted. "I'm on my way to get you."

Chapter 24

Anastasia and I walked into Tyang's Nail Shop at 1:45 p.m. on Saturday afternoon. Ten minutes later we were relaxing and sitting side by side in massage recliners, with our feet soaking in warm water. Our backs vibrated, and so did our feet.

A young Korean girl with beautiful jet-black, straight hair came and sat on a stool in front of me. "Fee feyal okay?"

I hated talking to foreigners because I had to ask them to repeat themselves about twenty times before I understood what they were saying. "Excuse me?"

She dipped her hand in the water and patted my big toe. "How fee feyal? Fee feyal okay?"

I nodded my head. "Oh yes, my feet feel good. Thank you," I said.

She lifted my left foot from the warm water and dried it on a soft white towel, then examined my toenails. "This yo'ah fir pedicu'a?"

Here we go again. "Pardon me?"

"When lat tie you get toe done?"

"About a month ago," I answered.

"Who do yo'ah toe fo yu?"

I looked over at Anastasia for help.

"She wants to know who did your last pedicure," Anastasia said to me.

I looked at the Korean girl. "I went to a sister who owns a nail shop in my neighborhood."

"I tell she no Korean," she said, examining my feet with a turned-up nose. "Koreans do gud wok. Yo'ah toe not gud wok. You wan cute toe, comah heeyah. You wan jack-up toe, go to yo'ah sista."

Anastasia heard the Korean girl and hollered. I looked over at her as she sat next to me.

"I can't be sure, but I think I just got checked," I said.

"You definitely got checked," Anastasia responded.

Thirty minutes later Anastasia and I were at side-by-side nail stations. We got our nails filled in with acrylic coating. Little fans beneath the table were blowing on our freshly painted toenails when the wind chimes over the door to the nail salon rang. In walked Sharonda and Leticia, the broads who were with Malcolm and his boy, Ivan, at Mr. G's Club last week.

I whispered, "Stacy."

She looked at me. "Huh?"

"Remember the girls that I told you about that were at Mr. G's with Malcolm?"

"Uh-huh."

"They just walked in."

Anastasia directed her attention toward the front of the nail salon, where Sharonda and Leticia had sat down in two chairs to wait their turn. Anastasia and I were about fifteen feet away, so they hadn't seen me yet. I remembered the club was dark and dim on the night I approached their table. Even though I had got a good look at them, maybe Sharonda and Leticia hadn't gotten a good look at me.

"The one with the micro-braids is Sharonda," I said to Anastasia. "She's the one who was darn near sittin' on Malcolm's lap. The girl next to her is Leticia. She had on that same outfit last week at the club. That same halter top is the reason Ivan's eyes were focused downward as she talked to him."

"Look, Rhapsody, don't start nothin', 'cause I'm some-body's mama. Okay? I can't be out in these streets, fighting."

"You ain't gotta worry about me, Stacy. If *they* don't start no crap, it won't be no crap."

A minute later another Korean lady escorted Sharonda and Leticia to the same massage chairs Anastasia and I had sat in for our pedicures.

Leticia was the first to notice me. She looked at me kind of funny but turned her head. Then she looked at me again and squinted her eyes, like she was trying to figure out if she'd seen my face before. Then her eyes widened a bit. That was the expression that let me know she had finally realized where she'd seen me. She leaned over and whispered something to Sharonda, who looked dead into my face. She nodded her head at Leticia, confirming that I was definitely the one who had shown my butt and cussed them out last week.

Anastasia was watching all three of us. "Rhapsody, be cool."

I didn't remove my eyes from the broads when I spoke to Anastasia. "I *am* cool, Stacy, but I ain't no punk."

"I didn't say you were a punk, I said, 'Be cool.'"

Two Korean women had coated our nails with acrylic and had filed them evenly. Now they instructed Anasta-sia and me to wash and dry our hands, then select the nail polish color we wanted. The racks that housed the hundreds of bottles of nail polish were adjacent to the massage chairs in which Dumb and Dumber sat. With our backs to them, Anastasia and I compared nail polish colors.

I held up a bottle of bright pink polish with glitter. "This color would look nice on your fingers, Stacy."

"Yeah, it would, if I were in kindergarten," Anastasia said. "Put that crap back."

"Put that crap back, trick." The echo came from behind us. We didn't know if it was Sharonda or Leticia who had mocked Anastasia, 'cause when we turned around, both of them were looking down at copies of *Jet* magazine, with smirks on their faces.

We brought our attention back to the nail polishes. I mumbled, "I'm trying to be cool, like you asked, Stacy."

"I know. Let's just pick a color so we can get out of here."

Anastasia selected a nice neutral beige color.

"That's a pretty color, Stacy. What number is it?"

"This particular bottle isn't numbered. It's called Sahara."

"It's called Sahara, trick." We heard an echo again.

I was surprised at how quickly Anastasia lost *her* cool after instructing me not to lose mine. She turned around and asked, "Is there a freakin' problem?"

Leticia and her oversize boobs spoke up. "What?"

"Y'all messin' with my girl, and when you mess with her, you mess with me."

Sharonda stood and stepped out of the water her feet were soaking in. "Well, we can take it outside."

I took a step toward them. "Let's *do* it, then."

In the next second, one of the three Korean ladies approached us. "No, no. No fy in heeyah. I call polee."

This time I understood what she said without asking her to repeat herself. "We ain't gonna fight in here. We're gonna take this outside."

"No, no. No fi outsy eeda. Comah ovah heeyah an get yo'ah nail paint." She grabbed Anastasia's elbow and guided her back to our stations. She turned and looked at me. "You too. Comah ovah heeyah an seet down."

After our nails were polished, Anastasia and I sat under a nail-drying table. At that time Sharonda and Leticia were getting their toenails painted. My cellular telephone rang, and I was excited to see Malcolm's name flashing on my caller ID.

I pressed the TALK button and brought the phone to my ear. "Hey, Malcolm. What's up, baby?" I purposely spoke loud enough for Sharonda and Leticia to hear.

Anastasia looked at me, rolled her eyes, and exhaled. "Aw, heck. Here we go."

"You miss me, boo? I miss you too," I cooed to Malcolm. "I'm at the nail shop with Stacy. I can't wait to see you tonight."

From where I sat, I saw Sharonda take her cellular telephone from her purse and dial a number. Two seconds later I heard a click in my ear; then Malcolm told me to hold on.

"Hey, Malcolm baby," Sharonda said, loud enough for *me* to hear.

I didn't even remember moving out of my seat, but my fist went flying across the nail shop and slammed into Sharonda's face. Leticia came to her defense and jumped on my back. Anastasia must've been on my heels when I first sprang up, 'cause next thing I knew, she pushed Leticia off of me.

Sharonda leapt out of her chair, thinking she was gonna get the best of me. She was in for a rude awakening, because as soon as she came at me, I grabbed a handful of her micro-braids and slung her from the east to the west. I looked over my shoulder to see how Anastasia was doing. Leticia was a big girl, but somehow Anastasia had managed to bring her to her knees. Then they started rolling on the floor. I took Sharonda's braids and rammed the back of her head into the wall of nail polish, and every bottle tumbled to the floor.

I saw that Leticia had gotten the best of Anastasia. She was straddling my friend, tryin' to hit her face. I let go of Sharonda and ran into Leticia. I bodychecked her like I was a football player charging at a player on the opposite team. She went airborne before she slammed into the floor. I heard the door chimes ring, and suddenly six policemen had all four of us in handcuffs.

One cop asked a Korean lady who had started the fight. She pointed right at me. "Tha one wit da big mou."

It took three hours for a lady cop to come open the cell at the jailhouse on Twenty-Sixth Street and California Avenue to tell me and Anastasia that we were free to go. We walked out to the vestibule and saw Trevor. To say that he was livid would really be putting it mildly. Anastasia and I took one look at his face and knew we were in trouble.

"What the heck was y'all doing, fightin' in a nail shop?" Trevor's eyes were the size of golf balls. He wouldn't let us answer. He turned away from us. "Let's go!" he yelled.

As Trevor drove to my house, Anastasia and I didn't utter a word. He glanced at his wife, who was sitting in the passenger seat, and said, "Are you gonna answer my question?"

"It was two girls against Rhapsody, Trevor. What was I supposed to do? Let my best friend get her butt kicked?"

He positioned his rearview mirror to look at me sitting behind him. "What happened?"

I exhaled. "There were two girls at the nail shop who had a beef with me. They were talking crap to me and Stacy."

"Rhapsody, the police said the girls were nineteen years old. What kind of beef could they have with your grown behind?"

"I had kind of a run-in with them before, Trevor."

"That didn't answer my question," he said.

"They were mocking us, and it got on my nerves, so I stole on one of them."

"What was up with the cell phones?" Trevor asked.

I played dumb. "Huh?"

"The police said something happened with somebody's cell phone."

Anastasia turned around in her seat and looked at me. "You may as well tell him, Rhapsody."

Trevor looked at me in the rearview mirror. "Tell me what?"

I rolled my eyes. I didn't feel like getting into that right then.

"I'm waitin'," Trevor said to me.

I didn't have a choice. Trevor wasn't gonna let up. "I called my man, and while I was talking to him, he got another call, and he put me on hold. One of the broads from the nail shop had called him, and she made sure I knew it."

"Hold up," Trevor said. He looked confused. "Those girls were teenagers." Trevor glanced at me in the rearview mirror. "One of them is messing around with a dude *your* age?"

Anastasia looked at the embarrassed expression on my face. I did not want Trevor to know the age difference between Malcolm and me.

"Nope," Anastasia answered for me. "Rhapsody is messing with a boy the girl's age."

Thank God we were wearing our seat belts, because the way Trevor slammed on the brakes, I thought all three of our heads were going straight through the windshield. *"What?"* He looked at me in a way that made me feel ashamed. "What the heck is wrong with you, girl?"

I didn't say nothing, 'cause I couldn't say nothing. No words would make the situation right in Trevor's eyes. I turned to look out the window and kept my stare there until we got to my house.

Chapter 25

When I walked in my front door, I saw Malcolm sitting on the living room sofa. He glared at me.

"Don't say a word to me, Malcolm." I walked past him, and he got up and followed me.

"What are you walkin' in here pissed at me for?"

I stopped walking and turned to him. "'Cause this is *your* fault."

Malcolm went to the front door and slammed it shut. I hadn't realized that I had left it open. He came back to me. "*My* fault? Did I tell you to punch Sharonda in her face?"

I put my hand on my hip. "First of all," I began, "this is *my* house, and the only one who slams doors around here is me. Second, who told you I punched her in the face?"

"We were on our cell phones, Rhapsody, when the crap hit the fan. I heard Sharonda say hi to me, and the next thing I heard was her cell hittin' the floor and a whole bunch of shufflin' and arguin'. Then Sharonda called me twenty minutes later and told me what happened. You better be glad I was able to convince her to drop the charges."

My eyes got so big, I looked like a deer that had been caught in the headlights. "What do you mean, I better be glad?"

"If Sharonda hadn't dropped the charges, you *and* your girl would still be locked up."

"So, what did you have to do to get her to drop the charges, Malcolm? Huh?"

He walked away from me. "Rhapsody, don't start with me, okay?"

I followed him into the kitchen. "I'm gonna start and finish it. What's up, Malcolm? Are you screwing Sharonda?"

He stopped abruptly and turned to face me. "I'm not doing this with you, 'cause you're crazy."

Malcolm went into my den, plopped down on the futon, and picked up the remote control from a table next it. He turned on the television and found a basketball game on the ESPN channel. I guessed he called himself dismissing me, but I went and stood directly in front of the television.

"You didn't answer my question. Are you screwing Sharonda?"

"Look, Rhapsody, I stood on my feet for nine hours today. I don't feel like dealing with this petty crap."

"Oh, so now I'm petty?"

"What you did today was very petty," Malcolm said to me. "Sharonda is nineteen years old. You're a grown woman. Don't you feel the least bit stupid?"

"I *feel* like slappin' the heck outta you, that's what I feel. All I wanna know is if you're screwing her or not."

When he didn't answer me, I folded my arms across my chest. "You're procrastinating, Malcolm. You got somethin' to hide?"

"Sharonda and I grew up together."

My eyebrows rose. "And?"

"And nothin'. We're only friends now. Would you move out of the way?"

"Malcolm, you must think I'm a fool. I saw her almost sittin' on your lap at the club last week."

"That's a lie, Rhapsody."

"I know what I saw."

He exhaled loudly to let me know that I was getting on his last nerve. "Sharonda is a friend of mine. In fact,

I have many women friends. Okay? So don't trip. I consider *you* a friend."

"Except you're screwing me."

"And you're the *only* friend I'm screwing. Now move out of the way. I'm trying to watch the game."

"I'ma let you watch your game, Malcolm, but this conversation ain't over."

I went into the kitchen. I was sitting a pot of water on the stove in preparation for spaghetti when I thought I saw someone move through the bushes outside my kitchen window. My screams brought Malcolm running to me.

"What's the matter?" he asked.

"I think somebody is outside, in the bushes."

Malcolm removed one of his gym shoes and quickly ran out my back door with it in his hand. Within two minutes, he was back in the kitchen. "I didn't see anybody."

I looked at him. "What the heck were you gonna do with your gym shoe? I said I saw a person, not a roach."

At three o'clock on Sunday morning I got out of bed to pee. In the dark I walked into the bathroom, half asleep, with my eyes closed. I'd been living in that duplex for five years, so I knew that the toilet was four steps away from the bathroom door. After taking the four steps, I turned around, lifted my T-shirt to my waist, and squatted. When it dawned on me that I was squatting lower than usual and that it was taking longer than it normally would for my butt to connect with the toilet seat, it was too late.

Swoosh.

Malcolm had left the toilet seat up, and my naked butt was cold and wet. I looked like a two-year-old getting potty trained, with my butt way down in the toilet and my legs dangling.

"Malcolm!" I hollered at the top of my lungs.

Immediately, he came to the bathroom door, turned on the light, saw me, and started laughing.

"You left the toilet seat up, and what are you laughing at?"

Malcolm was laughing so hard, he could hardly get his words out. "You look like a munchkin."

To him, it was funny, but it wasn't funny worth a darn to me, because I was truly stuck down in the toilet. I was short and had an oversize butt. No matter how I tried to raise myself up, I couldn't do it.

"This is not funny, Malcolm."

He was hollerin' and laughing. "Yes, it is."

I felt my blood begin to boil, and my ears were getting hot. I was mad as heck 'cause Malcolm saw me trying to free myself, but he just stood in the doorway and got his laugh on at my expense.

"Malcolm, I'm stuck," I said seriously. "Will you help me up?"

"Hold up. I'll be back," Malcolm said and went into my bedroom.

"What do you mean, 'hold up'? What are you doing? Come on, Malcolm. This water is ice cold on my butt."

Suddenly there was a flash of bright light in my face. The fool had taken a picture of my desperate situation with his cellular phone.

"Oh, my God!" I said. My heart was beating overtime. "No you didn't, Malcolm! I know you didn't do what you just did."

He was still laughing. "I had to. This is a Kodak moment."

I was pissed on top of pissed. "This ain't funny!"

I was so hot and bothered that I didn't want Malcolm to touch me. I was determined to get out of the toilet on my own. He stood laughing while he watched me work up a sweat as I squirmed.

Malcolm stopped laughing when he saw tears streaming down my cheeks. My shoulders jerked, and I had to suppress terrible words that wanted to escape my throat. Malcolm didn't question why my shoulders shook vigorously. I guess he thought I was crying uncontrollably. That was when he came and wrapped his arms under my arms and instructed me to wrap my arms around his neck. His feet were spread two feet apart when he took a deep breath and hauled me up from the toilet. Cold water ran down the backs of my legs. I didn't say anything to Malcolm. I pushed him away from me and started the water in the shower.

"Come on. Don't be like that," he said to me.

"Leave me alone," I said with much attitude. I raised my T-shirt over my head and took it off, stepped in the shower, and snatched the shower curtain closed. Malcolm left the bathroom and shut the door behind him. Minutes later I heard the door open again. Malcolm pulled the shower curtain back and stepped in behind me.

He leaned close to me and whispered in my ear, "I'm sorry."

I still didn't say anything to him. We stood under the cascading water, with Malcolm's arms wrapped around me, for ten minutes before he took the sponge from my hand and gently washed my body thoroughly.

If my shower walls could talk, I would never show my face in public again.

Chapter 26

I rolled over and looked at my alarm clock. "Oh, my God," I said. I had mistakenly slept until noon on Sunday. I had had every intention of going to church. Morning service at World Deliverance Christian Center began promptly at ten o'clock. I imagined that Bishop Art Clark was probably opening the doors of the church.

It was the first Sunday in July, and the saints had probably taken Holy Communion already. "I know it was the blood. I know it was the blood. I know it was the blood for me," I could imagine the church folks singing.

Lord knows that I needed to take Communion, but it wouldn't make much sense for me to get dressed and to drive thirty minutes to church. As soon as I arrived at the church, the benediction would probably be over. It would be a waste of gas.

I looked at the right side of the bed and saw that Malcolm was gone. I threw the covers off my body and sat up. I must've done it too quickly, 'cause I got dizzy for just a second. The whole bedroom had shifted. I sat on the bed for about ten seconds, then stood and went into the bathroom to brush my teeth and wash my face. Afterward, I left the bathroom and glanced in the den and didn't see Malcolm. I walked to the living room window and parted the mini-blinds and saw that his Navigator was gone from my driveway. I knew for a fact that Malcolm didn't have to work, so I wondered where he had gone.

In the kitchen I saw fried bacon and scrambled eggs on a plate wrapped in clear plastic wrap on top of the stove. On the counter, next to the stove, was a note with my name written on it.

Hey, sleepyhead,

I'll be at Brainerd Park, shooting hoops with Ivan and the boys, till around two o'clock. Hit me on my cell if you need me.

Mal

I laid the note back on the counter and unwrapped the plate. Immediately, I got sick to my stomach from the smell. I knew I wouldn't make it to the bathroom, so I opted for the garbage can in the kitchen. Everything that I had eaten the day before came up with a fury. I literally puked my guts out. I went to the stove and picked up the plate and brought it to my nose. I didn't know if it was the bacon or the eggs, but the smell made my stomach turn. I had just bought the Canadian bacon two days ago and wondered if it had soured already.

I was worried that Malcolm was feeling ill as well if he had eaten the bacon. I dumped the food on the plate in the garbage, got the remaining uncooked bacon from the refrigerator, and dumped it also. Then I removed the bag from the trash can and tied it shut. I went back to the bathroom and brushed my teeth again and rinsed my mouth with Scope. I heard the telephone ring, and I went into my bedroom, sat on the bed, and picked up the receiver.

"Hey, girl," I answered when I saw the name TREVOR BAKER on the caller ID.

"Hey, whatcha doing?" Anastasia asked me.

I exhaled. "Not too much of nothin'. I just got up."

"Really? Did you and Malcolm have a late night?"

I thought about the events that had taken place in my bathroom early that morning. "Girl, you don't even wanna know," I said.

"Please spare me the nasty details."

"No, it wasn't nothin' like that. Malcolm left the toilet seat up, and I fell in the toilet bowl. It was pure drama after that. I cussed, screamed, and hollered. And the fool had the gall to take a picture when he saw that I was stuck down in the toilet."

Anastasia laughed out loud. "Girl, what? You better hope you don't end up on Instagram for the world to see."

"I was so doggone mad, I wanted to kill him."

"That's why you're supposed to look before you squat. I know I have to."

"That's because you share your bathroom with a man. I live alone, so my toilet seat is always down, Stacy."

"And for a week you have to share your bathroom with a man," she reminded me. "Why weren't you at church today? Bishop Art Clark preached for about fifteen minutes and, girl, we were out of there. It's the Fourth of July weekend. I guess the bishop had a barbecue to get to."

"I was gonna come to church this mornin', but I forgot to set my alarm clock."

"Mmm-hmm," Anastasia moaned. "Are you sure that's all there is to it, or was it a young tenderoni occupying your time?"

"No, seriously," I said. "I was really goin' to church, but I overslept."

"I'm dyin' to know what happened when Trevor and I dropped you off yesterday. How did it go with Malcolm?"

"It went all right. I asked if he was screwing Sharonda, and he said that he wasn't."

"Did you really expect him to admit it to you, Rhapsody?"

"No, not really, but what can I do, Stacy? I don't have any proof that he is."

"Is he there?"

"No. He went to play basketball with his boys. I'm gonna put a rump roast in the oven, and I guess I'll make macaroni and cheese for dinner today. Did *you* cook?"

"Trevor got up this morning and said he had a taste for beef stew, so I cooked my meat before we went to church. I just gotta add the veggies and make the corn bread."

"Ooh, I love your beef stew, Stacy. Save me a bowl, okay?"

"Okay. Listen, I want you to make a frappé tomorrow for the barbecue."

"Why can't you make your famous homemade vanilla ice cream?"

"Because I don't feel like it. I got enough stuff to do. Making the frappé is the least you can do for having me fighting and going to jail with you."

She had me cornered. "Okay, you're right. I'll make the frappé."

"Well, let me get in the kitchen and season the ribs while Chantal is taking a nap."

"Is she drinking the formula yet?"

"Yep. That hungry hippo couldn't hold out for too long."

I chuckled. "Stacy, you are too crazy. I'll talk to you later."

After talking with Anastasia, I heated my oven to four hundred degrees and seasoned my rump roast. I cut eight white potatoes into small chunks, sprinkled them with seasoned salt and lemon pepper, and placed them, along with the roast, inside a plastic bag and sealed it tight. I put the roast in the oven to let it cook for an hour and forty-five minutes. On the back of the note Malcolm had left me, I wrote, "Ginger ale and rainbow sherbet," and then placed it under one of the magnets on the refrigerator to remind me to stop at the mini-mart on the way to Anastasia's house tomorrow.

With my Sunday dinner in the oven, I showered and put on a fresh nightgown. I lay across the futon in my den, turned on the television, and flipped to the Lifetime channel. The movie *Who Will Love My Children?* starring Ann-Margret, had just come on.

I'd seen this movie twice before and had cried throughout each viewing. Ann played the role of a woman stricken with a rare type of cancer who had only five months to live. She lived on a farm with her husband of fourteen years and seven children ranging in age from six to seventeen. Ann's husband had been crippled in the knees for many years and needed her help with planting the crops and plowing the fields. When she received the news of her cancer, Ann knew that she had to find homes for her children and a long-term care facility for her husband, and that she had to sell their land within the next five months.

By the second commercial break, I was already crying. You would think that since I'd seen the movie more than once, I could sit through it without getting emotional. I got a box of tissue from the linen closet and sat it on the table next to the futon. I peed again, the second time in an hour, and then lay on the futon.

The first of Ann's children to be placed in a foster home were her two youngest boys. They were six and seven years old, and she was able to place them with a man and a woman who were seeking to adopt. Ann was grateful she could keep the boys together. The boys didn't know where they were going with a suitcase in each of their hands. It wasn't until the caseworker knocked on the door of their new home that Ann said good-bye to her sons.

"Where're you goin', Mama?" the six-year-old asked.

Ann choked back tears. "Mama has to go away."

The seven-year-old placed his hand in hers. "Can we go with you, Mama?"

Ann knelt down to face them. By that time the foster parents had opened the front door. The caseworker stood behind Ann and placed a hand on her shoulder for support. Ann wiped her tears, which she couldn't prevent from falling from her eyes. "I wish I could take both of you with me, but I can't."

"Why, Mama?" they asked at the same time.

Watching Ann cry her heart out, I had to blow my nose and wipe my own tears. There was no easy way to tell your children you had to leave them. A mother's love was priceless.

I thought about Lerlean and what she had done for me when I was a child. Yeah, I loved my father, and I was grateful that he had always been in the home, where my brothers and I needed him to be. He had made sure we always had a roof over our heads, clothes on our backs, shoes on our feet, and food on our table. And, of course, he had been there to whup our butts when punishment was due. But it was Lerlean who had met us at the door with milk and cookies every day after school. It was Lerlean who had blown strong air into one of Walter's nostrils to force the bead he had had no business pushing up there to come shooting out the other nostril. It was Lerlean who had applied the balm to Daniel's knee when he'd fallen off his bike. It was Lerlean's bosom I had laid my head against when the li'l boy I had had a crush on told me I was fat.

I didn't know what I would do if my mama told me she had a disease that would take her away from me. I knew myself very well, and I couldn't handle it. That was why from that day on, I prayed that God would allow me to die before Lerlean died, and if He didn't grant me that wish and forced me to attend my mama's funeral, I would jump right on top of her casket as they lowered it into the ground and tell them to bury me too, because without Lerlean, there would be no Rhapsody.

I saw Ann turn and walk away from her boys, her pain evident. Simultaneously, they ran after her, and each boy wrapped himself around her legs and cried out.

"Don't leave us, Mama."

"Please take us with you, Mama."

With every ounce of strength she had, Ann picked her boys up and carried them to the door. She gave the fightin' and kickin' six-year-old to the man and the screamin' and hollerin' seven-year-old to the woman.

"No, Mama. Please, Mama."

"Mama, Mama. We're sorry for being bad, Mama."

Ann ran toward the caseworker's car. The tears were so thick in her eyes, she could hardly see where she was going.

"Mama, Mama," the boys cried after her.

"Don't go, Mama. *Please* don't go."

The caseworker opened the passenger door and sat the distraught Ann inside the car. The new parents had gotten the boys inside the house. Before the caseworker drove away, Ann looked toward the house and saw her boys in the living room window, beating their fists against the glass, crying out to her. She read their lips and knew what they were saying.

"Come back, Mama. Please come back."

During the next commercial break, I realized snot had dripped onto my nightgown. I blew my nose, wiped my tears, and got up to pee again. I didn't know why I was peeing so much. I hadn't drunk anything at all. I checked my roast by poking a fork into it. It wasn't as tender as I liked it to be, so I let it stay in the oven longer. Then

I called my parents' house, 'cause I needed to hear Lerlean's voice.

"Hey, Mama," I said when she answered.

"Hey, baby."

"Whatcha doing?"

"Getting ready to go to the flea market with your daddy. You wanna go with us?"

"Nah. I got cramps," I lied.

"You got Midol?" she asked.

"Yeah."

"Well, take two pills and lie down. You'll be all right. Your first two days of your period have always been the worst for you."

"Yeah, I know," I said sadly.

"What's the matter?" Lerlean had always been able to read my moods. Even if I was smiling and joking, if something was bothering me, she knew.

"Ain't nothin' wrong, Mama."

"Okay, well, your father is outside, blowing that horn like a darn fool. I already told him that I was on my way out. This is why I cuss him out every chance I get, 'cause he don't listen. I done told him before not to be blowing no horn for me. I said, 'James, just sit your old senile behind in the car until I get out there.' But I see he forgot, so now I gotta cuss."

"Mama, you know the flea market sells out of the good stuff real fast. You got to get there early. It opens at seven, and it's almost two."

"They don't ever sell out of the crap your father buys. He goes for the seersucker pants, the satin shirts, and the fat white belts with the big chrome buckle. Don't nobody buy that outdated crap *but* your daddy. Whether we get there at seven in the mornin' or ten at night, that crap will be there."

I heard the horn blowing through the telephone line, and my mother lost it and yelled out the front window, "James, if blow that horn one more time, I'ma stab you!"

"Mama, just go. I'll talk to you later."

"I'm so sick of him. I swear before the Lord, come Tuesday, I'ma call around to see if I can put him in a retirement home somewhere."

"Daddy's too young to be placed in a retirement home."

"He ain't gotta go to a retirement home, but he gotta get out of here."

I heard the horn again, and my mother yelled out the window, "You wanna die, James?"

"Bye, Mama," I said.

"I'll call you when we get back, okay? Don't forget to take the Midol."

"I won't. Hey, Mama?"

"What, baby?"

"I love you."

"I love you too, Rhapsody."

After speaking with my mother, I lay back down on the futon in my den and continued to watch the movie.

Ann found foster homes for each of her seven children except the oldest, her seventeen-year-old daughter, who would turn eighteen in a few weeks. Ann and her husband allowed her to move in with her best friend's family.

Four months passed, and the FOR SALE sign was still in the front yard. Ann had grown very weak due to the chemotherapy and radiation treatments. Every single strand of her hair was gone, and she'd gone from 120 pounds to 95 pounds. She was sitting on the front porch of her home when a white van drove up the driveway. Next to Ann sat her husband in his wheelchair, with a small brown suitcase on his lap.

He looked at her and said, "So, I guess this is it."

Ann looked at her husband of twenty years with tears in her eyes. "I wish it didn't have to be this way."

Two male nurses exited the van and approached the porch. Though she was very weak, Ann raised herself from her chair and kissed her husband's forehead. She pressed his head into her bosom and held it there. When a tear dropped from Ann's chin, he felt it run down the side of his face. She looked at the nurses, nodded her head, and motioned for them to come forward. She stood on the porch and watched the strong men in white uniforms carry her husband away. Ann died a week later.

I cried my butt off. I went through a whole box of tissues. I blew my nose and peed again. I wondered if I had taken a water pill and didn't remember doing it. By the end of the movie my roast and potatoes were nice, juicy, and tender. It was now 2:45 p.m. Where in the heck was Malcolm? Just as I picked up the telephone to call him, I heard him come in the front door.

"Hey, sugar baby bubble gum," he greeted me in the kitchen.

He was as high as a kite. Malcolm's eyes were glossy and bloodshot. He leaned forward to kiss me, but I turned my face away, 'cause I could smell what he'd been doin'.

"What's wrong, thickums?"

"Who in the heck is thickums?"

Malcolm was so high, he had to lean against the wall in the kitchen to keep his balance. His speech was slurred. "Aw, boo, it's all good. I like my women cute in the face and fat in the waist."

I was about ready to grab a butcher knife and cut him. It dawned on me that he was holding a paper bag full of chips and all types of candy.

"What is all of that, Malcolm?"

He put the bag on the table. "Brotha got the munchies, boo."

"That's 'cause you're full of weed. Don't you know you gotta take a drop Tuesday?"

"What's a drop?"

"A pee test, fool. Did you forget you have an interview with Audelia? You know you gotta be clean, Malcolm."

Malcolm scratched his bald head and looked toward the ceiling like he was tryin' to figure something out. "Aw, man. I forgot about that." He looked at me. "I messed up, didn't I?"

I was so disappointed in him. "Get outta my face, Malcolm."

By my expression, he knew I was serious. Without another word, he went into my bedroom and fell across the bed. Malcolm was sawing logs in less than thirty seconds.

I decided to get out of the house for a while and go to the grocery store for the frappé and ginger ale. I threw on a white tank top and denim shorts. I slipped into my Gucci denim slides, which three months ago I chose to sacrifice my cable and electric bills for. I grabbed the matching denim purse and my keys and walked out the front door. I couldn't get to my car because Malcolm's Navigator was blocking my one-car garage. I searched my key ring to make sure I had my set of keys to the truck. I'd never driven anything that big, and just backing it out of the driveway looked to be challenging. I unlocked the door with the keyless entry remote and climbed in.

"Hello, Malcolm. Welcome to paradise."

I heard what the truck said, but then again I didn't hear it, because my nose was on alert. Perfume lingered in the air. I recognized the scent, because while Lerlean and I were out shopping yesterday, Filene's Basement had advertised the same scented perfume, called Shi. We both loved it, and I'd told my mother I'd get us both a bottle with my next paycheck.

I sat there, pissed at the thought of Malcolm having a broad in the truck that I had bought him. I had made it perfectly clear to him the day I bought the truck that no other chick was to sit her rump in it. I would deal with him when I returned from the grocery store. If I woke him up now, he probably wouldn't even know who I was.

I started the ignition and put the truck in reverse to back out of the driveway. My plan was to go to the grocery store to get the ginger ale and rainbow sherbet, since I had nothing else to do. As I looked over my right shoulder and backed the Navigator out of my driveway, something on the floor in front of the passenger seat caught my attention in my peripheral vision. I pressed down on the brakes and put the truck in park, then leaned over to see what it was. A pink chiffon scarf was almost hidden beneath the seat. I picked it up and sniffed it. Shi flowed through my nostrils.

I slapped Malcolm's face as hard as I could. "Wake up!"

Malcolm quickly opened his eyes and raised his head. He brought his hand to his face to ease the stinging pain. "Wha, wha, what happened? Who hit me?"

"I did."

He looked up at me, and I could tell he saw four of me. He rubbed his eyes and his cheek. "What you do that for?"

I threw the scarf in his face. "Whose is this?"

He studied the scarf for a moment. "It's yours, ain't it?"

I wanted to knock Malcolm's teeth out. He was trying to play me for a fool. That pissed me off more than anything. "Would I be asking you whose scarf it was if it was mine?"

"Rhapsody, I don't know what you're hollering about."

I snatched the scarf out of his hand and held it an inch away from his eyes and nose. "Do you see this scarf, Malcolm?"

He moved my hand away, and I brought it back to where it was. "Do you see this scarf?" I asked him again.

"Yeah, I see it."

"Can you smell it?"

He didn't answer, and I shoved the scarf against his nose. "Can you smell it?"

Malcolm pushed my hand away again. "Yeah, I smell it. So what?"

"Well, then, don't say you don't know what I'm hollerin' about. I'm hollerin' about this pink scarf with the perfume on it, which I found on the floor of your truck. I wanna know whom it belongs to. You got heifers riding around in the truck that *I* pay for?"

"Nah. It's probably my mother's scarf," he said.

"Your mother's?"

"Yeah. You know I take her to therapy and everywhere else she has to go. She probably dropped it."

I knew Malcolm was lying to me, but I couldn't call him on it right then. I stood and gave him a look to let him know I didn't believe his weak story. "Look, Malcolm, I'm the wrong one to cross, okay? Let me remind you of somethin' one last time. I want you to listen and pay very close attention to every word that's comin' out of my mouth, because I won't repeat myself. *I'm* paying the note on that truck. That means it belongs to *me*. The only other woman who is allowed to ride in it *is* your mother. If I catch another broad in it or within five feet *of* it, it won't end well for you. I promise you that I am not playing with you. Now, you can mess around and let what I'm saying go in one ear and out the other if you want to. If you're smart, you'll grow eyes in the back of your head, because you never know when or where I'll roll up on you. And if I see some crazy crap, I . . . will . . . kill . . . you." I spaced out the last four words to let each one sink deep down into Malcolm's brain.

He didn't utter a word; he just lay there and stared at me like I had lost my mind. And he would be right, 'cause at that very moment my mind was totally gone. I really hoped that I had put the fear of God in Malcolm, 'cause it would literally take an act of God to save him if I caught him cheating on me.

I turned away from him and left the bedroom. I didn't wanna hear anything Malcolm had to say, because it wasn't important. I went into the bathroom and got a pair of small scissors from the medicine cabinet and cut the scarf up. I threw the fragments in the garbage can on the side of my house. I didn't believe that it was Malcolm's mother's scarf, nor did I care. If it *was* his mother's, then, oops, my bad. She would just have to buy herself another one.

At the grocery store, I was standing in the frozen dessert aisle and trying to locate rainbow sherbet when a man came and stood next to me.

"Excuse me. Can I ask your opinion on somethin'?" he asked.

I didn't wanna be bothered with no one. I just wanted to get what I had come for and leave. But Anastasia had made me promise her that I would stop being cruel to the whole world when I was mad at one person.

"Sure," I said.

"My wife sent me here to get vanilla ice cream. Which brand do you think is best?"

"In my opinion, Baldwin is the best."

"She told me to get Breyers," he said.

I snapped, "Well, what are you askin' my opinion for? If your wife told you what to buy, then get what she said. Darn, why do you men always gotta be so stupid?"

I found what I was looking for. I opened the glass freezer door, grabbed a container of rainbow sherbet, and walked away. I left that fool standing with his mouth agape.

I swear, the older I got, the less tolerance I had for stupid folks. There were times when I really didn't understand the male species. A whole lot of marriages would last a lot longer if the husbands just did whatever their wives told them to do. Bringing home a different brand of ice cream, one other than what the man's wife had sent him to the grocery store to get, should give her license to put both her feet dead in his behind.

In a different aisle, I found a two-liter bottle of ginger ale. I paid my bill and walked out of the grocery store. That was when I met up with another ignorant fool, who was walking in my direction.

"Hello," he said to me.

OMG! Why can't these idiots just leave me alone? "Hi," I said dryly. I kept walking, without giving him any eye contact. My mother had taught me years ago that if I wasn't interested in a man, I should never make eye contact with him, because he would misinterpret it to mean that I wanted to engage in conversation.

"How are you doing?" he asked.

"Fine."

"I didn't ask how you looked. I asked how you were doin'."

His sorry behind couldn't do any better than that? That grammar school pickup line was played out.

I stopped walking and looked at him. "Look, I'm really not in the best of moods today, okay? I would really appreciate you backing off of me." I started walking again, and he followed.

"I don't wanna upset you," he said. "I just wanna talk. Can I carry your bags?"

"It's only one bag, and I can handle it." I had forgotten which aisle I had parked the Navigator in, so I had to activate the remote to set off the alarm. When I heard the siren, I started walking in that direction.

"Can I ask your name?"

The idiot was on my heels; he had followed me all the way to the truck. My temper was at level eight and rising by the second. I didn't wanna have to snap on him, but I had already told the fool he couldn't get any play. But he was irritating the heck outta me in the ninety-plus degree weather. Obviously, he was too dumb to know what no meant. He didn't even have to say another word to me, because just knowing he wasn't letting up caused my temper to rise two more digits.

I turned to face him and allowed my neck to dance, as though I was twirling a hula hoop on it. "No, you can't ask for my name *or* my telephone number. But I'll tell you what you *can* do. You can get outta my face, because I'm done talkin' to you."

Right then I knew I had to repent for the words that had come out of my mouth. I knew God was ashamed of me. But dealing with Malcolm's cheating behind, fighting Sharonda, Malcolm coming home high as heck, and finding the pink scarf had caused the ugly side of me to make an appearance.

The man I had just cussed out stood next to the truck, with a look on his face like he couldn't believe what I had said to him. I unlocked the driver-side door and threw the ginger ale and sherbet on the passenger seat. I climbed in, slammed the door shut, and started the engine.

"Hello, Malcolm. Welcome to paradise."

"Oh, shut the heck up!" I put the truck in reverse and darn near ran over the man's feet as I sped out of the grocery store parking lot.

Malcolm didn't get his butt up until ten o'clock that night. I was in the den, lying across the futon, when he appeared in the doorway.

"What's for dinner?" he asked while scratching his bald head. The wife beater and shorts he'd slept in were wrinkled. He looked like he stank.

There was a rump roast, potatoes, and homemade macaroni and cheese on top of the stove, but I was still mad, so I didn't tell him. I kept my attention on the news.

"Rhapsody, what do you got to eat?"

I looked up at him. "Why don't you go into the kitchen and see?" I said with much attitude.

"What's *your* problem? What you got your lips poked out for?"

I exhaled. I had already repented for my actions and words from earlier in the day. I didn't wanna have to go to God a second time and beg Him to forgive me for allowing the devil to overtake me. "It's *you*, Malcolm," I said to him. "*You're* the problem. *You're* the reason my lips are poked out."

"Well, maybe if you weren't pissed off all the time about nothing, we could have somethin' good."

My eyes bucked out of my head, and I felt my temperature rise. *Shoot him. Stab him now. Suffocate him in his sleep. Put rat poison in his mac and cheese. Kill him now.*

I rose from the futon, walked past Malcolm, went into my bedroom, and locked the door behind me. I fell on my knees and prayed for strength. I needed God to keep me from doing what the enemy had just told me to do, because I wanted to do all those things.

Chapter 27

I woke up early Monday with a queasy feeling in my belly. I jumped out of bed and ran into the bathroom. I was able to lift the toilet seat just in time. Everything I had eaten yesterday came up. I felt Malcolm's open palm caress my lower back as he knelt next to me.

"You a'ight, boo?"

I wanted to answer him but couldn't, because I was about to throw up again. When my face went down in the toilet, Malcolm ran his hand softly across my shoulders. I emptied my stomach a second time and sat on the floor and let my head fall back against the sink. I was panting.

"What's the matter?"

I wiped my mouth with the back of my hand. "I don't know. I felt this way yesterday too."

"Can I get you anything?"

I pointed upward. "The Pepto-Bismol from the medicine cabinet."

Malcolm gave me the pink bottle, and I brought it my mouth, turned it up, and swallowed two big gulps. I told him I wanted to brush my teeth, and he loaded my toothbrush with toothpaste and gave it to me.

"What time is it?" I asked him.

"A little after five thirty. You wanna go to the emergency room?"

"No. I'll be all right."

We went back to bed. Malcolm snuggled up and held me in a spoon position. We had spent our last night together. His mother would be home later today. Just the day before I was ready to send Malcolm back to his mother, but lying in his arms right then comforted me. I pressed the back of my head against his hairy chest, exhaled, and melted in his arms one last time.

I woke up again when the sun was up to Malcolm staring down at me.

I frowned and asked, "What's wrong?"

"You tell *me*. You were tossing and turning since five thirty this mornin'."

The next thing I knew, I was running to the toilet again. After I threw up, I sat against the sink again, panting like I was dying of thirst.

"Rhapsody, you need to go to the hospital."

I shook my head from side to side. "No, Malcolm. It's probably just a virus."

"So, what are you gonna do? Sit here on the bathroom floor all day?"

"I'll be all right," I assured him. "Just give me a minute."

"I really wish you would get checked out."

"I'm scheduled for annual examination tomorrow morning. I'll let my doctor know what's going on."

"You want something to eat?"

My belly did a somersault. I frowned at him and shook my head from side to side. "The thought of food makes my stomach turn."

Minutes later I was relaxing in my tub with the Jacuzzi jets beating against my muscles. Malcolm brought a glass of orange juice to me.

"Drink this."

I took a sip and thanked him. He sighed and leaned down next to the tub.

"My mother will be home this evening."

A huge sigh escaped my lips. "I know."

"You know I gotta be there, don't you?"

I turned my head away from him to stare at the tiles on the wall. With his first two fingers, Malcolm softly brought my face back to him. Tears flooded my eyes, and when I blinked, they fell onto my cheeks. I had gotten used to going to bed and waking up with Malcolm at my side. We were so close, and I felt like I was losing my best friend.

He leaned over to me and kissed my closed eyelids. "Aw, boo, it's gonna be okay. We'll get another chance to play house again."

I didn't know where Malcolm got the strength. He was much stronger than I thought he was when he picked me up out of the tub, dripping wet, and carried me to my bed. Hours later the telephone woke me up. It was Anastasia, and she was hollering.

"Rhapsody, it's two o'clock. Where's my darn frappé?"

I glanced at the clock on my nightstand. "Oh, my goodness," I said. I hopped out of bed with the telephone still pressed against my ear. "I'm so sorry, Stacy. We're on our way." I disconnected the call, threw the telephone on the bed, and shook Malcolm's shoulder. "Malcolm, get up. We're late for the barbecue."

We quickly showered and dressed. I grabbed the sherbet from my freezer and the ginger ale from the refrigerator. Malcolm and I were out the door in less than thirty minutes.

Not only were Anastasia and Trevor hosting a July Fourth barbecue, but according to the number of cars parked on their street, all their neighbors were hosting barbecues as well. Malcolm and I had to park a block and a half away from the Anastasia and Trevor's house.

We got to the door and rang the bell. As soon as Trevor answered, he grabbed me and hugged me tight. But before I had a chance to introduce Malcolm, Trevor embarrassed me.

"Hey, dude, if you're lookin' for Ray Jr.," he said to Malcolm, "he lives next door."

I wanted to lie down and die right there on the front porch. Never in my thirty-four years of living on earth had I been so uncomfortable. For Trevor to assume that Malcolm wasn't my date and had chosen the wrong house proved to me that I must've looked way older than Malcolm.

After I wiped the egg from my face and composed myself, I said, "Um, Trevor, this is my friend Malcolm."

Trevor looked as bad as I felt. "Aw, man, dude," he said to Malcolm. "My bad."

I stepped into the foyer, and Malcolm followed. Once inside he shook Trevor's hand. "What's up, man?"

"It's all good, dude. Y'all come on in. The food is ready, and everybody's outside in the back."

We followed Trevor through the living room and dining room to the patio doors in the kitchen that opened to the deck. On the way, I looked over my shoulder and whispered to Malcolm, "Sorry about that."

He smiled slightly, then put his hand on my shoulder and gave it a squeeze to let me know he wasn't fazed. When we got to the kitchen, Trevor took the ginger ale and rainbow sherbet from me and placed them both in the freezer. When I slid the patio door open, the smell of burning charcoal filled my lungs. The first thing I saw was Anastasia sitting at a picnic table, bouncing Chantal on her knee.

I walked straight over to them. "Gimme my godbaby."

Anastasia stood and met Malcolm and me halfway. She put Chantal in my arms and extended her hand to Malcolm. "You must be Malcolm. I'm Stacy."

He shook her hand. "It's a pleasure, Stacy."

"Rhapsody has told me so much about you. Now I can finally put a face with the name."

"Rhapsody talks about you too," he confirmed.

The smile vanished from Stacy's face. "Yeah, I bet she does. I can imagine what she says. Are y'all hungry?"

"I'm not," I said, bouncing Chantal in my arms. She had gotten ahold of my beaded necklace.

"What about you, Malcolm?" Anastasia asked.

He shrugged his shoulders. "I could eat."

Anastasia led us farther into the backyard, where rib tips, spaghetti, potato salad, macaroni salad, deviled eggs, chips, and baked beans were spread across a picnic table buffet style. She helped Malcolm make his plate, and I took Chantal and sat down at a card table with Anastasia's aunt Margaret, her brother Darryl, and his wife, Sharlene.

"Hey, Miss Margaret," I greeted.

"Hi, sugar. I asked Stacy if you were coming over today."

"I had a late start this morning."

"What's up, girl? Long time no see," Darryl said to me. He and I used to mess around back in the day, when we were in our early twenties. In fact, I had aborted a fetus at Darryl's expense, one that he had helped plant inside me, when I was twenty-three years old. No one, absolutely no one, knew about Darryl and me. I had never even told Anastasia about the five-month-long affair I had had with her brother.

"Yeah, it's been a while, Darryl." I looked at his wife. "How're you doing, Sharlene?"

"I'm doing good, Rhapsody. I like those chandelier earrings. I see they're coming back in style."

Just as she mentioned my earrings, Chantal let go of my necklace and grabbed my right one. I had to peel her fingers away one by one.

Margaret laughed. "That li'l girl is quick and as busy as she wants to be."

Malcolm came over to the table with an overloaded plate. Chantal and I moved over when Anastasia brought an extra chair for him.

"Mama, Darryl, Sharlene, this is Malcolm. He's Rhapsody's date," Anastasia announced.

Trevor had made me realize that Malcolm actually looked twenty-one years old. I was waiting for a stunned look to appear on everyone's faces, but to my surprise, everyone was cool. I wondered if Anastasia had given them the heads-up before Malcolm and I arrived at the barbecue.

After Malcolm greeted everyone at the table, he looked at me. "You wanna eat with me?"

I glanced at the ribs and potato salad on his plate and felt my stomach turn. I shook my head from side to side. "No, baby. I'm not hungry."

He leaned into me and whispered in my ear, "You need to eat somethin'."

"I will in a little while, I promise."

The patio door opened, and Anastasia's nineteen-year-old cousin, Gabrielle, stepped out onto the deck, wearing red Daisy Dukes shorts and a red tube top that was stretched to the limit. Anastasia had mentioned that Gabrielle was home from college for the summer. I knew her to be a bona fide hoochie. As Gabrielle approached our table, I, along with everyone else, could see her black, round headlights through her top.

"Hey, y'all," she greeted.

"Uh, Gabby, you couldn't find anything else to wear today?" Margaret asked.

She looked down at her attire. "What's wrong with what I got on, Auntie?"

"What's *right* with it?" Darryl asked.

Gabrielle ignored Darryl and placed her eyeballs on Malcolm. "Hello."

Malcolm was engrossed in his food. He looked up at her. "Hi."

She smiled. "I'm Gabby."

Malcolm laid his fork down on his plate and extended his hand to her. "I'm Malcolm. It's nice to meet you."

Gabrielle shook Malcolm's hand but then held on to it and squeezed it. Malcolm withdrew his hand from her grasp and glanced at me.

"Hello, Gabrielle," I said, pulling her eyes away from Malcolm's bulging biceps.

She didn't even look at me when she said, "Oh, hey, Rhapsody. So, um, Malcolm, are you a friend of Darryl's?"

He swallowed his food like a gentleman before answering her. "Uh, nah. Uh, I'm here with Rhapsody."

That blew her away. Her eyebrows rose sky high. She looked from Malcolm to me. "Oh."

I sneered. *That's right, ho. So back your hot-to-trot behind up.*

"Who wants some frappé?" Anastasia yelled from the deck. I looked and saw that she had mixed the ingredients and had brought the frappé outside in a huge white Tupperware bowl. Trevor was behind her with a package of paper cups.

Everyone at the table raised their hands except me. Gabrielle sashayed her almost naked tail over to the food table. I knew I was gonna have to watch her.

"How're your parents, Rhapsody?" Margaret asked. She and my folks were neighbors back when Anastasia, Darryl, and I were children. I had met Anastasia and Darryl when they first came to spend the summer with their aunt Margaret. But she had moved shortly after I graduated from high school. Anastasia and I were already close friends at that point, so we stayed in touch and actually became best friends.

"They're good. Next Saturday they're cruising to the Bahamas to celebrate their fortieth wedding anniversary."

"That's wonderful. Be sure and say hello to them for me."

"I definitely will," I assured her.

Anastasia came and sat five cups of frappé on our table. Malcolm took one and sat it in front of me, and it didn't take Chantal long to try to claim it as her own.

"I don't want any frappé, Malcolm." I pushed the cup of frappé toward the center of the table, away from Chantal's reach.

Malcolm twirled a forkful of spaghetti and brought it to my lips. "Eat."

He wasn't gonna let up until I ate something, so I opened my mouth and accepted the spaghetti. I loved it. I finished his spaghetti, plus a serving of my own.

Trevor brought me a bottle of formula for Chantal. "You wanna give Chantal her bottle, Rhapsody, or should I take her?"

"No. You ain't takin' my godbaby from me." I took the bottle from Trevor's hands and fed Chantal. When she had finished her bottle, she collapsed in my arms.

Other relatives of Anastasia's had come to the barbecue, and Margaret, Darryl, and Sharlene were mingling with them.

Malcolm glanced at his wristwatch, then leaned back in his chair and put his hand on my knee. He exhaled. "It's about that time, boo."

I knew what he was referring to. "Time for what?"

Malcolm looked into my eyes. "For me to go home."

I looked at my wristwatch. "It's not even four o'clock yet." I wanted to keep him with me for as long as I could.

"Cherise said they'd be home around five thirty. I gotta be there to help Sean get my mother in the house."

"Who's Sean?"

"Sean is my brother-in-law. And don't forget I have to take you back home and get my things."

I admired Malcolm for being the man he was. Taking care of his mother was honorable, and I knew she needed

him, but heck, I needed him too. For the past week I had
gotten used to falling asleep in Malcolm's arms and waking up with my head lying against his chest. Kissing his
lips before we parted ways in the morning, going our
separate ways to work, returning home in the evenings,
having dinner, then making love all night had spoiled me.
His mother had had him for twenty-one years; now it was
my turn.

"I don't like this, Malcolm."

"You don't like what?"

"You leaving me," I whined. "I ain't ready for you to go."

"Well, what do you expect me to do, Rhapsody? You
know my mother's situation, and you know what my responsibility to her is."

"I understand all of that, but—"

He cut me off. "No, I don't think you do, 'cause if you
did, you wouldn't be sitting here, giving me a hard time
about what you already know I gotta do."

"Why can't your sister take care of your mother, or why
can't you put her in a home?" The words were out of my
mouth before I had a chance to stop them.

The expression on Malcolm's face confirmed what I
already knew. I had pissed him off royally. His two eyebrows suddenly turned into a unibrow. I'd never seen him
frown that way before. It was terrifying. Malcolm turned
his entire upper torso toward me and brought his face
extremely close to mine. "What did you just ask me?"

I kept my mouth closed because I knew I couldn't fix
what I had just said to him. But it seemed as though my
silence only added fuel to the fire I had lit.

"Let me tell you somethin', Rhapsody. Lucille Ella-Jean
Washington is my world. No one comes *before* her, and
no one *equals* her. Understand? My mother doesn't live
with me. I live with *her*. How can I put her out of her own
house? And I don't care what her condition is or how old

she gets. I'ma take care of her 'cause that's what a son does for his mama. If she lives to be one hundred and I have to change her diapers, that's what I'll do, 'cause she changed mine."

He continued. "And as far as Cherise goes, she does more than her share when it comes to taking care of our mother. She comes over every mornin' before work and bathes mama. Plus, Cherise gets her out of the house on the weekends." Malcolm poked himself in the chest and said, "But I'm the one living under Lucille's roof, so I gotta do what I gotta do, and you just have to accept that."

"Is that right?" I asked sarcastically. "Well, what if I told you that I didn't care about your responsibilities at home? I want you to stay with me."

Malcolm let out a small chuckle, which made me feel like a joke to him. "You know, Rhapsody, the way you say that, it almost sounds like you're saying, 'To hell with my mother.'"

I didn't say anything. I let my silence speak for me.

"I like you, Rhapsody. I really do. We got a good arrangement, but don't make me choose between you and my mother. Trust me, you don't wanna do that. Now, I'm gonna go and thank your friends for having us over, and then we're leaving."

Malcolm left me and the sleeping Chantal at the table.

During the drive back to my house, I didn't say a word to Malcolm. I kept my focus on the scenery outside as he drove.

He glanced over at me. "Oh, so now you got an attitude?"

I didn't even acknowledge him at all. Thirty minutes of silence had passed before Malcolm pulled into my driveway. I was out of the truck before the wheels came to a complete stop. I opened the front door, entered my house, and tried to slam the door shut behind me, but Malcolm was on my heels. He caught the door and forced it back open.

He followed me into the living room. "Rhapsody, what is your problem?"

"You are, butthole."

"Okay, you know what?" he said. "I'm just gonna grab my stuff and go."

Malcolm's duffel bag was on the floor by the door, next to an end table. When he bent down to grab it, I snatched it up and threw it farther into the living room.

"What did you do that for? You better chill, girl. I ain't got time for this. I told you I gotta meet my mother at the house."

"Screw your mother!" I spat out.

Malcolm's eyes grew wide, and out of reflex he raised the back of his hand to send me flying fifty miles an hour. His hand stopped in midair. He didn't say anything as he glared at me. Malcolm lowered his hand and looked deep into my eyes, like he was searching for the woman who had just uttered those horrible words to him. It couldn't be the woman whom he'd made love to countless times in the past week. And it certainly wasn't the woman whose dreadlocks he had held back while she puked her guts out. "I can't believe you said that to me." He walked toward the spot where I had thrown his duffel bag.

I started shaking uncontrollably. I knew I was wrong. "Malcolm, I'm sorry. I'm so sorry."

He picked up his duffel bag and tried to walk past me, but I blocked his way to the front door.

"Malcolm, baby, I'm sorry." Tears had started to run down my face. "I didn't mean to say that."

His nostrils swelled with each breath he took. His chest heaved up and down. "Move out of my way."

I put my hands on his shoulders. "Baby, please don't leave like this."

He stepped to his left, and I stepped to my right. He stepped to his right, and I stepped to my left.

"Move," he said sternly.

"I said I was sorry, Malcolm." My right shoulder jumped up and touched my right earlobe. I tried to suppress the second tic, but I couldn't. My shoulder jumped at my ear again. I looked like Michael Jackson and the zombies when they did that move in his *Michael Jackson's Thriller* video.

Malcolm frowned at me. "What is wrong with you? Move out of my way."

I was at his mercy, and for the life of me, I couldn't control my shoulder. "Can't . . ." *Tic.* "We . . ." *Tic.* "Just . . ." *Tic.* "Talk?"

Malcolm moved two steps back from me. "What the heck is wrong with you?"

Bad words wanted to escape me. My head and neck jerked back and forth, as though I was trying to keep from vomiting. *No, Jesus! No. No*, I prayed silently. *Tic, tic, tic.* "Please, God, don't let me . . ." *Tic.* "Say . . . " *Tic.* "It."

Malcolm frowned at me. "Girl, are you crazy?"

Tears spilled from my eyes.

"Your tears don't move me, Rhapsody, and I ain't falling for your craziness. Get outta of my way. I'm not gonna tell you again."

All my self-respect, self-esteem, self-control, and self-confidence vanished. I placed my face in my hands and sobbed like a newborn baby. "Please don't leave, Malcolm. I don't want you to go." I snatched his duffel bag from his hand, threw it on the floor, and sat on it. I looked at him and said, "You ain't goin' nowhere."

He looked down into my eyes and scolded me with his. "I'm about to go to jail."

"Can we make love before you go?" I was pitiful, and I knew it.

His lips didn't answer me. Malcolm pulled my right arm and flung me across the living room like I was as light as a sheet of paper. He grabbed his bag and walked out the front door.

I lay on the floor, crying after him. "Malcolm, Malcolm. Please don't go. I'm sorry. I'm sorry."

I got up and ran to the window and saw the Navigator backing out of the driveway. My mood of regret turned into anger at the thought that he had really left me. I ran into my bedroom and picked up the telephone and dialed 9-1-1. I was gonna report that my truck had been stolen.

"Nine-one-one. What's your emergency?" the operator asked.

I couldn't do it. Even though I was mad as heck, I couldn't do it. But I knew I had to say something before the police came to my door. "I'm sorry," I said. "I dialed by mistake."

"Do you need assistance, ma'am?"

"No, thank you. I was trying to dial four-one-one for information. I'm so sorry."

"Very well then," the operator said.

I placed the receiver on its base and threw the telephone across the bedroom. My body shook. "Bbbbbbastard! Bbbbbbbastard!" I stuttered and screamed. I felt my stomach rumble. I ran to the toilet and threw up the spaghetti I had eaten.

Chapter 28

On his way home, Malcolm went over the events that had taken place back at Rhapsody's house. He couldn't wrap his brain around her behavior. He understood that Rhapsody had been upset that he had to leave her. They had a week together, but he had a commitment to his mother. Malcolm thought back to Rhapsody's shoulder, head, and neck jerking. "What the heck was that about?" he asked himself aloud.

He remembered Rhapsody's words. *Please, God, don't let me . . . say . . . it.*

Malcolm shook his head from side to side. "That chick is kray kray."

Malcolm had a decision to make. After what had taken place at Anastasia's barbecue and at Rhapsody's house, he concluded that maybe it was best that he give the truck back to Rhapsody and go on about his business. The Navigator was nice, and he looked good driving it, but it wasn't worth the drama.

Malcolm's Navigator and Sean's GMC Yukon arrived at the house at the same time.

Outside of the Yukon, Sean stretched his legs. "What's up, man?" he greeted Malcolm.

"You got it. How was the drive?" Malcolm responded as he climbed out from behind the wheel.

"Long."

Malcolm walked to the front passenger side of the Yukon, carrying his duffel bag, and stood next to his sister,

Cherise. He opened the back door of the Yukon. "Welcome home, Lucy."

"You want me to kick your behind, Malcolm? I done told you about that 'Lucy' crap," his mother fussed.

Malcolm turned around and bent over. "Here it is. Go ahead and kick it."

Both Cherise and Sean laughed, but Lucille wasn't amused. "Don't laugh at him, y'all. He ain't funny." She looked at Malcolm, who was acting a fool. "Get me outta this van, boy."

Cherise unfolded Lucille's wheelchair and placed it next to Malcolm. He lifted his mother and carefully sat her in it. Lucille reached up and slapped his bald head.

"Ow, Mama!" Malcolm yelled. "What was that for?"

"For talkin' crap. I may not be able to kick, but I can still hit."

Cherise noticed the duffel bag that Malcolm had sat down next to his leg. "Where are you coming from with an overstuffed duffel bag?"

"A friend's house, not that it's any of *your* business."

"Is it the same friend that bought you that truck?" Lucille asked Malcolm. "Now, I dare you to tell me it ain't *my* business."

"Yes, it's the same friend. Now, if y'all are done interrogating me, can we go in the house?"

Cherise and Sean carried Lucille's luggage to the front door and kissed her good-bye.

"Bye, Mama," Cherise said.

"Bye, baby."

Cherise and Sean turned and headed back down the driveway, but Malcolm stopped Cherise before she got to the truck. "Hey, Cherise. You're on vacation this week, right?"

"Yep," she said happily.

"Can you take Mama to therapy in the morning?"

Before Cherise answered, Lucille spoke. "Why can't *you* take me?"

"Because I got a job interview in the morning."

"An interview where?" Cherise asked.

"Downtown, in the Loop. It's with the CTA."

"That's good, Malcolm," Cherise said. "The CTA pays top dollar. Okay, yeah, I'll take Mama to therapy in the mornin'."

The entire house reeked when Malcolm and Lucille entered.

"Whew. What the heck is that smell?" Lucille asked as soon as Malcolm wheeled her into the foyer.

"It's probably the garbage."

"Why didn't you take it out, Malcolm?"

"Ma, I ain't been home in a week."

"Well, take it out and open up some windows. Wash that can with pine oil before you put another plastic bag in it."

Malcolm wheeled his mother into her bedroom, set her luggage on top of the bed, and went to empty the garbage. When he returned, he saw Lucille unpacking her clothes. He plopped down on her bed.

"So, how was your trip?"

Lucille took blouses and Capri pants from the luggage and laid them on the bed. "I had a good time, Malcolm. Everyone asked about you. It's not every year that the Washingtons gather for a family reunion, but your great uncle, Jesse, is the oldest living uncle. You really should have gone to see him. His health isn't good. He's battling rheumatoid arthritis, he has osteoporosis, and he's in the early stages of dementia."

Malcolm nodded his head. "Yeah, I should've gone with you, Cherise, and Sean." When Lucille had told Malcolm that she was going to Memphis with Cherise and Sean, Malcolm had seen this as an opportunity to escape his curfew and had decided to spend the week with Rhapsody. "I remember when Cherise and I were little, you'd send us to Memphis for the whole summer. As soon as school let out, Cherise and I were on the Amtrak train, heading south. Uncle Jesse was always there to pick us up from the train station. He'd come with a bag full of candy too." Malcolm smiled at the thought. "Those were the good ole days."

Lucille wheeled herself to the dresser and pulled out the top drawer. In it she deposited nightgowns that she hadn't worn on her trip. "Well, maybe you'll get a chance to get to Memphis before Uncle Jesse slips further into the dementia, Malcolm. I know he'll be glad to see you."

"Yeah, I definitely gotta make that happen."

"So, where have you been for the past week?"

"I stayed at Rhapsody's house."

Lucille wheeled herself back to the suitcase on her bed and removed lotion and perfume bottles. She wheeled herself back over to the dresser and sat them on top. "Tell me about Rhapsody."

She's crazy, Malcolm thought to himself. "What do you wanna know?"

"Where does she live? Where does she work? And why haven't I met her?"

"Rhapsody works for the CTA, directing traffic. She owns a duplex in Oakbrook Terrace and—"

"Oakbrook Terrace?" Lucille shrieked. "She's got money like that?"

"She's single, with no kids, and she makes a nice penny."

"Humph. I guess she does if she can afford to live in Oakbrook Terrace and to buy that big truck she got you. What is *she* driving?" Lucille said.

"Rhapsody drives a Benz."

"My, my, my," Lucille said. She looked at Malcolm, who was lying across her bed. "Do you love her?"

He frowned. "Who?"

"Who are we talkin' about, Malcolm? Rhapsody. Do you love her?"

"I like her."

"Humph," Lucille said again. "Does she love *you*?"

"I don't think so."

"Well, why are y'all wasting each other's time? The sole purpose for two people getting together is to build a future with one another."

"Ma, our relationship is not a normal relationship. Rhapsody and I understand each other, and we have an agreement."

"Which is what, Malcolm?"

"We're friends, and that's all we are."

Lucille exhaled. "Can we get deep here?"

Malcolm rolled his eyes. "Here we go." He knew that when Lucille asked to get deep in a conversation, it usually meant it was lecture time. But that was one thing Malcolm loved about his mother; she always told it straight and never sugarcoated anything.

"Can we get deep or not, Malcolm?"

"Yeah, Ma. Go ahead." Malcolm grabbed one of Lucille's pillows and propped it up to support his head.

Lucille rolled her wheelchair closer to the bed. "When am I gonna meet Rhapsody?"

Malcolm shrugged his shoulders. "I don't know." After that day's episode, Malcolm felt that there wasn't a need for them to meet. Once he returned the truck to Rhapsody, he would wash his hands of her.

"Malcolm, listen to me," Lucille said. "When a woman buys an extremely expensive gift for a man within days of meeting him, it usually means she's fallen head over heels for him and considers him to be *more* than a friend. Friends don't get automobiles. They may get jewelry or clothes, but not something that equals the value of ten years' worth of mortgage payments. Let me ask you a question," Lucille said. "What would happen to your truck if you decided to end your 'friendship' with Rhapsody?" Lucille made quotation marks with her fingers.

"It would go back to her," Malcolm said calmly. He was more than willing to do it.

"And you're okay with that?"

"Yeah, Ma. I knew that before I accepted the truck from Rhapsody. I told you we understand each other."

"Well, let me ask you another question so that *I'll* understand. As long as you're screwin' her, you can keep the truck. Is that right?"

"Who says I'm screwin' her?"

"Boy, don't play with me. My common sense does. I ain't forgot about the scratches on your back. And no thirty-four-year-old woman buys a twenty-one-year-old man a truck that big and expensive unless he's making her toes curl."

Malcolm hollered out and laughed. "What do you know about curling toes? You got a li'l freak in you, Lucy?"

"How do you think your behind was created? I done had my toes curled a time or two," Lucille said.

Malcolm sat up. "Okay, this conversation is over. I don't wanna hear about you gettin' your freak on back in the day."

"*Back in the day?* Honey, your mama is still a freak *this* day."

He closed his eyes and covered his ears. "Oh, my God. No. Please tell me you're joking."

Lucille laughed. "What is your problem? I'm still young and desirable. If this wheelchair could talk."

Malcolm hopped off the bed. "Who is he? What's his name?" He demanded to know. "I'ma go find him and bust a cap in him. Who is he?"

Lucille saw that Malcolm had taken her seriously and was really upset. "Boy, sit back down. I ain't doing nothing but playing with you."

He sat down on the bed again. "Don't do that, okay? Don't play with me like that."

Lucille put her hand on her hip and looked at her son. "What if I *was* gettin' my freak on, Malcolm? Ain't nothing you can do about it."

Malcolm shook his head from side to side vigorously. "Uh-uh, you're my mama, and you ain't got no business doing that."

"I'ma ask the question again. How do you think *you* got here?"

"I don't care. That was twenty-one years ago."

"And?"

"You ain't supposed to be doing that kind of stuff."

Lucille decided to get him riled up again. "You mean like lying on my bed, moaning loud, and scratching a man's back like Rhapsody scratched up yours?"

Malcolm jumped up and ran out of her bedroom. "I can't take this. I'm outta here."

Lucille laughed until her stomach ached and tears ran down her cheeks.

Malcolm needed to get out of the house and away from his mother. He couldn't handle the thought of her having sex. He really hoped that Lucille was pulling his chain, like she had done so many times before. Often the two of them joked and played around and got under one another's collar. But his mother having sex was a topic of discussion that Malcolm refused to banter about.

He jumped into his truck, drove away from the curb, and dialed Ivan's cellular number.

"What's up, fool? I ain't heard from you in a week. You still playin' house?"

"Nah, man, that's been canceled," Malcolm replied.

"You sound like it was a bad experience."

"Ivan, do you remember the night we sat outside my house, talking, and you said Rhapsody could be a fatal attraction?"

"Yeah. That was the night she busted your car window with a tire iron."

"You were right, man. She *is* crazy. Rhapsody is straight from the twilight zone."

"What did she do *this* time?"

"Have you talked to Leticia since Saturday?"

"Yeah. She told me what went down at the nail shop."

"Man, that was some wild crap," Malcolm said. "But check *this* out. Today Rhapsody and I went to a barbecue at her partner in crime's house. All week she knew that my mother was coming home this evening and that I needed to be home to help Sean get her in the house. So, around four o'clock this afternoon, I told Rhapsody it was time for us to leave the barbecue 'cause I had to take her back home, get my stuff, then go home and meet Mama. She goes off and says that she didn't want me to leave and that she didn't care what my responsibilities to my mother were."

"That's bold," Ivan said.

"You ain't heard the bold part yet. She had the gall to suggest that I put my mama in a senior citizens' home."

"What?" Ivan shrieked.

"Yeah, man, can you believe that? So, anyway, we rode back to her house in complete silence. When I reached for my duffel bag, she took it and threw it across the living room. But I didn't trip. I just went to get the bag and reminded her I had to go home and meet my mother. You'll never guess what she said to me next."

Ivan was on the other end of the telephone line, on the edge of his seat. "Tell me."

"She said, 'Screw your mother!'"

Ivan's mouth fell open. "She said *what*?"

"You heard me."

"I shouldn't be surprised, 'cause that's what she said to me the first time she saw me at Mr. G's. Remember?"

"Yeah, I do. She snatched my duffel bag out of my hand and sat on it to keep me from leaving. I told her that if I had to tell her again to give me my stuff, I was going to jail."

"What did she say when you told her that?"

"She asked if I could screw her before I left."

"Man, you gotta be lying, Malcolm."

"Nope, I ain't lying. That's how crazy Rhapsody is. She was shaking and jerking and saying crazy stuff, man. She's really loony."

"You ain't telling me nothing I didn't already know. I think she's bipolar. Where are you?"

"Man, I'm just out here, driving around. I had to get out of the house 'cause Mama was talking a bunch of yin yang I didn't wanna hear. You wanna go shoot some hoops?"

"Nah, man. I'm on my way to Leticia's house."

"A'ight then. I'll holla," Malcolm said.

"Peace."

Malcolm ended the call with Ivan, then dialed Sharonda's number.

"I knew I would hear from you today," she answered.

Malcolm smiled. "Is that right?"

"Uh-huh. What are you doing?"

"Thinkin' about you."

"Where are you?"

Malcolm turned left at the next corner. "If you're home right now, I could be en route to your house."

"For what?" she asked.

"For whatever. Is it a problem?"

"Nah, it ain't a problem," Sharonda said. "Did I leave my pink scarf in your truck?"

"Yeah, and I almost got killed about that."

She laughed. "Aw, did your granny find it?" Sharonda mocked the age difference between Malcolm and Rhapsody.

"Heck, yeah, she found it."

"What did she do with it?"

"Let's just say I'ma have to buy you another one."

"You let that broad cut up my scarf, didn't you, Malcolm?"

"I didn't *let* Rhapsody do it. She just did it. And that was after I lied and said the scarf belonged to my mother."

"Malcolm, that scarf was a Donna Karan original, and it cost me eighty-six dollars."

"Sharonda, I promise to buy you another one when I get paid next week. Okay?"

"No, it ain't okay."

"Look, Sharonda, I was in a good mood, but you're messin' that up right now. I said I'ma buy you another scarf next week. What else do you want me to do?"

"Let me beat you in a game of naked Twister," she teased.

"Where are your folks?"

"They're out and won't be home for a while."

Malcolm pressed down on the gas pedal. "Set the game up. I'll be there in fifteen minutes."

Chapter 29

By 9:00 p.m. I was a basket case. Malcolm had been gone for only five hours, but it felt more like five years. I lay across my bed, clutching the pillow he had slept on for the past seven nights against my chest. Every few minutes I'd sniff it to remind myself what he smelled like. I had vomited twice since I'd come from Anastasia's house. The ground turkey she'd used to make the spaghetti was probably spoiled.

I turned to lie on my back and stared up at the ceiling. I counted the lines of shadow up there from the glow of the streetlight peeking through my mini-blinds. I decided to call Malcolm. I needed to make things right between us. I wanted to let him know that I was wrong for the things I had said about his mother.

I was reaching for the telephone on my nightstand when it rang. I got nervous for a second, wondering if it was Malcolm calling to tell me that what we had was over and that he would return the Navigator to me. The caller ID showed Trevor Baker, and I let out a small sigh of relief.

"Hey, Stacy," I answered.

"Are you asleep?"

"No, just lyin' here in the bed, thinking."

"About what?"

"Malcolm. He went back home."

"When he said good-bye to Trevor and me at the barbecue, he seemed a li'l upset."

That's puttin' it mildly, I thought.

"Trevor told me what happened when he met y'all at the door . . . that he had mistaken Malcolm for one of our young neighbors' friends. Is that what was bothering Malcolm?"

"No, he was cool about that," I said. "We had words when he told me he was ready to leave the barbecue."

"Well, why did he wanna leave?"

"His mother had gone to Memphis for the holiday. She was due back this evening. Malcolm needed to be there to help his sister and brother-in-law get her into the house, but I wasn't ready for him to go just yet, and I told him that."

"I don't understand," Anastasia said.

"What don't you understand?"

"Last Friday you called me, all excited and giddy, and said that Malcolm was coming to play house with you 'cause his mother was going away for a week. You told me that he needed to be home when she returned to help get her into the house. So, what I don't understand, Rhapsody, is why you would try to keep Malcolm from doing what you already knew he had to do. Not only was that selfish of you, but it was also kinda childish, don't you think?"

I frowned. "Childish?"

"Yes, childish. Malcolm had already been with you for a week."

"It wasn't long enough," I said.

"Well, it should've been. Malcolm had already told you where he needed to be this evening."

"I don't see why his brother-in-law, Sean, couldn't get his mother in the house."

"Because she isn't *Sean's* mother, Rhapsody. She's *Malcolm's* mother. I'm sure Sean was there to assist, but it isn't his responsibility to aid Malcolm's mother." Anastasia chuckled sarcastically, then said, "I mean, I really can't believe I have to break this down for you."

"Malcolm's sister, Cherise, was there too, Stacy. How many folks does it take to lift a woman in a wheelchair?"

"Oh, my God. You're ignorant," my very best friend said to me. "Cherise probably can't lift her mother from the car and get her up the porch stairs. It takes a strong man to do that." Anastasia decided to use reverse psychology on me. "Let me ask you a question. What if Lerlean was confined to a wheelchair and needed you to bathe and dress her? You think it would be right for Danny's girl-friend, Antoinette, to do those things for your mother in-stead of you?"

I thought about that. "Antoinette loves my mother, and I know she'd be willing to do whatever she can for Ler-lean, but I wouldn't feel right. Lerlean is *my* mother, and I'm her only daughter, so of course I'd be the one to do those things for her, not Antoinette."

"Humph. I didn't think you would be able to do it, but you did."

I was confused. "What did I do?"

"You put yourself in Malcolm's shoes. Yeah, Sean could've lifted and carried Malcolm's mother, but how do you think it would make Malcolm feel? He would've felt just like you would've when it comes to Antoinette caring for Lerlean. Just like you're Lerlean's only daugh-ter, Malcolm is his mother's only son. You were wrong, Rhapsody."

I felt like a complete idiot. I had admitted to myself that I was wrong for the things I had said to Malcolm about his mother. But talking with Anastasia made me realize that I was also wrong for trying to get him to stay with me when I knew his mother needed him.

"Stacy, you are so right. I was selfish today, and I really need to call Malcolm."

"You're gonna apologize?"

"Not only *that*, but I just remembered he has a job interview in the morning. He and his boys got high yesterday, and Malcolm has to pee in a cup."

"Can he postpone the interview?"

"Nah. He ain't gotta do that. I know a way he can pass the urine test."

"What way is that?"

"I'll explain it to you tomorrow. I gotta call Malcolm right now."

Malcolm's cell phone rang seven times before he answered. "What's up?" he said very dryly. By the tone of his voice, I knew he was still pissed at me. If I wanted Malcolm's forgiveness, I knew I would have to beg my butt off, and I knew I had to sound sincere.

I took a deep breath, let it out, and said, "I'm sorry for acting like a fool and for being selfish today. And I'm really sorry for what I said about your mother. I was out of control, and I was way out of order. We had a great week together, but instead of being grateful, I behaved like a spoiled brat. I truly understand why you needed to be home to meet your mother. I had no right to try to keep you from being where you needed to be. I was wrong, Malcolm, and again, I am so sorry." I hoped those words were good enough, 'cause I meant them wholeheartedly.

There was a long pregnant pause before he spoke. I guessed he wasn't expecting me to say what I said. I could hear him thinking. "Okay."

That wasn't the response I had been bracing myself for. I was ready for him to let me have it. Had Malcolm said such nasty words to me about my mother, there wouldn't have been any forgiveness. I had given him just cause to cut me off and bring the Navigator back to me. I didn't know how to read his response. I needed clarity. "So, are we cool?"

"I don't know yet."

I had to accept that from him. At least he hadn't cussed me out or written me off, not yet, anyway. I knew I could still work on him. "You gotta take a piss test in the morning."

"Yeah, I know," he said. "I smoked some weed yesterday. I should probably call your friend and cancel. You think she'll let me come in a month?"

"Wait a minute, Malcolm. You knew you had an interview scheduled for tomorrow. Why would you do something so stupid? Marijuana stays in your system for six months. And an interview with the CTA is hard to get." I sighed. "Be here at my house at six in the morning, and I'll tell you what you need to do to pass the urine test."

"Are you going with me?"

"No. I have a doctor's appointment in the morning, before work. Mr. Duncan will be back from vacation. Make sure to wear briefs tomorrow, no boxers."

"Why?"

"You'll find out when you get here."

Chapter 30

Early Tuesday morning I turned the water off, pulled the shower curtain back, and screamed at the top of my lungs when I saw Malcolm leaning against my bathroom sink.

"What the heck are you screaming for?"

"What the heck are you standing in here for? Why didn't you tell me you were here?"

He scanned my naked body. "You look good when you're wet."

I pulled a large towel from the rack next to the shower, covered myself, and stepped out of the tub. Malcolm watched as I dried myself off.

He looked so fine dressed in a charcoal-gray pin-striped suit, an ivory silk shirt, and an ivory silk necktie. It looked like one of the suits that Eddie Murphy and Richard Pryor wore in *Harlem Nights*. I looked down at Malcolm's feet and saw Bill Blass gray silk shoes.

"You're a bit overdressed, but I guess it's okay."

"I didn't know what to wear but figured I couldn't go wrong with a suit."

I nodded my head. "There's a condom on my night-stand. Get it and bring it to me."

"What for?"

"Just do it, Malcolm."

He fetched the condom and brought it to me. I finished drying myself off and hung the damp towel back on the rack.

"Take it out of the package," I instructed him.

I had a small measuring cup with a spout on it sitting on top of the sink. I picked it up and straddled my toilet and squatted halfway down.

Malcolm frowned at me. "What are you doing?"

"Making sure your piss test turns out right." I held the cup between my legs and peed in it. I was happy to finally be able to relieve my bladder. "Whew. I've been holding that since I got up this morning."

I instructed Malcolm to stretch open the rim of the condom over the sink, and then I poured my urine into it. I emptied the cup and threw it into the trash can next to the tub. I opened my medicine cabinet and took out a sewing kit. I found a small spool of white thread and cut off about twelve inches of it, then tied the strand into a knot at the top of the condom.

"Pull your drawers down, Malcolm."

"Why can't I just carry the condom in my pocket?"

"Because the pee has to be body temperature, that's why. You can't give them a cup of cold pee, Malcolm. I know what I'm doing, okay?"

He pulled his pants and underwear down to his knees. I knelt before Malcolm and placed the urine-filled condom between his testicles and inner thigh. "The hem of your drawers will keep it in place. How does it feel?"

"It's okay," he answered as he pulled his clothes up.

"Try not to walk too fast, so that the condom doesn't shift. A doctor will give you a cup to pee in. When you pour the pee in the cup, be careful not to spill any. Flush the condom and string and make absolutely sure they don't float back up. Stand there and watch them go down the toilet, and then flush it again."

Chapter 31

I signed in at the receptionist's desk at the Loyola University Medical Center in Maywood. "I'm Rhapsody Blue, and I have an eight-thirty appointment with Dr. Scimeca," I told the receptionist.

"Yes, Miss Blue. I'll let the doctor know you're here." After she took my ten-dollar co-payment from my hand, she pointed to a row of chairs behind me. "Please have a seat."

I sat and noticed that I was the only patient waiting to be seen. I saw magazines lying across the table in front of me and picked up the latest issue of *New Parents* magazine. I scanned through the first few pages before I came to an article about breast-feeding. A color photo showed a black woman nursing her baby. I wasn't really sure why, but for some reason, I felt a connection to the photo. I saw how the baby attached his small lips to the mother's nipple and suckled. I wondered if I'd ever get the chance to breast-feed my own baby.

A nurse snapped me out of my thought. "Miss Blue?"

I looked up at her.

She smiled. "Dr. Scimeca is ready to see you."

The nurse escorted me through a door that led to many examination rooms. Outside of the room where my exam was to take place was a scale. The nurse instructed me to remove my shoes and step on it. I saw that I weighed 179 pounds. I stood five feet two inches tall, which meant I was short and fat. I picked up my shoes and followed the nurse into the room. I sat on the examination table, and she noted my weight in my chart.

Miss Blue, you're overweight," she said to me.

"I know that!" I snapped. "I got mirrors in my house. I can see what I look like."

Her eyes bucked out of her head at my tone. "Excuse me?"

"What has my weight got to do with my Pap test?" I asked her.

"Miss Blue, it's standard procedure that we record your weight and blood pressure."

"Well, recording them and telling me about them are two different things. I'm not here for a weight consultation. So, just take my blood pressure, write it down, and send Dr. Scimeca in here to examine me. And tell him to hurry up, because I'm running late for work."

The nurse realized I was ignorant, so she stopped talking to me, which worked just fine for me. In silence she took my blood pressure and my pulse. After that she inserted a small white plastic thermometer under my tongue. She then flashed the light from a tiny silver flashlight that looked like an ink pen in both of my eyes to look for whatever. The thermometer in my mouth beeped, and she gently pulled it out of my mouth and recorded my temperature in a logbook she held in her hand.

From a cabinet next to the table I was sitting on, she removed a hospital gown and laid it on the examination table, next to my leg. Without looking at me, she said, "The opening goes in the back." She walked out and slammed the door behind her.

"Screw you too, ho!" I said loudly to make sure she heard me.

Ten minutes later Dr. Scimeca brought his old wrinkled behind into the room with my chart in his hand. He did my Pap test every year. Dr. Scimeca had delivered all three of my mother's children. Walter, the oldest, was almost forty years old. Dr. Scimeca should be about ready to retire.

"Hello, Rhapsody. It's good to see you," he greeted.

"Hi, Dr. Scimeca. How are you?"

"I'm doing well. Thank you."

"How's the wife?" I asked.

"Barbara's fine. We welcomed our sixth grandson last Friday. Our youngest daughter, Jen, announced her engagement a month ago. Our oldest boy, Bill, is in his last year of law school. My middle boy—"

I didn't have time for what he was talkin' about. "Uh, excuse me, Doctor Scimeca. I would really love to hear about Barbara and Jen and Bill and the descendants of the Scimeca clan, but time won't permit it. I gotta get to work. Can we please get on with my exam?"

"Oh, sure, sure," he said as he walked over to a table and laid his chart on it. "Please forgive me. I do that all the time."

I knew the routine, so I lay back on the examination table and scooted my butt all the way to the end.

Dr. Scimeca placed my feet in the stirrups, sat on a stool in front of me, then spread my legs wide apart. "My goodness, you have quite a discharge here. Are you always this way?" he asked me.

"Only when I'm close to my period."

He inserted something long and cold inside of me. "When *was* your last period?"

"About six weeks ago."

Dr. Scimeca stopped what he was doing and looked up at me. "Six weeks? You haven't had a period in six weeks?"

"It could be four weeks. I don't keep up with it. It comes whenever it comes."

He went back to what he was doing. "Are you on any birth control?"

"No."

"Are you active?"

I hesitated. "Yes, but with only one man."

He continued my exam in silence. When it was over, Dr. Scimeca gave me a clear plastic cup from the same cabinet that housed the hospital gowns, and sent me to the bathroom to fill it. When I got back to my examination room, a different nurse received the urine-filled cup from me. Dr. Scimeca was completing his notes on his chart. He told me to get dressed and then said that he would return in ten minutes.

I had gotten dressed and was sitting on top of the examination table when Dr. Scimeca came back into the room.

"Doctor," I began. "I saw on the news the other day that there's a new pill on the market that women can take that'll only let them have their periods four times a year. Can you prescribe it for me?"

He looked at me. "That won't be necessary, Rhapsody."

"Why not?"

"Because you're pregnant."

My heart skipped a thousand beats. "Wha? Huh? Did . . . What?" I was so disoriented, I couldn't get any words out, and I couldn't see clearly. I shook my head vigorously from side to side. "Uh-uh. No way," I said to Dr. Scimeca. "That broad must've switched my pee with another woman's pee."

He frowned at me and chuckled at the same time. "What broad?"

"The first nurse that came in here. She had an attitude, and I gave her one right back. I know she's behind this. I want another test," I demanded.

"Rhapsody, to suggest that a staff member would do such a thing is ludicrous."

I was not leaving there without another test being taken. "I don't care. The urine test is wrong. I want you to draw my blood and test it."

Dr. Scimeca didn't argue with me. He stuck a needle in my arm and filled three vials with my blood. He told me to sit and wait, which I did, for another fifteen minutes. I knew I was extremely late getting to work and Mr. Duncan was probably wondering where I was, but I didn't care. I had to make this imaginary baby go away.

Dr. Scimeca came back and told me that my blood test was positive as well.

"But I've been having sex with Malcolm for only two weeks," I said to Dr. Scimeca. Before Malcolm, I had gone three months without having sex with an actual man. But I did have plenty of toys that I had entertained myself with.

"Rhapsody, with today's technology, a pregnancy can be detected within twenty-four hours after conception."

No matter how tightly I squeezed my butt muscles together, I couldn't control it. I pooped on myself right then and there.

I left Dr. Scimeca's office with stains on my panties and a prescription for prenatal vitamins. I couldn't believe it. Over the past two weeks, Malcolm and I had screwed like rabbits, but it had never dawned on me that I could or would get pregnant. I had got so caught up on how good Malcolm made me feel that I had totally dismissed the fact that he could also make me pregnant. At thirty-four, I didn't wanna be a single mother, and Malcolm was just a kid himself. I knew he'd go through the roof when I told him.

Chapter 32

"So, you basically wanna get away from the whole fast-food thing, huh?" Audelia asked Malcolm.

He nodded his head. "There's no money in it. It's time for me to change my career goals."

"What would you like to do here at the CTA?"

Malcolm shrugged his shoulders. "I don't know. Maybe drive a bus?"

Audelia nodded her head. "The starting pay for bus drivers is about nineteen dollars an hour."

Malcolm became excited, but he didn't want to show Audelia his emotions. Nineteen dollars an hour was way more than he had ever imagined he'd make. As a manager at Burger World, Malcolm was paid only $14.75 an hour.

"In about four years," Audelia continued, "you'd reach full pay of up to twenty-eight dollars an hour."

He tried with all his might to keep his composure, but Audelia was blowing Malcolm's mind big-time. "That sounds cool," he said calmly.

"But you're gonna need your CDL license. Do you have one already?"

"No, but I'll get it. That ain't a problem."

Audelia smiled at him. "I like you Malcolm, and since I owe Rhapsody a favor, I'm going to forgo all the written tests. But you must take *and* pass a urine test. After that, you'll be taken to Dan Pontrelli's office. Dan is our job placement coordinator. He'll give you your test results and get you on the payroll as a full-time bus driver after you secure a CDL license. Any questions?"

That was music to Malcolm's ears. The fact that he didn't need to take any written tests was great. Rhapsody had made sure the drug test wouldn't be a problem. All he needed to do was get a CDL license and he would be on his way to making big money. "Nope, no questions at all."

Audelia pressed her intercom button, and her secretary was there in moments. "Please escort Mr. Washington to the examination area," Audelia instructed the secretary.

Before he left her office, Audelia shook Malcolm's hand. "Welcome to the Chicago Transit Authority family, Malcolm."

He took her hand in his own. "Thank you. Thank you very much."

After following Rhapsody's instructions exactly the way she had said, Malcolm was asked to sit in the lobby and wait. He would have never guessed that getting a job with the Chicago Transit Authority would be so easy. It really paid to have a hookup.

It took less than eight minutes for the results of Malcolm's urine test to come back from the laboratory. In his office Dan Pontrelli offered Malcolm a seat across from his desk.

"Mr. Washington," Dan said, "your test results showed no sign of drugs, which is great, but there's one problem."

Malcolm frowned and looked concerned. Everything had been working out perfectly. What could have gone wrong? "What's that?"

"You're pregnant."

Chapter 33

No sooner had I got in the car than my cellular telephone rang. I saw it was Malcolm calling, and my heart raced. I nervously answered. "Hello, Malcolm."

"Hey." He sounded like how I felt.

"You don't sound too good. How did the interview go?"

"The interview with Audelia went great."

I was glad to hear Malcolm's good news before I gave him my bad news. "Wonderful. So when do you start, and what are you gonna be doing?"

"Are you still at the doctor's office?" he asked me.

I started my engine. "I'm leaving just now. I'm going home."

"You're not going to work?"

"No."

"Why?" he asked.

"I just don't feel like going." I couldn't go to work with poop in my panties.

"How did your exam go this morning?"

"It went okay."

"Did your doctor run other tests?"

I took my foot off the brake pedal and sat still. *Could he know?* "Other tests like what?"

"Did you tell your doctor that you were throwing up over the weekend?"

My palms became sweaty. He had to know, but how could he? "Malcolm, why are you asking so many questions? I wanna talk about your interview."

"I'm on my way to your house. I'll see you there." He disconnected the call.

I sat in the driver's seat and tried to figure Malcolm out. Why had he asked so many questions about my appointment? Something was up, and it made my stomach rumble. I felt the contents of my stomach coming up. I opened the door and puked on the concrete in the parking lot.

I got on Interstate 290 and headed home. I called my boss on the way.

"Hello, Mr. Duncan. Welcome back," I greeted.

"Hi, Rhapsody. Are you stuck in traffic?"

"No, I'm headed back home. I won't be in today. I woke up pregnant this morning."

"Pregnant?"

"Yeah. I just found out at the doctor's office, Mr. Duncan. I need the day off to process it. But I'll definitely be in tomorrow."

"So, I guess congratulations are in order."

I exhaled. "I don't know about that. Maybe they are. Maybe they're not. It depends on how my baby's daddy will receive the news."

I ended the call with Mr. Duncan just as I was turning onto my street. I saw Malcolm's truck parked in my driveway. When I exited my car, I noticed him sitting behind the wheel, smoking a cigarette. I walked over to him.

"Why are you smoking a cigarette?"

"My bad," he said and looked at me. "A cigar would be more appropriate for the occasion, huh?"

I hung my head, then looked up at him. "How did you find out?"

Malcolm started to speak, but I cut him off.

"Not out here. Come on in the house."

We went inside, and I headed straight for the bathroom. I stripped and showered. After the shower, I put my soiled clothes in the washing machine. I put on my blue terry-cloth robe and slipped into the matching slippers. I walked in the kitchen and saw Malcolm slouched down in a chair at the table.

"You know that pee you gave me?" he asked me. "It was pregnant pee."

So, that's how he knows. I leaned back against the kitchen sink and folded my arms across my chest. "Oh, my God. The urine test. What did Audelia say?"

"Besides the fact that she was pissed, because she thought we tried to get one over on her, she was cool. She told me to come back and see her in a year. She wants you to give her a call."

I went and sat on his lap. "I'm sorry."

Malcolm wrapped his arms around my waist and pulled me closer to him. "I just kissed nineteen dollars an hour away. It ain't your fault, though. We just like to screw, that's all. But it's cool," he said to me. "I ain't gonna let you go through this by yourself. I'ma hang with you every step of the way. And I don't want you to pay for nothing. I'ma handle this myself."

When Malcolm said, "I ain't gonna let you go through this by yourself," I thought he meant being by my side, holding my hair away from my face, while I puked my guts out and running to the convenient store in the middle of the night to satisfy my cravings. And when he said, "I'ma hang with you every step of the way," I thought he meant supporting my heavy thighs when I held them open during delivery and coaching me on breathing correctly, the way we would have learned in the Lamaze classes. But he threw me for a loop when he said, "I don't want you to pay for nothing. I'ma handle this myself."

I had 100 percent medical insurance coverage through my job. I didn't have to pay for the prenatal care, and neither did Malcolm, so what was he talking about?

"You're gonna handle what by yourself?"

He looked at me. "You know."

I looked right back at him. "No I don't. What are you talking about handling?"

"The abortion, Rhapsody. It's *my* responsibility, not yours."

I stood slowly because I didn't wanna make myself dizzy. "There won't be an abortion, Malcolm."

He looked at me like I had just told him that grape-flavored Kool-Aid had been discontinued.

"What?"

"You heard what I said. I'm not having an abortion."

He stood up. "Why not?"

I raised the tone of my voice to match Malcolm's. "Why would I?"

"I'm not ready to be a daddy. I don't make enough money to take care of a baby. Why would you put me in this position?"

"Because I'm too old to have an abortion, Malcolm. I may not have another chance to have a baby."

"Rhapsody, you can't be serious about this. What am I gonna do with a baby? I can barely take care of myself."

"Look, Malcolm, I'm having this baby. Whether or not you choose to be in your child's life is up to you, but the fetus that's growing inside of me is a keeper."

Malcolm turned from me and left the kitchen. "This is jacked up."

I followed him to the front door. "Where are you going?"

He stopped, looked at me, and raised his voice when he said, "You're keeping tabs on me now? Just because you're pregnant, you feel you gotta know my every move?"

I remained calm, because I understood the news of my pregnancy was a shock to him, but I wasn't gonna tolerate any disrespect from Malcolm. "Look, Malcolm, I don't care where you go, but you better lower your voice. I just thought we could go get a bite to eat and talk about this."

He shrugged his shoulders. "What's to talk about? You already said what you were gonna do, so I ain't got nothing else to say." He walked out and slammed my door behind him.

I went into my bedroom and lay across the bed. I guessed I could understand why Malcolm felt the way he did. He was young. Life, for him, was just beginning. I couldn't blame him for not wanting to be tied down, but my maternal clock was ticking loud as heck. I hadn't purposely set out to get pregnant, especially by someone who had to be in the house before the streetlights came on, but, hey, crap happened to a lot of people. I couldn't let the fact that Malcolm had walked out on me and my baby upset me. I had to be healthy.

As I lay there on the bed, I suddenly felt drowsy, and at some point I gave in to sleep. I had a dream so vivid, it felt real.

Malcolm returned at 5:00 p.m. Tuesday evening. He came into my bedroom and sat on my bed. He put his hand on my leg, which stirred me.

I opened my eyes and looked at him. "Hey."

In his hand were his keys to my house and the Navigator. He held them out for me to take, but I didn't wanna touch them.

"I can't do this, Rhapsody."

I sat up on the bed. "What are you saying? You wanna end our relationship because I won't get an abortion?"

"What relationship? We don't have a relationship. All we do is screw and fight."

I was at a loss for words. I couldn't think of a single word to say to Malcolm. He laid the keys on the bed, next to me, and stood. From his interior jacket pocket, Malcolm withdrew a folded sheet of paper and gave it to me.

I took it. "What's this?" I unfolded it and darn near screamed at what I saw. I was holding a marriage certificate bearing the names Sharonda Taylor and Malcolm Washington. According to the date and time on the certificate, they had gotten married at city hall two hours ago. My hands shook. "What is this, Malcolm?"

"I married Sharonda this afternoon."

"You're not ready to be a daddy, but you're ready to be a husband?"

"I felt it was the right thing to do."

I felt like I was talking to a total stranger. "How was marrying Sharonda the right thing to do?"

"Rhapsody, Sharonda is five months pregnant."

My eyes grew out of my head. Surely, I was being punked. There had to be a hidden camera in my bedroom, because there was no way this was happening for real.

"Five months? You don't wanna be a part of my baby's life, but you married Sharonda?"

"I'm in love with Sharonda, Rhapsody."

Malcolm left me completely stunned and horrified. He left me sitting on the bed and walked out my front door. I hopped out of bed and ran to the living room window just in time to see Malcolm get in on the passenger side of Sharonda's car. I saw her lean over and kiss him, then look toward my window and smile, like she could see me peeking through the vertical blinds. I ran to my bathroom, lifted the toilet seat, and emptied my stomach twice.

I woke up, drenched with sweat. My bedsheets were wringing wet, and my hair was matted all around my face. I looked at my digital clock on my nightstand. It was 5:15 p.m. I had slept the entire afternoon away. I searched my bed for Malcolm's keys, but they weren't next to me. I closed my eyes and silently thanked God that it was only a dream. I exhaled loudly and reached for the telephone on my nightstand and called Anastasia.

"Can you come to my house?" I sounded frantic, but I couldn't help it.

"Are you all right?" she asked me.

My voice shook. "No."

"I'm on my way."

Anastasia got to my house in record time. It was usually a forty-five-minute drive for her to get to me, but that time she did it in thirty minutes. She used her spare key, which I had given her years ago, and let herself in. I was sitting on my living room sofa, with my legs bent beneath me like a pretzel. Anastasia came and sat next to me.

After listening to me, she let her head fall backward on the headrest of my living room sofa and exhaled loudly. "Rhapsody, how in the world did you allow this to happen?"

"I don't know. I didn't plan on getting pregnant, Stacy. It just happened."

"That's some bullswanky, and you know it. If neither you nor Malcolm was using anything to prevent you from getting pregnant, it was planned. But I wanna know *why* you weren't using anything."

"Because whenever we get together, we never think about it."

"You mean, whenever you see each other, you tear your clothes off so fast that birth control is always the furthest thing from your minds."

"Something like that," I said.

"Humph," she said. "So, let's think about this a minute. Here we have a thirty-four-year-old woman who is pregnant by a twenty-one-year-old man who runs a hamburger joint and still lives with his mother. But now that the woman is pregnant, he wants nothing to do with her or the baby because he's not ready for parenthood."

I nodded my head, and Anastasia continued. "Another innocent soul comes into this drug-infested, overpopulated world without a daddy, and the mother is left to fend for the baby on her own."

Tears dripped onto my chest. I cracked a sorry smile. "Yep, that about sums it up."

I had honestly expected Anastasia to drill into my head how she had warned me not to get involved with Malcolm in the first place. But instead, she was the sister I needed her to be. Anastasia wrapped her arms around me and pulled me close. "It's gonna be okay, boo. I'll be your baby's daddy."

"I don't know, Stacy. Maybe I *should* get an abortion."

She pulled away and glared at me. "What?"

"I don't think I can do this on my own, and Malcolm—"

"Screw him!" she shouted. "You don't need him. You're a strong, independent black woman who can take care of herself. What's growing inside of you is a gift. I don't care how you made the baby. It's here now. Get yourself together, Rhapsody, and grow up, 'cause you have a huge responsibility on your hands."

Chapter 34

"Don't say a word to me," was the way I greeted my boss Wednesday morning.

Mr. Duncan sat behind his desk, looking at me as though I'd lost my mind. "Good morning to you too, Rhapsody."

I punched my time card and plopped down in my chair. "What's so good about it?"

He got up and brought me a beautiful mug he'd gotten in Jamaica. "You don't even deserve this, but I'll give it to you, anyway."

I loved the mug. I exhaled and looked up at him. "Thanks."

"I can see this is gonna be a long nine months," he said. "I don't know if this office is big enough for me, you, and your mood swings."

I looked into my boss's face and spoke as calmly as I possibly could. "If you don't say nothing to me for the next nine months, and you keep that toilet seat down, we won't have any problems."

He threw his hands in the air and went back to his desk.

I checked my morning report and was glad to see that no train or bus had been involved in an accident overnight and that the city of Chicago's public transportation system was running smoothly. My extension rang, and I answered the phone on the first ring.

"Good morning. You've reached the CTA's traffic room. This is Rhapsody. How may I help you?"

"Hi, Rhapsody. This is Audelia."

I was not ready to speak with her just yet. "Hi, Audelia. I was gonna call you today."

"You were?"

"Yeah. I want to apologize for what happened yesterday. Malcolm got high with his friends over the weekend, and I didn't want him to risk failing the urine test."

"Rhapsody, you should've called and told me. I probably could've gotten around him being tested." She paused, then said, "Um, you know you're pregnant, right?"

"Yep. I found out the same time Malcolm did. Audelia, I hope you didn't get into any trouble while looking out for Malcolm."

"Rhapsody, please. *I* run this office. Normally, we keep medical records and applications on file for a year, but I threw Malcolm's out. Have him come back to see me in six months, and I'll take care of him."

"Audelia, you are a godsend. Thank you so much."

"I know Malcolm's gonna be needing this pay with the baby coming and with you taking your six-week maternity leave. I can get him on the payroll just in the nick of time."

"We really appreciate everything, Audelia."

"Yeah, yeah, yeah. Don't look for a baby shower gift," she said and we ended the call.

Since the sole purpose of my job and Mr. Duncan's job was to redirect traffic in case of an accident, we really didn't have anything to do that day. And I wasn't about to sit up and look at him for eight hours. I grabbed my purse and keys. "Mr. Duncan, I'm gonna take a walk down Michigan Avenue. If anything jumps off, hit me on my cell, okay?"

"What if *I* wanted to go take a walk and enjoy the air?" he asked me.

I put my right hand on my right hip and shifted all my weight onto my right leg and glared at him. "Well, since both of us can't leave the office at the same time, because one of us has to answer the telephones, guess which one of us is staying? I'll give you a hint," I said. "It ain't me."

Without waiting for a response, I walked out of the office and slammed the door. I walked to the corner of Madison and Randolph Streets, where a Dunkin' Donuts shared its establishment with a Baskin-Robbins ice cream parlor. The aroma of dark roast coffee beans filled my nostrils as soon as I entered through the door. Yesterday Dr. Scimeca had warned me about drinking too much caffeine, because he knew I was a coffeeholic, but I didn't care. Without my coffee in the morning, I could be the devil's sister.

On the Dunkin' Donuts side of the café, I stood in line behind two men and waited my turn. It didn't take long for me to reach the counter and place my order for a medium coffee with extra cream and extra sugar. Because the thin red stirrers weren't strong enough to stir the sugar that settled in the bottom of my cup, I asked for one of the pink spoons that were given to customers who bought ice cream.

"Spoo fo I cree only," the man from Pakistan told me.

He spoke so fast that I couldn't understand. "Excuse me?"

"Buy I cree, get spoo. Spoo not fo coffee. Spoo fo I cree only."

Four people had come to stand in line behind me. "I don't want ice cream. I just want a spoon to stir my coffee."

The man pointed to the box of red stirrers that sat on the counter in front of me. "Stir coffee."

My temples started to throb, and while I massaged them, I looked at the Pakistani. "Sir, I just want a spoon. May I please have a spoon?"

By the many exhalations, I knew everyone standing in line behind me was getting frustrated, but, heck, so was I. I guessed the man behind the counter had got frustrated too, because he lost his patience with me and raised his voice. "I toe you. Buy I cree, get spoo!"

Immediately, I lost my self-restraint and raised my voice to match his pitch. "It's six thirty in the mornin'. Who in the heck do you think is gonna buy ice cream? Now, give me a spoon before I jump over this counter!"

He gave me two spoons.

With my coffee in my hand, I walked directly across the street to my favorite bakery and bought myself a cheese Danish. When I returned to the office, I saw a report on my desk that Mr. Duncan wanted me to scan through. I kindly moved it aside, set my breakfast in front of me, and bit into my Danish.

Mr. Duncan was sitting behind his desk, watching me. "Rhapsody?"

"What?" I asked nastily.

"Can you go through the report?"

"When I'm done eating."

"Are you taking an early lunch?"

Why was he getting on my nerves so early in the morning? I assumed he wanted to get cussed out. "Nah, I ain't taking an early lunch. I don't care what time of day it is. If I want to eat something, that's what I'm gonna do." I shoved the report aside again. "This doggone report ain't going nowhere, and if you're in such a hurry to get it done, then I suggest you look over it yourself."

For the next three hours, Mr. Duncan tried his best to keep from talking to me. At eleven thirty he asked if I wanted to order Chinese food for lunch. I declined, and he walked away from my desk like a good little boss. Just when I was about to make my way to the bathroom for what seemed like the fiftieth time, my extension rang.

"Good afternoon. You've reached the CTA's traffic room. This is Rhapsody. How may I help you?"

"Hi, baby girl."

I was so happy to hear her voice. "Hey, Ma."

"Your father and I got two more days till the cruise," she said excitedly.

"I know. You're excited, huh?"

"Yeah. We got so much stuff to take, we had to go out and buy another set of luggage."

"Are you taking your whole closet or what?"

"Well, we'll be gone for seven days, and I figured we'll change at least twice a day. The captain's ball is on Sunday night, and we have to dress formal for that. Your father has a tuxedo, and I'm wearing the royal blue gown that I wore to your cousin Sheila's wedding last year."

"That's a good choice. I like you in that dress. Make sure you and Daddy take lots and lots of pictures. How are you getting to the airport?"

"Walter will take us."

"You and Daddy have your passports?"

"Yep. We have everything."

"Okay, it sounds like you're ready. Have fun, let your hair down, and enjoy the moment. Cruises are awesome, Mama." I had been on a couple myself. "I want you and Daddy to have a great time and bring me back a whole bunch of stuff."

Lerlean laughed at me. "What kind of stuff?"

"Just stuff, and as soon as you get on the ship, send me a postcard."

"Okay. Well, I gotta go and pick up the refill of my arthritis medicine. I can't afford to leave that behind."

"I got to get my prescription too," I said without thinking.

"What prescription do you have to pick up? What's wrong with you?"

Shoot. I wasn't ready for her to find out yet. "Um, um . . ."

"Rhap . . . so . . . dy?"

Whenever Lerlean sang my name like that, I had to come clean with whatever I was trying to hide from her. I slowly inhaled, then exhaled. "Ma, I'm pregnant."

"What?" she shrieked.

"Yep, I'm pregnant. You'll finally become a nana."

I knew she wanted grandchildren, but I didn't know how she would take the fact that her unwed daughter, the youngest of three children, would be the first to give them to her.

"Oh, my God. Thank you, Jesus. Oh, thank you, Jesus," Lerlean squealed. "My very first grandbaby. I'm so happy, Rhapsody. When did you find out?"

Her acceptance was totally unexpected. "Yesterday."

"And you're just now telling me?"

"I'm not married, Ma, and I didn't want to upset you before your trip."

"Why would I be upset? I'm happy for you. But your father may be a different story. You know how he is about his baby girl."

"Yeah, I know. Don't tell him anything. I'll do it when you get back from the cruise."

"Who's the daddy?"

"A guy named Malcolm."

"I didn't know you were seeing anybody. When did you meet him?"

I hated to lie to my mother. But there was no way I could tell her I had met Malcolm two weeks ago and had probably gotten pregnant the same day I met him. "We've sorta had an on-again, off-again type of relationship for about eight months."

"Eight months and you haven't brought him around your family? Is he funny lookin'?"

I laughed. "No, Ma. I haven't met his family, either."

"Why not?"

"I guess the time hasn't been right."

"Rhapsody, your family and his family are about to share a baby. When *will* the time be right?"

"I don't know."

"Are you hiding something from me, baby girl?"

Yep, the fact that Malcolm is darn near a baby himself. "No, I ain't got nothing to hide."

"How far along are you?"

"Two weeks."

"Whew," she said. "You have a long way to go."

I sighed loudly. "Don't remind me. I wake up every morning with my face in my toilet."

"Get you some saltine crackers and sit them on your nightstand with a can of 7UP. As soon as you wake up in the morning, eat two crackers and drink a little of the 7UP. It'll settle your stomach, and you won't have the sickness."

"Ma, I have never heard of that before. Are you sure?"

"Girl, I had three babies. Just do what I tell you, and you'll be all right."

"Okay. I'll call you and Daddy tomorrow night, before you leave."

"You should come by the house this evening. I'll fry some catfish and make spaghetti."

"Ooh, that sounds good. You're gonna put your foot in it?"

She laughed. "I always do."

I drove up in front of my parents' house and saw that both of my brothers' cars were parked outside. I felt like putting the pedal to the metal and speeding away. I didn't wanna deal with Daniel and Walter. I hoped my mother had the catfish and spaghetti ready and she would allow me put some in a Tupperware bowl and leave.

I used my key, which I had had since I left home over ten years ago, and let myself in. I heard voices coming from the back of the house and assumed everyone had gathered in the kitchen. As I walked through the living room, I looked at all the family photos, including the childhood pictures of Daniel, Walter, and me, that my mother had kept throughout the years.

One particular picture of me drew my attention. It was my fourth grade class picture. I was smiling and was missing two front teeth. My hair was parted down the middle, with a twisted pigtail on each side. I picked up the picture and noticed how shiny my hair was. It took me back to the night before I had my class picture taken. Lerlean made me sit in the kitchen chair next to the stove while she pressed my hair with the green Ultra Sheen hair grease. I shivered because I could still hear the hot straightening comb sizzle when it touched the grease and got too close to my scalp.

"You see how ugly you were?"

I looked up and saw Walter standing in the dining room, cleaning the carcass of a piece of fried catfish.

I hollered toward the kitchen, "Mama, Walter is in your living room, eating a piece of fish."

"Walter!" she yelled. "Bring your greasy butt back in this kitchen. You know I don't like nobody eating in there."

"Ma, I ain't in the living room. I'm in the dining room," he hollered back at her.

"He's in the dining room now, Mama, but he *was* in the living room, sitting on your couch," I lied.

Lerlean came into the dining room with a broom in her hand and looked at Walter. "Boy, have you lost your mind? If you get fish grease on my furniture, I'll break this broom across your back."

"Mama, Rhapsody is in here lying on me," Walter complained. "You're gonna let her get away with that?"

Daniel came into the dining room. "Hasn't she always let her get away with everything?"

I sat the picture I was holding back on the table and went to kiss my mother's cheek, and then she and I went into the kitchen.

My folks had a big kitchen, the kind I wished I had in my house. My father was sitting at the table, eating a plate of catfish doused in Louisiana Hot Sauce and spaghetti. In a bowl, next to his plate, was a lettuce, tomato, and cucumber salad topped with French dressing, his favorite.

Mama went to the stove to prepare a plate for me, while Walter, Daniel, and I sat at the familiar kitchen table. It had been a long time since all of us had sat at that table together and had had dinner as a family.

I leaned over and kissed my daddy's cheek. "How ya doin', Daddy?"

He drank from a glass of grape Kool-Aid, then swallowed. "Hey, baby girl. How was work today?"

"Work was good," I said. "No accidents, so I was able to relax all day."

"I wish I could get paid for doing nothing. It must be nice," Walter said.

I gave that fool a sarcastic look. "Oh, it's very nice, but everybody can't have my luxury."

Lerlean sat a plate filled with two catfish fillets and a healthy portion of spaghetti in front of me. "Did you remember to get your pills?" she asked.

I looked up at her with bulging eyes, reminding her that right then was not the time to discuss my pregnancy.

Daniel caught the look in my eye and couldn't help himself. "What kind of pills are you taking?"

"Probably birth control pills," Walter answered for me.

My father almost dropped his fork. Even though I was fully grown, no man wanted to know about or even imagine his daughter having sex.

"Nah, they're the kind of pills to keep me from cussing y'all out."

Neither of my parents said a word. My father kept eating, while my mother stood at the kitchen sink, washing dishes. The looks on my brothers' faces was priceless.

"Daddy, did you hear what Rhapsody said to us?" Walter asked.

My father licked hot sauce off his fingers. "Uh-uh. What did she say?"

Daniel turned in his chair and tapped my mother's lower back. "Mama, did you hear what she said?"

"Yeah, I heard her."

My mother's nonchalant attitude was a surprise to Daniel. "And you ain't gonna say nothing to her?"

Lerlean turned around and looked at him. "What do you want me to say, Danny? If you and Walter stop messing with Rhapsody, she won't have to cuss."

I smiled to show my brothers that I still had what it took to win my parents over. It was something neither of them could ever do.

"I don't believe this bull—"

My father cut Walter's words off before he could finish his sentence. "You watch your mouth at this table, boy."

I laughed out loud. It was just like old times.

By 9:30 p.m. my brothers had left. My mother had gone to take a bath, and so my father walked me to the front door.

"Are you sick?" he asked.

"No, Daddy. I'm all right."

"What kind of pills are you taking?"

"Vitamins." I didn't lie.

"Regular vitamins?"

I had wanted to wait until after his cruise to confess to my father but figured that since he had asked, that was a good moment to come clean. I exhaled and blurted out the words, "They're prenatal vitamins, Daddy. I'm pregnant." I had hoped never to have to say those words without having a husband by my side.

If my father was disappointed, he didn't show it. He pulled me close to him. "Are you all right?"

Being wrapped in his arms made tears appear in my eyes. "Yeah, I'm okay."

"Who is he?"

"A guy named Malcolm."

"Where is he?"

"I don't know where he is right now. I haven't talked to him today."

"I want to meet him when I get back from vacation."

"Okay," I said, but I didn't think that was gonna be possible. Malcolm had made it clear that he wanted nothing to do with my baby or me.

I arrived home and found Malcolm's Lincoln Navigator parked in my driveway. The excitement I felt caused my heart to almost leap out of my chest. I prayed that his being there was a sign that he'd had a change of heart and decided to be a father to our child. I turned my key in the lock of the front door and pushed the door open. A string hanging from the ceiling in the foyer met me; a note was attached to it. I turned on the light and read the note.

I'm sorry. Come into the bedroom.

I smiled. I was as happy as a kid in a candy store. My bedroom was dimly lit, with candles burning on the dresser and the nightstand. Malcolm lay in the middle of my bed, wearing his birthday suit.

"It's about time you came home. I've been lying here for an hour."

It didn't even matter to me that Malcolm had walked out on me. I had my boo back, and that was all that mattered.

Chapter 35

I woke up early Thursday morning to find Malcolm gone. I hopped out of bed and headed for the shower, but not before I chewed two saltine crackers and swallowed half a can of 7Up. I loved my mother because she was very wise. She was right on the money about the crackers and soda. I felt no morning sickness whatsoever.

After my shower, I stood in my bedroom, facing the long mirror that hung on the back of the door. I studied my naked body and tried to imagine what it would look like in the months to come. I turned to the side to get a profile and stuck my belly out as far as it would go. I didn't like what I saw. It seemed as though my lower abdomen was already protruding, but at only two weeks, I knew it wasn't possible to be showing.

I shuddered at the thought of carrying around a whole watermelon. I thought of myself as being fat, but Malcolm said I was thick. To my knowledge, being fat was when you couldn't walk up a flight of stairs without busting a sweat, and that was me. Being fat was having on a pair of panty hose and folks could hear you approaching from a block away, and that was me also.

While I was driving to work, my cellular telephone rang and Anastasia's home number showed on my caller ID.

"Good morning. How are you feeling today?" she asked me.

"Really fat."

"Girl, you ain't even showin' yet."

"I *am*, Stacy."

"Rhapsody, you're not even a whole month pregnant. What are you showing?"

"I'm showing *fat*," I said irritably. "I looked at myself in the mirror this morning and almost cried. I don't think I can go through nine months of this."

"Well, it's too late for that kinda talk. You have no choice but to go through with it."

"Oh, I got a choice, all right. There's still time."

"What did I tell you about that? Just because Malcolm's dumb behind is acting crazy doesn't mean *you* have to act crazy."

"He apologized to me, Stacy."

"When?"

"Last night, when he came over. He was at my house when I got home from my parents' house."

"What was he doing there?"

"Lying in my bed, naked, waiting on me."

"To do what?" I knew she was vexed because her voice rose.

I didn't answer.

Anastasia exhaled loudly and paused a moment before she spoke. "Tell me you didn't do it, Rhapsody. Please tell me you didn't screw him."

My own voice rose because she was starting to get on my nerves. "Don't you screw Trevor?"

"Trevor is my husband!" she shouted back at me. "We are in holy matrimony. He pays my mortgage and car note. He buys my food and keeps my light, gas, and telephone on. He puts clothes on my back. He's my husband. I'm supposed to screw him. You, on the other hand, got played last night."

"Let you tell it," I said. "I'm gonna do whatever I have to do to keep Malcolm. Even if I have to pay."

"Pay?"

"You think Malcolm can afford the note on that truck he's driving, Stacy?"

That really pissed her off. "What?" she shrieked. "Girl, have you lost your darn mind? It's amazing to see how Malcolm can make you do this without puppet strings attached to your hands and feet."

"You really get on my doggone nerves, Stacy. You're so negative and always got something to say."

"That's because you keep doing crap you ain't got no business doing. And if you don't wanna hear the truth, then don't bother callin' and tellin' me anything about what you're doing." She disconnected the call, but I didn't care. I was tired of talking to her boojee behind, anyway.

I looked at the clock on my dashboard as I headed toward the Loop. It wasn't even seven o'clock yet, and already Anastasia had managed to screw up my day.

I was so irritated when I got to work, I didn't know what to do. But there was a God somewhere, because Mr. Duncan had come in early and had left a note on my desk, letting me know that he'd be in meetings all day. "Thank You, Jesus," I said out loud.

I sat at my desk and sorted through the interoffice mail. In one of the envelopes addressed to Mr. Duncan was a promotion the CTA was running for a trip to Cancún, Mexico. It was an all-inclusive package that included four nights and five days at a five-star resort and round-trip airfare for only $299.00 per person. A nonrefundable fifty-dollar deposit would reserve a suite with a view of the Caribbean Sea at the Caribe Real Resort Hotel.

I could really use a vacation, especially before the baby came. People always said that once you had kids, your life was over. I looked at the flyer again and saw how gorgeous the turquoise and blue water was in Cancún. Just as I was about to call Malcolm, my extension rang. I silently prayed that there hadn't been a bus accident or a train derailment. I exhaled and answered the phone.

"Good morning. You've reached the CTA's traffic room. This is Rhapsody. May I help you?"

"Hey, baby."

The sound of Malcolm's voice always soothed me. I smiled into the receiver. "Hey, boo. I was just about to call you. Are you at work?"

"Nah. I'm off. I have to take my mother to therapy today. What's up?"

"Do you have any vacation time?"

"I got a week coming to me. Why?"

"How soon can you take it?"

"Whenever I want."

"You got a passport?"

"Yep. I got it in my first year in college. Me, Ivan, and a few other students went to the Dominican for a week."

I glanced at the flyer I was holding in my hand. "The Dominican, huh? Well, how does Cancún, Mexico, sound?"

"It sounds good. Are we going?"

I smiled. "Yep."

"When?"

"How fast can you pack?"

I called the travel agent who was listed on the flyer and booked a suite for Malcolm and me at the Caribe Real Resort in Cancún. I charged $740.00 on my MasterCard. Since my bank account was low, I would have to use my credit cards and get cash advances. But it would be worth it. Our plane was scheduled to leave O'Hare International Airport at five o'clock the next morning. Our plane tickets would be waiting for us at the Southwest Airlines counter.

Mr. Duncan would have a cow when I told him that I was leaving town on such short notice, but he would be all right. With a baby coming, I might not have another chance to take a vacation. As soon as the travel agent gave me my reservation number, I called my boss's cellular phone.

"Didn't you get the note I left on your desk?" he asked irritably, like I had interrupted something important.

"Yeah, but I need to tell you something, Mr. Duncan."

"I'm in a meeting, Rhapsody. Can this wait till tomorrow?"

"I won't be here tomorrow. After today I'll be on vacation."

I heard him excuse himself from wherever he was. "What are you talking about?"

"I have three weeks of vacation time, and I'm taking one of them starting tomorrow."

"Rhapsody, you know the procedure for taking vacation time. You have to submit a request in writing at least one month prior."

"Apparently, you've misunderstood the purpose of my call, Mr. Duncan. I'm not asking for your permission. This is a courtesy call. I'm telling you what I'm going to do."

"I don't have anyone lined up to take your place."

I almost told him that I didn't care, but I held my piece. "I'm sure you'll figure something out. I ran this office all by myself while you were gone all last week. If I can do it, you can do it. Heck, you're the boss, not me."

"If that's the case, why are *you* telling *me* what you are and are not doing? I'm gonna have to write you up, because you're in violation of the rules."

I spoke very calmly to him. "Mr. Duncan, you can write me up, mail me up, or do whatever kinda *up* you wanna do. Oh, and I'm leaving at two o'clock today 'cause I got stuff to do."

"Two o'clock? You can't leave that early. Somebody has to be there to answer the phones."

"Then I suggest you hightail your behind back here, 'cause when this time clock strikes two, I'm out."

Without waiting for a response from him, I hung up the telephone. I did realize that I might not have a job when I returned from Cancún, but to be quite honest, I really didn't care.

"Hey, sweetness."

I turned around to see Willie Boston standing in the doorway.

"Good morning, Willie. What are you doing here?"

"I stopped by to see if you needed any more money."

"How much money you got?"

"How much do you want?"

I wondered if I could break even and have Willie cover what I had spent for Mexico. "About seven hundred dollars."

Willie pulled a wad of one-hundred-dollar bills from the front pocket of his work uniform pants. He unfolded seven of them and laid them on the table nearest him. I walked over to Willie, pulled him farther into the office, closed the door behind him, and locked us in. I picked up the money from the table and verified the amount. I folded the seven bills and placed them in my right bra cup.

"Of course, for *this* kind of money, the stakes are high," Willie said to me.

I closed the vertical blinds and let Willie have his way with me. When we were done, he said, "What will you let me do for a grand?"

"Do you *have* a grand?" Some extra spending money for Cancún would be great.

"I will in two weeks."

"Then come back in two weeks and find out."

Chapter 36

At four fifteen on Friday morning, Malcolm and I stood at the counter at Southwest Airlines. I gave the young clerk our passports. She took the documents from me but spoke to Malcolm, who was standing next to me.

"So, you're going to Cancún?"

"Yeah," he answered.

After comparing our names, she began to check our baggage, while at the same time admiring Malcolm's pectorals, which were bulging through his white tank top. "The weather is real hot down there, so be sure to use plenty of sunscreen."

This broad was acting as though I was invisible. She kept talking to Malcolm as she placed our baggage on the conveyor belt to be loaded onto our plane. "I wonder if it ever snows in Africa," she said directly to his chest.

I snapped at her, "What the heck are you talkin' about Africa for? Who gives a darn about snow in Africa? Just check the bags and shut up!"

The big-eyed broad got scared and didn't say another word.

Malcolm looked at me and shook his head from side to side. "Rhapsody, must you act a fool everywhere you go?" he asked as we walked toward the boarding gate.

"She was flirting with you. What do we care about snow in Africa? We're going to Mexico."

"She was just doing her job."

"Well, she needs to learn how to do it with her mouth shut."

"I know you ain't jealous of a li'l white woman, are you?"

"I don't give a rat's behind if she was orange. She talks too much. I started to hit that ho right in the top of her head." I stopped walking and looked at him. "And let me tell you one thang, Malcolm. Don't let me catch you looking at the bikinis in Mexico. You keep your focus on *me*."

"I can't make any promises about that," he said. "My grandmother was a churchgoing woman, and she used to say that my grandfather had the spirit of the wandering eye. It could be hereditary."

"Oh, yeah? Well, I got the spirit of crazy. Now, you can get to Mexico and piss me off if you want to. I will clown on you and those skinny, thong-wearing broads so bad, the governor of Mexico will have us banned from the country forever."

I saw the pure white sand and the turquoise-blue water as we flew over the resorts along the Caribbean Sea. Malcolm had fallen asleep during the four-and-a-half-hour plane ride to Cancún. I tapped him on the shoulder to show him the view from the air. We saw folks Jet Skiing and parasailing.

"Wow! I can't wait to Jet Ski," Malcolm said excitedly. "You're gonna roll with me, baby?"

I turned my nose up. "Heck, no."

"Why not?"

"Because I can't swim."

"Put on a life jacket. You'll be all right."

"Malcolm, I'm not getting on a Jet Ski."

"Well, can we at least go parasailing?"

"I'm pregnant. I can't be doing all that crazy stuff. Why can't we just have a fun, relaxing time on the beach?"

"I don't have a problem with that, but there's more to do than just lying on the beach all day."

"Of course there is. We can get massages and facials."

A frown appeared on his face. "Massages and facials? That's women's stuff. What about horseback riding and snorkeling?"

He made me feel really old. I should've known that I couldn't tame a twenty-one-year-old, especially in a city like Cancún. "Horseback riding is dangerous for a pregnant woman, Malcolm, and snorkeling is out because I don't like water in my face."

He sat back in his seat and sighed. "What did you bring me here for? We may as well have stayed in Chicago since you don't wanna do nothin'."

"Caribe Real is a five-star hotel. I'm sure there will be plenty to do."

He didn't say another word. Five minutes later, our plane touched down at the airport in Cancún, Mexico.

After we collected our luggage, we stepped outside the airport and were greeted by a Mexican man wearing a light blue Hawaiian shirt. He stood next to a van and held up a sign that read TRANSFER TO CARIBE REAL RESORT. He loaded our luggage in the back, and Malcolm and I climbed in the van with four other couples who were staying at our resort. Everyone introduced themselves, and we settled in for the twenty-minute ride.

The hotel was absolutely beautiful, and the interior of the lobby took my breath away. Because the weather in Mexico was fair all year long, there were no doors. A huge open archway welcomed us. Mauve-colored tiles decorated the floors and walls. To the immediate left of the entryway was a stage area, where a band played music and a pretty dark-haired lady sang a welcoming song in Spanish. We didn't know what the heck she was saying. Whether she was singing "Welcome to Caribe Real" or

"Here come the niggas," we didn't know. Malcolm and I were there to have a ball. We left our bags with the bell-boy and walked to the concierge at the check-in counter.

"Hola, señorita. Hola, señor." A tall Mexican man wearing a white shirt with palm trees on it greeted us. I could tell his smile was forced. I looked at another man and two women who were behind the counter, wearing the same shirt and checking folks in, and saw that their smiles were forced too.

Malcolm responded, *"Hola."*

"Hola," I said and informed him of who we were. He checked our reservations and then gave us two key cards, along with a list of the restaurants at the resort. After putting red rubber wristbands on our wrists, which signaled that we had an all-inclusive package, he gave us a map of the huge hotel, along with a list of activities that were featured daily. He pointed us in the direction of the elevator that would take us up to the fifth floor.

No word could describe how beautiful our suite was. In the middle of the room sat a *double* king-size bed. It was humongous. If Malcolm and I lay on opposite sides and rolled over toward the middle of the bed five times, we still wouldn't meet.

Next to the bed were mauve-colored his and her sinks. Across from the sinks was a closet that housed an iron and ironing board. On the top shelf of the closet we saw a small silver safe. To the right of the closet, a door led to the bathroom, which had a mauve-colored sunken Ja-cuzzi tub, a separate shower behind glass doors, and a rose-colored toilet.

"Rhapsody, come look at this view."

I went out onto the terrace and stood next to Malcolm. Down below, a large pool that could fit up to three hun-dred people was half full. A game of water volleyball was under way. Dark blue lawn chairs surrounded the entire pool. Three minibars that looked like little huts were very busy. Straight ahead was the Caribbean Sea in all its glory.

"Ooh, Malcolm, look at how pretty the water is."

The waves rushed up on the sand, and the water was crystal clear. About twenty feet into the ocean, the water was turquoise. Farther out, where the motorized sports took place, the water was royal blue. I looked up at the sky and saw that it matched the three colors of the ocean.

"Malcolm, our suite faces the east. So we'll be able to see the sun rise out of the water. Will you get up early with me to see it?"

"How early?"

"About four o'clock."

"Girl, you must be crazy," he said. "I'm on vacation, and I ain't getting out of the bed till the afternoon. Did you notice that there's no clock on the nightstand?"

"Yeah. Why is that?" I wondered out loud.

"Because when you're on vacation, time doesn't matter. You're supposed to do whatever you want whenever you wanna do it."

I stepped to him and wrapped my arms around his waist. "So, what do you wanna do now?"

He kissed my lips softly. "I don't know. You picked this resort. What do *you* wanna do?"

I shoved my torso into his. "You know."

Malcolm laughed at me.

When we stepped into the room from the terrace, there was a knock on the door. The bellboy stood in the hall with our luggage. Malcolm brought the luggage into the room, and I tipped the bellboy twenty dollars and sent him on his way.

"You wanna get something to eat before we have sex?" Malcolm asked.

"Let me teach you something, boo. Never eat right before you screw, 'cause you'll get full and tired. Always

screw before you eat. That way you'll work up an appetite."

Malcolm and I made our presence known to anyone
who was in the suite above and below us, next door and
across the hall from us. It was almost 10:30 a.m. when
we emerged from our suite, and according to the list of
activities the concierge had given us, we had a half hour
to make the breakfast buffet at two of the four restaurants
at the resort. I had slipped into a light blue, chiffon, flo-
ral, spaghetti-strap sundress and white flip-flops, while
Malcolm had opted for a short-sleeve khaki shirt, khaki
shorts, and a pair of black Tommy Hilfiger flip-flops.

I hadn't realized how hungry I was until I saw the buffet. I piled a plate with bacon, sausage links, scrambled
eggs, and French toast. I found a table that gave us a view
of the ocean while we ate. I assumed Malcolm was behind
me, but when I looked around for him, he was nowhere
to be found. When I sat down, a waiter was quickly at my
side.

"Hola, señorita."

I smiled. *"Hola."*

"Wha u ly fa dree?"

The look on my face must've told him I didn't understand, 'cause he repeated what he'd said. This time he
made the letter *C* with his hand and brought it up to his
mouth, as though he was drinking from a cup. "Dree.
Wha u ly fa dree?"

That time I got it. "Oh, what would I like to drink?"

He smiled and nodded his head. *"Sí, señorita, sí."*

I still didn't see Malcolm, but I ordered for him, anyway. "Two cups of orange juice, please."

The waiter walked away to fulfill my request. That
was when I saw Malcolm coming toward me, balancing
three plates. He placed them on the table, sat down, then
looked at my plate.

"That's all you're eating?" he said.

On one of his plates were bacon, sausage, and fried honey ham. On another plate were grits, eggs over easy, and hash browns. On the third plate I saw a stack of pancakes and French toast.

"Malcolm, that is so ghetto. Why couldn't you make one plate, eat it all up, then go back for seconds?"

"Because I'm hungry, and they're starting to remove all the breakfast foods. The mid-morning snack buffet is being set up now."

Our friendly waiter sat our cups of orange juice on the table, then shook Malcolm's hand. *"Hola, señor."*

"Hola," Malcolm said with a mouth full of food.

"R u hubben n wy?"

Malcolm understood him perfectly. "No, we're not married. We're just friends."

"Jus frees? An u come to play ly thees?"

"What do you mean, 'a place like this'?" Malcolm asked.

"A play fa peepa who n luv," he said and walked away.

Malcolm looked at me, and I looked at him. We stared at each other for a long moment. I didn't know if Malcolm was in love with me or not. But if I were honest with myself, I'd have to admit that I had, in fact, fallen in love with him.

Do you love me, Malcolm? I imagined myself asking him. I wanted to tell him that I loved him, but I'd be devastated if he didn't echo the words back to me.

After breakfast, Malcolm and I went to the gift shop at the resort to buy souvenirs. Even though I was mad at Anastasia, there was no way I could go back home without a gift for her. I saw beautiful brass wind chimes I knew she'd love to have.

Malcolm tried on a red bandanna, and I liked it so much that I bought four of them. Daniel and Walter didn't deserve a souvenir, but out of the goodness of my heart, they would each get a bandanna. Trevor was like a brother to me, so he'd get one too. The fourth one was for Malcolm, since he looked so good in it. For Chantal, I chose a straw doll wearing a sombrero. I got my father a box of cigars that had been dipped in cognac. I'd always loved the smell of that. I didn't know what to get for Lerlean.

Malcolm came over to me, holding up a white sundress with I'M HAPPY IN CANCÚN written on the front. "I think I'll get this for my mother," he said.

"Get another one." The dress was ideal for my mother as well.

I couldn't forget about Mr. Duncan. At first I wasn't going to buy him a souvenir, because he got on my nerves every day, but he did bring me a pretty mug from Jamaica. It was only right that I got him something. Besides, if I brought him back a gift, he might not fire me.

Mr. Duncan was a drinker, and I saw the perfect T-shirt for him. It showed a shot glass filled with a brownish liquid and had the words ONE TEQUILA, TWO TEQUILA, THREE TEQUILA, FLOOR on it. At the bottom of the T-shirt was a man who had passed out. Malcolm bought the same shirt for his friend Ivan. For his sister, Cherise, he bought a yellow jewelry box. When she opened it, she would see a porcelain ballerina twirling to soft music. A tan bucket hat with CANCÚN across the front was what he bought for his brother-in-law, Sean.

We stood at the counter and watched as the cashier took the time to carefully wrap each one of our gifts in newspaper or plastic to ensure they wouldn't get damaged when we packed them in our luggage.

"One thousen thendy-thee pesos," she said.

I understood the one thousand twenty-three part, but we didn't have any pesos.

"How much?" I asked with raised eyebrows and a high-pitched tone.

She smiled at me. "One thousen thendy-thee pesos, senorita."

"How much in U.S. dollars?" Malcolm asked.

"One hondud two dolla, dirty cen."

"Whew." I exhaled loudly, and to my surprise, Malcolm's hand came out of his pocket with the money.

We collected our gifts and headed to our suite.

"Who's caring for your mother?" I asked while we were on the elevator.

"She's staying at Cherise's house till I get back."

Once we had separated our gifts and had packed them away, we changed into our swimwear. Malcolm complimented me on my fuchsia one-piece. It was low cut in the back, and it had a little skirt around the waist to hide the dimples in my thighs. He looked nice in his navy blue swim trunks. I put our beach towels, sunscreen lotion in my beach bag and off we went for some fun in the sun.

I didn't know how much fun we were gonna have in the one-hundred-plus-degree heat. I spread my pink beach towel and Malcolm's blue towel across two lounge chairs on the beach. I squeezed sunscreen lotion in Malcolm's hand, and he rubbed it on my legs, arms, and back.

"You want me to return the favor?" I asked him.

"Nah. I'ma get in the water."

I turned to lie on my back and watched him dive in the water like he was a marathon swimmer. I put my shades on my face, leaned back, and closed my eyes. Before long I dozed off.

I didn't know how long I'd been asleep, but I woke up to laughing. It took me a minute to gain my focus and remember where I was. The beach had gotten more crowded. Not far from me, I saw a woman lying on a lounge chair, topless. Many people were in the water, and

I couldn't find Malcolm anywhere. I removed my shades and scanned the area for navy blue shorts and saw a pair that matched Malcolm's about five feet in the ocean, straight ahead of me. I knew that there was no way it was Malcolm in those shorts, because the man wearing them was snigglin' and gigglin' with a woman who looked half my age and was definitely half my size.

Before I allowed myself to move in their direction, I studied the man's features. Everything about him, from the bald head to the color of his skin to the way he laughed, was a replica of Malcolm. What really shocked me was the fact that he picked the almost naked broad up by her waist and dropped her in the water. She came back up, laughing, wanting him to do it again. It was Malcolm, all right, but I still didn't move. I lay there watching them.

I took my mind back to O'Hare Airport early that morning. I recalled the conversation I had had with Malcolm about bikinis. I didn't wanna get up from the lounge chair and go off if I wasn't absolutely sure that I'd warned him against this type of intolerable behavior, but I distinctly remembered telling him what I would and would not put up with. However, it shouldn't have mattered whether I had warned him or not, since he was old enough to know better. Some things should be common sense. But since Malcolm was acting like he didn't have any or was simply disregarding what I'd told him in Chicago, I had to do the fool.

I calmly stood from the lounge chair, folded both our towels, and put them in my beach bag, along with my shades and the sunscreen lotion. I then placed the bag on my left shoulder and walked toward the ocean. I got in the water and wormed my way through the people having fun and splashing water on each other. I snuck up behind Malcolm just as he was getting ready to pick the girl up and drop her again. I tapped his shoulder, and he turned around.

You could always tell when men were caught with their hands in the cookie jar by the expression on their faces. Malcolm looked like he'd seen a ghost.

"Oh, h-h-hey, baby," he said nervously.

I looked at him and asked very calmly, "What are you doing?"

"Oh, I was just, uh . . ." He looked at the girl. "We were just, uh . . ."

"*We*?" I asked with raised eyebrows.

The broad had the gall to come from behind Malcolm and step in front of him to face me. "I'm Precious, and *you* are . . . ?"

She tried to show me up. I took my beach bag off my shoulder and let it fall in the water, forgetting about its contents. I took a step closer to her. "Who am *I*? I'm the one that's about to whup your *precious* butt. *That's* who I am."

I had to give the girl her props, because she was bold. She was getting ready to come at me, but Malcolm stepped in between us. "Whoa. Hold on, y'all."

"No, *you* hold on," I said to him. "What did I tell you at the airport before we left Chicago?"

"Rhapsody, don't trip. Okay? We were just talking."

"*Talking*? What kind of language are you speaking when you're picking her up and dropping her in the water?"

"*My* kind of language," the broad said.

Malcolm saw the look on my face, and he knew me well enough to know I was getting ready to react violently. He quickly turned to her. "You might not wanna say nothing else, 'cause she *will* jack you up out here in this water."

"Screw both y'all," she said and waded away.

I looked at Malcolm and said, "Let's go."

"Go where?"

I picked up my floating beach bag and saw that everything in it was soaked. "Up to the room. It's time to take a nap," I said over my shoulder as I made my way back to the sand.

"But I'm not sleepy."

I stopped walking, turned around to look at him. I balled up my lips and gritted my teeth. "Well, get sleepy!"

On the elevator up to the suite, I didn't say a word to Malcolm. I waited till we were away from the public and in our suite before I spoke to him. I didn't want any witnesses to my threats, 'cause if he was found dead, floating in the ocean, I would scream and holla and do everything else a woman did when she had lost the love of her life. "You got off easy, Malcolm. The next time I won't do no talking. I'm just gonna stab you."

Malcolm got undressed and climbed under the covers. "Girl, you ain't gon' do nothin'."

I didn't comment. I didn't need to. I figured I could show Malcolm better than I could tell him. I stepped out of my sundress, got in bed, and snuggled next to him. We were both snoring in less than five minutes.

Chapter 37

We had arrived in Cancún on Friday morning, and by Sunday night I was ready to take my behind back to Chicago. Malcolm was wearing me out. I felt like I was his mother the way I had to keep telling him over and over again not to do this and not to do that. I got tired of hearing my own doggone voice.

"What are you lookin' at her for . . . ?"

"What did she say to you . . . ?"

"Why are you smilin' in that broad's face . . . ?"

"Why did it take you so long to come back from the bathroom . . . ?"

"Why do you gotta go back to the gift shop . . . ?"

"Who is the gift for . . . ?"

And I could've sworn I'd heard him call out Sharonda's name in his sleep last night. It had taken all that was within me to keep from smothering Malcolm with my pillow. I'd vowed to myself that if I found out that he was screwing Sharonda, in hell would I lift my eyes, because I would kill him.

It was Monday morning and our last full day in Cancún. Since we'd got there, Malcolm had been moping and pouting, saying that I had been a Debbie Downer the whole trip. He wasn't lying next to me when I woke up. I slipped into my robe and found him sitting on the terrace, looking down at the folks doing water aerobics in the pool. I sat in a chair next to him.

"I'm sorry that you're not having a good vacation."

He looked at me. "Rhapsody, don't think that I don't appreciate this vacation, because I do, but when you told me we were coming to Cancún, I was geeked because there's so much to do here, but you won't let me do nothing."

He was right, and I knew it. Being paranoid and insecure wasn't fair to him. "Okay, Malcolm, it's our last day, and I'll do whatever you wanna do except horseback ride. It's too dangerous for the baby."

I thought I saw a little excitement in his eyes. "Are you for real?"

"Yep. Whatever you wanna do. We'll call this Malcolm's Day."

He was definitely excited. He sat up from his slouching position and rubbed his palms together. "Okay, cool, cool. How about we hit the Jet Skis first? After that, we'll check out parasailing. And yesterday I heard a tour guide tell another couple about a safari trip we can take to see animals in the wild. And there's a water park about two miles from here, with all kinds of twisted slides we can ride."

Just sitting there listening to Malcolm made me wanna throw up. I was thirty-four years old and pregnant. All the crazy crap he wanted to do was out of my league.

He saw the distraught look on my face and frowned. "What? You don't wanna do it?"

I faked a smile. "Yeah, boo, I promised you this would be your day. I'm game."

He hopped up from the chair and whistled his way to the shower. I sat on the terrace, looked out over the ocean, and shook my head from side to side, wondering what I was gonna do.

Twenty minutes later Malcolm was dressed and ready to go. I, on the other hand, was taking my own sweet time.

"Dang, Rhapsody. What's taking you so long?"

"I'm moving as fast as I can, Malcolm."

"Baby, you've been brushing your teeth for twenty minutes. Come on."

I dreaded leaving the suite. I took my time, Malcolm's time, and everybody else's time getting dressed. And that morning the saltine crackers and the 7Up didn't work; I vomited three times. I swooshed a capful of Scope around in my mouth and spat it into the sink. "Okay, Malcolm, you're always rushing me. I'm almost ready."

"I'll just meet you down on the beach."

"You just wanna look at the bikinis. You're gonna mess around and make me stab you for real, Malcolm," I warned him. "Wait for me. All I gotta do is put on my T-shirt and shorts."

It was another hot day in Cancún. Malcolm was so hyped about *his day*, he could barely eat breakfast. Watching me eat like a turtle, he drummed his fingers on the table, looking bored as heck.

"Will you quit that?" I asked, glaring at his fingers.

"Will you hurry up? You're eating slow on purpose. You know I'm ready to hit the waves."

I drank the last sip of my orange juice; then Malcolm and I headed to the beach. It wasn't long after we got to the beach that I found myself listening to an instructor give me and Malcolm the dos and don'ts regarding the Jet Skis. He pointed far out into the ocean to a neon orange cone floating in the water.

"Do go tha fah. Tha wheyah shar. Wen get ta con, com bak."

I leaned into Malcolm. "What is he saying?"

"He said not to go past the orange cone, because there are sharks."

That was it. I was done. "I ain't going."

Malcolm exhaled loudly. "Rhapsody, don't start. Ain't nothing gonna happen to you. Put a life vest on and let's go."

I had never been so scared in my life. At that point, I was willing to tell Malcolm to go and find that broad he'd been splashing in the ocean with and invite her to ride with him. "Why can't you go by yourself?"

"Because you promised me you'd hang with me today." He marched over to Jet Ski we'd been assigned.

Those who were standing around waiting for the next available Jet Ski found my hesitation humorous. Malcolm got on first, then waited for me to climb on behind him. When I hesitated, he said, "Okay, Rhapsody, get on behind me."

With tears in my eyes, I climbed on. I looked at the lady who was next in line. Tears dripped onto my cheeks when I spoke to her with a shaky voice. "My name is Rhapsody Blue, and I'm from Chicago. If I don't come back, call my mama, Lerlean Blue, and tell her I got about six hundred dollars in my bank account, which she can have. And tell her to bury me in my new lilac suit I got from Neiman Marcus."

I was really sincere, but those who heard me, including Malcolm, laughed their butts off. The Jet Ski sounded like a motorcycle.

Once Malcolm and I were secure and set to go, the instructor approached us. "Hit way reeyah ha an go reeyah fas so no tur ovah. Go reeyah fas, reeyah fas."

I understood everything he said, and I had to throw up real bad. I wrapped my arms around Malcolm's waist and held on for dear life. I pressed my face into the back of his neck. The next thing I knew, we were flying at one hundred miles an hour in just eight seconds. I started screaming.

Malcolm was having the time of his life. "Woohoo! Yeah! This is da bomb diggidy."

"Slow down, Malcolm!" I yelled.

Either he didn't hear me or he chose not to obey. A big, gigantic tsunami wave was coming at us.

Malcolm sped up. "*Yeah!* Get ready, boo. We gon' hit this wave like champions."

I imagined being in a head-on collision and having my air bag inflate hard against my face. That was what it felt like when the wave rushed into us. Malcolm was out of his mind, yelling at the top of his lungs.

"Yeah! Yeah!"

We were both drenched, and I could barely see. We were coming up on the orange cone, and Malcolm knew he had to turn around, but instead of slowing down, like he should've, he did the turn at eighty miles an hour and the Jet Ski capsized. We both landed in the water, and I started kicking and screaming.

Malcolm knew I couldn't swim, and he was immediately at my side, reminding me of the life vest I was wearing. When I realized I wasn't sinking, he left me alone to get the Jet Ski upright. In my peripheral vision, I saw something bright orange in color and remembered what the instructor had said about the sharks, and I lost my self-control.

I was delirious. "Jaws is out here, Malcolm. Come get me. Come get me!"

He climbed onto the Jet Ski and came over to where I was. He saw that I was hysterical. "Calm down before you drown out here."

I kept crying, "Jaws is out here! He's gonna eat me."

Apparently, Malcolm thought my dilemma was funny. He was laughing when he pulled me from the water. When I was safely on the Jet Ski, I started hitting him re-peatedly on the back of his head. "Get me off this water!"

He tried to duck and dodge my blows, but I kept hitting him until my feet were back on the sand. Those still waiting their turn had seen what had happened, and they applauded my safe return.

"We knew you could do it," someone said.

We turned in our life vests and walked away. Malcolm grabbed my hand.

"Wasn't that fun?" he said.

"No, not even a little bit."

Our clothes were drenched through and through, but it was still hot. I saw that Malcolm was leading me to the parasailing section on the beach. I witnessed a small white sailboat leave the shallow water at a rapid speed; then two people attached to it by a long rope flew into the air behind it, sitting on what looked like a swing seat. A gigantic light blue kite sailed up above them.

I stopped walking. "Nope."

Malcolm looked at me and smiled. "Come on, Rhapsody."

I shook my head from side to side. "I ain't gon' do it."

Malcolm squeezed my hand, then pulled me toward his chest and hugged me tight. "Boo, it's gonna be all right."

I wasn't giving in to him that time. "No, Malcolm, no."

He didn't say anything else. He held me, squeezed me tight, then looked down into my eyes. "I love you."

My heart melted because he hadn't said those words to me before. *Can it be true?* I wondered.

"Do it for me," he pleaded.

"What did you say?"

"I said, 'Do it for me.'"

"No, before that."

He thought for a moment. "I said, 'I love you.'"

By then I was ready to walk through fire with Malcolm. He loved me.

When the instructor strapped us into the swing seat, he saw tears streaming down my face.

"Wy u cry, senorita? U no wan fly?"

"She'll be all right," Malcolm said sternly.

The instructor stepped away and gave the driver of the boat the cue to step on the gas.

I looked at Malcolm, sitting next to me. Through my tears, I saw three of him. "I hate you for making me do this. . . . Ah, Ah! Jesus, Jesus!" We were in the air, flying high, and I was acting like a fool. "Oh, oh, oh, Lord. Jesus, Jesus, Jesus, Jesus. Jesus, Jesus, Jesus."

Malcolm laughed at me so hard, he was crying himself. I closed my eyes so tight, my eyelids looked like they were glued together. I didn't wanna see nothing.

"Open your eyes, Rhapsody."

I didn't do it. I *couldn't* do it. I knew if I looked down, I would faint.

"Boo, open your eyes."

"Shut up!"

We must've hit an air pocket, because we took a quick dip, and my stomach dropped. "Ah, ah! Jesus, Jesus, Jesus."

Malcolm kept on laughing.

I decided to make a deal with God. "Lord, if you let me get off this thang, I promise to never do nothing this crazy ever again." I didn't think God heard me, because we hit another air pocket. "Ah, ah, ah! Jesus, Jesus, Jesus, Jesus."

After parasailing, we went up to our suite to change into dry clothes. I was starving and couldn't wait to see what the lunch buffet consisted of. Malcolm and I both wore white. He dressed in white denim shorts, a white T-shirt, and tan flip-flops. He wore a white bucket hat on his head. I pulled on a white, asymmetric linen tank blouse, a long white linen skirt, and white flip-flops. I pulled my hair back from my face and tied a white scarf into a bow on the top of my head. We were gorgeous and looked good together. We got on the elevator and met a woman who was coming down from a floor above us.

"You two look cute," she commented. "Did you get married today?"

That made me feel good, but I said, "No, we didn't."

"You look like a couple who's very much in love with one another."

That was the first of many compliments we received on our way to the buffet. When we walked into the restaurant, someone asked, "When's the wedding?" Another woman said, "You must be on your honeymoon."

It blew my mind when a couple who was on their honeymoon came to our table and asked us to pose for a picture to show the folks back home in Atlanta how many newlyweds were in Cancún, at the Caribe Real Resort, at the same time as they were.

Since I had clowned and acted like a fool during the parasailing and Jet Ski excursions, Malcolm forgave me my promise to go to the water park and on the safari. He said he couldn't take any more of my screaming and hollering. Once we had eaten, we left the restaurant and walked hand in hand along the beach. It was mid-afternoon, and the temperature had already reached ninety-six degrees.

"Thank you, boo," Malcolm said to me.

"For what?"

"For doing what you do best, which is taking good care of me and always looking out for me, and for giving me great sex."

I laughed. "Is it great, Malcolm?"

"Mmm-hmm. Each and every time."

I let go of his hand to write our names in the sand. I got as far as *Mal* before the water came ashore and washed it away.

"Hold the water back, Malcolm."

"How in the heck am I supposed to hold the water back?"

I moved farther up on the sand, higher on the beach, where the water wasn't able to reach, and wrote my message.

Malcolm Luvs Rhapsody.

Malcolm held his camera in his hand, and I asked him to take a picture of our names in the sand, but I could tell he didn't want to. The expression on his face kinda, sorta told me that what I had written in the sand was a lie. In his expression, I saw a question: he was asking me why I had written a lie. When he saw how I was examining his expression, Malcolm snapped the picture, but the truth was out.

"You lied to me earlier," I said to him.

"What are you talking about?"

"Before we parasailed, you told me you loved me, but that isn't true, is it? You said that only to get me in the air."

He exhaled. "Rhapsody, this is our last day in Cancún. Can we please not argue? If I said I loved you, I meant it."

I shrugged my shoulders and frowned at him. "What do you mean, if you said it? You told me that you loved me, but that was a lie, wasn't it? I read your face when I wrote it in the sand."

Malcolm didn't comment. His silence confirmed what I already knew. I walked to our names in the sand and erased the word *luv* with my feet. In its place I wrote the word *hates*.

"How about that, Malcolm? Is that a better word to explain how you feel about me?"

Malcolm stood three feet away from me and made tight fists with his hands, then released them. I could tell he was really pissed and was trying not to hit anything. "That was uncalled for, Rhapsody."

I walked past him, and he grabbed my arm firmly. "I'm talking to you. Where are you going?"

I snatched my arm away from his grip and ran to the hotel. I went up to our suite, fell facedown on the bed, and cried myself to sleep.

There was no clock in our room, so I didn't know what time Malcolm inserted his key card and opened the door. It was dark outside, and the band that played by the pool had retired its music for the night. I was lying on my stomach when Malcolm came and put his hand on my butt.

"Rhapsody?"

I was awake, but I didn't move.

He shook me. "Rhapsody?"

I turned over to lie on my back and saw Malcolm's silhouette standing over me.

He stretched out his hand toward me. "Come with me," he said.

Malcolm's speech was slurred, and I knew he had been drinking. I put my hand in his, and he pulled me up from the bed. Without saying a word, I followed Malcolm down to the beach. I knew it was past midnight, because the moon was high in the sky and the beach was deserted. It was just me, Malcolm, the moon and the stars, and the waves rushing against the shoreline. I didn't see another soul anywhere.

"Where are we going, Malcolm?"

He placed his index finger against his lips to silence me. "Shhh."

We came upon a brick wall. Behind it was a secluded place that couldn't be seen by anyone walking by. Malcolm pulled me behind the wall and began kissing me passionately and wildly. I tasted tequila on his tongue. He must've been downing shots all afternoon and evening.

He drew my tongue into his mouth and savored it. From just the kiss alone, my body became weak. He backed me up against the wall and lifted me up for me to wrap my thighs around his waist. I wasn't even concerned that someone would walk by and see us.

Malcolm kissed my entire face. "Do you believe I love you?"

He was drunk, and I knew it was the alcohol talking. I would never forget the look on Malcolm's face when he saw what I had written in the sand. But at that moment I needed to feel him inside of me. Against my better judgment, I said the exact opposite of what I really felt.

"Yes, Malcolm, I believe you love me. Please make love to me right now."

He laid me down on the sand, and with each stroke, Malcolm told me he loved me. Tears came to my eyes because I knew he was lying, and come the next morning, while he was nursing a hangover, Malcolm wouldn't even remember what we'd done or what he'd said to me.

I looked up at the full moon through teary eyes. I tried to convince myself that Malcolm was making love to me, but I knew better. The stars didn't lie. They told me Malcolm was only screwing me.

When he had finished, Malcolm collapsed on top of me and said, "I love you, baby. I swear I do."

Everything within me knew better than to believe him. But my heart had already been sold to the devil. I was in love with Malcolm, and deep down in my soul, I was convinced that I was in love all by myself.

Chapter 38

Very early Tuesday morning we were packing our things when the concierge called our suite and informed us that a van would be at the hotel in an hour to take us to the airport. Our large suitcases sat open on the bed. Malcolm was at the bathroom sink, gathering his toiletries, when I looked on the floor next to the bed and saw that he'd forgotten to pack his tan flip-flops.

I picked the flip-flops up and put them on the bed. That was when I saw pink material in the bottom right corner of Malcolm's suitcase. It was folded with the T-shirt he'd bought at the gift shop. I was curious why the color pink would be in his suitcase. I pulled the material from beneath the T-shirt, and in my hand was a scarf. It looked similar to the one I had found on the floor of his truck, the same one I'd slashed.

When Malcolm came out of the bathroom with deodorant, toothpaste, and mouthwash in his hands, I held the pink scarf up for him to see. "What is this?"

He looked at the scarf, then at me. "Why are you going through my stuff?"

"Never mind that," I said. "Who is this scarf for?"

"Who do you *think* it's for?" he asked, biding time to come up with a good answer.

I shifted all my weight onto one leg and glared at him. "I don't know, Malcolm. That's why I'm asking."

"It's for my mother," he said. "I gotta replace the one you cut up. Now, put it back and stay out of my suitcase."

I folded the scarf neatly and put it back where I had found it. I knew he was lying, but I couldn't prove it yet.

Because all our meals, drinks, and excursions were included in our trip, and because we didn't make any calls from our room, we had a zero balance at checkout. We turned in our key cards, and the concierge removed the red rubber wristbands from our wrists. The moment we stepped outside the hotel, the driver made his way toward us with the van. I guessed that the other couples who had arrived with us had left earlier or were staying longer. Malcolm and I were the only two headed to the airport.

I didn't say anything to him on the ride back to the airport. I purposely gazed out the window, away from him. After we checked our luggage at the airport, I sat waiting for our flight number to be called, with my eyes closed. It wasn't until we were on the airplane, buckled in our seats, that he spoke.

"So, what's your problem?" he asked.

"You."

"How am I your problem?"

"Let me ask you a question, Malcolm. Do you want this baby?"

"If I didn't want it, I wouldn't be with you."

That answer didn't satisfy me. "No, I want you to tell me that you want this baby just as much as I do."

He paused. "All right. Since you wanna get into this right now, then let's get into it. I can't say that I'm looking forward to becoming a father at my age, but I do accept my responsibility *as* a father."

I really wanted to know what he meant by that statement. "And what's your responsibility, Malcolm?"

"Providing for the baby and raising it. Making sure the baby has whatever he or she needs."

"As far as what?"

"As far as food, clothes, Pampers, and stuff."

"Well, can you provide a roof over his or her head?" I knew he couldn't. Malcolm didn't have a pot to piss in or a window to throw it out of, but I wanted to make him feel less than a man. I wanted him to hurt like I was hurting. I hit him below the belt, but he played it cool.

"No, I can't. But there's a roof over *my* head, and as long as I got one, then my child will have one."

"Do you remember what happened last night?"

He frowned and knit his eyebrows, trying to figure out what I was talking about. "Last night?"

"Early this morning, rather. Down on the beach."

He smiled. "Oh, yeah. It was good. We have great sex."

I cocked my head to the side. "*Sex*? We weren't making love, Malcolm? Do you even remember what you said to me?"

"Rhapsody, I said a lot of crap to you. Refresh my memory."

A lot of crap? I knew Malcolm's words were a lie. "How about I refresh your *drunk* memory? You got me out of bed in the middle of the night, took me down on the beach, and screwed me, but in your drunken state, you tried to convince me that you loved me. And those were your exact words, Malcolm. You told me you loved me."

He drew back from me quickly, like he was afraid to touch me, like I had a deadly disease that would kill him if he got too close. "I said *that*?"

My stomach dropped. *Oh, my God. Oh, my God.* When he asked the question like that, I wanted God to abort the fetus I was carrying right then and there.

Rhapsody, I said a lot of crap to you. Malcolm's words echoed through my brain. I threw up on the floor of the airplane.

Chapter 39

I woke up on Wednesday morning with a migraine headache. Because Malcolm's mother thought he would be in Cancún until Saturday, he'd stayed with me last night. I'd wanted to tell him to take his butt home, but his manhood had got to my womanhood before the words were able to come out of my mouth. Malcolm was my weakness; I couldn't deny that.

I sat up on the bed and ate two crackers and swallowed a half a can of 7UP, then lay back down and listened to him snore for five minutes before I got up to wash my face and brush my teeth. In the kitchen I chased a prenatal vitamin down with a glass of orange juice. I went back into the bedroom and listened to my voice mail.

"Baby girl, it's Mama. Your daddy and I made it to the boat. I dropped your postcard in the mail today, but the cashier said we'd be home before you even get it. We love you, and we'll see you in a week." *Beep.*

"It's Tuesday morning, and I was waiting to see how long it would take for you to call me. It has been six days, so I guess you still got an attitude. I have been calling and calling, and if you would have answered your telephone, you'd know that your goddaughter caught a bad case of the chicken pox and had to be rushed to the emergency room early Sunday morning. If Chantal could have asked where her godmother was when she needed her, I would've told her that you weren't available." *Beep.*

I erased both messages and immediately dialed Anastasia's house. She answered on the third ring. "Hello?"

"It's me, Rhapsody."

"Rhapsody who?"

"Don't play with me. How's Chantal?"

"Oh, *now* you care?"

"I left town on Friday morning, Stacy. I got back late last night, and I just got your message. How is Chantal? Is she still in the hospital?"

"I wouldn't be home, talking to you, if she were."

"And you say *I* got an attitude? Just tell me how my goddaughter is."

"If you cared so much, you'd have your behind over here, seeing about her, instead of calling on the darn phone."

I hung up on that crazy heifer. I swore, Anastasia made me wanna strangle her sometimes. I opened the top right drawer on my dresser and grabbed a matching bra and panty set and took them into the bathroom. I laid my underwear on top of the sink, then pulled my locks back and wrapped a rubber band around them. I brushed my teeth, then took a shower.

When I stepped out of the shower, Malcolm was still asleep. I got dressed and walked out the front door, with Anastasia's, Trevor's, and Chantal's gifts from Cancún in my hand.

Twenty minutes later I stood on Anastasia's porch and rang her doorbell.

After a few moments I heard, "Who is it?"

I knew she was watching me. "Ain't you lookin' through the peephole, skank? Who do you think it is?"

Anastasia swung the door open. "If you're gonna have that type of attitude, then don't bother comin' in my house."

"You're the one with the attitude," I said. "I called to see how Chantal was doing, and you act like I didn't return your calls on purpose."

"Well, where have you been for the past six days?"

I cocked my head to the side. "Can we discuss this on the inside?"

Anastasia moved out of my way, and I headed straight to Chantal's nursery. She was in her playpen, chewing on a rattle. Red bumps decorated her face like it was a game of connect the dots. I sat the gifts down next to the white wicker rocker Anastasia used to put Chantal to sleep at night and went to her.

"Hey, godmommy's baby."

She smiled, dropped her rattle, and reached for me. I picked her up and hugged her close to me.

"I missed that baby. Yes I did."

Anastasia stood in the doorway of the nursery. She leaned against the wall, with her arms folded across her chest. "Well, she can't tell."

I ignored her and sat down in the wicker rocker. I reached in the bag and pulled out the doll I had brought back from Cancún. "Look what godmommy has for you."

"Yeah, that's right," Anastasia began. "Go ahead and kiss Chantal's butt to try to make up for not being here when she needed you to be."

I looked at Chantal as she played with the doll. "Your mama is gonna make me cuss her out if she don't shut up."

"Don't say that to my baby, Rhapsody."

I looked at Anastasia. "She don't even know what I'm saying to her." I shooed her away with my hand. "Leave us alone. Go in the kitchen and cook something. I'm hungry."

Anastasia raised her eyebrows, and she dropped her arms at her sides. "Ho, you still ain't told me where you been, and you got the nerve to ask for something to eat?"

"Me and Malcolm took a vacation to Cancún."

She took a step farther into the nursery, raised her eyebrows higher, then folded her arms across her chest again. "You and *who*?"

"I didn't stutter. I said, 'Me and Malcolm.' And don't say nothing, 'cause I don't wanna hear nothing."

I couldn't believe Anastasia left it alone and walked away. I could tell she was pissed, 'cause I heard the kitchen cabinets slamming shut and dishes clashing.

Chantal felt a bit warm to me. I placed my palm on her forehead and got worried. I stood and took her into the kitchen. "I think she's running a fever."

Anastasia came over to us and felt Chantal's forehead. "Yeah, she is. I'll get her medicine." She left the kitchen and was back in seconds with medicine Chantal's pediatrician had prescribed and a bottle of calamine lotion.

"I'll give her the medicine," I said and took the bottles from Anastasia's hand. I sat in a chair at the kitchen table with Chantal on my lap and gave her a half teaspoon of the liquid medicine. Afterward, I dabbed calamine lotion on her sores.

Anastasia gave me a bottle of milk. "You wanna feed her?"

I took the milk and Chantal back into the nursery and sat in the rocker. I fed my goddaughter and rocked her to sleep. I laid her in her crib and returned to the kitchen and saw Anastasia sitting at the table, in front of a bowl of grilled chicken Caesar salad and a pitcher of iced tea.

"She fell asleep really quickly."

Anastasia nodded her head. "It's the medicine. It keeps her drowsy. She'll sleep for about three hours, but I won't let her sleep that long. I'll get her up in an hour."

I sat down at the table and filled my plate with salad. "What happened Sunday morning?"

"She woke up choking. She had a temperature of one hundred one, and her neck was red and swollen. I got scared, 'cause I didn't know what to do. I called my mother, and she told me to get her to the emergency room. I got Trevor up, and he drove us to West Suburban Medical Center. Her pediatrician met us there. She diagnosed Chantal with chicken pox."

"She's not waking up choking anymore, is she?"

"No, it only happened that one time. But now I'm paranoid. Every ten minutes that Chantal's asleep, I go into her room and check to make sure she's breathing."

I nodded my head 'cause I understood how Anastasia felt about her baby. I'd do the same thing.

We both ate in silence for a few minutes before I remembered the gifts I had brought with me. I went into the nursery, grabbed the gift bag, then returned to the kitchen.

"I brought you and Trevor something back from Cancún."

"You mean from your freak fest."

I chuckled. "I ain't gonna lie. Malcolm and I did plenty of that."

"Did y'all do it on the beach?"

"Yep."

"That's what I wanna do," Anastasia said. "I think it's very romantic."

I shrugged my shoulders. "I'm sure it is if you're with a man who loves you, but I wouldn't know."

Anastasia looked at me curiously. "What?"

"Nothing," I said and gave her the bag. "Yours is the wind chimes, and Trevor gets the bandanna."

She pulled the things from the bag and smiled. "Oh, thank you. And I'm sure Trevor will thank you himself. He doesn't wear bandannas, though. But you might start a trend with him."

"When Malcolm tried it on in the gift shop, I liked it on him. I bought Walter and Danny bandannas too."

"So, what brought on Cancún?"

"I was at work Wednesday, going through the interoffice mail, and saw a promotional flyer advertising a cheap package for CTA employees, and I just ran with it."

"And you couldn't call and tell me you were leaving?"

"What was I gonna call you for? You didn't wanna talk to me. The last time we talked, you hung up on me, remember?"

"That's beside the point, Rhapsody. You know you have a goddaughter, and that's a responsibility like having a child of your own. Heck, anything can happen. Something *did* happen."

I couldn't argue with that. "Yeah, you're right."

"I mean, if you're gonna fall out with me, then keep it on me. Don't take it out on my child, Rhapsody. Chantal didn't do nothing to you. I needed to get in touch with you on Sunday morning, and unbeknownst to me, you're down in Mexico, shakin' sand out your coochie hairs."

I knew Anastasia was seriously trying to make a point, but I couldn't stop myself from screaming out in laughter. When she realized what she'd said, she laughed herself.

"Okay, that didn't come out right, but you know what I meant," she said.

Trevor came home for lunch to check on Chantal. That didn't surprise me, because he was a good husband and father. I wished Malcolm could adopt Trevor's character.

He walked into the kitchen and kissed his wife's lips and my cheek. "How's my girl?"

"I'm fine," Anastasia answered.

"I mean my baby girl."

Anastasia stood from the table. "She's better. I was just about to check on her."

"That's okay. I'll do it," Trevor said and left the kitchen.

I sighed. "I wish I could look forward to that."

"What?" Anastasia asked me.

"Malcolm coming home from work in the middle of the day to check on his baby."

Anastasia sat back down. "Rhapsody, Malcolm is young and inexperienced. But I promise you, the moment he sees his baby's face, there won't be anything you, his mother, or even God could do to keep him away from it."

"I hope so, Stacy. But remember when you were eight months pregnant and Trevor came home and found you gone? Remember how he called your cell phone and tracked you down? Remember how he waited by the front door for you to walk in just so he could kiss your big belly? We knew you were carrying a girl. Remember Trevor telling you that he needed to know where both his girls were at all times?"

She smiled at the memories. "Yeah, I remember."

"I left Malcolm asleep in my bed three hours ago. I know he's up by now, and he hasn't called my cell phone to find out where I'm at or to check if I'm okay."

"Rhapsody, the worst thing you can do is to compare Malcolm to Trevor. You have to remember that Trevor has fifteen years on Malcolm. Mentally, they are on opposite ends of the earth. Every man has to find his own way in life. But can I tell you something without you getting pissed at me?"

"Say what you gotta say, Stacy."

"You gave Malcolm all of you too soon, and what I mean by that is, you exposed your heart to him, and now he knows he's got you. You already showed him that you ain't going nowhere, no matter what he says or does. That's a dangerous mistake to make in a new relationship."

I nodded my head up and down. "Stacy, you just preached, girlfriend."

Malcolm's Navigator wasn't in my driveway when I returned home from Anastasia's house, and truth be told, I was relieved. Witnessing Trevor's love for and dedication to his wife and daughter brought tears to my eyes. And because of that, I didn't wanna look at Malcolm.

I wished I hadn't told my parents I was pregnant, because I still had time to get an abortion. I could have the procedure done first thing in the morning, take the rest of the week to relax, and be ready to hear Mr. Duncan's mouth on the following Monday.

Malcolm's luggage was missing, and I hope it was a sign that he'd gone home. We'd been joined at the hip for the past six days, and I was thankful for the breathing room. He hadn't made up my bed, and that pissed me off. I had told him time and time again always to make my bed when he got out of it.

He'd left the toilet seat up in the bathroom, and that pissed me off some more. And what really fried my behind was the fact that the rug around the base of the toilet had wet spots, which meant he couldn't pee straight. I snatched up the rug and tossed it in the washing machine. My kitchen had been clean when I left. But I found a cereal bowl and a spoon in the sink. Why couldn't Malcolm leave the kitchen the way he'd found it?

I unpacked my suitcase and put everything in its place. I sat the empty suitcase in the closet, went into my den, and lay across the futon. I turned on the Lifetime channel and found the movie *Who Will Love My Children?* on again. I watched it. I couldn't help myself. I wept like a two-year-old. By the end of the movie, my mind was made up to keep my baby. There was no way I could abort it or give it up for adoption. I pressed the OFF button on the remote and turned onto my side and sighed. I got up and rearranged the furniture in my den, living room, and bedroom. It was five o'clock in the evening when I finished.

Later I heard Malcolm come in the front door. I was sitting at the kitchen table, pouring caramel icing on a cake I had baked, when he walked in and stood next to me.

"I thought I was in the wrong house," Malcolm said, referring to the new look of the place.

"I moved the furniture around, and hello to you too."

He sat down and tried to stick his finger in the bowl of icing, but I smacked his hand away.

"Don't do that," I fussed. "Ain't no telling where your hands have been."

"They've been in your panties."

I looked at him and rotated my neck. "And who else's?"

"What's that supposed to mean? And where did you go this morning? You were gone when I woke up."

"Humph. You must not have been too worried, because you sho didn't call my cell to inquire about my where-abouts."

"You ain't leave a note, so I figured you didn't want me to know."

"I went to Stacy's house, but since you wanna come up in here investigating *me*, where *you* been all day?"

"Are you gonna give me some of that cake or what?"

"Don't try to change the subject, Malcolm. Answer my question."

"What question?"

"You're playing games with me, but I am not amused. You still screwin' Sharonda?"

"What do you mean, 'still'? I ain't never messed with Sharonda."

"Yeah, okay. That's what your mouth say. I bet if I asked your testicles that same question, I'd get a different answer."

"Girl, cut me a piece of that cake and stop all this bull. All you do is fuss and moan. Dang, I'm getting tired of that."

I stood from the table and pulled the largest knife I had in my kitchen from its cutlery holder and sliced a very thin piece of cake and sat in on a saucer and served it to Malcolm.

He looked at me as though I was crazy. "What's that?"

"You wanted a piece of cake, so I gave you one."

"Didn't your mama teach you how to cut a cake?"

I looked at that fool. "No, but she taught me how to cut a man."

"Rhapsody, quit messing around and cut me a piece of cake."

I threw the knife on the table, and it landed an inch from Malcolm's elbow. "Cut it yourself."

I walked past him, went into the laundry room, and started a load of laundry. Five minutes later I heard my front door slam. When I saw that Malcolm had taken half of my caramel cake, I called his cellular telephone.

"Why did you take half of my cake?"

"I didn't take half," he lied.

I was livid. "Malcolm, half of my cake is gone! Why did you do that?"

"You want me to bring it back, Rhapsody? I can't believe you're hollering at me over cake. This is exactly what I meant when I said all you do is complain."

I was so sick of him, and I wanted to be done with the conversation. "You know what, Malcolm? Keep the freakin' cake and don't come back here tonight. I don't wanna talk to you no more today."

"Oh, is it like that?"

Without answering him, I hung up the telephone. I massaged my temples, because I felt another headache coming on. I lay across my bed and thought about the mess I was in. I wasn't sleepy, so I got up and sat at the kitchen table and balanced my checkbook. I wrote out checks for my mortgage, my house insurance, Malcolm's car note, and my tithes and offerings for the two Sundays I had missed at church. I put stamps on the envelopes and drove to the post office and dropped them in an outside mailbox.

On the way back home, I stopped at the Barnes & Noble bookstore next to the Oakbrook Mall and bought another copy of the novel that I had ruined in Cancún. When I got home, I sliced a huge piece of cake and took it, along with a glass of milk, and laid on my futon for some good reading.

I got through the first chapter in three minutes and was disturbed by what I read. I was disturbed not because the novel wasn't excellently written so far, but because that female character was so much like me, but the author hadn't interviewed me or asked for permission to write about my life.

By the end of chapter five, I was fit to be tied. The novel was about me; it had to been. The female character met a guy the same way I had met Malcolm, at a fast-food restaurant. From the way the author described the guy, it was Malcolm in every way. The female character also had a best friend who was always in her business and was trying to run her life, and if that wasn't Anastasia, I didn't know who was. The only difference between our lives was that the character in the novel was telling her story from a jail cell.

I finished the novel in four hours, and again I tipped my hat to the author for another job well done. I must say that I was disturbed by the ending of the book, because it was finally revealed why the character was telling her story from behind bars.

Chapter 40

I was lying in bed and swallowing two crackers and drinking 7UP when my telephone rang on Saturday. WALTER BLUE appeared on my caller ID.

"Are you dying, Walter?" I asked when I answered. "Are you on your deathbed?"

"Nah. Why?"

"Because if you ain't knocking on death's door, you shouldn't be calling my house this early."

"If your pregnant, evil behind rolled over and looked at the clock, you would know that it's one o'clock in the afternoon, but witches always sleep half the day away."

It dawned on me what Walter had said to me. "Did Lerlean tell you that I'm pregnant?"

"Nope. She didn't have to."

I sighed. "You better tell me what you want before I hang up."

"I need you to get Mama and Daddy from the airport."

"Why can't *you* do it?"

"I got two patients delivering this afternoon."

"Well, what about Danny? He doesn't work on Saturdays."

"Danny and Antoinette are in Detroit this weekend for her family reunion."

I sighed again. I didn't feel like doing nothing. "What time?"

"Their plane lands at Midway Airport at two forty-five."

"Two forty-five? I'm all the way in Oakbrook. Why didn't you call me earlier?"

"I was planning on going myself until I got the calls from my patients."

"Are you sure about Midway? They flew out of O'Hare."

"Yes, Midway Airport at two forty-five on American Airlines flight number three-ten."

I got up to wash my face and brush my teeth. I slipped into a pair of size twelve Levi's jeans but couldn't button them. My pink nylon Fila jogging suit with the elastic waist fit much more comfortably. I remembered my mother telling me that she and my father had bought an extra luggage set to add to the seven pieces they already had to take on the cruise. There was no way the three of us, plus all that luggage, would fit in my car.

I didn't wanna deal with Malcolm, but I needed his truck. I called his cellular telephone and got his voice mail, but I hung up without leaving a message. I was pressed for time, so I called Anastasia.

"I need a favor, Stacy."

"What's up?"

"I have to get my parents from the airport, but all their luggage won't fit into my car. I can't reach Malcolm for the Navigator, so I'm hoping I can use your minivan."

"Yeah, that's fine. Trevor is out playing golf, and he'll be gone all day. Drive to my house, and Chantal and I will ride with you in the van."

Chapter 41

"Ma, I got a taste for your famous bread pudding," Cherise said.

Sean rubbed his belly at the thought of Lucille's desserts. "Ooh, me too."

"Well, I got everything but vanilla flavor," Lucille said to Cherise.

"I'll run to the grocery store and get it," Cherise offered. "Malcolm, can I drive your truck?"

He looked at Cherise. "Why can't you drive your own car?"

"Because I wanna ride in the Navigator."

He tossed her the keys. "Be careful."

Lucille rolled her wheelchair into the kitchen to prepare the bread pudding, Malcolm and Sean opted for a game of one-on-one on the backyard patio, and Cherise pulled the Navigator away from the curb.

Chapter 42

As we sat at the stoplight at Fifty-First Street and Cicero Avenue, I glanced at Anastasia, who was sitting in the passenger seat. "Stacy, I really appreciate you letting me use your van today. I don't know where Malcolm is."

"Girl, don't worry about it. Chantal could use the fresh air. Her doctor said it's safe to take her outside now."

I glanced at Chantal through the rearview mirror and saw her sitting quietly in her car seat, playing with her toes. "The chicken pox is almost gone."

"Yeah, her skin is clearing up real good."

What Anastasia said to me went through my right ear and came directly out my left. I was focused on a silver Navigator in the left turning lane, adjacent to where we sat in the van. I saw a light-skinned female sitting behind the wheel. She had long black hair, and she wore dark sunglasses and ruby-red lipstick. On the temporary license plates I saw D701357. While sitting at the stoplight, I fumbled through my purse for the set of keys to Malcolm's truck. They were attached to a key chain that held the information on the Navigator.

"What are you looking for?" Anastasia asked me.

"My keys to Malcolm's truck. I wanna see if the numbers on the key chain match the numbers on the temporary plates on that silver Navigator that's about to turn left."

I found the keys and looked at the numbers on the key chain. D701357 stared back at me.

"Oh, hell no," I said loudly.

Anastasia grabbed my right arm. "Rhapsody, calm down."

The green arrow appeared, and the Navigator made a left turn directly in front of us into a Mariano's grocery store parking lot. I was in the far left lane, heading south on Cicero Avenue, but I put my right turn signal on and turned right, crossing the cars in the middle and right lanes.

Anastasia held on to the door handle for dear life. "Rhapsody, I got my baby in this van! What are you gonna do?"

"You'll see," I said.

"I don't wanna see nothing. I ain't going to jail with you again."

I ignored her and followed the Navigator into the grocery store parking lot. I watched the woman park in a slot between a Pontiac Sunfire and a Suzuki Forenza. When she stepped out of the Navigator, I saw she was wearing a very short blue jeans skirt and a light blue tank top with white ankle socks and white gym shoes. I got more pissed because I had that exact blue jeans skirt in my closet but couldn't fit into it anymore. The fact that she was really cute in the face *and* in her waist didn't sit well with me.

"That ain't Sharonda," I said. "That's a different chick."

"Rhapsody, let's go," Anastasia pleaded.

"Calm down, Stacy. I ain't gonna touch the skank."

When the woman entered the grocery store, I pulled up behind the Navigator and got out with my purse and keys.

"Girl, what are you doing?"

"Taking my truck. Just follow me. We ain't going far."

Anastasia was mad at me, but she moved to the driver's seat of the van. "You're too old for this, you know that?"

I used the remote and unlocked the driver's door to the Navigator and got in. I drove it five blocks east on Fifty-First

Street, parked it on a residential corner, and got back into the driver's seat of Anastasia's van.

"Now I'm gonna wait till Malcolm calls me and says the truck was stolen either from his job, his mother's house, or Ivan's house."

Anastasia looked at me. "And then what?"

"Then I'ma stab him for letting a broad drive the truck that *I'm* paying for. Then I'ma stab him again for lying."

Chapter 43

"What?" Malcolm yelled into his cell phone when Cherise called.

"The truck is gone, Malcolm. It's not where I parked it. I searched the entire parking lot. It's not here."

Malcolm couldn't believe his ears. "You're saying somebody stole it?"

Both Lucille and Sean spoke to him at the same time. "What happened?" they chorused.

"You want me to call the police?" Cherise asked.

"Nah. Hold tight. I'm on my way." Malcolm disconnected the called and looked at his brother-in-law. "We gotta go get Cherise. Somebody stole my truck."

When Malcolm and Sean arrived at the grocery store, they saw a distraught Cherise. "Malcolm, I'm so sorry. I was only in the store for ten minutes."

Malcolm called the police from his cellular telephone. He dreaded making the second phone call. It was to Rhapsody.

Chapter 44

At around six o'clock Saturday evening, my mother was showing Anastasia and me the different souvenirs she and my father had picked up during a shopping spree on one of the Bahamian islands when Malcolm finally called my cellular telephone.

"Baby, I got something to tell you, but don't get mad, okay?"

I was calm, cool, and collected. "Okay." I blinked my eye at Anastasia to let her know that it was Malcolm on the telephone and that the crap was about to hit the fan.

"Somebody stole the truck."

At that moment I could've been nominated for a best actress award by the way I yelled into the telephone, "What do you mean, 'somebody stole the truck'?"

Anastasia laughed her butt off, but Lerlean was clueless.

"I let Cherise drive it to the grocery store. When she came out, the truck was gone."

I was holding my mouth, laughing, but when Malcolm said it was his sister who was driving the truck, I stopped laughing. I sat up straight on the sofa. "Cherise was in the truck?"

"Yeah. She said she locked the doors, and I don't see how somebody could steal a big Navigator from a crowded parking lot in broad daylight."

Anastasia saw the look on my face. She mouthed the words "It was his sister?" to me.

I nodded my head at her and spoke to Malcolm. "Don't worry about the truck. It has a tracking device on it, and it will be found a half hour after you call the police."

"Yeah, I already did that, but the truck is registered in your name, so you need to notify whoever and get that taken care of."

"All right, Malcolm," was all I said. I disconnected the call. Then Anastasia, Chantal, and I left my folks' house.

On the way back to Anastasia's house, I received a call from the police that the truck had been found right where I had parked it, but the passenger-side window had been broken. The stereo system and all four tires were gone.

Anastasia looked at me and said, "You should feel real stupid. Now what are you gonna do?"

"Pay to get the window fixed and buy a set of tires and a stereo system."

I dropped Anastasia and Chantal off, got in my own car, and called Malcolm to tell him what the police had told me.

He wasn't happy. "Aw, man. Are you serious?"

"It's okay, Malcolm. The truck is insured, and it's being towed to a body shop right now."

"I need to see you. Come to my mother's house." Malcolm gave me his address. I keyed it into my navigation system and pulled away from the curb.

When I arrived at his mother's house, I honked my horn for Malcolm to come out, but he opened the door, stepped onto the porch, and waved for me to come inside. I looked down at the jogging suit I was wearing. I had pictured myself wearing something more appropriate when I met his mother. I got out of the car and walked up the steps.

"Hey." He greeted me with a peck on the lips. "Come on in. I want you to meet my mother."

My heart was pounding against my chest. I stepped into the living room and saw a dark-skinned, slightly overweight woman with a salt-and-pepper, short-feathered haircut, and I could tell it was freshly done. She sat in a wheelchair, wearing the white sundress Malcolm had bought for her in Cancún. White house slippers were on her feet.

"Mama, this is Rhapsody. Rhapsody, this is my mother."

She was smiling at me. "My name is Lucille, sugar."

I walked over to her and knelt to hug her. "It's so nice to meet you, ma'am."

"It's nice to meet you too," she said. "Malcolm talks about you all the time. I'm glad you're a pretty girl."

I fell in love with her in that moment. I knew she and I would get along just fine. "Thank you."

Lucille offered me a seat on the living room sofa, and I sat down.

When I sat down, she said, "Malcolm, did you see how Rhapsody sat down when I offered her a seat? Did you notice that she didn't tell me she already had a sofa at home?"

They both laughed, but I didn't, because I didn't know what she was talking about. She filled me in when she saw that I was clueless as to why they were laughing.

"I'm sorry to hear there's a sister that dense," I said, referring to Deidra.

"Not only was she dense," Lucille replied, "but I guess she had been constipated for a while, because the heifer clogged up my toilet before she left here."

I covered my mouth. "Ooh, no she didn't."

"Yes she did, and I told Malcolm that she is never to darken my doorstep again."

"Okay, can we change the subject?" Malcolm said.

"Yeah, we can change the subject, but while Rhapsody and I change it, go and get us a glass of Kool-Aid." She looked at me. "Are you thirsty?"

I shrugged my shoulders. "Uh, yeah, kind of."

Lucille reminded me of my own mother. The way Malcolm quickly moved at her command let me know that she didn't take any crap, and I liked that about her.

"I see you're wearing the sundress we got in Cancún."

She nodded her head and looked down at it. "And it's so comfortable."

"I bought my mother one just like it. Did you like the pink scarf?"

She frowned a little bit. "Pink scarf?"

"The one Malcolm bought for you in Cancún. I accidentally damaged the pink chiffon scarf you left in his truck. In Cancún he bought you a pink scarf to replace it."

Lucille shook her head from side to side. "I've never owned a pink chiffon scarf."

At that exact moment my ears got hot. It felt like somebody had lit matches to them. Malcolm came back into the living room and extended a glass of Kool-Aid to me, and it took every ounce of my self-control not to take it and throw it in his face. I was in his mother's house, so I couldn't show my behind, but I was ready to go.

"May I use your bathroom?" I asked Lucille.

"Oh, sure." She pointed toward the rear of the house. "It's straight through the dining room and the first door on your right."

I stood up and gave Malcolm a stern look before I left the living room. I went to the bathroom and shut the door. I started pacing the floor. I was pissed beyond words. My head jerked back and forth as I tried with all my might to keep my anger in. "Freakin' dirt bag!" I tried to stop it. "Dirty toilet tissue breath."

I needed a reason to leave, because if I didn't, I would tear that bathroom up. I flushed the toilet and ran the water in the sink for ten seconds. When I got back into the living room, I said that my period had started unexpectedly and I needed to leave.

Malcolm looked at me like I was crazy, but he couldn't comment or question me, because his mother didn't know that I was pregnant.

"We can send Malcolm to the store and get you whatever you need, if you want," Lucille said. "I was just about to cook us something to eat."

"I ain't going to a store to buy that crap," he said.

She snapped at him. "What the heck you mean by 'crap'? And you're gonna do what I tell you to do."

Lucille was trying to become my new best friend. "No, that's okay," I said. "I need to change my underwear, so I should go home." I picked up my purse from the sofa and kissed Lucille's cheek. "Thank you for the Kool-Aid. And I'll be back for that meal you promised to cook for me."

Malcolm didn't have a clue why I was leaving so abruptly. He looked at me strangely but didn't question why I was in such a hurry to go.

"Okay, sugar," Lucille said to me. "You take care and call me sometime."

"I only have Malcolm's cell number."

"Our number is two-three-nine-six-one-seven-four," she blurted out.

I didn't look at Malcolm to see his reaction to the fact that his mother had given out their home number. To humor Lucille, I stood in the living room and programmed the number into my cell phone. Then I said good-bye and walked out the front door with Malcolm on my heels.

"What was that all about?" he asked when we had reached my car.

"I asked your mother if she liked the pink scarf you bought for her in Mexico."

Malcolm hung his head, 'cause there was nothing else he could do.

"That's right. You're busted. Now I'ma ask you this question one time and one time only. Who was the scarf for?"

"It's for my mother. I just ain't gave it to her yet."

Malcolm stood in my face and lied so effortlessly. I looked toward the living room window to make sure my new friend wasn't looking out at us before I balled up my fist and punch him in the center of his chest with all my might. It caught him by surprise when his chest caved in.

"You lying bastard! She told me she never owned a pink scarf." I got in my car and drove away from the curb.

Chapter 45

When I got home, I found a large white envelope on my doorstep. My name had been written on it in calligraphy type with a gold ink pen. I picked it up and unlocked my front door. I walked into the living room, threw my keys on the cocktail table, sat down on the couch, and tore open the envelope. The first thing I pulled out was a message written on a sheet of white carbon paper in calligraphy with the same ink pen.

Rhapsody Blue,

Here's a gift for you.
It's something that'll make you really tic.
Guess who's suckin' your man's d . . . ?

So Malcolm had told that stank broad about my illness. The next thing I pulled out of the envelope was an eight-by-ten color photo of Malcolm lying naked on a bed, smiling at Sharonda as she knelt over his waist and gave him pleasure. I saw that her arm was extended outward, and I could tell that the heifer had taken a selfie. The only item of clothing she wore was a pink scarf around her neck.

Immediately, I started to sweat. I'd warned Malcolm over and over again that I wasn't to be played with. But since he liked to play with fire, I was gonna set some stuff off and let it burn. I went to my closet, pulled down a white shoe box from the top, and drove back to Malcolm's house.

Chapter 46

Ivan and Malcolm were sitting on the front porch, talking. "Dang, Malcolm. She just stole on you out here in the street?"

"Yep," Malcolm said, rubbing his chest, which still burned. "I'm slippin', Ivan. I should've bought two scarves and given one to my mother."

"I think you just need to go ahead and leave that crazy old broad alone."

"I can't. She's pregnant."

That was shocking news to Ivan. "What? Y'all wasn't using nothing?"

"Nah. But when I talk to Rhapsody tonight, I'ma tell her that I ain't taking no more of her crap."

"Then what do you think will happen?"

"Then I'll probably wake up, because you know I'll only say something like that in my dreams."

They both laughed out loud.

I turned the corner onto Malcolm's block and saw him and Ivan sitting on the porch, laughing. They were probably laughing at how Malcolm was getting away with playing me. I slowed my car down as I crept up to his house.

I saw the concerned look on his face when he noticed my car. I was sure he was wondering what I was doing back there. I got to his house and let down my driver-side window. He said something to Ivan, then stood to come my way. When Malcolm got within ten feet of my car, I raised my .22 semiautomatic Beretta and aimed it at his chest. It was a gift my father had bought me for Christmas the year I'd moved out on my own.

Malcolm stopped dead in his tracks. His eyes popped out of his head, and he turned to run from me. I couldn't let him get away. I pulled the trigger and opened fire. I don't remember how many bullets pierced Malcolm's back, but I do remember seeing him fall on his face. Ivan stood and ran to Malcolm. I sped off.

Epilogue

I tried to kill Malcolm, but he was in the hospital for only two weeks. Three bullets had struck him just beneath his left shoulder blade. I should've made sure he was dead before I drove off. That way I would feel that being locked up was justified. It's almost like robbing a bank and getting caught with only twenty dollars in your possession. You have to ask yourself, "Was it worth it?" My answer would be, "Yes."

Shooting Malcolm is definitely worth the years I'm facing ahead of me, because I've proven my point to him. I am not to be played with. My trial doesn't start until after my baby is born, which will be in three months. Malcolm threatened to sue and have me declared an unfit mother. He wants the state to award him full custody of the baby. The word on the street is that Malcolm and Sharonda got married and are waiting on the birth of my baby, whom they plan to raise as their own.

I get to talk to my parents for three minutes every day, and all my mother does is cry for the whole three minutes. My father won't say it, but I know he's ashamed of me. He had such high hopes and dreams for his baby girl.

Walter and Daniel came to see me the day I got here. Both of them cried. But that was the first and last that I saw of them.

My attorney said that the maximum I'll get is seventeen years for attempted murder. With good behavior, it'll probably get reduced to twelve and a half years. She's also using my mental illness as a defense. Dr. Buckles has already agreed to testify on my behalf. She's convinced that Tourette's syndrome played a huge part in my actions. My attorney feels strongly that I will probably get off by reason of insanity. While I'm locked up, I'm required to see Dr. Buckles once a week. She's even upped my medication. I also attend an anger management class on Tuesdays and Thursdays.

I hear that women's prisons are much worse than men's prisons. So I guess I'll be doing the whole seventeen, 'cause I already know that I'm gonna have to fight for my life in here. There's a broad in the cell next to mine who keeps looking at me like I'm a pan of peach cobbler. But she'll have just one time to grab my boobs or pat my butt. And when that happens, I'll just prove to her what I had to prove to Malcolm.

So, God willing, nobody in here will have to see the ugly side of me.

Book Club Discussion Questions

1. Malcolm was thirteen years younger than Rhapsody. Do you believe that he was too young for her?
2. Why didn't Malcolm tell Rhapsody the truth about why he couldn't stay the entire night with her?
3. Do you believe that Tourette's syndrome was to blame for Rhapsody's actions?
4. Was Rhapsody justified when she confronted Malcolm at the club, in front of his friends?
5. Why was Rhapsody's relationship with her brothers, Walter and Daniel, so strained?
6. Do you believe that Anastasia was a true best friend to Rhapsody? Why or why not?
7. On vacation in Mexico, Malcolm told Rhapsody that he loved her. Do you think that was true?
8. Rhapsody bought Malcolm a brand-new Lincoln Navigator. Why do you think she went to great lengths to keep him in her life?
9. What was Rhapsody's breaking point? Why did she shoot to kill Malcolm?
10. What do you think the future holds for Rhapsody, Malcolm, and their child?

UC HIS GLORY BOOK CLUB!

www.uchisglorybookclub.net

UC His Glory Book Club is the spirit-inspired brain-child of Joylynn Ross, Author and Acquisitions Editor of Urban Christian, and Kendra Norman-Bellamy, Author for Urban Christian. This is an online book club that hosts authors of Urban Christian. We welcome as members all men and women who have a passion for reading Christian-based fiction.

UC His Glory Book Club pledges our commitment to provide support, positive feedback, encouragement, and a forum whereby members can openly discuss and review the literary works of Urban Christian authors.

There is no membership fee associated with UC His Glory Book Club; however, we do ask that you support the authors through purchasing, encouraging, providing book reviews, and of course, your prayers. We also ask that you respect our beliefs and follow the guidelines of the book club. We hope to receive your valuable input, opinions, and reviews that build up, rather than tear down our authors.

What We Believe:

—We believe that Jesus is the Christ, Son of the Living God.

—We believe the Bible is the true, living Word of God.

—We believe all Urban Christian authors should use their God-given writing abilities to honor God and share the message of the written word God has given to each of them uniquely.

—We believe in supporting Urban Christian authors in their literary endeavors by reading, purchasing, and sharing their titles with our online community.

—We believe that in everything we do in our literary arena should be done in a manner that will lead to God being glorified and honored.

We look forward to the online fellowship with you.

Please visit us often at:

www.uchisglorybookclub.net.

Many Blessings to You!

Shelia E. Lipsey,
President, UC His Glory Book Club

Notes

Notes

ORDER FORM
URBAN BOOKS, LLC
97 N. 18th Street
Wyandanch, NY 11798

Name (please print):_____

Address: _____

City/State: _____

Zip: _____

QTY	TITLES	PRICE
	3:57 A.M Timing Is Everything	$14.95
	A Man's Worth	$14.95
	A Woman's Worth	$14.95
	Abundant Rain	$14.95
	After The Feeling	$14.95
	Amaryllis	$14.95
	An Inconvenient Friend	$14.95
	Battle of Jericho	$14.95
	Be Careful What You Pray For	$14.95
	Beautiful Ugly	$14.95
	Been There Prayed That:	$14.95
	Before Redemption	$14.95

Shipping and handling-add $3.50 for 1st book, then $1.75 for each additional book.
Please send a check payable to:
Urban Books, LLC
Please allow 4-6 weeks for delivery

ORDER FORM
URBAN BOOKS, LLC
97 N. 18th Street
Wyandanch, NY 11798

Name (please print):_____

Address: _____

City/State: _____

Zip: _____

QTY	TITLES	PRICE
	By the Grace of God	$14.95
	Confessions Of A preachers Wife	$14.95
	Dance Into Destiny	$14.95
	Deliver Me From My Enemies	$14.95
	Desperate Decisions	$14.95
	Divorcing the Devil	$14.95
	Faith	$14.95
	First Comes Love	$14.95
	Flaws and All	$14.95
	Forgiven	$14.95
	Former Rain	$14.95
	Forsaken	$14.95

Shipping and handling-add $3.50 for 1st book, then $1.75 for each additional book.

Please send a check payable to:
Urban Books, LLC
Please allow 4-6 weeks for delivery

ORDER FORM
URBAN BOOKS, LLC
97 N. 18th Street
Wyandanch, NY 11798

Name (please print):_____

Address: _____

City/State: _____

Zip: _____

QTY	TITLES	PRICE
	From Sinner To Saint	$14.95
	From The Extreme	$14.95
	God Is In Love With You	$14.95
	God Speaks To Me	$14.95
	Grace And Mercy	$14.95
	Guilty Of Love	$14.95
	Happily Ever Now	$14.95
	Heaven Bound	$14.95
	His Grace His Mercy	$14.95
	His Woman His Wife His Widow	$14.95
	Illusions	$14.95
	In Green Pastures	$14.95

Shipping and handling-add $3.50 for 1st book, then $1.75 for each additional book.
Please send a check payable to:
Urban Books, LLC
Please allow 4-6 weeks for delivery

ORDER FORM
URBAN BOOKS, LLC
97 N. 18th Street
Wyandanch, NY 11798

Name (please print):_____

Address: _____

City/State: _____

Zip: _____

QTY	TITLES	PRICE
	Into Each Life	$14.95
	Keep Your enemies Closer	$14.95
	Keeping Misery Company	$14.95
	Latter Rain	$14.95
	Living Consequences	$14.95
	Living Right On Wrong Street	$14.95
	Losing It	$14.95
	Love Honor Stray	$14.95
	Marriage Mayhem	$14.95
	Me, Myself and Him	$14.95
	Murder Through The Grapevine	$14.95
	My Father's House	$14.95

Shipping and handling-add $3.50 for 1st book, then $1.75 for each additional book.
Please send a check payable to:
    Urban Books, LLC
Please allow 4-6 weeks for delivery

ORDER FORM
URBAN BOOKS, LLC
97 N. 18th Street
Wyandanch, NY 11798

Name:(please print):_____

Address: _____

City/State: _____

Zip: _____

QTY	TITLES	PRICE
	My Mother's Child	$14.95
	My Son's Ex Wife	$14.95
	My Son's Wife	$14.95
	My Soul Cries Out	$14.95
	Not Guilty Of Love	$14.95
	Prodigal	$14.95
	Rain Storm	$14.95
	Redemption Lake	$14.95
	Right Package, Wrong Baggage	$14.95
	Sacrifice The One	$14.95
	Secret Sisterhood	$14.95
	Secrets And Lies	$14.95

Shipping and handling-add $3.50 for 1st book, then $1.75 for each additional book.
Please send a check payable to:
    Urban Books, LLC
Please allow 4-6 weeks for delivery

ORDER FORM
URBAN BOOKS, LLC
97 N. 18th Street
Wyandanch, NY 11798

Name: (please print):_____

Address: _____

City/State: _____

Zip: _____

QTY	TITLES	PRICE
	Selling My soul	$14.95
	She Who Finds A Husband	$14.95
	Sheena's Dream	$14.95
	Sinsatiable	$14.95
	Someone To Love Me	$14.95
	Something On The Inside	$14.95
	Song Of Solomon	$14.95
	Soon After	$14.95
	Soon And Very Soon	$14.95
	Soul Confession	$14.95
	Still Guilty	$14.95

Shipping and handling-add $3.50 for 1st book, then $1.75 for each additional book.

Please send a check payable to:

Urban Books, LLC

Please allow 4-6 weeks for delivery

ORDER FORM
URBAN BOOKS, LLC
97 N. 18th Street
Wyandanch, NY 11798

Name (please print):_____

Address: _____

City/State: _____

Zip: _____

QTY	TITLES	PRICE

Shipping and handling-add $3.50 for 1st book, then $1.75 for each additional book.

Please send a check payable to:

Urban Books, LLC

Please allow 4-6 weeks for delivery